I, Mona Lisa

I, Mona Lisa

NATASHA SOLOMONS

HUTCHINSON
HEINEMANN

1 3 5 7 9 10 8 6 4 2

Hutchinson Heinemann
20 Vauxhall Bridge Road
London SW1V 2SA

Hutchinson Heinemann is part of the
Penguin Random House group of companies whose addresses
can be found at global.penguinrandomhouse.com.

Penguin
Random House
UK

Quote on p. 91 from *The Story of Art* by E. H. Gombrich (Phaidon,
London 1950). Used with permission.

First published by Hutchinson Heinemann in 2022

www.penguin.co.uk

A CIP catalogue record for this book is available from
the British Library

ISBN 9781529151299 (hardback)
ISBN 9781529151305 (trade paperback)

Typeset in 11/15 pt Sabon LT Std
by Integra Software Services Pvt. Ltd, Pondicherry

Printed and bound in Great Britain by Clays Ltd, Elcograf S.p.A.

The authorised representative in the EEA is Penguin Random House
Ireland, Morrison Chambers, 32 Nassau Street, Dublin D02 YH68

Penguin Random House is committed to a sustainable future for
our business, our readers and our planet. This book is made from
Forest Stewardship Council® certified paper.

For my parents, Carol and Clive

GALLERY GUIDE

Renaissance Room

Mona Lisa – Leonardo da Vinci's most famous painting

Leonardo da Vinci – Florentine inventor, polymath and painter of genius

Salaì – Leonardo's chief assistant at the *bottega* and also his lover

Francesco Melzi also known as Cecco – another of Leonardo's assistants, latterly his amanuensis, editor and collator of his manuscripts and Salaì's bitter rival

Lisa del Giocondo – a renowned Florentine beauty and the model for the Mona Lisa

Francesco del Giocondo – a wealthy silk merchant and Lisa's husband

Niccolò Machiavelli – a politician, operator and occasional friend of Leonardo's

Raphael Santi – a young painter from Urbino and a confidant and admirer of Leonardo

Michelangelo Buonarroti – sculptor, painter, grouch and adversary of Leonardo

Leda – Queen of Sparta and Leonardo's most magnificent and beautiful painting; friend of Mona's

Il Magnifico or Giuliano de' Medici – of the legendary Medici family of Florence; powerful patron of Leonardo in Rome

Pope Leo X – brother of Giuliano; passionate about food and music as well as God

King Francis I – teenage King of France, latterly patron of Leonardo Da Vinci in France and the purchaser of Mona Lisa, Leda and other paintings

La Cremona – the most famous courtesan in Milan, also a poet and the model for Leda

French Galleries

Room of the Sun King

Louis XIV the Sun King – admirer of Mona Lisa, Leda, absolute monarch of France

Queen Marie Thérèse – his pious Spanish queen

Madame de Montespan – Louis's official mistress and the mother of at least six of his children

Françoise, Madame de Maintenon – the royal governess, and latterly the mistress who succeeded Madame de Montespan

Revolutionary France

Louis XVI – King of France

Marie Antoinette – his extravagant wife; a woman of great passion and style

Citizen Fragonard – exuberant Rococo painter beloved of Marie Antoinette, who fell out of favour after the Revolution

Twentieth-Century Room

Pablo Picasso – painter and friend of Mona Lisa

Sigmund Freud – psychoanalyst and art lover

Vincenzo Peruggia – thief and kidnapper of the Mona Lisa; Italian Nationalist

Jacques Jaujard – brilliant chief curator of the Louvre during WW2; never seen without a cigarette

Jeanne/ Agent Mozart – French Resistance agent, film star and Jaujard's lover

Prologue

Louvre, Paris, Today

*I*n the beginning I listened in darkness. When I was new, I had no eyes and could not tell night from day. But I discovered that I liked the music – the brisk joy of the *lira da braccio* and the flute – and the raucous studio chatter. The tickle of the charcoal. The steady warmth of his fingertips, all nudging me into life, layer upon layer. I came into being, not all at once but like the build-up of smoke in a room, one wisp at a time. His breath against my cheek as his brush blew life into me. I swam into consciousness as if from the bottom of the deepest ocean, cool and black. I was aware of voices, like the grinding of the rocks against the waves. But I was always listening for his voice. He whispered to me. He willed me into being, coaxed me out of the poplar wood. Until then I was content in the dark. I did not yet know there was light.

My face came first, edging into view against the spinning layers of white lead. He conjured me forth with tonal shadows and blocks of shading in dark washes. I was coated again and again with a layer of *imprimitura*, translucent as a butterfly's wing. My skin was ghostly, not pink flesh, so he added a small portion of red lake and yellow and shaded me with burnt umber. My hands and dress and veil and hair were nothing but thoughts in charcoal, waiting to be. There were the first ink lines of the cartoon. The sharp point of the needle picked out my new contours, ready for the charcoal *spolveri*. His fingers massaged in the rubbing powder through the tiny holes in the paper. I was an outline, a mirror image upon wood. A collection of parts. Chin. Breasts. Finger. Nose. And with my new eyes I looked about me. The busyness of the day and the stillness of the night. I marvelled at it all. The stars flickered beyond the window lit like the studio candles – perhaps a celestial painter laboured, the Leonardo of the heavens, on a new constellation commissioned by the gods.

While Leonardo was painting me, giving me shoulders and lips and creating the cascades of my hair and the translucence of my veil, he talked to me.

'Painting is superior to music as it does not perish immediately after its creation. This song on the lute, although sweet, has already vanished and yet here you are.'

I listened in rapture to these intimacies as something began to stir deep within me – the first seeds of love.

At first, I used to gaze at Leonardo rapt and silent. Then one day he confided to me the secrets of the heavens, saying, 'People believe there is a man on the moon, but there are only seas. Its surface is awash with saltwater.'

I heard a voice speaking the question I wanted to ask.

'There is truly no man on the moon?' said the voice.

Then, to my astonishment, I understood that this was my voice. I could speak. I did not know.

Leonardo stared back at me, astounded. He leaned forward until his eye was level with mine. Stroked my lip with his brush.

'Are you really there?' he asked me.

'Yes. I am,' I answered.

'Who are you?' he asked, studying me in wonder.

I looked back at him and replied, 'I am yours.'

My Leonardo was many things – *imaginativa*, generous, fastidious – but he was not fast and, in the time it took to conjure me, he confided in me a great many more things. He conceived new worlds in a single leaf. There was only ever one Leonardo. And there was only one painting like me. The other pictures could be looked at but none of them could see. When I was young, and my paint fresh and my varnish uncracked, I was a revelation in white lead and *imprimitura*. No one painted in the same way after me. Or no one who was any good. The lacklustre, soft-cocked, grey souls went on for half a century producing whey-faced Madonnas by the yard for altar panels in provincial churches. But after looking upon me, even the poets returned to the world with a sharpened tongue.

Please understand that I am not the pretty bourgeois wife of a silk merchant. I am not Lisa del Giocondo. I can hear her now as she was then, her voice petulant and anxious. The rattle of her worries. *The studio is stifling. Can the window not be opened?* Lisa. Lisa. Her name is like a hiss of steam. Did I have to begin with her? To be made in the image of someone so ordinary. But as the brilliant lapis lazuli resplendent on a thousand Madonnas' robes are mined from limestone, so was I cajoled from the unyielding and reluctant Lisa.

For a short while, like mother and a foetus, she and I shared a soul. Then, I was not yet myself. The soft curl of Lisa's hair, rubbed out. Drawn, anew. The first curve of her cheek. The shape of her skull. Leonardo's thought and his intention. I was more Lisa and Leonardo than myself. But little by little, stroke by stroke, I became. My soul my own. I looked about me with my own curiosity. I saw the lemon trees glistening in their pots lining the loggia. The dust on their leaves. Perspiring musicians playing to keep Lisa smiling. To make me smile. And just like that, we were no longer the same, she and I. Praise the Madonna and all the saints in Heaven. My smile is not hers. It never was. She always needed the punchline to every joke explained. Poor, good, dutiful Lisa.

Now, as I look out of my glass prison in the Louvre, it has been hundreds of years since I saw her last. She lies in her tomb, and I in my glass coffin. Most prisoners have committed a crime. Not I. A gilded palace, no matter how splendid or filled with silent treasures, is still a jail when one cannot leave. The visitors to the Louvre queue for hours and then gawp without seeing me. I am now a fixture in the travel guides and the package tours of Europe. I've become ill-tempered and full of black bile in my old age, but the manners of the tourists are despicable. They complain to one another how small I am, or that my smile is more of a grimace. Once, I used to jostle with hundreds of others in an undignified dormitory of pictures, half-forgotten except by those who came to seek me. Yet nowadays I am everywhere, so you no longer see me even when I am right before you. You all come here to linger in my presence, to pay homage for your allotted seconds, before you are hurried on by my jailors. Still you choose to record on your phones the moment of your not looking while your back is turned to me.

Well, if you will not look at me at least do not search for the other Lisa. I am real. That is the secret. Frankly she isn't worth the trouble. The pious, prattling wife of a vain and self-promoting merchant. She is dead. Her bones lost, dust in a convent. Listen instead to my history. My adventures are worth hearing. I have lived many lifetimes and been loved by emperors, kings and thieves. I have survived kidnap and assault. Revolution and two world wars. But this is also a love story. And the story of what we will do for those we love.

From the very beginning I was his, for like Prometheus he breathed the fire of life into me. At first this held no fear for me, for I did not understand what I was, and that as a painting of wood and pigment I was different from a man of flesh and blood and bone. I did not know what it was to be mortal or that he must die. I only knew that I loved him, and that in time he must come to love me too. We were together many years and he confided in me his many secrets. His jealousies. The disquiet of his ambition.

And in the end we made one another immortal, he and I. Yet now he is gone and I watch in silence, alone. The cell walls might be made of glass, but it is bulletproof, two centimetres thick and sealed from the outside world. I can hear almost nothing but muffled babble. No one troubles to speak to me any more. Even if I call out, no one listens.

Listen now.

Florence, 1504

Winter

At fifty-one Leonardo is still a handsome man. He wears a short, rose-coloured tunic and a cloak of deepest green velvet gifted to him by Ludovico Sforza, Duke of Milan. In his tunic and his cloaks, Leonardo appears every inch the celebrated artist from Milan blown in amongst the conservative Republicans of Florence in their plain gowns and sensible haircuts. His beautiful curling hair is now streaked with grey and carefully styled, reaching down to the middle of his chest. The silver lends him an added air of gravitas. He visits the barber regularly and his cheeks are smooth. His eyes are like those of the birds he loves, an *aquilone* perhaps or a kite, observing every detail, dark windows thatched beneath thick brows. I watch those brows. They are the internal weathervanes of the studio. This morning, Zephyrus must be sending a warm wind as, to Leonardo's delight and my dismay, Lisa del Giocondo arrives with her maid. I observe as the assistants stop grinding pigment to watch her, startled each time by her beauty. In between visits, even I forget her loveliness and am taken aback, until she frowns, irked, and the illusion of the mortal goddess is spoiled. She surveys with distaste the peeling magnificence of the Sala del Papa, and the stripped and scraped skins of kid goats and calves splayed across the tiles and benches; they are waxy translucent and ready cured for vellum. It's clear to me Leonardo's forgotten that she's coming, but he is all charm and attention and sits her down in the best chair. I am resting upon my easel at the far side of the hall, where I have a good vantage, but Lisa is too busy fussing with her layers of shawls and does not notice me.

'Dearest Leonardo, I brought you a present,' she says, handing him a small package.

He crouches beside her, apparently touched by the gesture.

'Well,' she smiles, 'aren't you going to open it?'

Leonardo dutifully unpeels the paper to reveal a prayer book. He holds it up to the light and I perceive that every page is bedecked with crude and doom-laden woodcuts of sinners in torment. He stares at her in fond puzzlement and she clasps her hands tightly.

'I worry about your eternal soul, maestro. Please, I beg of you, read it.'

'If I read without belief, I'm not sure it will have the necessary effect, Madonna Lisa.'

Her lip quivers.

Leonardo bows. 'I will study it carefully. If anyone can save my soul, I'm certain that it's you.'

I have no stomach and yet I feel sick to it. Leonardo's soul does not need saving. He has his own unique faith. And if his soul ever needs saving, it will be me who does it and not Lisa del Giocondo, for all her piety. I am a painting that can see and hear: I have been touched by the divine. Even if, now and again, I'm also touched by earthlier arrows of loathing and disdain.

'Salaì. Vin Santo. Biscuits.' Leonardo stands, signalling to his chief assistant.

Salaì. What can I say? He is a thief. Liar. Obstinate. Glutton. Yet, all this Leonardo forgives, because Salaì makes him laugh and he is beautiful. Beauty makes Leonardo overlook a great deal. This is true of both Salaì and Lisa. Salaì means 'Little Devil' and he is Leonardo's perpetual favourite, with his long ringlets like a string of polished chestnuts, and his impish grin. He looks like an angel longing to discard his wings and misbehave. Darling Leonardo cannot resist. It is my task to watch Salaì closely, to try and limit the havoc the wretch can and does wreak on us all. I warn Leonardo again and again, but he hardly ever listens. He is in thrall to beauty.

Lisa shivers. It is absurd. The studio is deliciously cool. The ceilings are high and the windows shaded. The oil paints react to extreme heat and Leonardo needs a steady, even light to draw. Lisa is never content.

'May we have a fire lit?'

'Of course, Madonna.'

Servants bustle in an instant. Everyone wants to please Lisa. It's tiresome. Even the flames in the grate burst in an instant, as if under her spell, daubing a rosy glow on her cheek. Leonardo leans forward, entranced. He signals for his brushes and his palette, determined to match my cheek to hers. To my satisfaction, the fire is built of damp logs and so begins to ooze smoke and poor Lisa coughs, covering her mouth and pearlescent teeth with a small white hand. Her eyes liquify with tears. Leonardo scrutinises every part of her face, unblinking in his fascination as though she is the Madonna herself.

She glances around the studio, restless as a sparrow. The chatter is subdued, all laughter muffled. Even Salaì behaves. She's searching for something. For me.

'Oh,' she says, as she spies me at last, her face stricken. 'It still isn't finished.' Her exquisite nose wrinkles. 'And it doesn't look like me.'

What she means is, she doesn't like me. Which is fine. As I don't like her either. Leonardo is far more diplomatic. He places a reassuring hand on hers. She recoils. He is not her husband, and she frets when he touches her.

'A painting is visual poetry.'

Lisa looks at him, puzzled.

He tries again. 'When I paint, I paint two things. I paint a man, or here, a woman. But I also paint a mind – my mind, my ideas. This portrait is not simply of you, but also of my mind and my ideas. That part of the picture will appear to you as stranger, as she is not you, but me.'

And me, I think, but this is not the time to argue.

Leonardo gestures to his assistants to set my easel before him and Lisa, and she examines me with strained dislike. He glances between us.

'No one has created a painting like my Lisa before. She is Eve and not Eve, and the Virgin but also every woman. Petrarch's Laura and Dante's Beatrice and all Beloved Ladies. But she is also human, with tones of flesh. If you reach out and brush her cheek, you expect it to dimple. She is the lustre of life itself, filled with warmth. She's enveloped in light and shade. She's the legitimate daughter of nature and the kin of a god who speaks and breathes.'

Lisa leans forward closer and closer until her eyelashes almost brush mine, straining to see what Leonardo sees, how he sees me. Each day, I look out at the world through the eyes he gave me, while the world winks back at me. Glimpsed through our eyes, the universe is a marvel.

Lisa doesn't see it. She can't. She stands before me and continues to study me intently, her face troubled. I stare back at her, meeting her eye. Why should I look away? Her lip curls in aversion.

'This won't do at all. I need you to at least pretend a smile, or I can't paint,' complains Leonardo, half-amused.

'Oh, I much prefer her like this,' I object. 'The frown suits her.'

Leonardo does his best to ignore me and concentrate only on the other Lisa.

'Messer Leonardo, I thought you were going to paint me in profile? The pose is insolent ... '

'Not at all. Her gaze is direct. Intimate,' suggests Leonardo. There's a note of pride in his voice.

I may be a woman but when you stare at me, I dare to stare back, resolute. I am not like the others who have come before who glance demurely at the floor, or their coyly clasped hands, or to the side. Look at me, and I see you too. All Leonardo's *bottega* know he's painted something revolutionary. That I am a revolutionary. I am a marvel and I will change the world, but only for those who wish to see. Lisa del Giocondo is not one of them.

How can she honestly believe that she and I still have any connection? The paper chain piecing us together snaps.

'What will people think? I am looking right at them. It isn't modest. It isn't virtuous.' Her voice is soft, worried.

'It's an intimate portrait to hang in your villa. No one need see it apart from your husband. I expect he will be so proud, he'll invite all his friends and acquaintance to view it.'

She gives a tiny smile.

Leonardo pats her arm again. This time she doesn't flinch. 'But my Lisa isn't finished. Look, her hands, her arms. The dress. All are only traced from the cartoon. I have barely begun the landscape behind her. You needn't worry. Not yet. Not for a long while.'

Not ever, I think. I am never, ever, going to live in the Giocondo villa. My place is here with Leonardo. I am not worried either. What Leonardo says is true. It takes him a very long time to finish anything. If he finishes them at all. I am not sure that I want to be finished and taken away from him.

Leonardo is angry with me.

'Why can't you be kinder to Lisa?' he chides. 'You tease her whenever she sits for us.'

'What does it matter when she can't even hear?' I object. 'Only the greatest artists can hear my *voce*. Those with true *ingegno*. Lisa is ordinary. Dull.'

Only the master himself hears my voice. At first I did not know this and unwittingly I would call out to the *garzoni* in the studio, tell a joke to Tommaso, or shout an insult to Salaì. I believed Salaì ignored me, and it took a little time for me to understand he could not hear. It was both a release from the pretence of courtesy and a disappointment. I was at liberty to be as rude as I wished, but every insult fell as if upon the wind. Leonardo and I wondered if ours was a unique bond formed between creator and his creation. But then one day Raphael de Santi, the painter from Urbino, came to visit the studio. I remarked to Leonardo how young Raphael was, how brilliant his drawing, and, unthinkingly, he bowed to me, and murmured his thanks.

It appeared that Raphael could hear me too. That night, Leonardo and I decided that it seemed artists of true vision and genius, blessed with *ingegno*, can hear my voice. For now, it is a source of pride that only the most brilliant can hear me speak. Leonardo himself, Raphael. I wonder if there will be others. I do not care. As long as I have Leonardo, I shall never be lonely.

Leonardo grunts, still displeased with my manners towards Madonna Lisa. He is never unkind, and he is always patient with those more stupid than himself, which is all of us.

'You might be cleverer than Lisa, but your smile lacks the sweetness of hers. As does your temper.'

'She is made entirely of cold and phlegm. Like a frog.'

Leonardo sets down his brush. Tonight, his work is not going well, and I am not helping. He is drawing and re-drawing my hands in charcoal. The primed white lead of my panel is full of his *pentimenti*, or regrets, where he has rubbed away the *spolveri* dots and keeps adjusting the angle of my fingers again and again. If we don't make peace, I might end up with no hands at all. I know I ought to plead forgiveness but it sticks in my throat. I want him to devote himself to nothing except me, but he is distracted and interested in many things. His sketches and designs are scattered across the studio. Salaì saunters past and Leonardo catches his hand and places a kiss upon the tender flesh of his wrist and I'm needled by jealousy, both that he has hands and that the master wishes to kiss them. But not even Salaì can placate him, and he scrubs out my fingers again, leaving only smudged stubs.

Perhaps there is prescience in his wretchedness tonight, as the door to the studio catches in the wind, a January squall, and in puffs Niccolò Machiavelli, master of misfortune wearing the pretence of friendship. We owe our present studio, lodgings and a new commission for a vast mural of the Battle of Anghiari in the council chamber all to Machiavelli. We are all in debt to him. I warn Leonardo again and again to be careful of Machiavelli's barbed benevolence. His preferred currency is neither gold ducats nor florins but favours, and he takes great pleasure in demanding their repayment. I study the black hair slicked wetly to Machiavelli's white skin, and his skull-tight smirk. Payment is due.

'Leonardo! My great friend.'

Leonardo rises from his easel and embraces him with genuine pleasure, paying no heed to my concerns. He's glad of a distraction and Machiavelli amuses him. He is clever and witty. His mind marvellous. That it relishes in dark delights, doesn't trouble him. Every aspect of life's shades fascinates Leonardo.

Machiavelli manoeuvred the Florentine Council into commissioning Leonardo, and also allowing him both studio and living quarters in the refectory at Santa Maria Novella. The Sala del Papa was built for the comfort and pleasure of visiting popes and it is suitably magnificent on the outside, with brilliant white-and-dark green-striped inlaid marble, a harmony of geometric shapes that gleams bone bright. Yet inside it is dilapidated and dingy and parts of the outer room are in poor repair. Perhaps it's the luminous frescoes of the former Florentine rulers, the exiled Medicis, that makes the council reluctant to fix the roof as Leonardo requested and now the rain thrums in various buckets and pools on the herringbone brick floor. The rosy faces of the Medici boys stare dolefully from the walls amongst blooming rosettes of damp, the ghosts of Leonardo's youth. Several windows leak; rivulets stain the yellow walls like tears.

Machiavelli sees me set upon my easel, and Leonardo's pigment-stained fingers, and scowls.

'You're messing around with Francesco del Giocondo's wife,' he tuts.

'The boys are working on the commission,' says Leonardo, ignoring the innuendo.

This is mostly true. But the council are paying for the master himself. Machiavelli looks around, observing the skins of preparing vellum and bubbling vats of gum arabic, as well as the laughter from the retinue of assistants and apprentices spilling over from the large room next door. Pine logs crackle and sputter in the grate. A bowl of fat figs rests on a low table beside a large pecorino and a haunch of ham, glistening with glossy white fat. It looks posed and set up for a still life for the apprentices.

'You spoil those boys,' complains Machiavelli.

'Only sometimes,' I object. 'In between the charm, he's furious at their incompetence and untidiness.'

Machiavelli ignores me. Everyone does except Leonardo.

'I take pleasure in their joy,' says Leonardo. He has no time for Machiavelli's smug parsimony. 'The painter is a gentleman. He wears well-cut clothes of fine fabric. He eats good food. Only then can he try to paint beauty and capture the human soul.'

Machiavelli raises an eyebrow but voices no further objections. 'In that case, is there anything else you need?' he asks, solicitous as an innkeeper angling for a handsome tip.

'Salaì? What's on the list?' calls Leonardo.

Salaì dances noiselessly over to them, placing down two goblets and pouring wine. 'Towels, napkins, candlesticks, a feather mattress, a couple-ladle, lamp stands, inkwell, ink.'

'You can't get these things yourself?' asks Machiavelli, dubious. 'The advance I negotiated for you ought to be sufficient for ink and napkins.'

Leonardo shrugs. 'You offered. And I suspect this visit is going to cost me in the end. What is it that you want? You didn't come here to do my shopping.'

Machiavelli grins his crocodile smile. 'I need your assistance and expertise. I'm going to divert the Arno. Take it away from Pisa and deprive the city of their route to the sea. Everyone says it's impossible.'

'And you know I like impossible things. You're trying to tempt me.'

'Of course. I wouldn't lie to you, Leonardo.'

Now it is Leonardo's turn to laugh, but it's no good. I can see he is smitten. Diverting the Arno is an engineering scheme on the scale of the gods. I sigh. Machiavelli understands how difficult Leonardo finds it to finish a painting, especially one as monumental as this great mural. But Niccolò Machiavelli can also hear the steady drum of war, and he's sniffed a route to victory against Pisa, and he does not really care about painting or Leonardo except when it can help him realise his own endless ambition. I study Leonardo. There's a frenzy of excitement about him.

'Do you have accurate maps? What is the soil type?' he asks.

Machiavelli produces a folded-up document from his satchel. 'They are not as good as anything you could draw. You must come and see it for yourself. Make new maps.

'Imagine it, my friend. Florence with a canal! A triumphant city with a route to the city. At last we would be a republic to rival Venice or Rome herself. Create the designs, and I swear to you that I will see to it that they are followed.'

Leonardo regards him with longing. He wants to believe him. He has submitted tender after tender to the grand dukes – architectural designs for duomos, or designs for machinery of war – but while his ideas amuse and are admired, he has never had anything commissioned on this vast scale. Ambition and desire flare within him. I can see it. He glows like Icarus, catching in the orb of the sun.

'We will be the creators of the new Florentine Republic,' declares Machiavelli.

The politics of the scheme mean nothing to Leonardo. It's the engineering wonder, the possibilities of altering the face of the earth. He is lost to this new scheme.

'Leonardo! Negotiate your terms,' I chide.

He nods, and glances at Machiavelli. 'I shall submit a bill for my expenses. My drawings and my travel.'

Machiavelli grunts. 'Of course. I take it the advance for the painting commission has gone?'

Leonardo doesn't answer.

Machiavelli stands and gapes at me. 'I don't like the way she looks at me. It's the way her face is just there against the background. She needs some clothes. And hands. When are you going to finish her?'

'Never,' says Salaì, appearing again to clear the glasses. 'Because then he'll be obliged to hand her over to Francesco del Giocondo.'

Salaì does not like me. Until I appeared, he had no rival for Leonardo's affection. He might not be able to hear my barbs and insults, but he senses that I am no ordinary painting. I unsettle him.

Machiavelli scrutinises me again. 'She's uncanny. She might just be a face. But something about her is so lifelike.'

He turns his back on me. He has no manners.

'Oh, and here is the formal contract for the mural,' adds Machiavelli. 'I've negotiated excellent terms. A monthly stipend of fifteen florins. They'll cover all the costs of materials, of course.'

He pushes over a piece of paper and Leonardo signs without reading.

'It's to be completed by next February, no exception or excuse accepted. That's not a problem?' says Machiavelli, sly, pricking at Leonardo's vanity.

Leonardo waves away his concern. He always begins each work with great optimism. It slowly leaks away over time like wine from a cracked flagon.

Salaì laughs, incredulous, and shakes his head. For once I agree with him.

The studio without him is a summer's day without sunshine. We are all irritable and indolent; we lack any purpose. Leonardo has left Salaì in charge, but the other assistants resist his command and squabble. Leonardo has taken on a new pupil, a slender boy of about thirteen. The rumour is we owe his father money. According to the gossip of the *bottega*, his father is a Lombardy nobleman but, despite the debt, still agrees to pay Leonardo five lire a month for his son. Salaì enters the sum in the accounts book. The boy has elegant clothes; his tunic is lambswool dyed a brilliant red and in the chill of the evening he produces a dapper cloak of grey velvet that even Leonardo would wear, the folds catching in the firelight. Salaì bullies him endlessly. The night after Leonardo leaves, Francesco Melzi no longer wears the cloak, but Salaì preens in it beside the hearth. Francesco sits silent, feigning indifference, hot shameful tears unshed. He understands his place in the *bottego* hierarchy. Alicia our maid, helped by two other serving women, comes in to clean and provide meals but is disgusted by the disorder and mutters in discontent, and shows her aversion by banging dishes and sweeping with more vigour than necessary. The piles of discarded plates. The rotting fruit.

Salaì immediately covers over the windows with thick, rough paper as instructed – the light must be even and cool. More workmen and carpenters arrive, bringing five *braccia* length of elm wood ready to build a platform and a ladder and all the various devices in Leonardo's plans so he can reach the high places along the wall where the paper for the vast preparatory cartoon for the council chamber is to be secured. The studio is rapidly becoming a building site. Salaì struts and yells, self-important as a rooster. Two of the serving women leave in tears. Leonardo would never allow this. The maestro rules not through threats but charm and tenderness. We all long to please him. A huge ream of paper arrives for the cartoon. Salaì orders the boys to begin gluing it together. The constant smell of rancid and boiling rabbit skin bubbling in the cauldron on the fire for the glue is revolting. Francesco is burned when Salaì drips glue on his wrist. I'm not certain it's an accident. Alicia vomits from the perpetual stench. I long to complain to Salaì, and launch a volley of curses that he cannot hear, and almost as if he senses my disapproval, he lifts me off my three-legged easel and lugs me into Leonardo's bedchamber. I object vociferously. He justifies moving me to an absent Leonardo.

'It's for her own good. The heat, steam and fat from the glue will spoil her paintwork.'

He places me assiduously on the linen covers, although I sense that he'd prefer to hurl me down. He peers at me for a moment.

'It will be good to have a few days without your supercilious look. As if you always know best. Sanctimonious hag.' He breathes the insult under his breath as he walks out banging the door.

I am alone and furious. I stare at the ceiling. A spider's web is strung across the beams. My anger cools into curiosity. This is the first time I have been inside the master's chamber and I'm thrilled to have such an intimate peek. The room bears the imprint of Leonardo, shaped to fit him like a discarded calfskin glove. The riot of papers and familiar bound notebooks. The smell of rosewater, lavender and turpentine. The cedar chest of clothes. The linen on the bed is smooth and unmarked. The down of the pillows unrumpled, musty from weeks of disuse. Leonardo has the best bed, lavishly carved with wall hangings draped from the beams. The others all sleep on mattresses, or share several to one box bed. Although, Salaì sleeps here more often than not. I picture him wrapped in the master's arms, Leonardo toying with his curls, the naked line of his back, anointing the lobes of his ears with kisses. I am awash with envy.

Yet while he is away, even Salaì does not dare to slumber on his bed, to dream his dreams. Leonardo will not object to me resting my head here on his pillow. It is different between he and I. His affection for me will endure beyond a season, it is a love that transcends flesh and one day I am determined he will prefer me even to Salaì.

Several weeks later, when Leonardo arrives back from Pisa exhilarated and exhausted, he doesn't even notice the progress. He barely inspects the sketches. I hear him call out for me at once. I am dizzy with pleasure.

'Where is Lisa? Where is my Lisa?'

He hurls open the bedroom door, lit up with happiness to see me. I smile back.

'Well, what was it like?' I ask.

'Wet. Muddy. But there are possibilities.'

His face is flushed, but beneath the excitement he looks drained and weary, like the white lead is scraped and showing beneath the bright pigment on his cheek. He orders Francesco, who has become our little 'Cecco', to carry me and the easel into the studio. I'm relieved to be back amongst the crowded *bottega* and cannot resist smirking at Salaì, who huffs at the sight of me.

'Master, will you not look at the preparatory sketches for the murals?' he pleads.

Leonardo kisses him lightly upon his lips and ruffles the gold of his hair, but then dismisses him with a wave. I preen.

'A glass of wine. Some cheese. And, Cecco, are the colours ground and ready? Black, umber and a little lake.

Bring me the measuring spoons. No. This is for my Lisa. I'm not using tempera to bind. I'm using oil. Hasn't Salaì been teaching you properly?' He grumbles, journey-worn and yet eager to paint me.

'Leave the boy alone. He's taken good care of me. Unlike Salaì,' I complain, as Cecco races back with the brushes.

Leonardo ignores my snipes about his favourite. I regard the studio with interest. The builders have finished construction of Leonardo's scaffolding and it teeters around the edges of the room with hanging platforms and pulleys and hoists resembling great siege mechanisms. Leonardo, however, for once pays no attention. He stares only at me. He plucks at his brush and begins to mix paint, blending carefully.

'I studied the blood flow of the Arno, but I was also thinking of you, *mia amata* Lisa.'

He has not called me by such an endearment before, and I'm touched. I recognise that something has shifted between us during his absence. He has missed me, and in his mind he's been thinking of me, holding my face in his mind, and so for now at least, he wants to devote himself only to me. All other routes and distractions lead him back to me, show him how to finish me.

He stands for a moment and, reaching into his satchel, pulls out a hand-painted map and unfurls it, holding it aloft so I can see. The tributaries of the rivers splice apart and sluice across the paper in blue and brown, curling and rippling in a vigorous frenzy of ink. Leonardo taps the page with a long finger, but he scrutinises me.

'The *vene d'acqua* of the earth is like the blood flow of a woman. The life cycle of a woman is short while the earth is eternal, but still they reflect one another. As a man, or indeed a woman has bones inside her, the supports and armature of flesh, so the world has the rocks, foundations of the earth. As a woman has in her a lake of blood, where the lungs rise and fall in breathing, so the body of the earth has its ocean sea, which rises and falls every six hours as if the world breathed.' He looks at me and smiles. 'We must give you breath and a pulse. Or make it seem very nearly so.'

He thrusts the map at Cecco and reaches instead for a measuring spoon and, like an alchemist, adds a pinch of lake and a smear of oil and mixes it with a blunt palette knife on the board.

'But even that isn't enough.' He frowns, reaching for something else beyond my understanding. 'You, my Lisa, are different from other women. You are the Universal Woman. Eternal like the earth. I'm painting every woman and the earth herself at once, glimpsed, I think, over your shoulder. Woman and the earth itself and the very forces that give her life.'

I tingle with possibilities. It is like that with Leonardo. He sees the correlation between all things, and as long as I am in his presence, I sense them too. When he leaves the room, the light of understanding extinguishes.

He reaches out with his brush and begins very slowly to smooth more layers around what will become the waves of my hair. He murmurs as he works, half to himself.

'The curls of your hair move like the waters of the Arno.'

He tickles along my hairline, where it touches the sky.

'Fetch a mirror!' he calls. 'She wants to watch.'

It's true. I do. Who else is privileged to witness their own creation and, even more, to remember it?

I stare back at myself in the glass as Cecco props it up before me, on a waiting easel. We smile shyly at one another. Two Madonna Lisas. It is too easy to call us beautiful. Our eyes are hooded and knowing, our hair is smudged charcoal *spolveri*, the edges of our gowns edged in chalk over the layers of gesso and waiting to be painted. Leonardo confides softly as he works.

'You will wear a veil. Dark and needle fine. Translucent and the boundary barely visible against the tinge of blueish sky. In nature the air has darkness behind it and appears blue,' says Leonardo.

I gaze back at him, only half-understanding. He sees the connection between all things. Nature, painting. Life and death. Shade and light.

He tells me with pride that I began for him as an experiment. Vexed by what he insists upon calling the unfortunate and sorry paintings of Sandro Botticelli, he determined to create me. I reveal what is possible in the science of painting and *prospettiva*. But that's not good enough for me. I don't want to remain as an experiment. I want to be more than an *invenzione*, however astonishing. He confided to Lisa del Giocondo that I am Petrarch's Laura and Dante's Beatrice. Yet if I am a beloved lady, then I must be loved. And I want to be loved by Leonardo.

Salaì abandons waiting for him to comment on the mural sketches and disappears to bed, muttering and disgruntled. I notice him filch a bottle of the good wine to take with him, the reserve vintage kept for guests. For once, I choose to say nothing. Still, he glowers at me with loathing. Tonight his bed will be cold and empty. Tonight Leonardo belongs only to me.

*

Salaì's temper does not improve. Over the next few days, Leonardo pays scant attention to the preparatory drawings for the mural. It is to depict the wild triumph at the Battle of Anghiari, the skirmish of screaming horses, warriors and billowing flags. Before he left for Pisa, Leonardo had completed dozens of sketches of horses and howling warriors, and schooled the assistants as they attempted similar studies, but now he has lost all interest. He desires only to paint me. He sends back to the apothecary all the paint for the mural. At that, even I protest. The mural must be finished. We need to be paid and we need somewhere to live.

'I'm experimenting with a new recipe of oils and pigments. I don't want to paint *Anghiari* in tempera or in fresco,' answers Leonardo.

At this Salaì loses his temper. 'Maestro! You don't think it might be helpful to confide your plans to me rather than to a … than to her! I'm trying to run your *bottega*.'

Leonardo fixes him with a look of measured disdain. 'She listens and doesn't argue.'

Actually, this isn't true at all, but it infuriates Salaì deliciously. To my disappointment, the row is cut short by the arrival of Lisa del Giocondo. Today Lisa is pale, and more fretful even than usual. She sits in the upholstered chair beside the fire and fusses, unable to be still. Leonardo places her carefully in the requisite pose, leaning her left arm upon the armrest and laying the other on top, to signal our virtue. Her slim fingers toy with the velvet of her sleeve. Leonardo presses his hands upon her shoulders, twisting her, angling her right shoulder further back, and her face turns out directly towards him, frowning. He takes out his brushes and tries to work but it's no good. She fidgets and sighs, impatient.

Leonardo offers her a glass of Vin Santo, the fire to be stoked up or raked out. No, no, she wants nothing. Yet still she cannot settle. She is peevish and unhappy. Even so, I recognise she is lovely, and I appreciate now, having glimpsed myself in Cecco's mirror, that it's true, she's more beautiful than I. Nevertheless, Leonardo is not interested in reproducing a simple copy of female charms.

However, I have no sympathy for her wretchedness. All work in the *bottega* has halted for Lisa, for this, and here she sits sighing and crossing and uncrossing her feet in her fancy embroidered slippers. I agree with Salaì – I cannot bear this woman bringing her tedious troubles to our studio. Her fretful children, the duplicity of her servants. We have been forced to listen whilst she has whined about them all. Nothing pleases her. Yet Leonardo displays no such exasperation. He sets down his brush and leans forward, his countenance grave.

'What's troubling you, Madonna del Giocondo? We are friends, I hope,' he says. 'Have the servants been stealing buttons again?'

'No … '

Tears, round and fat as Medici diamonds, somersault down her cheeks. I have never seen her cry before. I have only observed the livid sobs of the maids. These clear, wobbling tears, and her rasping, catching breath, is new. I am fascinated.

'Please,' she murmurs. 'They must go.'

Leonardo dismisses the assistants with a gesture.

He asks no questions, only waits. His expression is kind, brimful with concern.

'Come, Lisa. What is the matter?' I ask.

Leonardo pours her a glass of wine, presses it into her hand and wipes her tears with a square of silk.

'My sister,' she says at last. 'She was denounced in a *tamburazioni*.'

Leonardo takes her hand and murmurs in sympathy. 'What did it say?'

She swallows and mutters, unable to look at him. 'The accuser says that four men went to the convent of San Domenico in the middle of the night where two nuns were waiting for them and stayed there three or four hours … and you must imagine the rest. It's rank with sin.'

'And your sister is one of these nuns?'

'Sister Camilla Gherardini. There is to be a trial.'

She begins to sob again.

'Florence is full of convents and full of bawdy men longing to tell lascivious stories. It doesn't mean that it's true.'

She shakes her head. 'The allegation in the *tamburazioni* is full of details about the … the indecencies.'

Leonardo shrugs. 'So the anonymous wretch who dreamed up the denunciation has a lewd imagination. He scribbled down the filth in his mind and then popped it in the drum.' He sighs and pats her hand. 'Madonna Lisa, simply because someone writes it or speaks it, doesn't make it true. I am sure your sister will be found not guilty.'

She gazes at him with gratitude that is close to adoration. There is the sound of a scuffle from behind a door, and it is clear from my vantage that Salaì and the other assistants are prying. Leonardo is outraged, but he can't betray his fury without revealing to Lisa that the assistants have been listening and know her humiliation.

'A rat. They have caught the rat that has been raiding my larder. Don't kill it now, boys,' he calls, his voice hard. 'I want to make it suffer later. I don't like sneaking vermin.'

Lisa shudders at the thought of the rat. Silence falls from outside the door.

After she has gone, Leonardo calls them all into the studio. They file in shamefaced and stand before him. He is angrier than I've ever seen him. The assistants are lined up together, quaking like captured enemy soldiers. Tommaso, handsome and with his tomato-red hair. Pimpled Giovanni, surprisingly plain for Leonardo's studio. The master prefers to surround himself with beauty, but beauty falls from Giovanni's brush. Ferrando, who until little Cecco's arrival didn't do much else but grind colours.

'Boys, you have disgraced me. And you,' he says, turning to Salaì, 'you are the one who knows how I too was denounced. I was barely older than you and accused in an anonymous *tamburazioni*. Charged with sodomy. Arrested. Placed in a prison cell. I was fortunate that the charge was not upheld.'

I stare at him, frightened, and wondering how he managed to get away with it. I have little doubt he was guilty.

He admonishes us, furious and defiant. We are all ashamed. We have taken vicious delight in the salacious. None of us loves Lisa, but now we are all envisioning a young Leonardo terrified and suffering in a foul jail cell and someone else enjoying his mortification.

'Where is your compassion?' he says, his voice soft with fury. 'And you, my Lisa, need to learn more humanity.'

I stare back at him, stung. I long to cry. I wish that I could have plump tears tumble down my cheeks like Lisa del Giocondo.

Spring

I hear the rains outside the windows day after day. Cecco might not hear my *voce* but he senses that I'm not like other paintings, and he enjoys my companionship. He confides in me, and I listen to the young boy's confessions of loneliness, which are all the more frank because he can only imagine my reply. He likes to come and sit beside me as he sharpens chalk or prepares the pigments, mashing up buckthorn berries into powder for delicate yellow lake for skin tones and grinding cochineal beetles ready for all the bloody carmine the master will need for the battle scene. I won't let Salaì torment and belittle him. I even told the master he'd stolen the boy's velvet cloak, and he returned it, stained with vine black out of spite.

Leonardo asks Cecco to lift me up so I can see. Little Cecco doesn't question the order, accepting it as an expression of the master's genius and peculiarity. His slim arms tremble as he holds me aloft – he is still more child than man. The water sloshes down from the sky in rivulets and pours along the streets, turning them into tributaries of the Arno. Children sail toy boats amongst the horses and market stalls. Cabbages bob past. I watch a cardinal hitch up his robes and reveal his pallid, skinny ankles. I am lowered to my easel.

We stay safely indoors. Salaì finally gets his way and Leonardo has returned his attention to the mural of the Battle of Anghiari. The commission is already late. The office of works at the palazzo grumbles when Leonardo collects the monthly stipend alongside extra money for the vast amount of paper and wood for the scaffolding.

They pay him in pennies to belittle him, to make their point about how slow he is, and he rejects the fee entirely, complaining that he's not a 'penny painter' and declaring that he'll resign the commission. The same afternoon, an emissary is despatched to the studio with the money owed in decent silver ducats, and assurances are extorted from Leonardo. He'll fulfil the contract.

At last he's immersed in the work, lost. The refectory walls of the Santa Maria Novella are smothered in paper, sixty *braccia* in length, and another eighteen *braccia* in width. When the mural is finished, it will be twice the size of *The Last Supper*. The baker brings eighty-eight pounds of sifted flour to coat the cartoon, and a blacksmith arrives with iron pins and rings, and hammers out rings and wheels – the sparks and furnace fires are like knockings from hell – but now Leonardo has a platform on wheels so he can slide around the area as he works on the massive drawing.

Over the weeks, Cecco and I sit side by side surveying the growing cartoon in dread and wonder – the Milanese armies advance from the left-hand side while a fierce cavalry skirmish rages in the middle of the room. The walls are covered with the snarling mouths of warriors, the rearing backs of horses, the brutishness of war. Beyond the brief outline of a gully, Salaì tries and fails to draw the strategic bridge and the massing Florentine cavalry. He can't perfect the perspective, even with the master's help. 'See,' I tell Cecco, 'even Salaì grapples and fails.' The boy happens to notice and giggles, exulted.

The composition is complex, and Leonardo reworks each detail in careful studies before copying them onto the cartoon. Everyone is tired and snappish. Cecco is still not permitted near the cartoon but only to skivvy for the others. He's despatched to the apothecary for sponges and endless charcoal and more chalk. Leonardo is never satisfied with the work of the assistants and corrects it again and again.

'Tommaso, the cannon balls must have a train of smoke following their flight. Salaì, if you show one who has fallen, you then must show the place where his body has slithered in the bloodstained dust and mud.'

Leonardo has the doorway to his bedchamber demolished, so that he can walk directly to the cartoon, and he paces blinkered, arms folded. Some days he doesn't draw at all, merely walks to and fro and murmurs for hours on end. He gropes towards certainty and composition. As I stare at the emerging cartoon, I can almost hear the din of battle, the agony of men's dying and screaming of the horses as they rear up and stomp the earth.

Leonardo arrived in Florence pummelled by war with Borgia. I am the only one who hears Leonardo's dreams at night, when he cries out at the horrors of what he's seen. Cesare Borgia. The man is a stain on the human race. He cracks open the ribs of his enemies, splits them with a wedge like the carcass of a bullock or a pig, until the cobbles are slick with blood. He leaves their severed heads brooding on their chests like a hen upon her hatchlings. I know, because Leonardo tells me these things, restless in the dark while the others sleep. But I am awake, always, and I stay with him, listening and trying to comfort him. 'War, my Lisa, is the most brutal kind of madness,' he says, his face damp from the night sweats. I urge him to sketch away his fears. I wish I could be more like Salaì; I long for hands that could touch and caress, proffer comfort. It's always from his arms and from his bed that Leonardo rises. The love I can offer is only of the mind, not of the body.

Leonardo draws in charcoal and then burns half of them to dust on the candle flame, but it doesn't work. The foul images remain, branded on us both. Now, he uses cleansed visions from the campaign in his cartoon. I still smell blood and viscera rising from the paper.

I lose all sense of time. Alicia carries in meals and then takes them out barely touched. Leonardo sleeps fitfully and rises at midnight to work again. The battle leers nightmarish by candlelight. The assistants daren't slumber while the master labours. News that Leonardo is at work on another masterpiece has started to travel far and wide, and we begin to receive letters from Milan and Rome and Mantua from ever-hopeful patrons eager for portraits and commissions.

'Ask Cecco to reply,' I tell Leonardo. 'He has a fine hand. You should let him scribe for you.'

We shan't be too precise. I know, even if Leonardo himself does not, that there is scant chance of an actual portrait. If they are extremely fortunate, they may be able to purchase a Madonna or a Salvator Mundi produced by the studio and overseen by the master, but even that seems hopeful.

Cecco draws out a chair, some paper and ink, moistens his quill and settles down at the table. I can see that he's relieved to be given a task that doesn't involve dashing about through the rain. The hem of his tunic is perman-ently sodden. Yet the boy never complains. Leonardo rarely drafts his own correspondence. He writes with his left hand, close and methodical but in a mirror lettering difficult for others to decipher. I dictate the letter, full of puff and flattery, but careful not to promise what will only later disappoint and enrage. Leonardo repeats my words to Cecco.

Cecco is finishing the letter when Alicia hurries in, the door banging behind her. For a moment, I'm startled, half-imagining that a fuming patroness has arrived all the way from Mantua to demand her portrait. But there is no woman of charm and choler here. It's Niccolò Machiavelli.

'Maestro,' he calls, but his tone lacks all civility.

He's drenched and water from his saturated boots causes a puddle to form on the tile floor. His skin is stretched too tightly around his skull as though death is peeping out from his small black eyes.

Leonardo doesn't notice him at first. He is up on the scaffolding, twelve *braccia* in the air, seated on a wooden platform. He's lost to the detail of a horse's foot, trying to perfect the movement of the earth flinging around its galloping hoof. When finally he glances down and sees Machiavelli, he fails to register the malevolence of his greeting, his cadaverous looks. The work is going well, so Leonardo perceives nothing but his own joy reflected back at him like sunlight off a looking glass. He continues to draw, grasping his chalk, the wind sneaking in through the gaps in the leading and causing the paper to flap and rustle.

'Come down!' calls Machiavelli.

'A moment.'

Machiavelli stamps his foot on the floor, a rare display of temper. 'At once!'

Finally, Leonardo recognises the wrath and fear on the politician's face and climbs down.

'Your wretched plan is a fiasco,' says Machiavelli. 'You are cosy and cosseted, while I'm there in the swamps.'

'Then sit by the fire. Eat something,' says Leonardo sensibly.

Machiavelli ignores him. 'There's been a storm. These vile rains. The boats guarding the mouths of the ditches were wrecked. Eighty souls lost. Drowned. Dead because of you and your absurd plan.' He spits the words.

Leonardo stares at him aghast and says nothing for several minutes, just continues to stare in horror while the colour drains from his face.

'We have no choice but to withdraw. The walls of the ditches have collapsed. The entire plain is flooded. Farms ruined. Cattle all drowned. It's a disaster and of your making.'

'I believed the canal would work,' Leonardo stutters at last, running his hands through his hair, streaking it with chalk. He murmurs, still unable to believe it. 'Eighty souls lost.'

'And more than seven thousand ducats.'

'Eighty men … n-never mind the cost.'

'No! The cost is never anything to you!'

Salaì, Cecco and Tommaso regard Machiavelli with loathing and revulsion, but they daren't utter a word. I am not so craven.

'Leave him be. You begged him for his designs. No one else would do!'

Machiavelli snorts. He sounds like one of the horses on the cartoon. He speaks only to Leonardo. 'I intend to keep my head on my shoulders and my position as Chancellor of the Signoria.'

Leonardo glances up at the massive cartoon. The war-riors leer, the huffing horses churn the dirt. Art must be his clemency. He will have to draw and paint his way out of this disaster.

Machiavelli leaves the chamber, shoving Alicia aside in his anger. The room is suddenly empty and cold; nobody speaks. I watch Salaì. He too can see that Leonardo has made an enemy of Machiavelli. There is more ill fortune to come.

The rain continues to hurl against the glass and gusts batter the shutters. This is the swirling deluge that has ruined Florence's dreams of a route to the sea. Oh, if the canal had worked, it would have been the marvel of our age, but now it lies in ruins and death. The master himself is staggered by guilt, filled with bile and melancholy. He stands unmoving, unseeing, fixed upon some unfathomable desolate reverie. For the eighty drowned souls we can do nothing except pray. We see them floating in the dugouts and waterlogged swamp as the rain sweeps everything away. Fingers wrinkled and eyes open, bodies hauled out of the brackish waters and laid upon the muddied banks. Stacked up ten deep. Yawn-mouthed. No-named. They'll be buried in another soggy ditch. Common men like those won't be carried home.

They will remain always, a bloody stain upon Leonardo's conscience.

For seven nights Leonardo neither works nor sleeps. He barely eats. He sits and stares. Cecco says he's certain that he prays but I am convinced he does not. I wonder sometimes if Leonardo is a heretic. I plead with him to speak to me, but for once he doesn't seem to hear. Guilt eats away at his soul like maggots. We tell him that it wasn't his fault. He was not responsible for the men; he was not there. I lose patience.

'If you are certain that you're guilty of a sin, then go to confession.'

He sits unmoving.

'Let Cecco fetch a priest,' I say.

He whirls round. 'No priests.'

I think I've reached him at last, but when I press him again he slumps back into his gloom and refuses to say another word.

While I worry about Leonardo, Salaì worries about the *bottega*. Niccolò Machiavelli has been pleading his case to the Florentine Council, doubtless insisting that he carried out Leonardo da Vinci's plans impeccably, and that he, Niccolò, is blameless in the ensuing catastrophe. Soon we hear that Machiavelli has been ordered to take leave of his post. We have little hope for Leonardo. But he has not been summoned to the council to defend himself. Neither has he been asked to leave the Santa Maria Novella and the commission for the mural has not been cancelled. Yet, now when it is expedient for work to continue speedily and with Leonardo's customary divine *ingegno*, he has stopped entirely.

Salaì prepares to resume the day's work on the cartoon, marshalling the assistants, but they're a platoon without a captain and the scene has barely progressed. They scratch at the edges, spoiling the cleanness of the lines. It seems hopeless. Then, late one morning, Alicia ushers in Lisa del Giocondo and her maid. Leonardo stands and bows, but he doesn't show her to the best chair and does not order wine and instead slumps back down. She must have been warned that he is in great torment, as she displays no surprise on seeing him so dishevelled and seats herself beside him. Salaì watches her closely, and I realise he must have summoned her. I'm torn between annoyance that he dare consider Lisa might be able to help Leonardo, and hope that she will.

To my surprise, Salaì then heaves my three-legged easel so that I'm opposite the master too. Leonardo glances between us both. He looks gaunt and hasn't visited the barber for some days. His eyes are sunken and he is not dressed with his usual fastidious care. Lisa and I both stare at him.

'I hear you killed eighty men, Maestro Leonardo,' says Lisa at last. 'That you caused the rains to fall steadily for three months and the ditches to collapse and drown them all.'

'I might as well have done it,' says Leonardo. 'I should have known.'

'No. You do not know everything,' says Lisa sharply. 'Because you seek to understand all secrets of the universe, you flail and come apart when there are things that you do not. You cannot understand why this terrible thing has happened. I know. God willed it.'

There is silence for a moment and she pauses and shrugs. 'I understand that I am not supposed to understand anything much at all. I am small and stupid. You certainly all think so.'

As she glances around the chamber, Salaì, Tommaso and even spotty Giovanni shift uneasily, trying not to meet one another's eye. I'm glad they don't look at me.

'I know I am stupid beside you and certainly next to God. Even you are stupid compared to God, oh great Leonardo. You need to surrender a piece of your will and all your pride and accept this calamity as His will.'

Leonardo is very still, but he's listening.

'Lisa is right. She is stupid. But she is still right. You are not God. You're not that powerful,' I say.

Lisa rises and smiles. 'God forgives you all your sins. Those poor men's deaths are not your sin. It is pride to think so. Now pride is a sin.'

I believe Lisa is trying to make a joke. It's a shame that it's neither funny nor appropriate. To my irritation, Leonardo almost smiles. He takes her hands and bows deeply.

'You are a woman of perfect *virtù*.'

She smiles. 'Then listen to me.' She gestures to me. 'I'm always watching you. Or my *virtù visiva* is.'

Leonardo brightens for a moment. 'So you are starting to like the portrait?'

Lisa doesn't answer, turning with an elusive smile, as her maid fastens her cloak.

After she has gone, he returns and sits back down beside me with a sigh. I may not be fond of Lisa, but she is a friend to Leonardo. I will allow her that single virtue.

'Come, maestro, you're punishing the others too. Salaì. Our little Cecco. What did *il ragazzo* do? If you fail to deliver this commission and we're run out of Florence, they'll suffer too,' I say.

Leonardo doesn't move.

'You're supposed to be teaching them. Salaì's adequate. Cecco's dreadful. If you're not going to help the poor boy, I think it would be kinder to let him go to Michelangelo Buonarroti or Sandro Botticelli.'

To my gratification, I observe him wince. I swell to my theme.

'Yes, Sandro would be best. He has such patience, I've heard. And look at that angel over there. That's Cecco's.'

A sheaf of drawings flutters across the table. Several of Leonardo's own horses rear and gallop along the page, while in one corner Cecco has attempted a feeble angel of the Annunciation. Her neck is short, her shoulder lumpen and the angle of her arm is twisted and wrong.

I sigh. 'A pity. Such a sweet boy. But he's not talented. Sandro Botticelli could help him, I think.'

Leonardo explodes. 'I recently saw a Botticelli Annunciation in which the angel looked as if he wished to chase Our Lady out of her room. In fact, Our Lady seemed in such despair, she appeared as if she was about to throw herself from the window.'

'Oh, so then perhaps Botticelli isn't the fellow to help our Cecco with his Annunciation? If only we knew some other painter of immeasurable talent,' I say, serenely.

'Why did I paint you a mouth? I've had no peace since,' he grumbles.

I decide it's prudent for once to remain silent.

Leonardo picks up the paper, examines it closely, sighs with anguish and hollers for Cecco, gesturing for the boy to sit. I watch while he painstakingly makes corrections to the angel's arm as the boy observes, amazed.

The next day before the morning meal, Leonardo appears before us renewed. I see he's deftly shaven, his hair is trimmed and he surveys the cartoon on the wall.

'Lower the horses,' he says, impatient, pointing to the skirmish of cavalry in the central section.

He considers the bemused assistants with profound dissatisfaction. 'What have you all been doing? Idling? You've muddied the profiles on those warriors. Amend them.'

At once, with a snap, work begins again. I watch, fascinated. I'm not sure whether it was Lisa or me, or both of us together, who made the difference. Soon, the chambers of the church fill with dark and murky air; I inhale the smoke and filthy dust of war. Everywhere are feverish cries of death. I'll be relieved when this commission is finished. I want him to return to painting me. It's been weeks since he touched me with his brush. I miss his hand. I want him to rise in the night, unable to resist adding another layer to my lip, my hair.

In the early evening as the light fades, I notice a man lingering, watching from the doorway. He hesitates, a package under his arm. Then, reaching a decision, he presses into the room. He's luxuriantly dressed if disordered, his cloak haphazard. I recognise him. A fleshy and petty Florentine nobleman of middling years. He purchased a Madonna several months before. If I'm not mistaken, the parcel he clutches is the same size as the panel on which she was painted. His cheeks are rouged with mortification. I'm intrigued. He shuffles into the refectory and stares up at the cartoon, discomfort momentarily forgotten in awe at the vast drawing, half-concealed behind the elaborate scaffolding. It's gathering dark, the candles are unlit, and in the shadows and half-light monstrous figures, part human, part gorgon, writhe amongst the battle scene.

'Messer Leonardo?' he calls, at last.

The master turns and peers into the gloom. Seeing the figure, he blinks in confusion.

'Baron Luigi?'

The Baron is a forlorn figure. His wife bore him eight children and died birthing the ninth. He has been offered several other young women as suitable for his next wife, but he's refused them all. I listen to the studio tittle-tattle. On seeing him, Salaì instantly bustles. Alicia is summoned. Wine is poured, more candles are lit, candied fruit brought from the larder, and ham sliced and laid out on boards with wedges of cheese. A fire pops and smokes in the grate. Leonardo and the Baron sit in chairs beside the nascent flames. The young assistants hover, anxious and intrigued. Why is the Baron here himself? Why hasn't he sent a servant in his place, or summoned Leonardo to his palace near the Ponte Vecchio? Yet I notice it is the nobleman himself who appears ill at ease. He takes none of the proffered refreshment. He twists his gold signet ring round and round on his pudgy finger.

The parcel now sits on the table, bound in cloth. The Baron's gaze falls continually upon it.

'Is that the Madonna with the guelder rose?' asks Leonardo gently. 'Has there been some accident? Do you need me to make a repair?'

With the tenderness of a midwife, Leonardo begins to unswaddle the panel from its many layers. The Baron flinches. The Madonna is laid bare. She smiles serene and benevolent, from the poplar wood. Much of the painting is by Salaì and Giovanni, but the sumptuous layers of robe, the liquid way the fabric falls on her sleeve, I can see is by the master himself. The Madonna's face has the touch of the master, and there is something particularly gentle and sweet about her expression. Her billowing curls have fallen from his brush. And, as hard as I look, I perceive no damage to the picture.

Neither does Leonardo. Something else is wrong. He dismisses the assistants with a wave.

'I truly don't know whether I should speak to you or a priest,' says the Baron finally, his head in his hands. 'I find myself in front of her in the night. She is so lifelike. I kiss her and speak to her.' He glances up at Leonardo, his expression desperate. 'You must think me mad.'

'I do not.'

'It's blasphemy,' he says softly. 'Save me, Leonardo.'

Leonardo leans forward. 'Baron Luigi, what is it that you want me to do?'

'I cannot love the Madonna. Not like this. It's unholy. My soul.'

He gives a cry of anguish, and I feel pity rise within me like cool water from a well. 'Please, remove the signs of her divinity. Let me kiss her without guilt.'

Leonardo is silent for a minute, considering. The un-seasoned wood in the fire hisses and spits and weird shadows leer at us from high on the walls.

'I will do it, if that's what you really want. I am only your servant. But, Baron Luigi, I fear for your conscience. The guilt will never truly be gone. Perhaps it would be better to banish the painting from your house entirely. To rid yourself of temptation.'

The nobleman nods miserably. A man with plague told to swallow medicine. It is futile, a tonic to salve the doc-tor's sense of helplessness rather than ease the sick. Baron Luigi already fears he's doomed by his unholy passion for a holy painting.

Leonardo stands and removes the wrappings from the picture.

'There is a chip to the varnish in the top right-hand corner,' he fibs. 'I'll make the repair and then you can let me know where you want it sent. To your brother's villa, perhaps?'

The Baron doesn't reply but acquiesces meekly with a look of wretchedness. He stands, ready to leave.

'Escort the Baron safely home,' says Leonardo, calling to Giovanni and Tommaso.

They hasten after him. Wealth cannot insulate a man from unhappiness. The ill-fated man grieving for his beloved wife and now enraptured and enchanted by a painting. I study Leonardo through the darkness. It takes powers of divine genius to make a painting of such beauty that a man loves it as though it were a real woman. Yet, in me, he has created something else entirely. I am a new miracle. I am a painting who loves the painter.

Summer

*L*eonardo doesn't want to go to the party. He conjures up a dazzling swirl of excuses, but we all know the truth. The thought of Michelangelo Buonarroti is a bag of stones in his stomach and this is Michelangelo's night. It's the grand unveiling of his new statue of David and Leonardo is seething. He paces through the cloisters of the Santa Maria Novella, weaving to and fro beneath the arches, hissing with fury.

'Instead of the brave yet docile Hebrew boy of legend, Michelangelo's carved a marble colossus. It's supposed to be the monster Goliath who's *il gigante*, not the shepherd boy. The entire conceit is absurd.'

All the doors are thrown wide to the refectory beyond, and I watch him through the opening.

'That spoiled block of marble lay ignored in the *fabbriceria* of the duomo for years. They were going to offer it to me. Then they gave it to Michelangelo instead.'

Salaì coughs. 'They did offer it to you, maestro. You told them that it had been botched by Agostino di Duccio and they could stick it.'

Leonardo glances at him, expression laced with reproach. 'Don't remind me of the inconvenient truth, my friend, when I wish to feel slighted. It's unkind.'

Salaì demurs and pours him a glass of wine by way of apology. Leonardo slumps on the bench in the courtyard beside him, laying his head on his shoulder, absently toying with Salaì's curls. Catlike, Salaì nuzzles into him. If I was a statue like Michelangelo's *Il Gigante* and not a painting, then at least I would have form, and Leonardo could sit beside me too, stroke my cheek, slide his arm around my waist, but he is dismissive of the sculptor's art. I am a higher form of art, if a lonelier one.

The night is warm and infused with lilac and I can hear the first of the cicadas. Leonardo sighs and huffs.

'I told the works department it's a mistake to put the statue in the loggia. They ought to put it behind the low wall where the soldiers line up. It's absurdly oversized. People will fall over it in the middle of the piazza.'

He takes a long sip of wine.

'They've had to break down the door of the works department to get out the colossus. It's vandalism!'

None of us remind him that he smashed a doorway between his bedroom and the refectory so he could reach the *Anghiari* cartoon more quickly.

'Four days and forty men to move the creature on fourteen greased beams.' He shakes his head, feigning dismay, but this is a feat of engineering ingenuity and even Leonardo sounds intrigued rather than appalled.

He's dressed tonight with particular care in a silk tunic in shimmering damask. The evening is mild, the sun still high and he wears a cloak of the lightest lambswool. Salaì fastens it tenderly on his shoulder with a golden brooch shaped like a laurel leaf, brushing away his long hair so it doesn't tangle in the pin of the clasp. His fingers brush his cheek, and Leonardo catches them and kisses them. For a moment his anger dissipates like mist in the wind. I feel a familiar tingle of envy towards Salaì.

'I don't know why I'm bothering. I should go as a beggar, then I'll look exactly like the man of the hour, in his dog-skin boots,' complains Leonardo.

'A sculptor is a workman, but the painter is a gentleman,' I call out, interrupting, reminding him of his own words. 'Now go. If you're late, you'll seem bitter. You must be magnanimous. Your usual charming self.'

Leonardo obeys. He collects his hat and comes inside and bows to me, then strolls out into the evening air in the street beyond, the carnival notes of music already floating up to us. Salaì and Cecco join me inside. Beneath the music we can hear the shouts of the gathering crowds and the grunts of the horses and men. We are torn between loyalty to Leonardo and the prickle of excitement. I envy the others. At least they will get to see the marble *Il Gigante* in the Piazza della Signoria; if not tonight, then in the coming days and weeks. I must depend on their cast-off descriptions.

Leonardo returns at midnight having lost his hat. Cecco and Tommaso are despatched to search. We have little hope of its recovery. It will have been thieved long since. Leonardo has drunk a good deal of wine. He saunters into the refectory and stands there swaying like a cypress tree in the breeze.

'Well?' I demand. 'How fares Michelangelo's *Il Gigante*?'

He considers for a moment. Blinks several times. Hiccups. 'The body should not look like a sack of walnuts. *Un sacco di noci*,' he says with a hint of mischief. 'Nor a bundle of radishes.'

Yet he is studying the cartoon of *Anghiari* with tremendous concentration. His fingers twitch, restless, and he lights an oil lamp – one of his own design – and reaches for chalk. He begins to make alterations to the musculature of one of the warriors' torsos. Even hazy with wine, he's precise with his pen, too eager to wait till morning. He might loathe Michelangelo, yet he remains impatient, determined to uncover what he can learn from him. Tommaso and Cecco return without the hat, Tommaso as red as his hair, full of contrition and apologies. Leonardo doesn't hear, much less care. They are drooping with tiredness and vanish to bed once it's clear the master will be working until morning. I wait in silence. The only watcher in a house full of sleepers.

At last, as the rose-pink fingers of dawn begin to probe between the slats in the shutters, he stops and yawns. He drinks a glass of wine, devours a peach and sits again, snatching up a piece of paper on which he quickly begins to draw. He turns it round and shows me. In black chalk he's sketched the naked figure of a muscular young man clutching a slingshot, turning slightly to the side, proud face tilted upwards. Unseen wind ruffles his hair. He pins up the drawing so I can admire it.

'For you,' he says happily. 'After *Il Gigante*.'

I am touched. He knows how I longed to see the statue.

He slumps down once more on the wooden bench beside me and tugs off his boots. Through the open doors we can see the fading stars and the sun rising in her slow sailing across the heavens. The sky is clear and cloudless and the sun bloody as a split pomegranate. I ask him to take me outside so I can see better. He laughs but obliges.

'Look. Is it day or night?' I say. 'Venus is still twinkling.'

'I am not even sure that the flicker of a star isn't really in the eye, and not the star at all. Sometimes, I wonder if the earth is a star.'

I search his face in the weird crepuscular light, the furrows of his brow. Restless, interested, always searching for answers to questions that no one else thinks to ask. Halfway through an answer he breaks off to ask another question. Nothing is quite finished. Not even me. And one day I should like a dress. Hands.

'Was Lisa del Giocondo there last night?' I ask. I usually can't bear to mention her, but he hasn't painted me for weeks, not even an eyelash.

'Yes. And her husband,' he says. 'They were both there. She is coming to see us for another sitting.'

Of course she is. Despite his restless mind, Leonardo always comes back to me in the end. Even though he is busy with *The Battle of Anghiari*, Leonardo still wants to paint me. I am his David. Michelangelo talks about freeing his sculptures from the marble, but Leonardo freed me long ago. We sit awhile in silence, companionably not speaking, listening to the steady whir and tick of the cicadas in the courtyard.

'Forty years ago, when I was a *bellissimo* boy in Verrocchio's studio,' he says at last, 'I was the model for his sculpture of *il David*.'

'Was it any good?'

'Yes. No. It was definitely smaller than Michelangelo's. The mild boy of scripture, not a giant. It has that in its favour.'

As we sit in the quickening light, I come to understand that the two versions of *il David* – Verrocchio's and Michelangelo's – are forcing the master to confront his own mortality. While once he was the inspiration for a sculptor's David and the very image of impetuous youth, now he is ageing. He might remain extraordinarily vital, but he is well beyond middle years. Michelangelo is the wild youth of Florence, rude but tolerated because of his uncanny brilliance. Who else could wrestle *Il Gigante* from a despoiled piece of rejected marble, lying forgotten for years? A brilliant upstart. The sort of man that Leonardo used to be, long ago. Michelangelo's conquest of his city wounds him. Leonardo's own greatest triumph, his *Last Supper* in Milan, is already fading, the Apostles withering into ghosts as his experiment with a new recipe for pigments fails.

'One day, when I die, what of me will remain? Not my *Last Supper*, it seems,' he says, a note of desolation in his voice.

'Me. That's why you must finish me.'

He smiles at me with affection. 'When I began you, I did not know in your eyes I would find love.'

For a glorious moment, I think he is declaring his love for me, and I feel a space open up within me. In that second it does not matter that we cannot touch, or that he will always lie with others and desire their bodies; it only matters that he loves me, adores me. And, then as he blinks, I realise that he is speaking of my love for him and I am maddened. How dare he gobble up my love like air, taking it for granted, assuming it will always be there, surrounding him? And then my anger is gone, blown out like a candle, because it is true. As long as I have thoughts, they will be of him and of love.

As I glance across at the page fluttering in the candle-light I realise how differently Leonardo and Michelangelo see the world. How differently they want us, the viewer, to perceive our world. I imagine that sketch of the David in marble, massive and bold and magnificent, a feat of daring from the prodigious Michelangelo. His vision of art isn't like Leonardo's. *Il Gigante* is aggressive and brash, swaggering with his slingshot. Nothing is hidden. A glorious exterior displayed for all to admire. Leonardo is opposite. He always instructs Cecco and Tommaso to tell stories with their pictures but to leave something as a mystery, something hidden. It is more enticing, more de-lightful, when a secret is concealed. The viewer must bring part of themselves to the painting.

The sun has floated upwards now, cherry red, daubing the cloisters rose pink.

'I'm better than any giant,' I tell him.

'Of course you are,' he says.

'I'll make you more famous than that sack of walnuts. And *Il Gigante* doesn't love Michelangelo.'

Leonardo leans close, whispers to me a secret, one he's never told me before. The place where my heart would be pulses and flutters. But I won't tell you what it is. You must imagine it or at least make a guess, for I am not like *Il Gigante*. I am Leonardo's creature after all, and some of my secrets are hidden, and when you come to me, you must bring a piece of yourself.

One day, he will tell me that he loves me. Those are the words I want to hear most of all. But for now, I laugh. I hold it deep within me, our shared confidence more precious than any wedding jewel.

To my joy, Lisa del Giocondo cordially requests that Messer Leonardo call upon her at the Giocondo villa in the hills above Florence, instead of coming to the studio. I have never left the city before. Salaì wraps me carefully in cloth, before placing me into a fitted pine box lined with soft leather for the ride up and out of the heat and the summer stink of Florence. My box is cramped and coffin dark. To my disgust, I am strapped to the side of the horse. It's my first time and, despite Leonardo's re-assurances, I'm sure it's going to bolt or roll and crush me to splinters. As we leave Florence I can hear the ring of its iron hoof upon the rutted stone change to a softer sound as it pounds the sun-baked mud. I feel the steady motion of the animal as it canters in the heat. Leonardo loves horses and only ever keeps the best. He's right that it doesn't bolt and instead its movements are fluid, smooth and strong. He reins it in, pausing to let it drink at a stream, and calls out to me as he slaps the horse's flank.

'So, my Lisa? How are you faring?'

Still I don't answer. It's dark and hot. The horse huffs and scrapes the ground, tail slapping at the flies. I am in the murk for half a morning and three thousand steps.

We reach the Giocondo place before midday, and the sun is already aggressive. A groom takes the horse which huffs and snorts. Salaì unfastens me and carries me in my box round to a loggia, and there, in the dappled shade of draped vine, releases me, placing me upon my three-legged easel. I look about me, dazzled. The bright, clear sky, pure and costly aquamarine. The lemon trees trimmed in their tubs, their leaves curling in the fierce sunlight. The rows of low combed hedges of box, angular and straight. The scent of bay and pine. A rill trickles beside a gravel path, leading down towards a mirror pond, where a Grecian Narcissus kneels, gazing in awe, transfixed at his own beauty. Rose bushes tremble in the warmth. Neptune snarls at us from the largest pool as fat carp swoosh around his ankles, unafraid of the trident held aloft. In the distance, nestled in the palms of a pair of hills and edged by a grove of olives, I can see the orange roof of the duomo and the golden orb of the spire catching in the light. Kites fly overhead, surfing on high currents.

The trill of birdsong is punctured by the laughter of several children who tear across the loggia in a torrent of giggles. A nurse chases after them on fat ankles, scolding and breathless. The children take no notice and Leonardo laughs.

'Children are all the same, whether they come from the loins of peasants or kings.'

Servants hurry with jugs of wine and plates heaped with freshly plucked melon and grapes, fatty hams and yellow cheeses, round as a full moon. A spread is set out on a cloth covering a marble table on the larger of the loggias. A bearded musician picks up his bow and begins to play the *lira da braccio*. As I stare at the city cradled below through the furze of the olive trees, I wonder if I am about to see Beatrice appear as my guide and this is not earth at all but *paradiso*.

Yet, despite the hospitality, Lisa del Giocondo is missing. We have come here not to feast nor to marvel at the wonder of the view. Salaì eats and drinks with relish, tearing himself more bread, and dripping slices of melon, but Leonardo casts about uneasily for Lisa. He has come for her. He frowns, questioning. Now I see that I ought to have wondered why we have been summoned here and she hasn't come to the studio. Before, I was too thrilled at the prospect of a journey to ask why it was necessary.

Leonardo beckons a servant. 'Madonna del Giocondo?' He gestures to the sky. 'The light is good.'

It's a lie. The light is much too fierce, even out here on the loggia. It won't be good until four or five o'clock. Until then, we'll need to retreat to the shade inside, find a cool, north-facing room.

The servant shakes her head and hurries away, tongue clicking. Something isn't right. Salaì stops eating; he looks at Leonardo, head cocked. Then she appears, led out like a widow on her husband Francesco del Giocondo's arm. Her head is covered in a veil of translucent black, air downcast. She looks shrunken, folded in on herself, and she barely picks up her feet, instead shuffling along. I am shocked to see her. We must have been summoned here because she is ill, or has been ill and is now convalescent. I wonder with what sickness. It can't be plague or she'd be hidden away.

Leonardo stands, walks towards her and bows, unafraid. She startles, apparently surprised to see him.

'See, it's the great painter, your friend Leonardo,' bellows Francesco del Giocondo, patting her arm as though she is a small dog. 'He is come here to see you.'

She blinks, wincing in the brightness of the sunlight at Leonardo, her face blank, as though she cannot remember who he is, or who he is to her.

'Madonna Lisa, it is a privilege and an honour, but I fear you are not well,' says Leonardo.

He takes her hand and leads her gently to a chair. For once unresisting, she allows him to settle her tenderly. Leonardo stares at Francesco questioningly and with considerable concern.

'Our youngest daughter, Piera, has gone to live with Our Lady in Heaven,' says Francesco del Giocondo, his voice not entirely steady.

His glance shifts from side to side and he accepts Leonardo's condolences quickly, chafing to speak of other matters. I look at Francesco and remember how much I loathe him. When I am in his presence, I almost pity Lisa. He rocks on his heels, restless and eager to be gone, to hand his wife over to us, even though we are nothing but familiar acquaintances. We do not love her, but he cannot bear her grief. He is straining to be away from it. Back to his business – anything, anywhere but here amongst the beauty of the lemon trees and the agony of his wife's despair for her dead daughter.

Lisa looks up at Leonardo, her face bloodless. 'She was two years old. Always naughty and always laughing. I keep thinking that I hear her with the others. But her voice is missing. How can I bear it?'

'I don't know,' he says, taking her hand. 'I have no idea at all.'

Francesco del Giocondo stands there, rocking from foot to foot, saying nothing. I scrutinise him, trying to see if his face divulges any signs of inner turmoil. He is twenty years older than Lisa. His face is now fattened with good fortune and an entitled sense of his own prosperity, and he will not allow even this to crack the façade. He glances back at me with a critical eye.

'She is wearing very ordinary clothes in the painting.'

Leonardo shrugs. It doesn't seem important, particularly at present. He will not be pressed by Francesco del Giocondo. The nurse reappears with the five surviving children, all now subdued and scrubbed. They are brought to the table and introduced to Leonardo.

'Bartolomeo, our eldest,' says Lisa, gesturing to a tall boy of nine or ten with messy hair, darker than the rest. 'Then, Piero, Camilla and Marietta.'

A boy of eight and two girls of seven and six, both gap-toothed and fair-haired, grin at the painter and hide behind their nurse. The youngest sucks her plaits.

'And then there would have been Piera, but now there is only Andrea.'

A plump baby, as unlikely as most cherubs adorning chapel ceilings across Florence, wrestles and writhes on the nurse's broad hip. A sheen of sweat appears like down above her top lip from the effort of restraining him.

'They'll be taken back to the nursery,' says Francesco quickly. 'They won't be allowed to interrupt.'

'Must they?' pleads Lisa. 'I like them around me, at the moment.'

'No, of course they can stay,' says Leonardo. 'Salaì loves to play with children.'

To my surprise, Salaì makes no objection and produces a shining coin from his pocket and, after showing it to them, then instantly makes it disappear, leaving their mouths little round 'o's of wonder.

Relieved that his duties have been dispensed with, Francesco del Giocondo escapes. The nurse and Salaì attempt to keep order and, as I watch, another, younger nursemaid appears and, taking the baby, suckles him. Lisa surveys them all, distant and melancholy. Camilla rushes over and presses her face into her mother's lap, crying bitter, bitter tears. Lisa takes a handful of her hair and inhales its incense deeply, rubbing it between her fingers, kissing her, and murmuring into her ear, and then, a minute later, the girl scampers away to join the others.

'Camilla's hair is almost like Piera's was but not quite. Piera's was finer, whiter. Like gossamer.'

We watch the children. They toss a leather ball high into the air, and Salaì heads it into the pool so it is speared on Neptune's trident; the children clutch themselves with laughter, entranced. Salaì pretends horror and rolls up his tunic and, shaking off his sandals, wades into the pool to retrieve it, grovelling apologies to the god. The children swoon with pleasure. Even Lisa smiles. Leonardo takes out his brush.

'The children are sad. They miss their sister, but children cannot stay sad for long,' she says.

'Children must play like the sun must rise,' says Leonardo.

She turns and smiles at him, sweetly and sadly. Leonardo beckons to the *lira da braccio* player.

'Play for us, please. But only cheerful melodies.'

The musician nods and picks up his bow.

At once Lisa looks vexed. 'Now you sound like my husband. He cannot stomach my unhappiness. It chafes against him like a pebble in his shoe. If you won't let me be unhappy and full of rage, Messer Leonardo, go back to Florence.'

Her voice has fire in it, and she looks at him with real anger.

'I beg your pardon, Madonna Lisa. Tell me everything you can about Piera,' he says. 'Tell me again about her gossamer hair and the way it moved.'

He sets down his brush and listens. She talks for hours as the sun filters through the vines, mottling the tablecloth, and sails across the heavens to the west. He says little, pausing here and there to ask a question, but mostly he simply listens to a mother as she talks of the girl she loves and has lost and hopes to meet again in Heaven, but finds now, when she needs it most, her faith has a loose thread, and she can't help but tug, and worry at the seam.

'She was just an ordinary little girl. They die every day. But she was mine. And I loved her.'

Weary, Lisa stands. She has become thin, fragile as a reed. The other children have been taken inside long since by their nurse and Salaì sits again at the edge of the loggia swinging his legs. The ruddy afternoon sun catches on the golden roof of the duomo and it seems to blaze. Finally, she glances down across at me. She has quite forgotten why we have come.

'That's who I used to be,' she says with a frown. 'I'm sure I'll remember how to be her again, one day.'

Leonardo takes pity. 'She hasn't been you for quite a while.'

'No,' agrees Lisa.

We watch as she slowly walks back into the villa, a broken lost thing.

'Women lose so many children, they are supposed to mourn quickly, and out of sight,' says Salaì. 'We were only brought here as a distraction, as Francesco del Giocondo has had enough of her desperation.'

I consider Lisa afresh. I am not like her. I shan't bear children and I shan't lose them. Her sufferings won't be like mine. Yet, for the first time, this day, I feel something for her other than irritation and contempt. Her life might be small, but it is also full of sadness. Something pricks at me. It is not the sharp point of the needle making more *spolveri* but a new emotion – compassion, perhaps. I don't like her, yet I feel for her and her loss. She is marooned in her grief.

Dinner takes place on the loggia. I am seated behind Leonardo. The rapture of the view and the magnificence of the villa is tempered by the base manners and endless bragging of our host.

Francesco del Giocondo is unable to collect paintings by all the famed artists of Florence so he accumulates their debts instead. As we sit outside in the dusk, listening to the ribald frog chorus from Neptune's pool and watching the improbable zigzagging flight of the fireflies, he regales us with stories of how all the artists owe him money – Sandro Botticelli and even Michelangelo's father, if he's to be believed. Giocondo avows how he plans to manoeuvre these debts into works of art – although surely grudging and resentful ones. I envision sour-faced Madonnas and pouting, furious angels. Perhaps he ought to settle for a tortured St Jerome, suffering in the wilderness.

Giocondo is in his cups and revealing all his tricks to Salaì, who's not drunk nearly as much as his host believes.

Salaì's a thief and a rogue himself and he can recognise another. Giocondo is convinced that I'm already his, but I am never to be delivered into his pudgy fingers. Neither Leonardo nor Salaì has troubled him for a single golden florin, and perhaps he chooses to think of that as artistic eccentricity, or evidence of our poor business acumen. The truth is that Salaì, greedy as he is, will not let Leonardo take a coin from him. Salaì would dearly love to be rid of me, but he loves the master more, and as long as the master wants me, he will take care that I am safe. Giocondo must have no claim over me.

'Didn't Machiavelli introduce you to Lisa?' I whisper to Leonardo.

'Yes, Machiavelli indeed.'

Machiavelli, the most cunning of all souls. Next to him, Francesco del Giocondo is a mere apprentice. Giocondo pontificates on, congratulating himself upon the debt of the Buonarrotis. I must concede, a marble copy of *Il Gigante* would look marvellous gracing the villa garden; in the dusk it almost seems to float above the city. However, Giocondo lacks the sly wiles of Machiavelli. Even I know that Michelangelo loathes his father. He declined to raise the boy himself, and farmed him out to an impoverished family of stonemasons where he was starved and beaten. Francesco del Giocondo would have been more likely to squeeze a sculpture out of the great Michelangelo if he'd allowed his father to waste and malinger in debtors' jail. None of us tells this to Giocondo. Salaì smirks into his wine and sloshes more from the carafe into his host's glass.

As Francesco and the household retire, no one takes me inside, and I remain upon my easel on the loggia. As

I watch, Lisa weaves through the rosy evening like a spirit, tramping barefoot amongst the garden, feet mucky, dew-slick. The statues of the gods stare in imperious silence, pitiless. She draws her veil around her face. To them, she is just another mortal ghost. We cannot imagine what it is to give birth to something. To feel it kick forth, wet and bloody and glistening. To have it suckle and grow and laugh and die. Her lap is voided now, never filled no matter how often her other children sit there, wriggling. She pauses and sits down to perch on the edge of Neptune's black pool, hands busy with her rosary beads, frantic for consolation. It's no good. Even I can see that. I am glad I am not her. She is forsaken in her grief. The string on the rosary snaps and the beads spill into the pool like bread, and I picture the fish snapping and gobbling at them blasphemously.

A little after, Salaì emerges into the evening with Leonardo and begins to mix paints, taking out bottles containing powdered cinnabar and white lead, blending them with linseed oil. It's been some time since he mixed them for the master; usually it is little Cecco's task, but we've left him in Florence and Salaì doesn't seem to mind. Once he has finished, he retires to bed leaving us alone. Leonardo busies himself, preparing brushes, and then he works.

'There is something different about you this evening,' he says, his brush tickling my mouth. 'There is an uncanny humanity in your smile that has been eluding us both till now.'

He dips his brush again in cinnabar, red as dragon's blood, and blends it with white lead, shading it in the tiny shadow in the curve above my lip.

The light is dwindling. The moon is in full sail and the night is hot, the doors to the villa thrown open. The sound of the rill and the streams appear more boisterous, chuckling against the pebbles. How can Leonardo see to paint? A servant carries out an oil lamp. I hear Lisa's baby wail. Shutters are snapped closed. Sirius appears in the sky, a gleam of light.

'I thought I was different from Lisa del Giocondo and I am. In temperament and outlook, I am nothing like her at all. But today I've seen that we do share something. She has lost a daughter.'

Leonardo stares at me through the gloom, puzzled, his brush aloft.

I speak softly. There is a new pain growing deep within my chest. 'I may not have children but everyone I love will die. I shall outlive you all. Long after you all wither and decay, I'll look upon these stars, alone.'

Leonardo is silent for a long moment. He looks troubled and then he sighs. 'Foreknowledge brings sadness. For that I am truly sorry, my Lisa.'

I cannot be sorry; not yet, not while he is still here with me. His very presence is joy to me. But I know misery will come. I can hear it in the creak of the earth and the far-off tolling of the duomo bell.

Autumn

*I*t is a relief to return to Florence. The milk no longer sours before the afternoon, and now in the mornings the master allows the shutters to be loosened for a few hours and a warm light trickles into the studio. While Salaì draws and redraws the bridge at the edge of the

Anghiari cartoon, cursing that he is unable to get the perspective right, Leonardo retraces my dress. He has changed his mind on what I am to wear. Francesco del Giocondo objected to the simplicity of my attire, so Leonardo has decided to make my clothes plainer still. The beauty shall be in the perfection of their rendering. I observe with considerable interest as he sketches my new dress, making careful drapery studies for the sleeves. They flow like water. There are whorls of fabric that catch the light. I am enraptured. A whirlpool of reflection and shade. He transfers the new parts of the cartoon to the white lead with charcoal *spolveri* pouncing, but the outline of my old dress is still visible. His abandoned ideas and *pentimenti* are clearly seen, regrets yet to be painted over.

There is a serenity in the *bottega* despite Salaì's rhythmic curses – we're used to those. A drowsy warmth. Under Alicia's stern watch, the maids bake bread on the hearth and scurry about the refectory with brooms and vases of late-summer flowers of bird's-foot trefoil, blackberry and guelder rose that the master draws with keen interest, his thick eyebrows puckering. Young Cecco, overjoyed that we've returned, sits on his haunches and grinds paint with the pestle and mortar and burbles an old song that his mother taught him. Salaì is out of temper and tells him to hush. I take pleasure in the squabbling. We are family. We are content. It can't last. It doesn't.

Michelangelo Buonarroti smashes our happiness apart with one hammer blow, as though we are a rejected slab of marble. There are raised voices in the cloisters and then Machiavelli and Michelangelo stamp into the refectory, talking loudly, indifferent to the interruption they are causing. Leonardo stiffens. Yet, as they are ushered in by Alicia, he betrays no sign of annoyance except by offering them the second-best wine, instead of the very best.

Niccolò Machiavelli steams with smugness. I can't understand why Michelangelo is here. He despises all rivals and never visits another studio out of pleasure or interest. The genial atmosphere of moments ago has tautened like a string, and might break at any moment. Niccolò must have decided upon the method of his revenge.

Michelangelo grins. His teeth are stained like a dog's. He stands with his feet apart, bouncing from foot to foot, hardly able to contain his impatience and glee. He is small and sickly-looking but with strong muscled arms like a labourer and enormous calloused hands. He has a coarse and untidy beard while his nose is crushed like a biscotti – Salaì whispers to Cecco that it was gained from a fight with another sculptor. If I wasn't so worried about what is about to happen, I'd laugh. I've never seen an artist so unlike his creations. Leonardo is a beautiful man who produces beautiful creations. His clothes are elegant and refined and his apprentices, renowned for their skill and prettiness, are similarly attired. Leonardo impresses upon us all that the painter is a gentleman who listens to music as he works. According to Leonardo, the sculptor, on the other hand, looks like a baker, covered in dust. Michelangelo certainly does. The only feature he shares with *Il Gigante* is his large hands, but even they are rough from grasping a chisel and mallet. Along with the dust, he's coated with a layer of blackened grime. I glance at his feet and take in the shabby and reeking dog-skin boots.

'Seats for our guest,' commands Leonardo.

'Oh, I'm not a guest,' says Michelangelo, sitting down on a bench, perfectly at ease. He stretches out his skinny legs, and grimaces. 'I'm staying.'

Leonardo stiffens and looks towards Machiavelli, who crackles with satisfaction.

'Yes, it's all agreed with the *signoria*. Michelangelo Buonarroti is to paint the mural on the far side of the east wall of the council chamber,' says Machiavelli, with the look of a fox who has raided the chicken coop and guzzled the lot.

'*The Battle of Cascina* is to be beside your *Battle of Anghiari*,' declares Michelangelo. 'Afraid of a little competition?'

Leonardo only smiles and pours his rival a glass of wine, which he knocks back in a swallow, not bothering to wipe the crimson trickle from his beard.

This is punishment from Machiavelli for Leonardo's failure to divert the Arno. Leonardo brought shame and ignominy upon Machiavelli and the time has come for the reckoning.

'You must make room here in the studio for Michelangelo. He needs space to prepare the cartoon for his mural,' adds Machiavelli, waiting for Leonardo to object.

This is absurd. There are a hundred places in Florence that Machiavelli and the *signoria* could find for Michelangelo and his *bottega* to live and work. It is simply part of Machiavelli's revenge. He looks at Leonardo with his small black eyes like two burnt chestnuts. His skin is so pale it appears sap green. He is longing for Leonardo to complain, salivating for it.

'Say nothing about it,' I murmur to Leonardo. 'You'll only make matters worse. We need to make the best of it for now.'

Leonardo takes my advice. 'With pleasure,' he declares. 'My cartoon is almost finished. We can manage for a few weeks. Anything to oblige an old friend, Niccolò.'

Machiavelli looks at him with ill-concealed wrath. He longs to see Leonardo suffer. It isn't any fun if he doesn't. Salaì shows Machiavelli out, still full of blood and choler.

I scrutinise the famous sculptor, wondering why Michelangelo would agree to such uncomfortable and unnecessary conditions. There is no need for the two great artists of Florence to share a studio, however large. Leonardo's complex scaffolding has shrunk and darkened the chamber. Yet Michelangelo looks strangely enthused at the prospect. If I had to guess, it would be that he does not like Leonardo, and that he is taking satisfaction at the prospect of tormenting him. He meets Leonardo's eye and grins at him, revealing once more his mouth of jagged teeth, lead tin yellow.

Leonardo attempts to bestow upon Michelangelo the same kindness and attention he does upon everyone. Through force of will, he tries to push from himself his animosity and personal revulsion. Leonardo is fastidious, washing more than once each week, and in an attempt to overcome the stench of his new neighbour has the refectory filled with posies and nosegays and sweet poultices. At the *albergo* he orders Tommaso and Cecco to make room in their box beds for Michelangelo's assistants. Salaì is told to relinquish his mattress for the great sculptor, and Leonardo has the maids remake it with clean sheets.

'What's the point? They'll be black with grime in the morning,' complains Salaì. 'It will stink forever.'

He sulks and grumbles but Leonardo is resolute. Michelangelo might behave like a peasant, but his soul is *ingegno*. The man is touched by God.

'I thought he made the human figure look like a sack of walnuts?' Salaì presses.

'You should dream of those walnuts,' admonishes Leonardo.

It's no good. All of Leonardo's attempts at kindness are rejected. Michelangelo arrives back in the evening with his five assistants and surveys the refectory with scorn. He vibrates with aggression and ill temper, bouncing on the balls of his feet, fingers coiled into fists.

'Why would my apprentices sleep beside yours? Do you think to steal them like breeding bitches? My *garzoni* sleep with me. My father is a mouth-stinking worm but he taught me two things. Never to wash and *Non ci si può fidare di alcuno*.'

I almost feel sorry for this glowering man, filled with misgivings and contempt. I mutter, 'Trusting no one makes for a miserable and lonely life.'

Michelangelo looks round the refectory with dark eyes, narrow with suspicion. I observe his apprentices who, interestingly, appear unconcerned by his ill-concealed rage. They bustle, unpacking chalks, charcoals and spools of paper. They are as shabbily dressed as their master, yet are pink-cheeked and well fed. His gaze rests on them with something either like fatherly affection or hunting master towards his pack; then instantly, he's cantankerous again, sniffing at the air.

'What's that objectionable smell? This place reeks like a whore-house.'

He sneezes and then, marching to the table, seizes a poultice and tosses it into the fire, his neck reddening. He points to another nosegay draped on the windowsill. 'Do you usually decorate your *bottega* like a brothel, da Vinci?'

Leonardo ignores him. It is clear to me that the two men can't possibly work here together. They can only plague and torment one another. Michelangelo stalks the studio inspecting the *Anghiari* cartoon without remark. Finally, he notices me. He peers at me and comes closer still, his breath rancid.

'Who is she?' he asks at last.

'She was Madonna Lisa del Giocondo.'

'Was? I didn't know she was dead.'

'She has become herself. The ideal woman. Dante had Beatrice. Petrarch had Laura. I have my Lisa.'

Salaì casts me a look of sheer loathing. Michelangelo yawns ostentatiously and picks at his ears. 'She's lifelike but she's too quiet for my taste.'

At that, Leonardo chuckles. 'Sometimes I wish she was quiet, maestro.'

Indignant, I choose to keep my counsel.

Later in the evening, food is laid out by the servants. Rice, lamb roasted on a spit, and fatty sausages and tripe sizzle in pans on the fire, curls of smoke coiling up to the rafters. Boxes lay about us, half-unpacked. As far as we can tell, all of them contain paraphernalia for painting, drawing or tools for sculpture. They are wrapped with reverential care. I scour the gloom for the crates containing blankets, clothes, rugs or even crockery. Michelangelo is a wealthy young man. He could choose lavish finery almost equal to that of Leonardo if he wanted but it's clear he cares nothing for such things. He keeps a parsimonious lifestyle and many a monk lux-uriating in his overstuffed cell could learn from him.

Leonardo ensures Michelangelo's glass is always brimming with wine, determined to pursue a path to harmony within the studio, but the conversation falters. Michelangelo grunts and sometimes even appears to growl, choosing to ignore most of the master's questions or answering the others with a single word.

'How old were you when your mother died?'

'Six.'

'And you were raised by a family of stonemasons?' Leonardo pauses but there is no response, so he presses on, attempting to find common ground. 'I know what it is like to be on the outside. I grew up in my grandfather's house in Vinci. They're decent souls, but my father takes pleasure in reminding me that I'm not quite part of the family.'

Michelangelo scowls. 'My father is just a cunt.'

Leonardo chuckles but Michelangelo stiffens, apparently unable to tell whether Leonardo is laughing with him or at him. He turns on him.

'Unlike you, I'm not a bastard.'

'But if I wasn't a bastard, my father would have forced me to become a lawyer, and that would've been a much worse fate than being a bastard. I am happier by far as a painter than I would have been as a notary.'

He says it with a gleam but Michelangelo doesn't laugh.

Salaì, Tommaso, Ferrando, Giovanni and Franceso lurk in the shadows, sitting on benches in a neat row eating tripe sausages and listening, ears pricked like baby hares. Michelangelo's *garzoni* squat beside them, scooping up rice and licking lamb grease from grubby fingers. Michelangelo beams upon his *garzoni* indulgently. He looks as if he wants to toss them a bone and fondle their ears. His gaze rests on Salaì with abhorrence. The studio has divided into two rival camps, like the Papal and Medici. Leonardo clears his throat and tries again. This is agony for him. He has notebooks to fill, ideas to record and test. Usually the evenings are times of enchantment and gaiety for all of us in his *bottega* – he adores liminal spaces, and the boundary between light and dark, day and night, is no different. He often spends it trying out ideas upon us all, whether on paper or in conversation, but instead he is reduced to playing host to the most reluctant and irksome guest. Machiavelli selected Leonardo's punishment with diabolical care.

'Perhaps I should read Dante. We discuss Dante many evenings. You love Dante too, I believe?' he asks, his tone soothing.

Michelangelo's face contorts in contempt. 'Everyone loves Dante, unless they're an imbecile.'

Leonardo continues, serenely. 'Cecco here had a question. He wished a passage explained. Perhaps you would—'

'Explain it yourself. You who painted *The Last Supper* in Milan with oils so poor that they're already starting to spoil.'

Leonardo flinches. It is torment to him that his masterwork is already rotting upon the wall in Milan. Yet having found a weakness, Michelangelo won't stop. He jabs at the wound with glee.

'After that disaster, surely only a capon would hire you. Yet here you are – Leonardo da Vinci, the Grand Bastard of Florence.'

It's one thing to insult his parentage, but another his art. Leonardo finally rises from his seat. He snaps his fingers. 'Enough. We leave in the morning for the palazzo. The studio is yours.'

Michelangelo's expression shows neither remorse nor triumph. His pack of *garzoni* continue to guzzle tripe, indifferent to the scene. Perhaps they have seen similar ones play out before them so often that they have grown inured. I, on the other hand, cannot bear to see the man I love humiliated. Already, Leonardo senses Michelangelo's fame eclipsing his. Yet that is not enough for Michelangelo; he must tease and belittle him too, grind his victory.

'Goodbye, Michelangelo Buonarroti,' I cry. 'You are a *terribilità* man.'

Michelangelo considers me with new and sudden interest. He stands and comes close.

'Oh. You're right, Leonardo,' he says slowly. 'She isn't quiet. I like her. Yes. I like her very much. Good evening, Leonardo's Lisa. I am pleased to meet you.'

'Go to hell.'

He laughs, a deep rumbling in his chest.

I meet his gaze, pierced with exuberance in spite of my repugnance. The man is insolent and boorish and cruel, yet he is touched by God. He can hear my *voce*. He smiles at me and, despite his yellow teeth, it has surprising sweetness. He reaches out towards my cheek and I see the coarseness of his fingertips where they have been grated away by the stone.

'Don't touch her. You'll mark her paintwork,' snaps Leonardo.

Michelangelo withdraws. I'm thrilled by Leonardo's concern, his apparent jealousy. Leonardo watches us both, his face tight and unreadable.

Winter

*W*e escape to the Hall of the Great Council in the Palazzo Vecchio. The room is vast, large enough to seat the five hundred men of the council. Friar Savonarola commissioned it only a few years ago in deference to his own austere tastes, before he was dragged outside to be hung and burned in the Piazza della Signoria. His presence lingers here still, and perhaps it is the knowledge of his fate that unsettles us all. The Great Council of Florence, who sentenced him to die, want Leonardo to paint in vermilion and gold leaf over all traces of his stark aesthetic. Leonardo is to be the painter priest to exorcise the murdered ghost. He leaves me here the first night alone, while the others retire to sleep in lodgings, but I can't stand it. I wait all night for the restless spirit of Savonarola, hearing him in every moan of the wind, every squabble of the pigeons and creak of the settling wood. In the morning, I beseech Leonardo not to abandon me again. He teases me, having no patience for sorcery or phantoms.

The hall is plainly plastered in white but the ceiling is held aloft with massive oaken trusses thick enough to belong to the mast of a great galleon sailing across the Ligurian Sea. There are battalions of large windows, some with crystal and lead and others veiled with waxed paper. Leonardo's wall with his *Battle of Anghiari* is to be on the eastern side, and Michelangelo's mural of *The Battle of Cascina* to sit next to it, the two great works and rivals displayed side by side.

Leonardo's ingenious scaffolding has been painstakingly rebuilt in the chamber, each section lugged by hand or horse and remounted by carpenters, the towers and plat-forms and pulleys all fitted back together. We should be in peace, joy and accord restored, yet it seems that Michelangelo's animosity has followed us like a curse. Bad luck and misfortune chase us. Despite its grandeur, the palace is damp. The cartoon was split into five sections to transport it here and, even though it is now reglued and supported by linen, in the wet it keeps coming apart, snagged by the wind that sneaks in through gaps in the waxed windows that continually tear in the endless, un-seasonal gales.

The morning is wild, and the wind bawls and yet more waxed paper is ripped away from the high windows, and a flock of sparrows like quivers of high-flying arrows shoot into the hall. They soar around the ceiling, frantic, fluttering and shitting as they fly, so that the tiles are speckled and slippery with yellow and brown. Tommaso is atop the highest platform dusting charcoal pouncing onto the highest part of the wall, and he screams, surprised by the onslaught. The sparrows are brushing his arms, catching in his hair, singing, messing, flapping. There is filth and feathers everywhere. In his panic he slips from the platform, and for a moment he seems to hover amongst them, arms flailing, and then he smashes to the ground, and lies quite still on the floor. A rag-doll boy.

'Is he dead?' I cry. 'Please don't let him be dead.'

I like Tommaso, and I can see a glossy trail of scarlet lurking amongst his red hair.

Salaì scrambles to his side, placing his finger beneath his nose. 'He breathes!'

I murmur a prayer of thanks. The birds are still flying, weaving all over the hall, defecating as they go. The room grows dim as my vision mists in my left eye. The sparrows' song is panicked and harsh.

'Ferrando, fetch the apothecary,' commands Leonardo. 'Cecco, bring blankets for his head.'

Cecco hesitates, unwilling to sully fine lambswool with blood, but Leonardo snaps at him, uncharacteristically fierce.

'Never mind the stain!'

Salaì shakes Tommaso and he rouses, whimpering for his mother; mucous speckled with blood dribbles from his nose.

Birds continue to soar while others watch us dolefully from their perches upon the scaffolding. As Cecco shrieks, birds take flight again, sailing amongst the rafters, thud-thudding into the walls, colliding with the cartoon. The sketched warriors stare, mouths frozen in silent, muted cries. Half a dozen feathered bird arrows plummet to the ground. Tommaso struggles to sit upright, bruised and dazed. A dead bird lands on his lap. He stares at it, agape in horror. Salaì tosses it away.

'Open all the doors, fetch brooms and chase them from the hall,' orders Leonardo.

The assistants try but it's a futile task; the ceilings are far too high, and they're wafting at them uselessly. Yet, somehow, after an hour, most of the birds are either es- caped further into the palace, fled from the windows or dead in sorrowful piles. The apothecary arrives and dresses the gash on Tommaso's head in vinegar and paper, and starts to blend a poultice with oil of roses, egg and turpentine.

'Badly bruised. Nothing broken, I don't believe,' he pronounces.

'Wrap him in the blanket and place him by the fire,' commands Leonardo.

'Yes, but don't let him get too hot. See, he's already starting to tremble. Keep this poultice close to help his wounds heal.'

'It's an ill omen,' complains Salaì, with a shudder.

'Nonsense,' says Leonardo. 'Bad weather and bad luck.'

He won't allow any talk of sorcery or alchemy. 'Clear up the mess, boys. And stoke the fire.'

Salaì pauses long enough to realise that there is a sickly yellow trail of bird excrement running down my arm and in the corner of my left eye. This cheers him immensely.

'Ah, Lisa is fouled too. Besmirched and half-blinded.'

Salaì takes vicious pleasure in any misfortune of mine.

'I must clean her at once,' snaps Leonardo, not finding it amusing at all. 'The acid in the urine will blight the layers of varnish if I leave it. No one touches her but me.'

Salaì retreats to find a cloth and returns, passing it to Leonardo who tenderly dabs it over my arm and eye. It burns and I glance at the room through a film of fog.

'How is it, dearest one?' he asks, voice full of concern.

'Better,' I say, wishing I could blink, my eye stinging and smarting, and yet his anxiety is worth any pain.

When he is happy that my vision is safe, he sets down the rag, and picks up a basket and walks through the hall gathering up the tiny fallen bodies of the birds. There must be dozens of them. He stares at them, not repulsed, only interested. He pauses, plucking up a speckled, twitching corpse and stretching out its wings with acute concentration, examining the primary feathers and its coiled reptilian feet, clenched in death. He strokes its back and head and, ignoring the basket, lovingly tucks the sparrow into the leather pouch fastened upon his belt.

In the coming weeks, my easel is propped beside Tommaso. I like to think I keep him company. He is swaddled in blankets and watches out of bruised, blackened eyes. The others are hard at work. Leonardo sighs and plucks from the leather pouch the dead sparrow that, to my revulsion, I see has started to moulder, its feathers pilling and the bones exposed. Leonardo displays neither disgust nor surprise, but spreads out the wings, to reveal the intricate and delicate needle-like bone structure of the wing piercing the skin.

'Needs to rot more. The bones aren't sufficiently exposed,' he says, shaking off more loose feathers.

All the same, he grasps a piece of black chalk and starts to sketch the wing, making close observations of the feathers and starting to note the placings of the observable bones. He's humming. It's the happiest I've seen him in weeks.

'When Tommaso fell,' he says, 'he seemed to pause for a moment first, did you notice?'

'Yes,' I say, worried. I did see. He's planning some scheme, but I'm not sure what it is.

'If Tommaso had been wearing man-sized wings and he'd beaten them up and down, like this,' he says, sketching rapidly with his chalk, 'he wouldn't have fallen, he would have flown.'

He makes more quick sketches and lines in his notebook. 'Do you see?'

But he isn't looking at me at all; he's only looking at the page and the decaying wing of the dead sparrow.

*

The boys continue to apply colour to the walls, focusing on the central group of warriors. Leonardo paces, dissatisfied with the composition. The balance is wrong. It is too cluttered, too knotted. Everyone's temper snags on the smallest detail, humours out of balance, too full of phlegm. It's the percolating damp of the palace. No matter how hot the fire and how many pine logs are hurled into the flames and how fierce the blaze, the wet is in the air and has seeped into our animal spirits, until everyone is filled with an oozing lethargy. Whether there is something wrong with the linseed oil from the apothecary, or it's the Roman formula that Leonardo has insisted upon trying, or the damp of the hall, but the paint simply won't dry.

'Why can't we paint in fresco, maestro? Fresco *works*,' complains Salaì, for the hundredth time, looking with dismay at the moist faces of the horses, where sweating black beads of paint are forming messy globules on the surface.

'Keep the fires blazing and it will dry. Fresco is too quick. Oil gives us time for perfection,' answers Leonardo.

This is not perfection, though. This is close to disaster, the paint doesn't dry at all and we feel the quiver of panic.

It is past midday, but the light has a strange sepulchral tone and the writhing figures on the wall appear flatter and more lifeless still, half-shadow men. The hall dims, a cloak tossed over the sun, as the light fails, darkening as a colossal storm blows in.

'Put down your brushes, you cannot see to work,' commands Leonardo.

An hour later, the rains come. The earlier gales have already torn away most of the paper coverings from the windows and those that remain are ripped and hang there shredded and flapping. Water founts inside and drips straight onto a section of the painting near the top, where the still-wet colours begin to trickle and run onto the dry sections below, spoiling them. The bell in the law courts begins to toll, as the rain continues to pour, flooding in through the windows and soaking the wall.

'Light the brazier, stoke the fire!' calls Leonardo, his voice rising with panic. 'We must dry the picture!'

It's a futile, hopeless task. The paints are foaming and starting to bubble. Rivers of red and muddy grey and yellow are streaming down, vandalising the painting. The warriors scream open-mouthed, aghast, their teeth now awash with red, bloodied in apparent horror at what is happening as the horses writhe and trample the earth. The fire rages hotter and hotter as log after log is hurled into the furnace, but it does nothing but make clouds of vapour fill the air. Soldiers weep crimson tears and horses melt into mud. The painting is a near ruin. I wonder if Savonarola is haunting this accursed place, borne on the wind, tearing off the blinds from the windows with his dead hands, so that his vision of simplicity and purity won't be sullied.

'Take my Lisa out!' shouts Leonardo suddenly. 'The heat and water will spoil her.'

'No, I will not leave you,' I cry.

'There's nothing you can do,' he calls. 'And I will not have you destroyed with *Anghiari*!'

'Because you don't want your greatest *invenzione* destroyed?' I ask.

He looks at me and shakes his head, and when he speaks his voice is soft and pleading, filled with tenderness.

'No. I don't want anything to happen to you. I couldn't bear it. Please. For me.'

I allow Salaì to carry me outside to the antechamber. Alone, in the cool, I listen to the scuffle and shouts from the other side of the heavy doors. I wonder what of the painting, come morning, will remain.

My candle gutters out and I linger in the darkness for hours. There are shouts and cries from within. If Leonardo suffers, then I want to suffer with him. Instead, I'm alone in the blackness, listening. No one leaves the hall. A grey dawn shines in the small window, and the sound of the wind and rain fades. I wait for someone to return. Heavy footsteps fall on the stairs below. He's come! At last, I can console him. He wants me. Relief and hope course through me. A door snaps open.

'What the hell are you doing out here all alone? Lovers' quarrel?' says a voice from the gloom.

I scour the darkness and see the scowling face of Michelangelo.

'Be gone, you rotten prattler.'

He grins broadly, seemingly unoffended. He closes the door behind him and comes very close and stares at me with a frank appraiser's scrutiny, holding up his lamp so that he can see me better.

'You're quite something. I'll be honest, I didn't think the old fellow had it in him. If he doesn't get round to finishing you, come and see me.' He holds up a hand in surrender. 'I'm not trying to be rude, but we both know what he's like. If you get fed up, I'll see you right.'

'I'm his. Finished or not,' I say.

He shrugs. 'Whatever you want. Me. I like having hands.' He makes an obscene gesture. I ignore him.

'What's going on in there?' he asks, nodding towards the closed doors of the Hall of the Great Council.

I refuse to be drawn and Michelangelo, growing impatient, sets down his lamp, picks me up under one muscular arm and, with a thump, shoulders opens the massive door. The room is full of smoke and steam and it takes a moment for us to be able to see. The inferno has cooled but it's still hot as an August afternoon. There are puddles of water on the floor. Michelangelo steps forward, propping me against a bench in a dry patch so I can see. The scaffolding hides the mural at first, disguising the worst of the damage, but as I look it's clear that the picture has melted. The upper wet sections have dribbled onto the lower drier sections, ruining them as they flowed downwards. All definition, outline and shading has been lost. It's a disaster. I'm not sure what can be done except clean it off and start again.

Michelangelo shakes his head, running his short fingers through his beard. 'What an ugly mess. You poor old fool.'

Worse than Michelangelo's scorn and all his insults is his pity.

I look upon Leonardo's face and see that not only is the painting ruined, but something inside his soul has cracked and broken.

Leonardo can't bring himself to order the assistants to paint over the damage, but neither can they continue work on the wreckage beneath. Salaì instructs Ferrando and Giovanni to continue to paint the least affected areas, but we can see that they are labouring on the roof of a house that has no walls. Leonardo can't even look at the painting.

He only comes to the hall at night when it is mostly hidden in darkness. He sits and draws birds. Sparrows, kites. Some he draws in great observational detail, examining each feather, and others he paints straight upon the ruins of the painting, great shadow birds.

He starts to write a letter to his father. He reads it aloud to me.

'*My Dearest Father, I received the letter you wrote to me, which caused in me in a brief space of time pleasure and sadness: pleasure in that I learned from it you are well, for which I thank God, and displeasure to hear I have displeased you.*'

He pauses, uncertain what to write next, and then I see he has abandoned the attempt and has started to sketch the wing of a flying machine on the back.

'If Tommaso had wings, he wouldn't have fallen.'

'I know, Leonardo, you told me. But he is recovering well. He will heal. The mural can be mended. Finish the letter to your father.'

'There's no need. I have nothing to say. I only annoy and offend him.'

'That isn't true.'

He gestures to the wall, puts his head in his hands. 'No one can see this monstrosity.'

Then he stands, pacing again, and to my dismay I see that he has brought wood, glue and animal skin and has spread it all out on the floor of the chamber. Sections of it are already assembled in the rudimentary shape of a giant, featherless sparrow's wing. He looks feverish and wild.

'The scaffolding is at least good for something,' he says. 'I'm going to use it to fly.'

'And how did that work for Daedalus? For Icarus?' I remonstrate, full of fear.

He only laughs.

'I'm going to make the *Uccello*, the Great Bird, and master the skies! First using the scaffolding in here, but soon the roof of the Corte Vecchia. Don't look so worried, my Lisa. I'll use the side away from all the workmen. We'll keep it a secret until my great *Uccello* is triumphant. Then we'll fly across the sea with inflated wineskins as life rafts to help us float back.'

I look up at the looming scaffolding; it appears skeletal and sinister in the darkness and I envision him hurling himself from the top, his wings strapped to his back. His eyes gleam. I don't want him to die.

When morning comes, Salaì and little Cecco arrive pale-faced and disconsolate. The council have heard whispers of a disaster in the hall with the mural, and they wish to inspect the work. They have spent large sums of money upon this painting. Leonardo ignores everyone and continues to sketch his wings, retrieving the notebook from the pouch at his waist and scribbling a comment, and then fastening it again with a wooden toggle, oblivious to us all. Michelangelo struts into the hall.

'Have you come to gloat?' I call.

'No,' he answers, not entirely convincingly.

'I need you to write a letter for me,' I say. 'It's very important. Once it's written, you need to take it straight away to Raphael Santi.'

Michelangelo grimaces. 'I can't bear Raphael.'

'Of course you can't. He's one of the few artists as gifted as you. Possibly even more so,' I say.

Michelangelo scowls. 'I liked it better when I couldn't hear you.'

'Write the letter. Be as rude and vile as you please, but fetch me Raphael.'

Spring

I watch from the window as Raphael and Leonardo walk through the unkempt garden side by side, deep in thought, hands behind their backs, just beyond the villa. The few houses and farms that make up the hamlet of Vinci lie scattered in the shade of the olive groves. The olive leaves are silver-grey, appearing to glitter in the morning sunshine. The sloping Tuscan hills are thickly forested in Turkey oak, cypresses and sweet chestnut, all budding in the luminous shades of early spring. The church spire thumbs skywards towards the heavens. Leonardo pauses to observe a kestrel hovering high in the air; the mouse or snake busy in the grass below has no idea it has been marked by death above. He has notebooks brimming with drawings of kites, sparrows, bats, hawks, lowly pigeons. And also mechanical flying machines. He and Raphael amble back into the villa and Leonardo is flushed with excitement, still talking rapidly of his schemes of flight.

'The *Uccello* will take its first flight on the back of the Great Swan—'

Raphael frowns, puzzled; he's from Urbino and isn't used to the strange names we give places.

'The Great Swan? Monte Ceceri. Near Fiesole,' explains Leonardo, only slightly impatient. 'The universe will be filled with amazement. Everyone will write of its fame and Florence will be renowned for all eternity as the place of its birth.'

Raphael listens with reverence and fortitude. He is the prince of amiability, and in his presence Leonardo has relaxed and softened. He is sleeping and eating once more. The young painter, thirty years his junior, has tremendous kindness and love for Leonardo. Raphael nods to me and pulls out a chair and sits at the scrubbed table, waiting for him to finish. We have been at Leonardo's uncle's house in Vinci for some time. I've instructed Raphael to hide the letters from Salaì. He must manage as best he can for the next few weeks without us, try to make repairs. The council won't pursue us here. The worst they can do is write furious letters and cut off further payments.

Here, the two men spend days walking out amongst the hills and groves, drawing and talking. Well, mostly Leonardo talking and Raphael listening. It's already doing him good. He's lost that hunted look.

'My first memory wasn't of my mother. And it certainly wasn't of my father,' he says. 'It was of a bird. A kite. It seems to me that I was in my cradle and a kite came to me and opened my mouth with its tail and struck me several times with its tail inside my lips.'

'A kite? Like we just saw, wheeling amongst the clouds?' asks Raphael, somewhere between astonishment and disbelief.

'Yes. A kite. But of course, then I only knew it was a bird. A vast, terrifying, beautiful bird.'

'Are you sure it wasn't a dream?' I ask.

'A *ricordazione* or a dream. It doesn't matter. Since that moment in my cradle, flight and birds has seemed my destiny.'

Raphael is silent, his brows puckered in thought. He tucks a lock of dark hair behind his ear and leans forward. He has wide brown eyes, gentle and sweet like a child, but when he speaks, the master listens to him as an equal.

'I am sure that you are right, maestro. A man senses his own fate. But I also know that if you want to talk about destiny, she is here.'

Raphael picks me up and leads Leonardo into the cool interior of the villa where Lisa del Giocondo is seated on a chair. Raphael sets me down beside her on a waiting easel. Lisa rises to greet Leonardo, who takes her hands and kisses them.

'You haven't come to see me for some time, Messer Leonardo,' says Lisa.

'My apologies, Madonna.'

'Paint me,' she says.

'Paint *me*,' I say.

Leonardo laughs.

'Yes, paint your Lisas,' says Raphael. 'And while you do, I wish to make a copy.'

Lisa del Giocondo comes almost every day, walking down to the small farmhouse with her maid; I almost forget to dislike her. The next weeks are amongst the happiest of my life, but I don't know it as I am looking away across the Tuscan hills, watching as spring puffs into the valley. We sit outside on the cobbled veranda surrounding the villa. Perhaps thinking of the kite and his childhood, Leonardo starts to draw in the landscape behind me. He sets out a mirror so I can observe his progress. There's the curling track leading through the olive grove, but he alters the angle and changes it again. These aren't the green spring hills, where the peasants are starting to sow wheat and barley, but an internal visionary landscape. Leonardo paints my veil translucent black, and through it you can see the rugged terrain. He paints a land of marvels. A wild rocky wilderness of blue hills. A bridge. A river. A gorge. The blue sky, glimpsed through the dark passage of my veil. For him, I'm never finished. He's always looking, adding another layer and another. I'm the ideal woman, perfect and yet never perfected. As he works he talks, and every time he shares an observation on light or the colour of a rainbow, I'm transported. No one else would think to confide the secrets of the universe to me but him.

'The ancients, from the Egyptians to the Greeks, dreamed of bringing a statue or picture to life but I did it,' he says, his voice holding a note of pride.

'You breathed life into me from the end of your brush, and here I am,' I say.

'Here you are,' he agrees.

One afternoon, after Lisa del Giocondo returns home, Raphael sits before Leonardo and me on the terrace, copying me and talking as he works, telling jokes.

'You see, Madonna Lisa, I never usually paint just one woman at once. I must combine several to find ideal beauty, but you are perfect, just as you are.'

Leonardo snorts. 'That's because I've already done the hard work.'

'Excuse me, I have – I am myself,' I object.

'Exactly so, Madonna Lisa. Don't put up with him,' says Raphael with a grin.

I can't help noticing that he's added the pillars of the loggia to his version, and he's drawn the little church behind us, snug in the hillside.

'Madonna Lisa. You are his greatest triumph and his greatest joy. Even the great and diabolical Michelangelo covets you. Everything else is noise. There is only Madonna Lisa. Or there should be.'

Leonardo stares at him, and then at me. He smiles and it is the smile of love. I'm suffused with warmth and joy. A kitchen maid carries out baskets of fruit and jugs of wine. I am perfectly content. And, to my delight, it dawns upon me that Raphael calls me Madonna Lisa, as though I am a real woman of flesh and blood not poplar wood and pigment.

At last, we cannot delay our return to Florence any longer. Salaì's letters are increasingly frantic. We bid farewell to Raphael with real sorrow. Though I am not sure how much I like his portrait of me, which amuses Leonardo. From inside the confines of my velvet box, I hear him chuckling as we ride back to the city. I ought to be glad, because as soon as the iron hoofs ring upon stone to signal our return, his laughter ceases. I can feel him rein the horse to the slowest of walks, reluctant to reach the palace. Leonardo longs for Vinci. For birds and freedom and dreams of flight. Of endless days spent grinding his own colours and painting me. Yet Leonardo is a virtuous man, and the young men of his *bottega* need him.

The city is already hot. It stinks of mud and old fish. I can picture how the Palazzo Vecchio looms over the Piazza della Signoria, the Torre di Arnolfo casting an ominous shadow. Entombed in the vast hall within, *The Battle of Anghiari* and Leonardo's assistants all wait. There's nothing to be done. We go in. The boys greet him with unalloyed joy.

'Tommaso, let me see you,' says Leonardo.

The boy presents himself, barely limping. His bruises have gone.

'Can you see? Can you hold a brush?'

The boy nods, proud.

'He can paint just as well as before,' says Salaì. 'He's still awful.'

Leonardo beams and embraces Tommaso. 'I'm making you wings. So next time you won't fall.'

Tommaso looks decidedly queasy.

Salaì lingers, uneasy, waiting for the master's verdict on the mural. He's attempted repairs. He has reapplied gesso over the worst-damaged section and repinned the cartoon, and started to reapply charcoal pouncing. I can't see what else could be done. He is clearly anxious, pale and sweaty, and moving from foot to foot. Leonardo kisses him firmly on both cheeks.

'Let's get back to work,' he says.

None of us believe it will ever be finished. All pleasure has gone. They rise and paint, pausing to eat and sleep, but it is a joyless task. The warriors snarl and snap. The horses scream. But at least now the paint dries.

Machiavelli is sent by the council to inspect our progress, and once again he brings the unwelcome company of Michelangelo and his *garzoni*.

'We thought you'd be finished by now,' says Machiavelli.

'I didn't,' says Michelangelo.

His *garzoni* are hauling his vast cartoon in several reams. They unfurl the first piece and lay it out on the tiled floor. Leonardo and his assistants pause in their work and come and watch. Naked men bathe in the River Arno, cooling off in the heat, dawdling, splashing. The cartoon reveals soldiers at rest in the moments before the battle when they are simply men and boys, larking and playful. Then, suddenly, in the camp behind, the alarm is sounded. The attack is imminent and the men scramble to dress and rise from the water. Soldiers again. Frantic. It's a piece of absolute drama, conveying both the moment of calm and then the panic. Some men kneel; others pull on clothes; others are still languidly splashing, yet to hear the alarm; many halfway between one position and another. It exhibits the most difficult of foreshortenings, all of which Salaì has been struggling with for months. And here our rival has produced it, with seemingly little effort, in no time at all.

'It is a great work,' says Leonardo.

Michelangelo only sneers but Leonardo rebukes him.

'You should listen to me most of all. We are not friends. Don't listen to the petty compliments of your friends. It's your enemies who you must heed. A friend may be deceived by love.'

Michelangelo looks at him with interest.

'I am not your friend, and I do not like you, and still I tell you that it is a great work,' says Leonardo.

I look across at *The Battle of Anghiari*, splotched and muted. Leonardo stares at it with profound dislike. For the first time in Leonardo's face, I see the features of the old man he shall become.

A messenger lingers at the door. Machiavelli snaps at him.

'Is your message addressed to the door or to a man?'

'It's for Maestro Leonardo.'

Leonardo holds out his hand for the message. He reads. He looks up, bewildered.

'My father is dead.'

I cannot go with them to the funeral in Vinci. Of course I know I cannot, but I resent the others who go to comfort the master. Why cannot I have arms and legs and a lap where he could place his head and weep while I stroke his hair? He brought me to life, but is it only a half-life? Salaì and Tommaso and even Cecco follow in a sombre procession through the square. I am left alone in the hall with Michelangelo and his *garzoni* for company. I am furious and fret about Leonardo. I ought to be there to offer consolation. Michelangelo laughs at me.

'What would you have him do? Pack you in a leather bag? Take you out and prop you up on the pew beside him with a prayer book? Or better yet, slide you into the confessional so you can listen to the sins of the nuns.'

I hate him.

'Do not sulk, Madonna Lisa. It doesn't suit you. And you are even more radiant than you were before your journey. You are not quite beautiful. You know too much for easy beauty.'

'I hope you spend lifetimes of suffering in purgatory.'

'I do enjoy our chats,' he says with a grin.

He turns his back upon me, and I watch as Michelangelo directs his *garzoni* with easy confidence, hoisting the vast cartoon upon the wall and fixing it with glue. It is a masterpiece and the damage and flaws of *The Battle of Anghiari* are thrown into relief. They work until dusk, when the light fades and lamps are lit across the city. Michelangelo blows me a kiss as he leaves.

Leonardo and the others do not reappear until nightfall. He staggers into the room; he has aged in a single afternoon. He slumps beside me, clutching a candle. Michelangelo's bathers writhe and startle upon the wall above us, a drama in perpetual motion, the terrible warning bell always tolling, always surprising the men from their moment of tranquillity.

'My father died leaving ten sons and two daughters,' he says at last. 'But he has left me out of his will. At the very end he rejected me.'

He stares up at Michelangelo's drawing in wonder and horror.

'Michelangelo was right. I'm nothing but a bastard after all.'

His face is painted with dejection and despair. I understand as I study him that the *Anghiari* commission is never going to be finished. We need to find a new patron, far from Machiavelli and the council, far from Florence. Once we flee the republic, leaving the commission unfinished with hundreds of ducats already paid, and the hiss of scandal pursuing us, I am not certain if we shall be able ever to return. Leonardo might dress in the silken tunics of a man from Milan, but in his heart he is the boy from Vinci. His soul belongs to Florence.

I glance again at Leonardo's face. I cannot bear his misery. He is like a golden coin tarnished and soiled. I must buff him into happiness until he burnishes once again. There is no choice. I must drag him into exile.

Like a living being she seems to change before our eyes and to look a little different each time we come back to her.

E. H. Gombrich

Amboise, 1519

Summer

You must forgive me now for moving ahead a little while. I have lived so many years, and seen so much, that I do not always choose to tell events in the order of their happening. In truth, I do not want to tell the story in order, for then Leonardo must die before the end, and I want him to walk with me all through this tale. Leonardo is as the light of home to me, so I shall keep his life spinning and keep him with me. We will return to the hour I lost my love once we are better friends, you and I. This is my story and I am not yet ready to confide that part. I have lived with his death for five hundred years now, but his dying haunts me still, and I cannot be harried. Death will come. He is always following at our heels, waiting.

I want to go back to Leda now. Without Leda to talk to, the emptiness after Leonardo's death would have been unendurable. So long as I had Leda, I was not alone, for I still loved and was loved in return. She was a tiny light in the swallowing dark of those first months. My love, my girl. My Leda, the most sublime painting ever created, and my truest friend.

We lingered, Leda and I, in Leonardo's empty bedroom, his tossed blankets upon his stripped bed. The room sepulchral except for us: two paintings upon a wall. At least in my dark dress, I was suitably attired for mourning, but Leda was always perfect in her nakedness. Leda, mother of Helen of Troy, nude amongst the wild flowers; her four children emerging from their eggs at her feet; Jupiter, in the form of a swan, reaching around her waist. The shutters in the bedroom were kept fastened. I ached with loss, but Leda would sing to me, and I tried to take comfort in her presence. In the days and weeks after Leonardo's passing, I would forget he was gone and each morning I'd wait for him to wake and call to me but the greeting never came. This silence would last always. I would always be waiting for his voice, the beloved voice that no longer calls to me. Each day began with the reawakening of grief, like the re-slitting of a wound, and I found myself staggered with pain. My head throbbed and I longed to wrench in two my veil and for the serene mists behind me to change to thunder. I screamed until my throat was ragged with cries that only Leda could hear.

'My darling, Mona,' she said, again and again. 'I am here. You are not alone. We are together.'

King Francis came to admire me, marvelling at my serenity and calm beauty, when beneath the surface of my pigments I was rage and agony. At least when you grieve, you weep. Your eyes swell and redden, your cheek pales. Pity me, then, and my false mask of tranquillity.

They didn't take me to Leonardo's burial. Salaì and Cecco agreed on almost nothing else, but they went together to the funeral, a last display of unity. To me, it felt like treachery and I despised them for it. I had more right to mourn than any of them. I ought to have been allowed to see him laid to rest. I, above all others, who would spend half a millennium grieving.

The service was held in the Chapel of St Florentin – Leonardo still pined for home, and this was as close as he could come to returning. In pity, Cecco propped me beside the window and I watched the line of tapering candles wavering in the dusk, the procession of monks and friars. They sickened me. The well-fed clergy all paid to say Mass. Paid to mourn to propel his soul upwards to Heaven. My grief was freely given, gushing forth as from a wound.

Salaì wasn't there when the master died, delayed by supposed business in Milan.

'You should have been here,' said Cecco, rebuking him as they returned from the burial. 'He wanted you. He loved you till the end.'

'I was busy.'

'One is never too busy for Death. He comes for everyone.'

'Not for her.'

Salaì glanced with dislike at me, then surveyed the paintings of Leda and St John on the opposite wall. He was no longer the beautiful boy with curling hair, but a man of forty, with hardness in his eyes and wearing the lined ghosts of old smiles. Leda and I were unchanged, but it was St John who irked him the most. Salaì had posed for Leonardo's *St John the Baptist* when he was young, and now St John taunted him with the image of his perfect youth, the glint of a lascivious smile. I was not sure whom Salaì had tried to avoid most during his frequent trips to Milan. He abhorred Francesco – no longer little Cecco but a handsome and self-assured man of twenty-five. He'd bullied the boy into becoming his enemy as a man. Cecco had grown into Leonardo's confidant and amanuensis, and unlike Salaì – brigand and rogue – was an aristocrat paid an annuity of four hundred gold francs to Salaì's paltry one hundred. Salaì and I loathed one another; yet, in truth, I believe it was St John who kept him away, the boy he used to be idly taunting him from the walls in all his physical perfection. St John never looked to me like much of a saint – preening, vain and with a hint of the original's devilry.

'Where will you go?' asked Salaì. 'If you stay, the paintings will stay forever. Like Helen of Sparta stolen by Paris, the King will keep them in his fortress.'

It was true that the most high and excellent Prince Francis – By the Grace of God, Most Christian King of France, Duke of Brittany; Duke of Milan, Count of Asti, Lord of Genoa; Count of Provence, Forcalquier and the lands adjacent – had been teasing Leonardo for years, attempting to cajole him into selling me and Leda, and even *St John the Baptist*. Leonardo and Cecco quietly demurred. I was not for sale. None of us were for sale.

I wanted to remain in France after Leonardo died. The manor at Clos Lucé was sumptuous and moulded to the master's comfort. Like a glove he'd just discarded, it was shaped to him, it held his presence – his books, papers, clothes, the scent of his skin, everything except Leonardo himself. Of course I wanted to stay. I wanted to remain steeped in him, in the last place he had been, pretending his absence was temporary. That he'd slipped into the next room or out into the rose garden and not into the next realm. 'I want to stay,' I said to Leda.

'I don't,' she answered. 'It's too sad. I want fresh air and to see somewhere new. It'll do you good, my darling.'

What either of us wanted did not matter. The days were gone when there was someone who listened to our desires. We were now but objects of value, possessions to be passed amongst men. There was nothing we could do but hope they were kind and treated us gently.

'We leave tomorrow. I do not wish to test the King's generosity,' said Cecco. 'I've already been obliged to read his notary Leonardo's will twice since he died, and remind him that the paintings belong to me. And that I shall not sell them. Not for any price they offer.'

'What price did they offer?' asked Salaì, interest piqued.

'What's it to you? We're not yours to sell, old man,' I muttered. 'Go and retire to your farm, eat cheese, screw and get even fatter.'

'We're going back to Italy,' said Cecco. 'Where they'll be safe from the King.'

Salaì was silent, and I wondered again if, despite being the maestro's lover and favourite for twenty years, he was wounded that Leonardo had not trusted him with his legacy.

I looked around the room, frantic, trying to memorise the limewashed stonework of the fireplace, the soot stains above the lintel. The crimson hangings curtaining the master's bed. If I was a painter instead of a painting, then I could immortalise it all in a still life. The rustle of paper on his desk and the endless scratch of his pen had stopped. Most of all, his voice had gone. It would always be missing now.

*

Cecco supervised our loading into the wagon to recross the Alps. We each had our own special box, lined with paper and soft leather, cushioned and meticulously wrapped. To my relief, Leda and I were placed close enough together that I could talk to her. In the twelve years since Leonardo created her for me, we'd hardly ever been apart. I hated being away from her. The journey to Milan would take weeks, and I couldn't bear the prospect of so long in isolation. It was still dark, as we were loaded in, gently packed in the front of the vehicle in another large crate, and draped with furs and skins in protection against inclement weather. We were paintings by the great Leonardo, objects of tremendous value, and must be guarded against jealous looks as well as frost and the knocks of the road. Yet, shortly after we were packed into the cart, I felt myself lifted off again. I lurched from side to side. Someone was running, clutching me tight.

'Thief!' I shouted. 'Leda!'

My first thought was that the King was seizing us, refusing to adhere to his agreement with Leonardo, then I heard another, louder voice raised in outrage.

'Salaì!' said Cecco, muffled but furious.

Not the King. Another, lowlier thief. I felt myself snatched away. I was set back upon the wagon. Cecco's voice was raised in anger.

'Salaì! After all this time, you are still nothing more than a vagabond and a thief in your soul.'

'Francesco Melzi, I hate you like a dog,' replied Salaì, spitting the words between his teeth.

Cecco replied, his voice low with fury.

'That might be so, but you still have to adhere to the law. I'm going to read you Leonardo's will one more time, as I have to the lawyers of the Most Christian King of France. Here we are, this is you. *To Salaì, his servant, one half of his garden outside the walls of Milan in which the same Salaì has built and constructed a house which shall be and remain henceforth the property of Salaì.'*

There was the sound of a scuffle, and the wagon rocked and jolted.

'You can object all you like. You can hit me, break my nose, but it doesn't change the fact.'

'Makes me feel a damn sight better.'

'If they're going to fight, it's a pity we can't see,' muttered Leda.

The wagon steadied.

'*To Messr Francesco da Melzi, gentleman of Milan* – you hear that, Salaì? Unlike you, I'm a gentleman.'

I braced myself for the wagon to rock and for another outbreak of hostilities, but there was nothing but a litany of cursing. Cecco continued.

'*To Melzi, each and all the notebooks Leonardo is at present possessed of and the portraits appertaining to his art and calling as a painter.'*

I could picture him, looking up at Salaì, sharp and watchful. Leonardo loved Salaì, but he was careful to place us and all his notebooks in Cecco's care. We were his legacy to the world.

'You inherit the house and garden, Salaì. The notebooks and all the paintings belong to me.'

'I don't see why we belong to anyone,' I grumbled. 'I belong to myself. I am not a chattel.'

'For the love of the Virgin, Mona Lisa,' complained Leda. 'Do you want to go with Salaì? He'll flog you to the highest bidder at the first opportunity.'

Not in the mood to squabble with my friend, I didn't reply. It was true that I rarely kept my opinions to myself. But, while I adored Leda, we didn't always agree. She was a Spartan queen after all, and I am just a woman – even if a universal one, the Eve of all ages. I could hear Leda fussing about her children, confiding to them in soothing whispers about the journey.

In a few minutes the wagon was moving. Away from France. Away from Leonardo and his earthly remains. I was glad to be alone, hidden and unseen. Lonely and desolate and frightened by my grief, I thought of Lisa del Giocondo, her body wracked by sobs, her howls of desolation. Now I understood more properly her loss, we shared more than just a name or a face. The cart shook me to and fro. Those became my shudders of woe, the screeching of the metal wheels against the rock, mingling with my cries of misery.

Milan, 1523

Summer

We returned to the grand Melzi villa perched on the shores of the River Adda. The house was large and adorned with frescoes, several of which had been painted by Leonardo himself, and I could feel his presence here. I could trace the master's hand in the swirling ash and oak and mulberry leaves tangling the walls and ceilings. It was here a dozen years ago that Leda was born. There, on that loggia under the shade of those larches, I sat and waited and watched, a tender midwife as she hatched, a fully-formed goddess.

Cecco's wife Angiola plucked fruit to bring inside. Bowls of heaped mulberries lay on the table, their seeping juices staining the wood and everyone's mouths and blackening their lips and teeth so they leered like lepers. I tried to join in the mirth but there was always a hard pebble in my throat. The brightest day, the warmest fire; all was as winter to me. I was never warm and yet I couldn't shiver. I found it difficult to concentrate or follow the thread of conversation, only listening when they spoke of Leonardo. What was the use of talking of anything else? I did not want the pain to ease; instead I tended my loss over the years as carefully as Angiola did her garden, anxious not to forget a single memory.

Even though Leonardo had been like a father to him, Cecco's heartache was not the same as mine. He'd wed and the marriage bed had borne fruit. His sadness now mingled with joy. Cecco himself might die, but now his line would go on. He'd found a new comfort against the eternal abyss, both in the earthly and sumptuous bosom of his wife, and in the very existence of his children. He still devoted himself to the master's legacy, but when I sat watching him with Angiola gazing transfixed upon their noisy and dribbling babies, I understood his grief was different. Leonardo's death had freed him. He had discovered another love.

Cecco liked to address me, even though he couldn't hear my reply. It was his way of talking to Leonardo.

'Come, Madonna Lisa. We are still working upon Leonardo's treatise upon painting. You have always understood his ideas better than I.'

Of course I understood his treatise upon painting. Who better to appreciate it, than a painting herself? But it was more than that; it was I who was his confidant, the keeper of his secrets. His true confessor. Leonardo never needed a priest. He had me. He had spent his last sixteen years revealing his ideas to me.

I recalled him whispering, 'How many paintings have preserved the image of a divine beauty which in its natural form has been overtaken by time or death? Thus, the work of the painter is nobler than that of nature, its mistress.'

There, upon the wall opposite me, in red chalk was a drawing of Leonardo in profile. I startled. I could not bear to look at it. The picture was so true to life, it was as if my love was here again, waiting to speak. I nearly called out to him. Drawn by Cecco, it would always be his most distinguished work. The elegant and authoritative slope of Leonardo's nose, the flow of his beard and long hair – finished by the hand of the master himself – the fullness of the lashes and the depth and intensity of his gaze. He was a beautiful old man, refined and generous. Thoughtful, yet ready to laugh. I'd asked him what he was thinking about in that pose while Cecco drew him and he looked at me with a raised eyebrow and replied, 'Why, you, Madonna Lisa, of course.' If it was a lie, it had been a kind one and typical of him.

Leda sensed my melancholy. 'Don't think of him. He's wanted in paradise. Think of me. Look upon me and I shall drive all other thoughts away. It's not possible to be unhappy while admiring my charms.'

I laughed. Leda was so assured of her own beauty. However, she forgot who gave it to her. When I looked at her, I still saw him. It both comforted and saddened me.

Now, Cecco seized his pen and, smiling, glanced up at me, continuing to work until it grew dark and the first stars cast out into the sky. I tried to persuade Leda to join the discussion on painting, but she preferred to talk of her babies. Leda pretended interest and concern in Cecco and Angiola's children, but as soon as Angiola quit the room, Leda retreated into superciliousness: Angiola's children were loud and effluent. They filled the house at all hours with the sounds of their mewling and puking. Leda watched with horror and fascination as the wet-nurse suckled them from her vast ripe breast, pale and round as a veined cheese. Leda's babes were hatched from the seed of the king of the gods, divine in their perfection. Angiola's offspring would grow up into men and women, age and die. Leda's hatchlings – Helen and Pollux, Clytemnestra and Castor – would remain infants forever, and never ever leave her side. Leda's children kept her as a perpetual mother. She never belonged entirely to Leonardo, as she always had her children. Of course she adored Leonardo – we all did – but her grief was never so absolute as mine.

I glanced up at St John. He hung opposite a mirror, and could see himself in the glass, but like Narcissus appeared transfixed by his own considerable beauty: the spiral curl of his long hair, the play of light on his cheek. In St John, Leonardo had painted Salaì and the suggestion of what he considered his irreverence and wayward charm. For my part, I always viewed Salaì's main character trait as malice, but then I did not love him. St John is the beautiful and blinkered version of Salaì, seen through Leonardo's vision of love. Yet the truth still seeps in at the edges and the lascivious, distinctly unsaintly smirk is the Salaì I knew. St John always appeared as though he was about to confide a filthy joke – he seemed to me more Bacchus than holy man – and I spent hours cajoling and pleading with him to share but he never spoke. Still, sometimes I hoped and wondered if he might.

We worked into the night and then, after Cecco disappeared abed and into the arms of his wife, it was quiet in the hall. The full moon floated before the windows like a bubble. The embers in the fire dulled. The rattle and click of the deathwatch beetle in the oak ceiling beams.

The scrape and scuffle of the mice. Two of Cecco's paintings were set out on easels, unfinished. He was not without talent. If it hadn't been for Leonardo, he might have been considered gifted. It is a curse to be apprenticed to the greatest painter of the age. Cecco always considered it his noblest duty to devote himself to Leonardo's genius rather than cultivate his own talents.

I was mesmerised by Cecco's red-chalk drawing of Leonardo. Perhaps it was because I was so transfixed by the drawing that I failed to notice the thief. He was upon me before I had a chance to scream. In a moment I was unhooked from the wall, crammed into a bag, dark and stuffy, the sides pressing in on me. Then he took me and we were gone.

We ran through the deserted streets, his boots reverberating on the cobbles. I heard the heave and gasp of his breath. Through the gaps in the weave of the bag I could make out that we were veering away from the Melzi villa and the river and onto a narrow side street, where the buildings leered close together on each side, the shutters tightly shut like eyelids. I yelled and hollered but there was no one there to hear. He sprinted faster, hurtling around the corners, and I listened to his ragged, frantic breathing. I could hear horses whinnying; a wagon was waiting for us. I was loaded in. After some merry distance, I was lifted off the cart and carried through an open doorway into a panelled hall. I passed into new hands, and someone lifted me out of the sack.

'Hello, Madonna Lisa,' he said.

'Salaì. You foul creature. Of course it was you.'

He grinned, glad to see me.

'I hope they took care with you. If they damaged you in some way, it might lower your price.'

He carried me into a pleasant room, not as generous as Cecco's but decent. Several easels had been prepared. St John already rested serenely on one, his impudent half-smirk unblemished by the journey.

Before I could reply, another man hurried in carrying a furious Leda. 'How dare you, Salaì? We aren't yours. Give us back to Cecco this instant.'

I cried out in relief. Leda and I were still together. Salaì sat down on a chair beside the fire, stretched out his legs and began to quarter an orange, tossing the peel into the flames. I thought back to Cecco's exquisite red-chalk drawing of Leonardo, and wondered if I should ever glimpse it again. Considering his brilliance as a painter, when it came to his favourite, Leonardo had clouded vision. For him, Salaì's beauty had always masked his greed and wickedness.

A notary came to assess us in the morning. The entire process was ghastly and undignified. I did not want to be valued and picked over. Leda did not make the least objection. She liked nothing more than to be admired, gratified by the attention. Then, she was probably the most enchanting painting in the world. She stood quite nude, hip thrust slightly to one side; Jupiter in the guise of the swan, his wing hugging and caressing her waist. Her hands seized his muscular neck, Leda a *figura serpentinata* half-pulling him away and half-inviting his embrace while his lascivious open beak swooped upwards towards her shoulder, his eye beady and black, his swan's shadow falling on the perfect alabaster of her bare skin and the blown beads of her nipples. Yet Leda herself remained serene, her eyes downcast in the barrage of the god's lust. Her hair fastened in the perfect knot, only a few amber curls torn free in the wind, while she stared down with a beatific look at her children hatching from their eggs. It was both the moment of seduction and consequence. Leda remains maiden, seductress and eternal mother. Jupiter writhes in passion, the god earthed by the beauty of a mortal princess. Every white feather of his plumage perfect, ready for flight. Leonardo, who spent years trying to master the mysteries of flight, paints the ideal bird in the marvellous bird-god. The bulrushes quiver in the breeze. The churn of the water and the smell of river mud. The blue castle hums in the heat haze and the pink wild strawberries in the foreground wait to be plucked. Speckled snapdragons nod. A dandelion-seed clock tickles across Leda's wriggling toes. I can see her now and always.

That morning, the notary looked at her and expelled a quivering sigh. He was lost. If he could have given up his wife and children and law practice and traded places with Jupiter, he would have done so in an instant and without a thought. I heard Salaì stifle a laugh. He knew it too.

'Why would you part with her?' the notary whispered, his voice a rasp, through dry lips.

'I am to have a real wife. Of flesh. I'm tired of painted delights.'

'I'd never tire of her. She's beyond price.'

'Try,' snapped Salaì.

'Ten thousand *lire imperiali*.'

'That's absurd. Even a king would baulk at such a price.'

Leda laughed and preened. In that way, we were always different, but I loved her no less for it. The notary coughed, embarrassed, realising that in his excitement he'd been overcome and forcing himself to move away from Leda. He started to examine St John and then me, initially with reluctance, and then with wonder. He stared at me. I glared back, wishing I could stick out my tongue.

'By all the saints, she is nearly as lovely. Her beauty is less apparent, it doesn't come at you all at once, but I feel as if I'm only waiting for her to speak.'

'Don't wait too long,' said Salaì. 'Value?'

'Five hundred *lire imperiali*,' announced the notary, after a moment's thought. 'She's the famous Mona Lisa. *La Gioconda*?' He leaned in close, with a frown. 'Although, I'm not convinced she's so jocund. It's a pun but it isn't true. Her smile looks melancholy to me. She's thinking of something that gives her joy but also pain.'

Salaì groaned and rolled his eyes. 'I asked you for a valuation, not your opinion on art. Listening to a man who isn't an artist pontificate is like the squeal of a broken cartwheel. When you get home you can rub your crotch as you think of Leda and have wistful dreams of Madonna Lisa. I couldn't give a shit what you think of the pictures. Except what they're worth.'

The notary sniffed, offended, and stalked back to Leda, expelling another unrequited sigh, more suited to a wistful knight of Petrarch than a paunchy, clammy notary of advancing years.

'A thousand *lire imperiali*,' he declared, his voice hoarse.

'Are you certain?' asked Salaì, his forehead creasing with wonder and greed. 'That's more than all my property. More than the vineyard.'

'Yes, I'm sure. And your prince will pay it.'

Salaì led him to value several other paintings he had set up on easels or leaned up against the walls. To my disgust, I noticed the nude version of me with high breasts like tennis balls, sprouting just beneath her collarbone, that Salaì had attempted some years ago. It was crude and ungainly and I abhorred it. I was certain that he had executed it to annoy and insult me. His skill was limited, and even if he had wished to imitate the master and attempt to charm the gods themselves he could not have succeeded. In any case, the loathsome Mona Vana gawps, thick-necked and wide-eyed. She is mute and stupid and worthy of Salaì.

'What of her?' asked Salaì, with a hint of misplaced pride.

I wished I had hands that could slap him.

The notary signalled his disinterest. Even the bare breasts of the Mona Vana were nothing to him.

'Twenty-five lire.'

'No. That's a pittance,' objected Salaì, outraged. 'She's worth at least a hundred and twenty.'

'Then why ask me?'

'You're right. Sod off.'

After dismissing him, Salaì turned and scrutinised me and then Leda, peering at us, trying to see us through the notary's eyes. I glared at him, filled with rage and loathing.

'You never cared about what we were to him. We've never been anything but a chattel to you,' I hissed, furious, speaking as if he could understand.

Salaì yawned, but guilt at betrayal of Leonardo's wishes must have nagged at him for he said, 'What wall does it matter that you hang on? One's much the same as another. And I'm feeling generous; I'll even ask if you and Leda can hang together. Or are you sore, that your friend is worth twice as much?'

I did not want either of us to be viewed as mere objects to be haggled over, assessed in order to buy a bride. Leonardo would have wept to have his Salaì treat us so meanly. I had long been Leonardo's favourite, the one he loved the best. But Leonardo was dead.

Autumn

Salaì was marrying a wealthy bride bringing a plentiful dowry, and despite the vineyard left to him by Leonardo, he wanted to bring a substantial sum to the union. Leda, St John and I were nothing to him but the prospect of gold. Salaì might then have been more than forty years old and his chestnut curls laced with frost, but in his soul he was still the grubby peasant boy Leonardo had plucked from his hovel, insecure and belligerent. He was not an aristocrat like Francesco Melzi, nor touched with *ingegno* despite the decades spent learning with the great master. He had little to bring his rich and honied bride except his fading charms, a small farm and anecdotes of the greatest painter of the age – most of which he could not or ought not repeat. Yet Salaì, vagabond and operator, was not a man to accept fate. He would enter this union on his own terms; not as a grateful supplicant but as an equal, and a rich man. He dictated letters to Francis, the Most Christian King of France, informing him that the paintings of his beloved court artist that he had so long coveted were now available. At a price.

Yet I did not despair. The letter must cross the Alps, so while Salaì waited for a reply, I prayed to the Virgin and to St Luke, the patron saint of painters; there being no patron saint of paintings specifically, I hoped St Luke would suffice and have mercy. I knew Cecco would be scouring the city for news of our whereabouts. I prayed that he secured our return before the letter arrived from the King.

Salaì was filled with confidence and glee, and decided that it was time to hold his nuptials. He tucked the betrothal ring in his jerkin and went whistling to present it to Bianca Coldirodi d'Annono at her father's house, and later the same warm September evening the new bride was brought to consummate the union with her husband, brimming with happy tears and shy smiles. I pitied her.

A splendid feast was laid out on the long table in the hall where we all hung. A hog turned on a spit so that its skin split and crackled, the spitting fat freckling the flagstone hearth. Savoury stuffed partridge and quail lay plucked, roasted and plump in earthen trays, their skins brown and crisp. Baskets of shellfish glistened; red lobsters and rocky oysters on puckered beds of peeled yellow lemons. Bowls of walnuts and runny cheeses and figs, downy apricots and grapes, feathered pastries carried in from the bakery, and flagons of wine. The air was thick with smoke and grease and laughter.

Bianca stood apart, veiled by women, her faced flushed with excitement. She must have been fourteen or fifteen, and despite the sumptuary laws wore a crimson overgown of costly silk embroidered with pine cones and pomegranates to signal her fertility, with a flowing skirt, a matching silk belt and a fringed cowl. She contemplated her soon-to-be husband with adoration and reverence. He winked at her and blew her a kiss. Was it possible that he loved her, or even harboured the faintest tenderness towards her? I wished that he did, but I doubted it.

The hall echoed with eating and singing and dancing and the cheerful notes of the *lira da braccio* and the flute. A juggler sent polished oranges skidding all across the floor. A baby boy was pressed into Bianca's arms to be kissed as a herald of future sons. She and Salaì danced and whirled, her dark hair twinkling with pearls, and when she sat for a moment, flagging, to remove her pinching shoes, a gold coin was instantly slipped inside – a portent of good fortune.

All around the hall Salaì had displayed the *contradonora* of gifts that he would be presenting to Bianca after their marriage ceremony in church on Sunday. There were chests brimming with gowns of silk and velvet, pearl headpieces, shoes and a wooden box with jewels of emeralds and jet. His gifts must be nearly equal to her dowry. He didn't have anything like enough coin to purchase such trophies. It was clear to me that Leda, St John and I had been used to secure a loan, but for today he wanted the guests to believe that we were part of his wealth, and his gifts to Bianca. A public display of his worth and worthiness. Until this evening, Salaì had been careful as to who had glimpsed us. He knew Francesco Melzi was hunting for us, and he was a man of means and influence. To display us like this was brazen, overweening and foolish. Milan was larger than Florence, but Salaì was taking a great risk that Cecco would discover us. It gave me hope.

It was also a mistake; many of the guests were so busy marvelling at Leda that they quite forgot to admire the bride. I saw Bianca turn and look in the direction of the throng, the gathering of silent reverents slowly ignoring the feast and revelry. Her dark eyes settled upon Leda and narrowed with distaste. I had my own share of devotees. They neither ate nor spoke, but stood, watchful and still, in my presence. I wished I could shoo them back to the party, order them to feast and compliment the bride, but there was nothing to be done. They remained before me, gazing in open wonder, indifferent to anything but me. I looked at Bianca and saw that she studied me with a settled look of dislike. It is not done to outshine a bride upon her betrothal day. Nothing good comes of it.

At dusk, after the final toast, the guests departed and the bride was borne upstairs to the bridal chamber to be made ready for her husband. Salaì sidled up to me clutching a glass of wine, his teeth stained red. He was drunk and, all inhibition removed, spoke directly to me.

'Did you enjoy the party?' he asked.

'No,' I answered, even though I knew he still could not hear. 'And you shouldn't have displayed us. Bianca did not wish us here. We were a distraction.'

He was staggering and his words were slurred. I studied him closely. He looked sweaty and unhappy, not in the least like a bridegroom about to consummate the union with his young bride. He didn't love her, I realised. Like me, he still loved only one man and he was dead.

Salaì regarded me with disgust. He was silent for a moment and then continued to talk aloud, half to himself, half to me. 'He loved only me until you. I was with him from when I was barely ten years old. I was a little rat. I infuriated and enraged him and yet he always forgave me. Like a father or God himself, he named me Salaì. I was ordinary Giacomo Caprotti until Leonardo.' He paused and grinned. 'But, Madonna Lisa, you most of all know that the love between us was not that of father and son.'

He made a series of obscene grunts, and then lunged towards me, his face a finger's breadth from mine. I could feel his breath against my skin, see the blackened pores on his nose. His eyes were wide and bloodshot, but when he spoke, his voice was low and shook.

'I loved him too, Mona Lisa. And then you took him from me, piece by piece.'

He stared at me with perfect hatred. Our rivalry for the love of Leonardo survived death itself. Our loathing of one another had become a callous or sore that would never heal. Salaì slumped back onto the bench and drained his wine. As I watched him, drunk and wretched on his wedding night, I alone appreciated how much Salaì missed Leonardo too. His life could not be easy and filled with joy like Cecco's. A wife and even children could not ease that void. His arms were empty. He longed for kisses and caresses that would never come again. I knew what it was to yearn for those embraces, that touch, however impossible. For a moment, I almost had sympathy for him; we shared a sour kinship. He peered at me through red lids.

'He and I enjoyed what you never could,' he said with a leer. 'That always consoled me. In fact, I'm going to console myself now. I think you should watch.'

'No!'

He stood and, reaching up, lifted me off the wall.

He blinked at me, his eyelashes brushing my cheek. 'You are pristine. A virgin like the Madonna. Always untouched. Mortals are warm and soft. Mortals can fuck. You might live forever, but really what's the point, Madonna Lisa? No one can ever really love you, only the idea of you. Even him.'

'Be quiet! Don't ever say that. It isn't true,' I pleaded, even though I knew it was futile.

'You need to know what you're missing.' He started to carry me towards the stairs as I berated him uselessly.

I wished that he would stop. Bianca did not like me. She would not want me there. She only wanted him. But Salaì could not be decent. Even once. I was for once grateful for my inhumanity. Beside this marriage, Leonardo's love for me was ideal – honest and compassionate. Salaì took no heed of my complaints and hurried up the stairs to the bedchamber. The room contained Salaì's most valuable possession after his stolen paintings – a bed hand-carved from walnut, seven *braccia* wide, dressed with curtains and pillows of cloth-of-gold and a linen coverlet plump with goose feathers. Bianca knelt in prayer next to the bed dressed in her plain linen undergarments. Her sister and mother unpinned the pearls from her long maiden's plait.

'Leave us,' snapped Salaì.

Bianca looked up, her lashes heavy with tears. No longer weighed down with her heavy wedding clothes, she seemed little more than a child. Without a word, her mother and sister stood up to leave. Her mother bestowed a single kiss on her daughter's forehead and quitted the room. Bianca's breathing quickened with fear. Salaì was at least twenty-five years older than she, currently thick with wine and clutching a portrait of another woman.

'Why are you holding that picture?' she asked.

'Lisa wanted to watch. She looks demure, but she's actually very nosy,' he said, swaying gently like a ship in harbour.

I didn't want to watch. I longed to plead forgiveness of Bianca, but I could not. I wanted to beg him to put me back downstairs, but knew it was pointless.

The girl looked at Salaì in horror.

'I don't like her. She stares at me. Her eyes follow me,' she said.

'I want her here.'

He propped me against the wooden bedpost, climbed up and, removing an ornate and gilded *Madonna and Child* from the wall, hung me upon the nail instead.

'I like the *Madonna*,' said Bianca, petulant and troubled. 'She will bless our union. Bring us sons.'

'Madonna Lisa will bring us cash.'

'I don't like her here,' said Bianca, stamping her foot and trying not to cry and fiddling with the oversized rubies upon her thin fingers.

I longed for Salaì to stop. I wanted him to take me out. A man of experience was supposed to be gentle and kind with a young girl.

Salaì ignored us both and started to undress, fumbling with his embroidered buttons. To the bewilderment of his bride, he looked up at me as he did so with an expression of vindictiveness.

'Who is she? Did you love her?' asked Bianca, bewildered and hurt.

'You mean Lisa del Giocondo? Pious and dull?' Salaì threw his head back and laughed fulsomely until he had to wipe tears. He snatched at Bianca and kissed her; she moved away impulsively.

'No, little one, you're mine now.'

She began to cry.

I muttered a prayer to the Virgin for him to have pity upon Bianca. He was a brute but he wasn't usually cruel. Or only to me.

Through the haze of wine he slouched, ashamed, then slid to his knees and began to pray, not to the Almighty but to a different master, an earthly one, who had died and who he had loved.

'I am sorry. Have pity. And forgive me. I am nothing without you. You saw me at once for who I am and you did not care and loved me anyway. *Ladro, bugiardo, ostinato, ghiotto.* Thief. Liar. Obstinate. Glutton.'

Bianca knelt beside him.

'I would never say or think such things. And of course I forgive you, and I'm sure God will too,' she said, believing that Salaì was pleading for her mercy.

He did not correct her. He kissed her tenderly and softly as a bridegroom should. His clemency did not stretch to me. Bianca seemed to me like Persephone, languishing in the underworld regretting every seed of the pomegranate, while Salaì with his silver curls and black eyes was Hades himself. As he laid her on the bed and stripped her naked, her expression full of wonder and trepidation, he glanced up at me, full of callous triumph. He wanted me to suffer, to remind me of my inhumanity. To know that I could not turn my face to the wall even if I wished. I was forced to remain in their chamber the entire night. Even when the candle guttered out, I could hear their grunts and whimperings in the dark. After Salaì began to snore, tired from his exertions, I could hear the muffled weeping of Bianca. I did not try to comfort her. There was nothing

I could say, and even if I had the words, she could not hear them.

To my profound relief Bianca pleaded that I be removed from the bedroom, and Salaì relented. I was returned to Leda and St John and the hall. Leda called out to me, jubilant.

'Mona! It was dreadful without you. What did he do to you? That canker. That worm.'

I couldn't tell her all at once, and stuttered in my dismay over what I had been compelled to watch. Leda listened, for once hushed into horrified silence. 'Mona,' she asked at last. 'Is it worse to be a painted woman, or to be real, in the hands of a man? At his mercy?'

'I do not know,' I said. 'It depends on the man.'

When the man was Salaì, it felt dangerous to rest for a moment, so when Cecco called at the house some weeks later, I was the first to see him arrive.

He came and sat beside me. He looked fretful and thin.

'I'm sorry, Leonardo. You placed your trust in me to keep them safe and I have failed you. I could not come before. I needed to raise the funds to secure their release. Until I had the money, there was no point.'

'You were stupid and foolish,' snapped Leda. 'Why didn't you hire a watchman? You know what Salaì is.'

'Yes,' I agreed. 'We're not going to absolve you.'

'Even though Salaì has had one or two excellent parties, that was not enough to justify his wickedness,' added Leda.

Cecco sat, his head drooping with exhaustion. Salaì and Bianca appeared in the hall. Waking at once, Cecco stood and bowed and presented her with a small inlaid-ivory box. She opened it and inside was a bejewelled perfume bottle.

'A beautiful bride should have beautiful things. Felicities upon your wedding, Madonna Caprotti.'

She smiled, dimples appearing in each cheek. She had made up her mind to be cool and distant with Cecco, but he was too kind, too charming. Salaì was not so easily swayed.

'I'm still flogging my paintings to the King.'

'*My* pictures are not yours to sell.'

Cecco brought out a copy of Leonardo's will. Salaì wiped his nose with his sleeve and yawned. 'The thing is, Melzi, by the time your case reaches the courts, Mona Lisa, Leda and St John will be in France. I don't see the courts demanding that Francis, By the Grace of God, Most Christian King of France, Duke of Brittany; Duke of Milan, Count of Asti, Lord of Genoa; Count of Provence, Forcalquier and the lands adjacent, hand them back. Do you?'

Cecco sighed and was silent for a moment. 'Has the King agreed to pay your price?'

It was Salaì's turn to say nothing, and Cecco suppressed a smile. Salaì snapped at his wife. 'Bianca, see to the morning meal. Bring enough for our troublesome guest.'

The girl looked at her husband in surprise, but, turning, did as she was told and retreated to the stores to speak with the housekeeper.

'I will offer a fair price,' said Cecco.

'I don't want a fair price. I want a handsome one.'

'I'm sure. I heard your wedding feast was bacchanalian. The gifts to your bride extraordinary. You must have debts to pay off.'

Salaì shrugged, feigning indifference. 'They can wait.'

I could see from the crimson flush beneath Cecco's collar that he was growing angry, but trying to control it.

'You're a common thief and you lie as easily as you breathe, Salaì. These are my paintings, yet still I'm willing to buy them back, as I wish to honour our master's final wishes. Leonardo wanted Mona Lisa, Leda and St John to remain with me.'

I listened with growing weariness as they haggled, argued and traded insults for an hour. I longed to return home with Cecco. We had work to do – manuscripts to prepare for publication, and the master's legacy to pore over. I understood that I had many lifetimes ahead to be lonely, but so long as I was with Leda and Cecco examining Leonardo's writings, then during this lifetime at least, I would be in proximity to those that had known him and cared for him. I wanted to cleave to what little was left of him, for as long as I could. These were the last people who had seen him, touched him, borrowed his pencil, shared a meal or a joke with him. When Cecco died, all his memories of Leonardo would pass out of the world and more of him would be lost to the ether. Until that day, I hankered to be surrounded by his friends, his books, his drawings. I wanted to think and hear of nothing but him.

Salaì was naming higher and higher prices.

'This is *folle*!' complained Cecco.

'No. I shall not sell her to you. Not for any price.'

Cecco observed Salaì, troubled and bewildered. 'I don't understand,' he said. 'You need the money. I've raised it. You don't want the paintings, I do.'

I understood. Salaì was living up to his name. He was no longer a little devil, just a devil. Cruel and vindictive.

Leda and St John were nothing to him. He was jealous of me because Leonardo loved me, and I was a true rival. Not all love needs consummating, and love takes many forms, something Salaì never understood. Leonardo had refused to sell me, and now Salaì wished to punish me by selling me himself like common household goods.

Cecco balled his fists and looked for a moment as if he would strike Salaì, and then, thinking better of it, spat, 'I'll see you in court. I have the will. They are my pictures. They'll be returned to me and you won't get a single florin for them.'

Salaì shrugged. 'They'll be in France by then.'

Cecco came and stood beside me, his expression grave.

'I'm sorry, Leonardo. I'm sorry, Mona Lisa. I'll return for you.'

Cecco took his leave. Salaì signalled to the servant to pour him a glass of wine and settled in the low chair, stretching out his legs.

The door was not quite closed, and I glimpsed Bianca watching from the crack, and I wondered how long she had been lingering there.

It was soon time to harvest the vineyard, and there had been an outbreak of palsy amongst the peasants and there weren't enough men to bring in the grapes. Salaì went out seeking men in need of coin amongst the ragged German and Swiss mercenaries left roaming the streets in search of casual work and easy fights after the latest war. While her husband was busy on his errand, rather than occupy herself in the kitchens or stores, or even walk amongst the roses blooming amidst the vines, Bianca came into the hall. She padded beside the long refectory table, picked up a bunch of dusky grapes, popped two into her mouth. She stared at Leda for several minutes, then St John, before finally standing before me.

'Why do they speak to you, Mona Lisa? It's as though they believe you can understand them. You look as if you might reply.'

I said nothing.

'Why doesn't he speak to me?'

I couldn't tell if she might turn on me or cry. And then she looked up, her face full of resolve.

'There isn't room here for both of us. I want my husband to myself. This is my house. I need you gone. I won't wait until the King of France replies. Suppose he doesn't? Suppose he decides to start another war with Milan instead? What then?'

The girl wasn't stupid. It was entirely possible. Francis's passion for wars with Italy was even greater than his passion for Italian art.

'As long as you are here, my husband is full of phlegm and spleen. I want his balance of humours restored.'

I longed to tell her that Salaì had never been in good humour.

I looked at her and, although she was small, her cheek touched with the first bloom of youth, her voice had the resolve of a woman. The girl I saw on her wedding night had gone.

'You see?' complained Bianca, scowling. 'You've got me at it now, chatting to you. It's against God and I won't have it. I'm going to be free of you all.'

She glanced at Leda with abhorrence, then summoned the maid, who fastened her cloak, and together they hurried from the house.

I feared for myself, Leda, even silent St John, but most of all for young and impetuous Bianca. She might have disliked me, but the years had softened me. Her life already seemed brief and unhappy, the fleeting passage of a cloud before the sun.

Several days passed and Cecco did not return. Bianca and Salaì ate and drank and bickered. She did not speak to me again. Salaì plucked a Muscat from the vine early one morning and, bringing it into the hall, held it up, declared it perfect, and half a dozen men were summoned to harvest the grapes. They were forbidden from entering the house or speaking to the women. Salaì remained outside with them as it grew late, directing their efforts. The grapes must be in before the rains came, and the sky was darkening, clouds swirling around the moon like watery pools of black ink.

We expected Bianca to prepare the evening meal for the workers, but instead she lifted me off the wall and started to wrap me carefully in layers of cloth, while her maid did the same to Leda who immediately began to object.

'Where are we going? Not that I mind. I'm thrilled to be out of here.'

'I believe she has a plan to be rid of us. If I had to guess, it would be that she's selling us back to Cecco. Madonna Bianca isn't too fond of us,' I answered.

Leda sniffed. 'I can't think why. Everyone adores me.'

She was silenced, bundled into a sack. The maid was white with terror. Bianca smiled, her teeth like tiny seed pearls.

'Don't be frightened, Maria,' said Bianca. 'It will be all right. I've hired a man, a Swiss soldier, to keep watch over us. He'll protect us. He's got a gun, and if Francesco Melzi tries anything, he'll shoot. If anyone tries to follow us after we've the money, he'll shoot them too.'

'How can you trust a mercenary, Madonna?' asked the maid.

'I'm paying him lavishly. Far too much to risk hanging.'

She took the maid's hands and kissed her. 'Please, Maria, hurry. You take this one, I can manage the others.'

Together, the women bundled us up and hastened from the house. In her hurry, Bianca had not wrapped me as closely as Leda or St John, and I could see a little. I noticed that they were both dressed in Maria's clothes rather than Bianca's, a sensible precaution. A woman of Bianca's rank scurrying around the city at dusk unchaperoned might call attention, but two servants would not be noticed. I was filled with admiration for the cunning of Bianca Caprotti. She was a suitable wife for Salaì, a young woman of considerable wiles who might indeed make him happy if he cared to notice her shrewd charms.

Outside, the night was cool, but the rain had not yet started to fall. I could hear that the streets were busy and the two women slipped unobserved amongst the traffic of passers-by. The air was thick with the stink of rotting cabbage, excrement – horse, pig and human – as well as roasting mutton pies, proving bread, fermenting wine, ripe cheese, burning incense and the chanting of evensong. The two women fled into the narrower lanes, too small for wagons or carts, and as they turned into a deserted alleyway I heard heavy, male footsteps behind them and hoped that they belonged to the Swiss mercenary. He was either protecting them from a distance or selecting the moment to rob them. Bianca walked quickly, slightly ahead of the maid, and she was leading them along a route towards the river. I could hear the ragged sound of her breathing.

'I'm hot and I can't see,' complained Leda. 'Can you?'

'Not much,' I confessed.

I could glimpse only a little through a gap in the paper, and Bianca grasped me tightly beneath her arm and the world was askew, the ground at an odd angle and the sky upside down. The first few spots of rain began to fall. Bianca's slippers were filthy. She'd borrowed her maid's clothes, but her own rose silk slippers betrayed her. The rain swelled to a barrage, and they scampered towards the river, slip-sliding in the slick mud and grime now lining the streets.

There was a distant shout.

'Stop! Get back here!'

They ran faster. The paper covering me began to grow slimy and slide away. The roar of the river rivalled the pelting of the rain. The footsteps behind us gave chase, sprinting too. I could no longer hear the mercenary; only someone new, someone hunting us. The man called out again, his voice echoing through the dark, distorted through the roar of the deluge.

'Stop! Stop at once! Thief!'

A shot fired out in the gloom. A spark of light and there was a wet thump. The women carried on running for a moment, and then Bianca stopped and turned, and sensing something horribly wrong went back. A bloodied bundle lay heaped on himself, a puddle running out into the dirt. Setting me down, Bianca knelt and tugged back his hood. Salaì lay weak and dying, his face sluiced by the rain, a gaping wound in his guts, soaked with gore and viscera.

'You,' he said. 'You killed me.'

'No. It's not true. I won't have it,' she said, her face awash with tears. 'You mustn't die. I won't allow it.'

He gripped her hand and spat blood. 'You killed me and took Mona Lisa.'

'No,' she said again, shaking her head furiously as a dog trying to rid itself of fleas. 'I wanted her gone. I had to get rid of her. I hate her.'

'So do I,' he said, with a cough, and belched up blood. Bianca crouched, weeping at his side.

'We share that then,' he whispered, grasping at her.

'I'm sorry,' she muttered, wiping her tears and leaving a streak of blood across her cheek, black in the murk. 'It's just a scrape. A tiny wound.' She shook her head, murmuring, 'I wanted it to be us. Only us.'

'That sounds delightful,' agreed Salaì. 'An excellent idea. But a bit late now.'

She leaned forward and kissed him.

The paper covering me had entirely fallen away now. I remained propped against a wall in the alley and surveyed them, as they stared back at me in silence. Leda was still covered in her wrappings, set to one side, unable to see. A moment later, the mercenary trudged out of the shadows, the gun still clasped in his hand. He stared at Salaì in confusion.

'Why did you kill him?' asked Bianca, wide-eyed with horror.

'He was following you. I was protecting you. Like you paid me.'

'He's my husband. You murdered my husband,' she hissed, angry as a viper.

'No,' said the mercenary, shaking his head and sensing the noose or the axe. 'No. That can't be right. You said

Melzi couldn't be trusted. You didn't say anything about your husband. Killing husbands is extra.'

He looked from one to the other as he took in the situation: the dying man, the paintings and the distraught women. He was considering how to turn it to his advantage, or the least disadvantage.

Salaì gave a gurgle and a cry of agony, and Bianca cradled his head. 'Go,' she ordered the mercenary. 'Fetch a priest and direct him to us. My husband needs the last rites. You've sinned in this life. Try to atone for the next.'

The hulking man hesitated, a sly grin on his lips, the weapon twitching in his hands. But a moment later the maid Maria began to scream, piercing and shrill, and it seemed as if the shutters must snap open and locks rattle in the alley. He ran.

'Hush,' hissed Bianca to the maid. 'We don't want to bring the constabulary.'

Maria sat and snivelled in the gutter, biting her own arm to silence herself.

A lone figure hurried along the alley towards us.

'The priest,' said Bianca, with bitterness and relief, but it wasn't the priest. It was Cecco. Salaì groaned with agony and despair. Cecco knelt in the pool of blood.

'You were late and I came to find you. What in God's name happened?' he asked.

'A mercenary shot him. I hired him as protection against you,' she said, spitting the words.

Cecco recoiled. 'What kind of man do you think I am?'

'We need a priest,' murmured Bianca. 'Hurry, Melzi.'

'No,' said Salaì, his voice low and rasping. 'Priest or not, we know where I'm going. Bianca, forgive me. I was a wretched husband.'

The girl covered him with kisses and he groaned in pain.

'Melzi, you whore son, you're not getting my paintings.' He gave a whine of anguish.

In the guttering dark, Salaì glanced at me, just meeting my eyes. He was drenched in rain and blood and filth.

'Mona Lisa ... I've always wanted to tell you ... I ... ' but his breath ceased and whether his final words were of love or loathing, bile or spite, or some secret nurtured from Leonardo himself, I never discovered.

Bianca rocked forward onto her heels and wept bitter, furious tears and hugged his corpse close, coating his cheeks with kisses until she was saturated with blood. She thrust me and the sacks containing St John and Leda at Cecco.

'I don't care what he said. I don't want them. It's because of them that he's dead.'

Cecco sighed. 'I'm so sorry, Madonna Caprotti, more sorry than I can say, but Salaì was right. I can't take them after this. Some clever magistrate might realise it means I was here this night when he was killed. I don't want to hang for this. You too must hurry home and have your maid wash your clothes and tell everyone who will listen that you were at home all night. You don't want the constabulary coming for you. The murderer himself will be long gone.'

Cecco gripped her hand tightly. There was a tang of iron in the air. Salaì's mouth was yawning; rain fell onto his open eyes as he lay unblinking, gazing unseeing at the heavens he would not reach.

Cecco released her hand and stood.

'I'm going to call in at the taverns and whisper that I've heard Salaì was murdered by a mercenary in a brawl.

I'll tell it a little differently here and there. The whispers will take care of it. In a week, no one will know the truth. You'll be quite safe.'

She prodded me with her sodden slipper.

'I only wanted him to love me. Only me and not her.'

'His love for her wasn't the problem,' said Cecco.

He knelt beside me and glanced up at the heavens. 'Leonardo, I tried to fulfil your wish, to keep them with me. I have failed you and I beg your forgiveness.' He smiled at me for the last time. 'Mona Lisa, we must say goodbye.'

I looked upon his concerned, kind face. The droplets suspended on his lashes like tears, his grave expression. Cecco would live to be an old man, a grandfather, and all the while continue to nurture the legacy of Leonardo, but because of this night he must undertake it all without me. I could no longer take satisfaction in our friendship or melancholy pleasure as he recited old memories to Angiola. One day, yet to come, his son would squander his legacy and sell Leonardo's manuscripts, and the scattering and winnowing loss would begin. I did not know all this then, amongst the streaming cobbles and the blood and the stench of death and the bouncing of the rain on the roofs. All I knew that night was I had lost two more men: one I loved and one I hated, but both connected me inexorably to Leonardo, and neither would I ever see again.

I'd spent my existence abhorring Salaì, yet I couldn't imagine his absence. Leonardo adored knots. He enjoyed the pun of them. He told me how his name, Vinci, came from *vinco*, or the osier weavers, who use osier shoots to bind into baskets. But, as Leonardo whispered to me, trace

Vinci further back and you find its Latin roots. There, you are bound by 'sweet bonds', or *dolci vinci,* of love. The osiers' knot and the lovers' bond. Leonardo envisioned knots as his emblem or insignia and he liked to draw them again and again. Even now, I can see the exquisite knots of Leda's hair; the golden twists, like plaited corn, each strand fine and gleaming. That was how we were: Leonardo, Cecco, Salaì and me and Leda. Together we formed Leonardo's finest knots, twisted upon each other, bound as one. But, in the murk of that grim alley as rain pelted down upon us, we came undone.

Fontainebleau, 1530

Winter

I watched as, outside the windows, snow lay in feathered drifts. The celebrated fountain in the gardens
froze in an arterial spurt, the mixture of red wine and
water gushing upward and then suspended, bloody against
the pristine white, like another rendering of the Passion
of the Christ. Ravens circled above, glowering and stark.
Venus, Cupid and Mars stood sheathed beneath layers of
snow, an elbow poking out here, a bosom there, the icy
tip of a helmet. Yet I sweltered inside the *appartement des
bains* as the steam puffed from the ovens, slinking out
from the cracks in the windows and drifting across the
wastelands of white.

Even on the coldest of days, steam was conjured forth,
filling room after room. Francis, by the Grace of God,
Most Christian King of France, had purchased us from
Salaì's estate for a sizeable fortune and placed us in his
bathroom suite. The *appartement des bains* was a series
of rooms dedicated to the art of bathing. The chamber
to the east adorned with frescoed nymphs by Le Primace
was devoted to washing and waxing; while the one

beside it was for sweating, and the plaster peeled and sloughed like rotten orange peel, to the dismay of the painted mermaids who regularly lost their tails. There were cold rooms and kitchens, offices and statue-filled gardens for cooling off, and finally a series of sumptuous sitting rooms with gilded panelling in which to relax and admire and contemplate upon easels the Italian masterpieces of which the King was so enamoured. The baths were not merely to cleanse the body, but to invigorate the soul.

I was both fortunate and unfortunate. I was placed on an easel in the chamber known as the Queen's Cabinet, a sitting room furthest along from the steam room, where the insidious vapour still crept in towards us, dampening our wood, slowly warping us, softening our varnish and despoiling our gesso. Yet it was worse for Leda. She was the glory of the King's collection and crowned the mantelpiece in the very first sitting room, where the steam had not lost its heat, and she was to spend a hundred years cloaked in a slick of condensation.

The other misfortune we had to endure was that all admirers who came to visit us did so absolutely naked. Flaccid and hirsute bellies, moist bald men, pink and stout, white and wet, pinched and drooping, with dropsy, with acne, freckled, sturdy or stooped. Tall women, squat ladies plump as partridges set to roast, blue-eyed, clear-eyed, blind. All of them came without pomp or pageantry to stare at us while bare-bottomed.

A series of artists came to pay homage to me. The first of many to make copies of me; some commissioned by the King or wealthy patrons, others desirous to pay court to the brilliance of Leonardo and attempt by tracing his hand to discern the secrets of his genius. An impossible, futile task. It was hot in the Queen's Cabinet and unpleasantly humid when outside snow blanketed the earth, and even the artists were required to disrobe. While the skinny painters hunkered naked and sweating on their stools, the paints hardening as they tried to sketch me, I would call out to Leda, and we'd laugh at them. They could not discover the secret of me. They could not even share in our joke. But, as time passed, it seemed less and less funny. We no longer laughed.

Francis, the Most Christian King himself, often came to gaze upon me. He liked to visit at night. The chamber was lit with candles but snow cast a weird ghostly glow, strangely bright through the windows and illuminating the cabinet room within. He stood before me unabashed, regal even in his nakedness. The King adored hunting, and there were many statues and paintings of Diana. He was a connoisseur of art and women, Leda and I the zenith of both. Some nights he chose Leda, and some nights me, often bringing real women to cavort with before us. But sometimes, like tonight, he simply stood with one hand on his hip and another on the neatly plucked royal balls, and pleasured himself in a series of frenzied gasps.

I watched, unable to turn away as sweat formed on his lip. He groaned, his face contorting like the frescoed gargoyles, the divine monarch brought to earth like other men. Liquid spurted on the floor. A footman would hustle along before dawn to wipe away the regal seed and dispose of it with suitable reverence. The King straightened and leaned back against a golden panel; Diana resting on her easel and her bathing nymphs looked benignly upon him.

'I've always adored you, Mona Lisa. When you smile, do you think of past joys or hope for future happiness? In any case, you are mine now.'

'I am not yours.'

It was years since I was anyone's. It's not done to correct a king – people have lost their heads for less, but I did not fear for mine. He only smiled at me. Francis rarely smiled, but whether I wished to or not, I saw it.

He soon left me. I was alone in the dark, watching the steady fall of snow, the huff of steam. I thought of all the copies of myself venturing out into the world, seeing new places, new things, while I was here, the steam splitting my grain. The other Mona Lisas were unseeing, unthinking ghosts, nothing but echoes slinking out across the continent, ignorant of pleasure or pain. I considered the King's question. When I smiled, I only thought of past joy. I remembered Leonardo. I remembered love.

'Leda,' I called. 'Leda? Can you hear me?'

'Yes,' she answered. 'You're not alone.'

I cried out in the almost dark. No one heard but Leda. Harrowed with grief and rage, I began to scream. The sound built within me, until I howled and screamed so loudly that the poplar wood beneath my paintwork vibrated and I felt the layers of varnish crack and tiny fissures appear all across my hands and face.

'Mona,' she called. 'Mona!'

I could hear the fear in her voice.

'You say I'm not alone,' I cried. 'But I cannot even see you. And everyone else is dead. We're here until we rot and worms burrow through us.'

'Let's play a game, my darling,' she called back.

I was quiet, listening. My skin ached, tight with the tiny creases of the craquelure.

'Let's build ourselves a house. A house of dreams where we can be together. On the banks of the Adda. Listen, Mona my darling. Can you hear the river?'

'No. That's the hissing of the infernal steam rooms.'

'You're quite wrong. It's the River Adda. I can hear it rushing across the stones. And listen again: there are the shouts of those silly boys. Cecco and Giovanni and Tommaso. Can you see? Leonardo is sitting on the bank with his paper and his black chalk and a wry smile, watching them. The boys are diving and ducking in the shallows. They want us to join them. Everybody lives, Mona.'

'Everybody lives,' I whispered, willing it were so.

'Shall we swim with them?' asked Leda.

'How?'

'This is a *fantasia*,' she said. 'We are real.'

As real women we stepped out into the River Adda, gasping at its coldness, our feet slipping on the slick stones, taking pleasure in their sharpness. I was warm and soft, and even as I shivered at the shock of the icy water, the tightness in my skin faded, the cracks in my skin healed and became smooth. The boys laughed to see us, splashing us and swimming away. I watched Leda, her face shiny wet, the plaits of her hair dark against her skin as she tugged me down into the cool depths below. She placed her hands upon my shoulders and kissed me on the lips, and then blew out a stream of bubbles and together we watched them fly upwards to the surface like meteors.

In the pit of the throat, if one gazed upon it intently, one could see the beating of the pulses. And in this work of Leonardo's there was a smile so pleasing that it was a thing more divine than human ...

Giorgio Vasari, 1550

Milan, 1507

Summer

I want to take you now to a villa outside Milan, beside a fast-flowing river. It's the place where Leda is about to be born and I am yet to know or love her. Leonardo lives once more. He writes and sketches, trying to exorcise the loss of his father. Here, I am young again, my varnish uncracked, and I do not always have the right words, or know how to help him.

When you and I left Leonardo last, he was escaping Florence as it was too full of ghosts, but I start to worry that they have followed us here. We move into the Melzi villa on the bluff of the River Adda where there is ample room for the entire *bottega*. Cecco's father is living in another family property in Prato and the servants are instructed to open up the villa for Leonardo the Florentine. He no longer carries with him the bones of dead birds; instead he is driven to understand the machinery of the human body. He longs to peel apart the layers that make up the *corpo* of a man, to understand all the secrets of life and immortality. But Leonardo also spends hours glowering at the swirling currents of the river. Sometimes he takes a piece of chalk and sketches the eddies and the flow of the waters, and other times he just watches, unmoving. When he returns to the loggia I ask him what he's thinking and he replies, 'My late father' or 'Lisa del Giocondo and her lost daughter.'

He comes and slumps beside me and sighs. 'I grieve for my father, even if he didn't think much of me.'

'That isn't true.'

'Don't console me, my darling. I don't want it. Pain is our memory of love.'

'Yes, I remember Lisa's despair at her loss. Although I prefer not to think of it,' I say.

'Why?' asks Leonardo.

I believe he already knows the answer and wants to torment himself by hearing me say it.

'Because it reminds me that I shall be without you. That my grief must endure for all eternity. Lisa grieves for her daughter but waits to be reunited with her in paradise. Can I hope for as much?'

Leonardo is silent. Perhaps I should stop, but I don't. I can't. 'When you die, maestro, I shall be alone and without love. I shall only have the memories and the pain. No one will hear my cries when I weep. My desolation will be absolute.'

Leonardo buries his head in his hands. He whispers, 'What have I done? My God, what have I done?'

That evening, from my position on the loggia, I see a fire burning on the slope beside the Adda. Vermilion tongues lap at the sky. I wonder if the boys are making some revelry, but then Leonardo appears before me, his eyes sore from smoke and his forehead greasy with sweat. He seizes me and carries me down towards the river.

'Where are you taking me? What are you doing? Maestro? Leonardo?'

He sets me down upon the bank, and I can see his face is creased with suffering. The fire hisses and burns, the branches in the pyre cracking and sending up livid darts into the night. In its glow he looks haunted, hollowed out with agony. He won't look at me and rubs his reddened lids, smearing ash upon his cheek.

'What sin did I commit when I created you?' he says, his voice low, his shoulders starting to tremble. 'I was full of pride. Lisa del Giocondo saw it. I wanted to be a little God. I wanted to create the greatest *invenzione* in art, beyond anything in man's imagination. And I succeeded, Mona Lisa. You are everything. Beauty. The world. Every thought I ever had, every dream and life itself.'

He rubs at his eyes again and I see now they are moist and primed with tears. He's starting to pace, weaving to and fro. He seems erratic and lost, full of self-loathing. I call out to him, trying to summon him back to himself, back to me.

'But I love you for what you've done. For yourself and the life you've given me,' I say, filled with love and fear. For the first time in my existence, I don't know what he's going to do, and I'm frightened. I stare at him in wonder and terror. The fire cackles, hungry.

He kneels down before me, as if beseeching my forgiveness for what he's about to do.

'You're right – I've doomed you to torment. An eternity of misery and loneliness. A real woman I might try to protect and make provision for, but you? And for all time?

It's not possible. No. The only kindness is to destroy you, my love.'

He's running his hands through his hair until it's wild and dishevelled. I don't want him to hurt me. I'm filled with panic, for this isn't Leonardo but a madman. His face streaming with tears, he stands and, picking me up, strides towards the blaze. I scream and cry out. He's shouting now too and, hearing the commotion and seeing the flames, the boys start to run down to the river, yelling at the maestro, terrified he's lost his mind.

Leonardo stands before the blaze. The flames rise up. The heat is massive. His fingers grip my panel. A step closer and I'm lost. The boys are behind us on the bank.

'Please, Leonardo. A day with you, an hour, a moment, is worth the decades and the centuries without you. I will pay the price. And willingly,' I beseech.

I want to live. I don't want to die like this. I don't know whether he hears me or not, but he lowers his arms and steps back from the blaze and sets me down upon the damp grass and kneels before me again.

'I can't do it.' His voice cracks. 'I'm too selfish to live without you.'

His face is contorted with guilt. 'I should never have made you, and yet I can't regret that I did.'

He stares at me, haunted and desolate. Behind him the flames laugh.

'Can you forgive me?' he asks.

I look into his dear face, exhausted and stricken. He's frightened me and yet I'm filled with pity. He did not expect to love me. I was supposed to be a wonder for the world, but I am wondrous to him. My universe was black and grey until he coloured it. My smile is for him. Always.

'I forgive you, for I love you.'

He slumps in relief.

'But you must make me a family,' I say.

He looks at me in puzzlement.

'You must paint another like me. I want a sister.'

The gardens have been neglected for many years, but Leonardo orders orange and lemon trees to be placed along the terrace and a bower covered with a fine copper net to keep captive songbirds. The grassy banks leading down to the river are scythed, so we can see and hear the swell of the Adda. The waters are clear and shining, and fish leap and glitter in the sunlight and we watch the painted fishing boats and the ferry carrying travellers into the heart of Milan. Leonardo orders Cecco to set bottles of wine to cool in the shallows, and carefully sketches plans for more terraces, with willows and larch trees sloping toward the water. I bask on my easel set out on the loggia and survey them all. I am dizzy with his love.

There amongst the babble of the river and the tang of the watercress and the note of the captive songbirds, Leonardo turns to me and asks, 'Well, my Mona Lisa, who then shall I paint for you?'

'I don't wish for a holy companion. Not a sanctimonious Madonna.'

'A goddess?'

'So long as she's fun. Not a chaste and worthy Diana. And please, I beg you, model her on some amusing woman. Don't bring another Lisa del Giocondo into our lives. Not here.'

I indicate the gardens where Cecco, Salaì and Giovanni are stripping off and preparing to dive into the sun-dappled river, trying to catch eels in their bare hands and falling back into the waters, spitting with laughter.

'The kind of woman who won't flinch at the sight of a few men cavorting naked,' I say.

Leonardo nods, squinting in the glare of the sun. His hair is whiter now and reaches below his shoulders, and he sports a long beard, like thistledown. His skin is uncreased and smooth. He remains a beautiful man.

As we watch the river, a flock of swans circle, honking, the air creaking with the god-like thunder of their beating wings. They alight on the water like a quiver of white arrows, dazzling bright in the warm sunshine. They are unearthly in their beauty, the muscularity of their necks, the downy drifts of their backs. Leonardo unfastens the notebook from his waist, is already drawing.

'Leda,' he says, not turning away from the flotilla of birds now cruising in the waters. 'Leda seduced by Jupiter in the guise of a swan.'

Salaì brings La Cremona to the villa. La Cremona is renowned throughout all Milan for her beauty and wit. She has many lovers and publishes sonnets about them all, which are feverishly devoured as much in hope for salacious gossip as for their literary delights. Since the Count of Milan himself is rumoured to be one of her lovers, and the subject of her most celebrated and flattering sonnet, she is not compelled to wear the prostitute's yellow veil – La Cremona is a poet, not a whore. Her latest volume is dedicated, with permission, to the count.

The sky is a costly lapis blue with ribbons of lead-white cloud. We wait on the loggia, and Salaì ushers out the lady herself. She is veiled, demure as a housewife, although we all know she is the most celebrated *cortigiana* of Milan.

'This is La Cremona,' says Salaì with self-conscious pride. 'We were introduced at a salon in the city.'

We all laugh and tease him at once, diverted at the notion of Salaì at a salon, as though he were an aristocrat like Cecco. He flushes with rage and humiliation and Leonardo signals for all of us to subdue our mirth; we are behaving with ill manners towards our guest.

'I am so pleased that you made the journey to see us here in Vavrio. Our little corner of paradise.'

She surveys the scene, breathing the perfume of lemon trees and the trill of captive songbirds like Eve in Eden.

'Madame, I believe you are a poet,' he says with a bow.

'I am, maestro,' she says, glancing down.

Leonardo steps forward and clasps the silk of her veil. 'May I? If I'm to paint you, I must see your face.'

She nods.

I don't know what I am expecting. An angel of heaven. The Madonna herself. Instead, here is an extremely attractive woman of perhaps twenty-five or thirty with very bright cornflower-blue eyes. The veil creates an air of mystery and secrecy. She is a sorceress of presentation, and yet it is not merely the azurite blue of her eyes, but the intelligent laughter of their expression. No wonder she mostly looks down; men don't like to be laughed at. She is a wit who can read and write. I'm not aware of many women who can do either, and La Cremona, whore and poet, excels in both – as well, one assumes, as in other, fleshier pursuits. Her hair is dressed in the typical fashion of the *cortigiane*, wound in close knots around her crown, but there is a breeze today and golden tendrils float free and tease her cheeks and the perfect bow of her lips. The more I stare, the more her beauty seems to develop. Her nose is long, and not perfectly straight. Her eyebrows are plucked into constant surprise. She flushes under the master's scrutiny, and the glow to her cheeks adds to her charm.

'Well,' she demands, arch, 'will I do?'

Leonardo gives a low laugh. 'Mona Lisa. I am content, are you?'

'Yes. I like her very much indeed.'

'Oh,' says La Cremona, looking at me in astonishment. 'You talk to her.'

'Of course.'

Leonardo begins the sketches in the afternoon. Cecco fetches the wineskins cooling in the river, along with paper and chalk. We all sit on the loggia, Salaì and La Cremona drinking and eating fruit and cheese and telling jokes, while the master draws outlines of her face and hair. It is the woven knots, the golden threaded corn upon her head, that fascinates him. On the paper it flows like water. He sketches her hair and then the flow of the Adda rushing beyond the banks; the swirling movement on the page is the same. He murmurs as he works.

'Observe, Mona Lisa, the motion of the surface of water which conforms to that of the hair which has two motions. One responds to the weight of the strands of the hair and the other to the direction of the curls. This water turns in eddies. It's the same principle.'

La Cremona stops laughing and sets down her glass. 'You think in poetry. Do you always talk to the painting?'

'She's a good listener,' says Leonardo.

'And I have a name,' I say.

'She says that she has a name,' repeats Leonardo.

'My apologies, Madonna,' she says, bowing her head.

'Madonna *Lisa*,' I insist.

'I'm not repeating every word,' says Leonardo. 'I'm trying to work.'

La Cremona glances between us both and laughs, a sound like the rushing of the Adda herself. 'To you, maestro, she is absolutely real.'

'Does she not appear lifelike?'

La Cremona stares narrowly and scrutinises me. 'She does.'

'Well then. It is not my fault that you cannot hear her *voce*. Not many can. But simply because you cannot hear it, does not mean that it isn't there. Have you ever heard the voice of God?'

'No.'

'Do you doubt it?'

'I wouldn't dare.'

La Cremona smiles, a shaft of lightning, and then turns to me. 'Well, Madonna Lisa, I shall speak to you as if you can hear. Even if it's a game, it's a good one.'

'It's not a game. But I'll forgive you. Few women speak to me. I'm tired of so many men.'

'What did she say?' asks La Cremona.

Leonardo sighs. 'I'm not becoming a gossip and go-between for the afternoon.' He surrenders his chalk. 'She's tired of being surrounded by men.'

La Cremona claps her hands with glee. 'Of course she is! Living in a *bottega*. Madonna Lisa, I'm sure you tell Master Leonardo precisely what you think. Men like him value the view of discerning women like us.'

'I told you I liked her,' I say to Leonardo.

'You've drawn the back of my head. The most intricate and tiny knots,' says La Cremona. 'Why? You won't see those, surely?'

'I see them. When I paint, I paint an entire woman. All of her. Not merely a collection of parts. It so happens that on the panel you can't see all of her, but she is still there.'

'Her? Not me?'

'No. She is Leda. She starts as you, but she will become herself.'

La Cremona stares at him, unable to discern if he is in jest, but he is drawing again, busy with the coiled plaits of her hair.

The summer drifts by to the music of the Adda. La Cremona stays one evening, not returning to her apartment in Milan, and does not go home again. The Melzi villa is commodious enough for us all. Cicadas chirp all night long in concert with tiny green frogs which sit on the warmth of the low walls and croak until dawn, or until Salaì, outraged by the racket, sloshes them with the contents of the slop buckets to hush them and they hop away and croak reproachfully from the bushes. It's a haze of merriment. Wine. Late in the evenings Leonardo plays the *lira da braccio* and Cecco the lute, while Salaì sings bawdy songs. La Cremona recites her poetry. The unpublished, unprintable versions. I know the size and shape of the noble cocks of Milan. Salaì and Leonardo sit hand in hand, and I am filled with such joy that, when Salaì rests his head on Leonardo's shoulder and the master kisses him and rubs his thumb along the firm muscle of his inner thigh, the jealousy does not gut me with a wetted switchblade. Leonardo loves me, but he also adores Salaì, and the angel-faced youth shares his bed most nights. La Cremona sees me watching as Leonardo strokes his cheek, and she kisses Giovanni and then little Cecco who reddens with embarrassment and pleasure.

'You see,' she says. 'These two like women as well as boys.'

So does Salaì, I think. He just loves Leonardo above all else.

And every day, Leonardo and the apprentices draw La Cremona. Her curls. The curve of her cheek. Her downcast lashes. It's apparent that next he needs to draw her body, the shape of her figure. It's time for her to disrobe. She pads down to the water naked, her feet dewy and freckled with river mud. Her skin is as fair and smooth as the shell of an egg. Cecco, Giovanni and the assistants gawp. They are not just Leonardo's boys. La Cremona laughs, tossing back her head. She kneels but the pose is too awkward, and after sketching her, he asks her to stand again. The tiny coils of her plaits fly in the wind. The light dances on her skin. She stretches, unashamed. Her nipples are almost as pink as the wild strawberries growing on the bank. Two fishermen on the river forget entirely to fish, moving to and fro, poised with their rods on the stretch of water before the villa and a splendid view of La Cremona's nipples. Leonardo is busy with his pencil, but frowns, aware of the disruption we are causing.

'Perhaps this afternoon we will work inside. More comfortable, I think?'

'Yes, but not so much fun,' says La Cremona.

Leonardo has chosen for his Leda a courtesan and not a nun. And it's from La Cremona and Leonardo's brush that Leda hatches. Slowly. At first she's nothing but a thought upon the gesso and layers of *imprimitura* white lead on the walnut panel, and then, an outline of *spolveri* dots picked out in charcoal, the familiar line of her face appears. The long nose. A hint of a smile.

I love her at once.

Autumn

 here are some evenings when Leonardo disappears off alone. He has the groom saddle his horse, rides off into the city to the hospital and returns the following morning, exhilarated and reeking of death, blood and viscera clinging to his tunic, even his boots flecked with gore. Those mornings he neither works on Leda or upon me, but embarks upon a different kind of drawing. He sits in the hall of the villa at the long oak table in his foul clothes, his white beard stained with bodily fluid. His cheeks are flushed with dark delights.

'I sat with an old man as he lay dying. This old man, a few hours before his death, told me he had lived for more than a hundred years. He was aware of no malady other than general feebleness. And so, sitting on a bed in the hospital, without any sign of distress, he passed from this life. And, my Lisa, I made an anatomy to see the cause of a death so sweet.'

I suppress a shudder. 'How?'

'Truth must be reached through sawing bones. Cutting them in half and showing the hollow of each of them. Seeing which is full of marrow, which is spongy or empty or solid.'

He is drawing the heart and beside it the stone of a peach, where a tree is sprouting forth.

'But in the old man, the arteries are withered and thin, no longer feeding the heart and lower members.'

'But you are supposed to be painting my Leda,' I object.

Leonardo smiles. 'I am. When I paint, I start work from beneath the skin. The muscles, the arteries that are the trees of life. This is how your Leda will come to life.'

La Cremona slides into the hall in her gown, ready to eat her morning meal. She sees Leonardo, his beard and hands smeared with gore, and falters. He is not the genial and benevolent gentleman of whom she is so fond but some foul conjuror, or malevolent.

'I've been at the hospital,' he says.

'May the Virgin bless me and keep me safe,' she murmurs.

'The safety is in understanding,' corrects Leonardo.

'But we keep our friends by washing,' chastises La Cremona. 'You stink of death and excrement.'

Leonardo glances up and then surveys his clothes and their battle stains. He stands and bows in apology to La Cremona. He is usually fastidious in his attire but excitement has made him forgetful. He excuses himself and returns in clean clothes. La Cremona is sitting at the table eating bread spread with milky cheese. She watches him wryly. There is still a rime of dried blood beneath his nails. We both see it. He is too impatient to work to bother with such niceties.

La Cremona stands naked and resplendent on the long oak table in the hall swaddled in a silk cloth, so that the apprentices can practise drapery studies, the interplay of shadow on flesh. Leonardo sighs and corrects their attempts.

'Poor is the pupil who cannot surpass his master.'

We all know there is little chance of that, but affection makes him ever hopeful. Salaì is working on a study of a nude La Cremona. It's crude and awkward. Her breasts sprout from just beneath her collarbone like little turned wooden bowls, her neck is long and gooselike, and her face doesn't resemble the honoured *cortigiane* so much as mine, but seen through a veil of spite. Salaì, however, is immensely pleased with his grotesque and will accept no criticism, declaring smugly, 'I'll call her Mona Vana.' I abhor drawing and artist both.

La Cremona is growing restless and teases them all. Always Leonardo is busy on a hundred things at once. His own painting of Leda stands in the corner waiting while he scribbles another observation beside his illustrations of dissections.

'Why do you only draw men's bodies?' she wants to know. 'Are you afraid of women?'

Leonardo looks up, startled.

'What do you mean, my friend? I'm painting you as we speak.'

At present La Cremona is wearing nothing more than a white tablecloth around her wrist that hides nothing. She's also eating an orange, which is dripping from her chin onto her bosom and the sumptuous curve of her belly. Unabashed, she uses the cloth to wipe it, revealing the curls of hair between her legs.

'No,' she says, with a stamp of her feet, 'you're painting Leda. She's an ideal. Not a woman. A goddess. No hair.' She gestures to the walnut panel on its easel at the side of the hall where Leda stands coyly nude. 'The bodies you dissect are all men. You study the way light falls upon my skin, and Salaì stands beside me with a boom of feathers playing Jupiter, but,' she raises her arm to reveal a spray of black down beneath her arm, 'you ignore this, and this,' she gestures again to her nakedness. 'In the finished painting sensibilities must be respected, but you, maestro, are a student of humanity and truth. Which leads me to ask again, are you frightened of women?'

I look at Leonardo with considerable interest.

He is silent for a moment, mulling. 'You are right of course, La Cremona. You have identified a gap in my search for truth.'

'Would you like me to fill it with my gap?' says La Cremona, teasing.

Salaì chuckles. Leonardo can't meet her eye or anything else.

'Salaì, fetch pillows and blankets. I'm not lying on this table without something more comfortable,' she commands.

Salaì pauses, glancing at the master.

'Salaì, order the servants to do as the lady asks.'

Later, La Cremona sips wine, swaddled in a blanket. The servants are preparing partridge stew and dumplings on the pot in the fireplace and the aroma fills the house with scented steam. It is growing dark and this evening is the first we have needed a fire for warmth in each of the grates. Beneath the blanket La Cremona is still naked and she shivers. Her feet are bare on the terracotta tiles. Leonardo places the drawing on the table. The assistants gather to look.

'The wrinkles or ridges in the folds of the vulva indicate to us the location of the gatekeeper of the castle,' says Leonardo.

The assistants mutter in agreement.

I glance at La Cremona and she wiggles her eyebrows, but out of tact refrains from making a remark.

The men talk for some time using similar fortress metaphors while La Cremona rolls her eyes and I try not to laugh, and then, at last, they continue their conversation into another room. La Cremona remains with me. She plucks the drawing off the table and stands beside me. I observe the elegant cross-hatching showing her legs, and then a yawning cavern between them. La Cremona grimaces.

'He's a master. The greatest genius of Florence. And this is the worst drawing I've ever seen him produce. If my "citadel" resembled this, I would not be the most adored *cortigiana* of Milan. No gatekeeper would be required.' She pauses. 'Although he has drawn me a very pretty little anal flower.'

I'm not sure what to say, as I have no point of comparison. La Cremona's is the first cradle of Venus I have ever seen. As she posed, I watched with interest, for once more intrigued by the model than the drawing. I see this thought dawn upon La Cremona's face.

'You don't have a cunny hole. I'm sorry. I'm being thoughtless and unkind. You have nothing down there. You stop at the elbow. There's nothing below your frame. Nothing at all.'

'I am not nothing,' I object, put out.

Yet it's not only women whose nakedness Leonardo finds off-putting. I've heard him say before that the act of coition and the parts of the body involved in it are of such ugliness that if it weren't for the beauty of faces, and the powerful effect of reined-in desire, nature would lose the human species.

La Cremona looks again at the drawing, tosses back her head and laughs. 'Perhaps I was cruel. I oughtn't to have pushed him to draw cunny holes. I ought to have left him to his dead men.'

She refastens the blanket, gathering up her clothes in readiness to dress for dinner. After she has left me, there is a sound. A strange mew or cry as if from a kitten. I look about but it is coming from the corner of the hall, on the other side of a low table where all Leonardo's paints and paraphernalia are stashed, beside the easel and the panel of Leda. The cry comes again, but this time she has a voice and she calls out, 'Mona.'

The voice is coming from Leda.

She speaks.

'My darling. I am here,' I call.

'It was dark. But now I can see,' says Leda.

Her voice is music. Leda speaks and she calls for me.

My heart is full, bursting with love. She is unfinished, picked out in charcoal *spolveri*, but the smooth oils of her skin and hair already reveal the sublime beauty of her face. I might not have what La Cremona calls a cunny hole to push a child out of, but I think I know how a mother feels when she sees her child born; when she sees that child open its blue eyes, draw breath and give its first cry. Leda speaks, and it's my name that she utters.

'Leonardo! Maestro, come!' I call.

The master comes at a run, half-afraid of some disaster, fearful at the very least that a burning log must have set the hearth alight. Leonardo glances around the chamber, seeing at once that there is no fire, only the pot of stew, bubbling.

'Place me next to Leda,' I beg. 'She's awake.'

He picks me up and carefully sets me down beside her.

'Mona,' says Leda. 'Mona Lisa.'

He studies her with a smile. '*Buonasera, Leda.* We've been waiting and hoping for you. Don't be afraid.'

'Why should I be afraid, maestro?' she asks. 'Mona Lisa is here.'

'Of course she is,' he soothes.

Cecco hovers at the doorway, and Leonardo signals to the boy to prepare his brushes and palette. He's eager to start work at once. The delicate curve of her eyebrow, the translucent glow of her skin that blends into shadow, so we can't see where her eyebrow stops and the shade begins, built up by endless layers of smoky glazes applied by the mink brush. I watch transfixed. She has no edges; she is all light and shade. She is real. She is like me.

Leonardo pauses and looks at me. Leda is my gift. A friend. He will die and leave me, but now I have my Leda. We will be companions to one another all through our long existence. While I have Leda, I will have an echo of Leonardo, and neither Leda nor I will ever be alone. Leonardo cannot give me a child, but he has given me her in an act of love. Not all acts of love need cunnies or sexual organs of any kind; sometimes paint and imagination is enough.

We live under the protection of the Count of Milan. He enjoys having Leonardo here, and has gifted him a farm with a vineyard as well as an annual stipend. He only asks that La Cremona visits him once each moon to read him poetry. Or so she says. Leonardo works with the vitality of a man half his age. Cecco spends hours grinding up cinabrese, red lead and malachite. His fingers are permanently stained. The swans have left, and Leonardo berates the empty river, entreating them to return. I don't leave his side. He paints Leda, talking to us both as he works. Leda is shy at first, bewildered by the world, newborn. He sketches the wild strawberries that flourish on terraces and between the cracks in the loggia, instructing Cecco to grind up the tiny cochineal beetles for carmine for the berries and paints them at Leda's feet. The ferry delivers fresh linseed oil for binding the paints. Leonardo draws study after study of bulrushes that tremble in the currents of the Adda, and these are copied onto the panel. He watches La Cremona: her skin, the angle of her shoulder, her hip. She and Leda are no longer the same. Leda watches her babies, as they hatch, transfixed in adoration. In motherhood, she possesses a serenity that La Cremona does not.

Painters come from Milan to copy Leda. Already the rumours of her beauty are spreading and they stay a month or two or three. Cesare da Sesto. Bernadino Luini and half a dozen others from all across Lombardy and Italy who I quickly forget. Cecco and Salaì even attempt to copy her. Some artists are here to paint and learn from the maestro, earnestly rising at dawn to sketch and work, but others fall under the *lume particolare* of La Cremona and leave dazed after weeks with their panel unprimed, brushes dry, pigments never unbottled.

The leaves fall. First a few, then dozens all around. We are driven inside the villa by the rains and then the storms and cold. Some nights the coverings on the windows freeze. The fires blaze day and night. Leonardo takes a fallen leaf, an ash, and copies it, painting it sap green upon the limewashed plaster in the hall. Cecco is enchanted by the effect and pleads with him to paint a thousand more. Transform the four-square villa into a forest, like he did for Ludovico Sforza many years before. But if there are to be more leaves, they must be in fresco. And we need chickens to produce enough eggs to bind the tempera to the plaster. The ferry delivers them.

One leaf becomes a branch. Then a tree. Its branches spread into the next year. The ash grows into an oak and then a chestnut and the trees become a wood, and then, as the years pass, a forest. Leda and I watch. I teach her the names of all the pigments that are ground up and blended to make up her many parts. She learns to laugh and teases me and my desire to learn everything I can from Leonardo. 'Don't be so serious, Mona. No more lessons today.' She is full of playfulness and fun. She is no longer newborn.

An invitation comes from il Magnifico Giuliano de' Medici in Rome. The old pope has died, and the conclave of cardinals has elected Giuliano's brother Pope Leo X, the first Florentine pope. The Medici brothers want in their court the great Florentine artists and they request Leonardo's presence in Rome. The master doesn't wish to go. We are happy here on the outskirts of Milan in our villa of trees under the count's protection. Yet, for all our contentment, we fret that it isn't sensible to refuse il Magnifico Giuliano. It is unwise to decline the summons of a Medici. We ignore it for a little while. We sing and paint. We test the bounds of fate.

I, Mona Lisa

We wake one morning to find news that the Count of Milan is dead and that Swiss mercenaries are gathering outside the city walls. We ought to have left at once. No one ignores a letter with a Medici seal. They have unholy powers. La Cremona and Leda believe that we brought ill fortune by not departing immediately. Leonardo refuses to consider such nonsense and superstition.

La Cremona and Leonardo hold hands and whisper, humming with anxiety. They step out into the garden and peer through the mist; fires are being set in the distance by the mercenaries and blaze in a furious inferno of orange and red, the smoke mingling with the fog and drifting across the river. The Count was our patron and protector and the city is about to swarm with his enemies. We cannot stay here.

La Cremona kisses Leda and then me goodbye.

'This parting is easier for you than for me,' she says. 'You are taking me with you.'

'Only your looks,' I say. 'You and Leda are nothing alike.'

'I am perfected,' agrees Leda.

'I shall miss you all,' says La Cremona.

'Come to Rome,' says Leonardo.

'No. Venice is the place for me. I'll soon be as rich as a queen. I shall buy from you both Mona Lisa and Leda, and they'll live with me in a palazzo beside the Grand Canal.'

Leonardo only laughs but for La Cremona it is not a joke.

I worry for her in Venice. It is in Milan that she is renowned for her genius and grace. Venice throbs with hundreds of *cortigiane* and she is no longer the youngest. Her eyes are luminous with tears.

'*Cortigiana* or queen,' I say, even though she cannot hear, 'you are a woman of *virtù*. Of power and poetry.'

She curtsies and blows me a kiss. In less than a year she will be dead of venereal disease. I shall not see her again.

Rome, 1513

Winter

*W*hen I first glimpse Rome as we ride in, I fear it has been sacked and the Sultan has invaded from Constantinople. It seems to lie in ruins, rubble and stones heaped upon the streets, every church and edifice half-pulled down and entombed in scaffolding. Then, as I look, it's clear that the city is a building site, swarming with masons and carpenters, and artisans of every guild as Rome is built anew, repainted and restored to remind the people of her glory, and that not only do all roads lead here but the only road to salvation is through her shining gates.

Leonardo is given apartments in the new Belvedere Palace. From one window we look upon the never-ending construction. The noise starts at dawn and continues until dusk. The din maddens Leonardo, who summons a foreman and demands to know when the work will be done. The foreman shrugs and spits. He hasn't a clue. Perhaps it will be finished in twenty years. Perhaps fifty. The popes keep on changing their minds about what they want. And then dying.

Cecco plays upon his lute to distract from the racket and persuades Leonardo to look out of the other windows. The apartment in the Belvedere Palace stands on a hill amid vast wooded gardens, a wilderness in the heart of Vatican City, seemingly ancient enough for Romulus and Remus to still lurk with dryads in the sylvan shades. There are grottoes and orchards of plum and apple and cherry; the now bare limbs are skinny hands, baubled with mistletoe like emerald rings. From one window we glimpse pergolas and fish ponds brimming with gliding carp. Sombre statues shiver in the morning frost, and the smooth slopes roll down to the valley at the bottom. Leonardo pulls on his velvet cap and his blue tinted glasses against the spiked glare of the low winter sun and strides for hours amongst the trees, drawing his cloak about him, declaring, 'Nature is the mistress of all masters.'

Il Magnifico himself sends the Medicis' own architect to the apartment to make any changes Leonardo desires. Leonardo is out on one of his customary walks when the architect arrives and Cecco lists the requested alterations.

'Pine-wood partitions. And a framework for a new ceiling for an attic. This window is too narrow. The maestro needs more light to paint.'

The architect scribbles down notes.

'Four dining chairs, poplar. Eight stools. Three benches. And a counter for grinding colours.'

Leda and I consider him from our easels. He bows and scrapes, a supplicant to a new Medici favourite. He notices Leda and catches his breath. Drops his pen. Leda accepts his adulation as her due.

'She is a wonder. A rival to the marvels of Michelangelo and Raphael,' he murmurs.

Leda is displeased. She does not like rivals any more than Leonardo. She wishes to surpass them all.

'I prefer Leda to anything by Michelangelo,' I say, loyal. 'I've heard the Sistine Chapel's a miracle, the closest thing to God on earth, but at least when you gaze upon Leda, you can do so without getting a crick in your neck.'

'Quite,' says Leda.

The architect blinks and turns to stare at me. He's like a fish, opening and shutting his mouth with a popping sound.

'She's so lifelike. It's unsettling.'

Leonardo arrives back from his walk, gratified to find the architect here, measuring up with his stick. The architect is accompanied by a *cursore*, an official papal courier, in splendid crimson livery. Until now, he's remained silent, standing absolutely still beside the door. Now, from a belt around his waist, he unfastens a leather pouch and produces a letter folded over and sealed with crossed keys and Medici shield, the papal seal of Pope Leo. He hands the letter to Leonardo.

'I am to deliver the missive to you, Messer Leonardo. Into your own hands.'

Leonardo reads it quickly and nods, pleased.

'We are summoned to the Medici court in the Eternal City for an audience. All of us. Giuliano wishes to meet Madonna Lisa and Leda. He has heard the rumours of your beauty. He wishes to show you to His Holiness.'

Already Pope Leo is assigning commissions with a speed to rival his predecessor, determined to make his mark upon posterity and pave his way to Heaven. There won't be a blank wall or ceiling without a fresco in Rome. Now, living in the Belvedere Palace, we are stars in the orbit of the Medici and everything glints with golden possibility. Leonardo sketches on paper after paper an endless series of ideas for all the different paintings he yearns to undertake. It's been years since he attempted anything on an epic scale and he's impatient with possibilities. None of us dares to speak of *Anghiari*.

Salaì, always the man to hear the talk in the taverns closest to the Vatican, and knowing who to buy a drink for, hurries back with the news that Michelangelo has at last finished the ceiling in the Sistine Chapel. The radical and wondrous painting is complete.

'Good for him,' says Leonardo. 'The man is impossible, but I should like to see it. As long as he isn't there to sneer.'

'Or to smell,' I add. 'I doubt the man's washed since we saw him last in Florence.'

'You're missing the point, maestro,' says Salaì, impatient. 'Michelangelo has painted almost every *braccio* of the chapel under the patronage of the last pope; there is only one section left. But Pope Leo is determined to leave his own mark on history. He's ready to commission the final part of the chapel.'

'Well,' asks Cecco, 'what does he want?'

'Tapestries all around the walls depicting the Lives of the Saints.'

'The maestro isn't a weaver!' objects Cecco.

'No. The weavers are in the Low Countries. The Pope is commissioning cartoons, vast cartoons for the weavers to copy. The greatest and most ambitious in all the world.'

I look at Leonardo. 'Why do you think he summoned you here to Rome?'

I, Mona Lisa

We all stare at Leonardo.

He smiles; his face is brimful of hope.

The men attend Mass, and afterwards, while the Pope and his cardinals banquet, Leonardo and his boys hurry back to collect us and return with us to court. The Pope needs to see what the great Leonardo can achieve, and Leda and I are the pinnacle of his genius, paintings touched with the divine, so pleasing that we are beyond nature and something more than human. Cecco cradles me in his arms. Giovanni bears Leda. The evening is cool and fine, and we plead not to be swaddled, desperate to see, and Leonardo relents. He has chosen a portfolio of work to show the pontiff. He is jittery, and fiddles with the silk of his tunic and imagined creases on the velvet of his hose. He is wearing his favourite cap in midnight velvet. He hasn't seen the Medici brothers since they were boys in Florence.

Torches are lit along the paths leading to the Apostolic Palace and the flames gutter and spit. Papal Swiss Guards in the Medici livery of crimson and gold stand to attention as we walk up Palatine Hill. Already I can hear music. It isn't holy. There are lutes and keyboards, flutes, trombones, cornets and crumhorns. There are a host of singers, and while the sound they make is heavenly, the words are not. They are not Italian or Latin.

'What language are they singing?' I ask.

'English,' says Leonardo.

'It's barbaric,' I complain.

We walk through the courtyard, listening to the music of the fountain mingling with the voices of the singers. Papal Guards open the massive palace doors and we are led into the Cortile delle Statue, where the exquisite Apollo himself stands resplendent and ignoring us. Leonardo pauses to regard the perfect stone curls of his hair, the metamorphosis of marble into the soft cambric cloak falling on his shoulder. The Pope, it seems, is an admirer of many gods of Rome. An usher in a splendid livery with the Medici crossed keys and shields waits for us, gesturing for us to follow.

'When will His Holiness finish the banquet?' asks Leonardo.

'It's a fast day. Today they only eat fish,' rebukes the usher.

Yet the smells of sage and butter wafting outside are making Salaì and Cecco and Tommaso's bellies rumble. We are led back inside and taken through a maze of corridors and walkways to a large chamber with a coffered ceiling, each panel picked out with gilt and displaying papal shields. The walls are adorned with frescoed parrots and angels, and here and there, amongst false marble columns, I am sure I spy real parrots roosting. Pope Leo and il Magnifico Giuliano de' Medici and the ranks of solemn cardinals are still eating. The Pope is extremely fat. His face sits brooding like a chicken on a nest of chins. His crimson camauro squats on the top of his head. He peers around the room, short-sighted. His porcine fingers are salamis, drumming on the table to the music in perfect time. He closes his eyes in happiness. I wonder if prayers ever provoke expressions of such bliss upon the face of the pontiff as these peculiar tunes. A broken consort of musicians perform while they sup, as well as several apple-cheeked choirboys. These must be the Englishmen as, beneath their rouge, there is a gruesome pallor; yet the boys can sing. There is a jubilant exultation to their song.

We stand awkwardly at the back, listening. No one notices us; they are too busy with eating and music. I notice that the musicians are wearing bizarre outfits, physicians' gowns. Il Magnifico Giuliano de' Medici spots Leonardo. He throws up his hands with pleasure and rises from the table. The cardinals flinch, frowning at the interruption. Giuliano bows an apology to His Holiness, strides over and kisses Leonardo on each cheek.

'Leonardo from Vinci. A Florentine. Not a friend, a brother.'

Leonardo is taken aback by the affection and effusion of his greeting. We are all remembering the painting of the cherubic, curly-haired boy in the church at Maria Santa Novella in Florence. This man is tall and angular, with a neatly clipped beard and thin red lips, and handsome despite the prominent Medici nose.

'Come, come. I cannot wait. His Holiness will not mind.'

His Holiness doesn't even notice his brother leaving the room. His jowls are wobbling to the music.

Giuliano leads us from the chamber. He keeps touching Leonardo, as though to check he is really there and not some phantasm.

'I hope you like your apartments?'

'Most agreeable, Magnifico,' says Leonardo, bewildered by such attentions.

This man, who is half-skipping with pleasure in his company, is the commander of the papal troops: a soldier, a scholar and a prince. Even so, I detect the glint of Medici steel that warns of caution. Giuliano, despite his façade of charm and nonchalance, is a man used to getting his own way. We seem to be friends. We must remain so.

'Why are the musicians dressed in physicians' gowns, Magnifico?' asks Cecco with sudden daring.

Giuliano laughs. 'It is a little joke Pope Leo enjoys. They are dressed as physicians or *medici*. And we too are *Medici*. Especially as, unfortunately, His Holiness requires physicians. He suffers from a fistula. He eats too much.'

Giuliano has no sense that he ought not to be sharing such an intimate detail with us. We are appellants of his circle now. An usher in robes holds open the door to another frescoed chamber, smaller than the last, and Giuliano waves us inside.

'This is His Holiness's private study. He'll come here after he's finished eating. He might be some time. You can set out the pictures ready for him to inspect.'

Leonardo steps inside and looks in awe and wonder.

'Now do you not see that the eye embraces the beauty of all the world? Oh, Raphael!'

'Yes, indeed, this room was painted by Raphael of Urbino and his workshop,' says Giuliano.

It still smells of paint. The frescoes on the walls cannot long be finished. The domed ceiling is gilded with so much gold leaf that it casts a glow upon the cheeks of the men below, and in the reflection of the torches and candles it gleams like the light of the sun. I have never seen Leonardo silenced by the work of another artist.

Salaì, Cecco, Tommaso and Giovanni are setting up easels for Leda and me, reverently placing us upon them, laying the portfolios of drawings out on the table ready for the pontiff to examine. Leonardo pays no attention to them, still busy with Raphael's fresco of the School of Athens. Salaì comes to stand beside him and gives a snort.

'Look, everyone's there. Michelangelo glowering in his dog-skin boots. Ill-tempered as ever.'

'I'm glad I've never met him,' says Leda. 'He looks a perfect grouch.'

'And there's Raphael himself in the far corner,' I say from my vantage on the easel. 'Except his face is too thin, and I don't much like his hat. He's not flattered himself. And, master,' I exclaim, 'Plato looks just like you. He's even pointing his forefinger heavenward in the identical pose as your Salvator Mundi and St Thomas.'

'Does Plato have the look of me?' asks Leonardo.

'Too sombre,' objects Leda.

Salaì and Cecco step forward to look more closely.

'He does,' says Salaì. 'And the positioning of the finger and thumb is your motif.'

Giuliano glances between Leonardo and the painting. 'I've never noticed that before.' He flicks his fingers at an usher. He grins. 'Fetch Raphael. Let's ask him.'

Giuliano gestures for wine and then pours himself a glass from the carafe. He's lost interest in the Raphael; those he has seen before and is already tired of their brilliance. He wants to examine the Leonardos. First, he peers at Leda with a hoot of glee.

'I would trade places with Jupiter. The line of her hip. The wind in the bulrushes. Who is she?'

'It takes several mortal women to make a goddess, Magnifico,' says Leonardo. For all Giuliano's generosity, Leonardo doesn't want to tell him about La Cremona. Something about him sets one's teeth on edge, like the coming of rain or a metal drinking cup.

'Your breath smells of fish,' says Leda. 'Move back.'

Giuliano peers even closer at Leda and scowls, displeased. 'She isn't finished.'

'No, Magnifico. Not yet.'

He turns to me. 'Ah, Madonna Lisa.' He's rubbing clammy hands with imperious satisfaction. 'Your charms never fade. It's a pleasure to see you again.'

'We haven't met,' I object.

Giuliano grins and then lets out a sigh. 'I knew the chaste and beautiful Madonna Lisa del Giocondo in Florence. When we were children, and then again after we returned, triumphant and glorious.'

He thumps his fist against his thigh and gazes around at us, as though we must share with equal pleasure the return of the Medici to our home city.

'I did not know you were acquainted with Madonna Lisa del Giocondo, Magnifico,' says Leonardo.

'A fine-looking woman. Her husband is a bore but loyal to the cause.'

As he talks, Giuliano drinks his wine while gazing at me with frank, unabashed admiration. I am relieved we are not alone.

The usher opens the door, announcing 'Raphael of Urbino!'

We all turn to him with relief and joy. It has been years since we have seen him and the boy is now a man, yet he retains his diffident manner and a youthful spring in his step. He embraces Leonardo and bows to me.

'Mona Lisa, you are even more glorious than when I left you,' he says.

'See! Even Raphael speaks to her as if she's real!' says Giuliano, amused.

I continue. 'Raphael, you've been busy. Between you and Michelangelo you've frescoed every wall and ceiling in Rome. And you've grown a beard.'

He smiles. 'Well, what do you think of the beard?'

'There was nothing wrong with your chin.'

Raphael laughs and turns to Leonardo. 'You see, it doesn't matter how many paintings I undertake. There is only one Mona Lisa. I've missed you, Madonna.'

I'd forgotten the beguiling charisma of Raphael. He is tanned and slight, his eyes dark and quick, flickering between us, but his presence is like the glow from a log fire. It isn't simply his talent and divine gifts that gain him so many commissions. It has been many years since I spoke to one besides Leonardo, one touched with *ingegno*. Loneliness is like the winter's chill; it seeps into your soul.

'And, Raphael, you've not met Leda,' I say.

'Mona has wearied me with your charms. But, it seems, she did not embellish her stories,' says Leda.

Raphael steps forward, rapt, to admire her. 'Goddess, marvel. Oh, Leonardo. She too breathes and speaks!'

Giuliano yawns and raps his knuckles. 'Tell us, Raphael. Is your Plato modelled on Leonardo from Vinci?'

Raphael nods a reluctant apology to Leda, but he must answer il Magnifico. 'When I last saw the maestro, he didn't have a beard either. But I painted Plato as I imagined our friend Leonardo in maturity and wisdom.' He turns to Leonardo, gesturing to his long whiskers. 'And I see you have done me the compliment of not contradicting me. Do you remember the words you had inscribed over the doors to your *bottega* in Florence?'

Leonardo grunts. 'Let no man enter who knows no geometry.'

'See!' exclaims Raphael. 'A prophet of art and mathematics.'

Leonardo frowns. 'Common sense, not philosophy. You must understand geometry and mathematics to produce art.'

Raphael's mouth is twitching with laughter. 'I couldn't decide for a while between Plato and Aristotle. I settled on Plato.'

Leonardo shifts, thinking. 'I do like Aristotle. "Good men possess a natural desire to know."'

For a moment, Raphael appears winded, unsure if he has made a mistake in his choice. Despite the esteem of two popes and the adoration of an empire, it is the approval of this man that he seeks.

'Do you like the finger?' he asks, eager.

'Very witty.'

Salaì stares at Raphael with open dislike. He's always loathed him for his extraordinary talent and now for his public homage to Leonardo. Salaì will only ever be a mere disciple, one whose light will extinguish beside the master's flame. Raphael is his own genius and Leonardo respects him as such, and Salaì can't bear it. His fists coil at his sides.

Raphael has walked to the table and is examining the portfolio of drawings; several of them are preparatory sketches for the cartoons of the Lives of the Saints for the Sistine Chapel. Salaì snatches them from him, his face contorting with rage.

'You're his rival for the commission. You cannot look!'

Raphael steps back, confused. 'I intend no slight, Salaì. They are exquisite drawings, I wished to admire them. That's all.'

'Salaì. Go home, you forget yourself,' orders Leonardo. 'Apologise.'

Salaì seizes Raphael by the shoulders and looks as if he's about to crack his head with his own, but then kisses him on the cheek, and leaves without a word.

'Always, you inspire devotion, Leonardo,' says Raphael, rattled. 'For which commission are we rivals?'

'Yes indeed,' wonders Giuliano, a puzzled expression on his face.

'The Sistine Chapel tapestry. The cartoons,' says Leonardo.

Raphael shakes his head. 'I've already been honoured with that commission. But,' he adds hurriedly, 'I would be glad of your advice. I see from your drawings that you were considering for a subject the miraculous draught of fishes. I adore these herons.'

'Raphael, do stop,' I say. 'You're veering close to condescension.'

Leonardo's shoulders slump; he's utterly dejected.

'What commissions are there that you or Michelangelo haven't taken?' I ask. 'There are other rooms in the private apartments.'

Raphael squirms. 'I'm painting the private apartments. Well, with my studio. There are so many rooms.'

'Of course. There are so many!' I say.

'You never told me that Raphael was greedy,' says Leda.

'No,' I agree. 'He didn't used to be.'

Raphael cringes at our rebuke.

'Then why am I here, Magnifico?' says Leonardo, turning to Giuliano. 'Why does His Holiness desire my presence in Rome?'

Giuliano beams at Leonardo with a courtier's practised smile of flattery. 'We are great admirers of your work. And we are the Medici of Florence, so it is only natural that we desire all the celebrated Florentine artists here at court.' He gestures to Raphael's mural. 'See, you're Plato.'

None of us points out that he didn't even know this till a few minutes ago.

'And you saw how much my brother enjoys music and pageantry. Tonight was a trifle. Englishmen and other buffoons dressed up in robes. We need a grand celebration to mark his ascension. The first Florentine pope. And it must be done by a Florentine.' He pauses. 'Is it true you made a mechanical lion?'

Leonardo bows. 'Yes, in gold for the Duke of Milan. It walked, and when it stopped, its heart opened to reveal mulberry leaves for Milan.'

'You must make a Lion of Florence for His Holiness.'

'With pleasure.'

'And, most of all, we desire you to plan and to create the entire spectacular to mark His Holiness's ascension to the papacy. You must design the pavilions, scenery and costumes.'

Leonardo bows. 'You bestow upon me a great honour, Magnifico.'

The doors are thrown open and the Pope waddles inside, cardinals trailing behind him like ducklings.

'Have you asked him?' he demands. 'Is he delighted?'

'Thrilled, Your Holiness,' declares Giuliano.

We walk back to the Belvedere Palace in silence. Michelangelo has sculpted the immortal tomb of the last pope and adorned the Sistine Chapel. Raphael is painting every room in the Apostolic Palace and Leonardo, the greatest genius in the Eternal City, is planning a party.

Spring

*P*lans for the pageant lie on every surface. There are elaborate stage sets of mountains that open with a complex series of pulleys to reveal His Holiness on his throne, with celestial skies above and the heavenly hosts. Designs of costumes in red and gold for the processions, while Salaì and Tommaso and Cecco paint scenery and instruct the carpenters on how to construct the mechanisms in the staging. Leonardo leaves most of the work to his assistants. The gardeners at the Belvedere Palace all know him now. One of them finds an odd-looking lizard and saves it for him. Leonardo brings it back to the *bottega* beneath the apartment, with tremendous excitement, and attaches wings to its spine with a mixture of quicksilver. They are made from scales stripped from other lizards and fish and quiver as it walks. He gives the creature a tail and horns and a crimson beard and feeds it scraps of meat to tame it and keeps it in a box next to those of his beloved cats. Whenever visitors call, he tosses meat out and the beast hurtles forth, terrifying the unsuspecting.

'You're bored,' I reprimand, when he has frightened the third papal courier.

Leonardo and Leda are in fits of laughter.

The maestro has also purged the fat from the guts of a bullock and made them so fine that they rest in the palm of Salaì's hand like the silk of a spider's web. He attaches the bellows to one end and fills them with air so that they expand to fill the entire space, crushing all the occupants into a corner. He skins lizards, frogs and snakes and inflates them with air and then suddenly releases them so that they puff and fly around the room.

'They are *scientia* experiments.'

'You're playing pranks like a schoolboy.'

Only Leda is amused, thrilled by the absurdity of his games, but soon his attention turns to other, darker pursuits. Beneath the apartment is a cavern of alchemy. There are plants and a distillery filled with hissing steam and bubbling pans. I watch while he works, attempting different distillations for varnishes and glazes based on old Roman recipes. Some days he retreats to the hospital at Santo Spirito and performs dissections on flayed corpses and returns, invigorated, his fingers blotched with ink and bodily fluid. I long to go with him. The mortals slumber but I cannot, and I remain in the *bottega*, listening to the hiss of the pots and waiting for him. La Cremona's words have lingered with me. All his drawings are of men. I see the flayed and separated cords of men's thighs, shaded and hatched in chalk and yellow wash to show the vessels and organs. I lack a body of my own and I want to see a real woman's again. I have only glimpsed La Cremona's, and I long to see another, to see how the parts are layered. The next time I see him draw his black cloak about his stained and foul britches, I call out to him, pleading.

'Take me. Please take me with you.'

He pauses, startled.

'I cannot. Of course I cannot.'

'I want to see how a woman is put together. A real, flesh and blood woman. Leda has children. I don't. I want to understand how a woman works.'

He hesitates and I know I have caught him.

'I heard your words to Raphael. Aristotle? "Good men possess a natural desire to know." Well, so do good women.'

He stares at me, not in revulsion but in acceptance. He recognises my need to grasp at knowledge.

He merely asks, 'How?'

He assembles a special case for me out of oak, plain but stout. We hope that it will protect me from the spray and viscera, but he drills small eye holes for me to observe the dissection. We test it in the studio, and from inside my case I still have an excellent view of the cauldrons and stacks of notebooks. To anyone who is curious, he will claim that the case contains paper and drawing implements. In the morning, I am like a lark laughing with excitement. I could take flight.

'Why are you so happy?' demands Leda.

I explain that I am to go to the hospital with Leonardo and watch his anatomy dissections.

'It isn't fair. I want to go.' She simmers with jealousy. 'I want to know what it is to be human too.'

'My love, I shall tell you everything,' I soothe. 'But come, you have your own babies to tend.'

I watch Leda, serene and flawless, the blue mountains hazy behind her in the morning light.

'Tell me everything. Swear it.'

'I swear.'

I shall remember it all for her. Every garnet of blood. Each fingernail and bone puzzle. She will remain here in the *bottega* with the hissing vials, and the deflated snakeskins, listening to the hammering of the carpenters and apprentices above, while I shall venture out into the world.

I'm calling upon the dead with Leonardo to uncover the secrets of life.

We ride to the Ospedale di Santo Spirito, a massive yellowing palazzo on the banks of the river. Leaving his horse with an orderly, Leonardo carries me in my new case into the Ospedale through the so-called Gate of Paradise and as we pass I observe a nun retrieve from a hatch inside a brick chamber, a tiny bawling infant, speckled with dirt. Leonardo tuts and shakes his head with pity.

'This is not the gate to paradise, or not on earth,' he mutters. 'Some end up in paradise much too soon.'

He hurries us on into the immense hall of the Ospedale, an octagonal tower at its heart with windows spilling light down onto the nuns and friars and poor suffering souls below. The walls are adorned with magnificent frescoes, and high above in niches sit saints indifferent to the welter of agony beneath.

I can hear the wailing of the sick and dying on the wards above the chant of prayers of the nuns. There is a stench of flesh and death and disease. Flies halo the saints.

A young professor of anatomy is waiting for Leonardo in the hall. He is slight and bearded and reminds me of Raphael. He doesn't remark upon the fact that the maestro is clutching an extra case. No one notices the pair of holes Leonardo has bored into the side so I can watch. The doctor leads us away from the hall of the Corsia and down a long corridor into another part of the Ospedale.

'I have a criminal for you, my friend. An interesting grotesque. A club foot,' says the professor.

I see Leonardo waver. But I made him promise. He knows what I wish to see, more than anything.

'Marcantonio, I would very much like to make a drawing of a foetus in the womb.'

The young professor baulks. 'Criminals are one thing, maestro, but a young woman? A mother?'

'I yearn to understand all things, Marcantonio. If we cannot observe, how can we learn?'

The younger man is silent, considering. He reaches a decision. 'Come. A woman died in childbed in the night. Destitute. There is no one to claim her body.'

He quickens his pace and Leonardo hastens to keep up. We are brought to the medical faculty. The smell hits me like a wall. I can taste it, sweet and sticky and foul. Candles and lanterns and incense are burning but nothing can stop the stench. I see rats and they peer back at me. They know something is in the oak box. Leonardo sets me down upon a bench. I'm glad it's not upon the floor, as it's slick with gore. From my vantage, I can make out high windows, all befouled and stained with effluence of every sort but light eases in, aided by the lamps and candles. Paintings of the Madonna and saints are hung askew on every wall. All are ugly and all are sprayed with bodily fluids. A body is laid out upon the table. A man. Yellow and gaping in death. His club foot swollen and gnarled.

'Wait,' says Marcantonio. 'I'll have the woman brought.'

Leonardo stands. No one would sit in this place. It is inhuman, repulsive. A skeleton jangles on a rack, its jaw agape as if seized in perpetual hilarity at some macabre joke.

'Madonna Lisa,' he calls softly. 'We can leave at once. You can change your mind. Men of great courage have had their nerves fail. Or been impeded by their stomachs.

Or the fear of living through the night with the thought of corpses quartered and skinned.'

'No,' I reply. 'I'm not afraid. I want to see. Else how can I understand?'

The conditions are sordid but my curiosity is unsatiated. I can also hear music.

'What is that?'

'They play music to soothe the dying.'

It doesn't seem to work. Even down here, the sombre tones of the strings war with the groans of the sick, a profane ensemble. At last Marcantonio returns with an orderly pushing a cart with a body draped with a bloodied sheet. I see the swell of her belly. The three men heave her onto a table.

Marcantonio lays out the anatomist's instruments upon a wooden bench. There are knives of every size – from huge carvers to palette knives – scissors, saws, mallets, sponges, strings, long gouging nails and pincers, all coated in a thick coating of rust. I realise the rust is encrusted blood.

He lifts the sheet.

The woman can't be dead, merely sleeping; her skin is colourless, so still; her hands clasped in fists. There are bloody marks on her lip where she has bitten it in agony, but now she is motionless, released into perfect peace with her never-to-be-born child. Her massive belly is a pristine snow-covered mountain. This silent woman, whose name none of us knows. To cut into her, to peer into the watery depths of her in order to peep at this child who she never got to hold, is an affront. I know it. I look at Leonardo and the young doctor, the huddled wall of their backs, and see that they know it too. We can never pay penance enough for this. Yet the need for knowledge pushes us on into the unconscionable. Leonardo and the doctor tell themselves that they are men of learning and *scientia* pressing for understanding the mysteries of the body on behalf of all men, but I know that they are as selfish as I. The desire to possess and understand a knowledge like this is greedy and venal. The path to truth feels very close to that of sin. In silence instead of prayer, Leonardo makes the first cut.

The woman with no name lies on the table. An assortment of parts. The child is perfect in every way except that it is dead. I think of Lisa, weeping for her daughter. At least this mother does not have to grieve. The dissection complete, the doctor has left Leonardo to make his drawings. Leonardo clasps a folio sheet and sketches, his face puzzled.

'The length of a child when born is usually one *braccio*. But the uterus is half that size.'

He draws the boy coiled, head tucked into his knees, the umbilical cord wound around his ankles, as when we disturbed him. There is something unconscionably sad about the flawless boy and the woman and the fetid room.

'You must describe the form of the womb, and how the child lives in it,' I say softly. 'And see if you can fathom in what way it is given life and food.'

Leonardo's chalk flies across the page.

The stink is putrid. The other bodies around us are ripe. At least the day is cool. After some time Leonardo sets down his chalk and picks up his pen, ready to make annotations.

'In this child the heart does not beat and it does not breathe because it rests continually in water, and if it breathed it would drown. And breathing is not necessary because it is purified and nourished by the life and food of the mother.'

'Yes, Leonardo. But what of the child's soul?'

He is silent, considering the question. 'One and the same soul governs these two bodies.'

'Then we must take care that they are buried together as one being, one soul. Promise me that you'll see to it.'

'I promise.'

Setting aside his paper, he takes out a syringe and fills it with wax and begins to inject the blood vessels of the woman's leg, in order to make it easier for him to do further drawings of the tangled passages of blood. I wish that I had hands that were capable of clasping hers, even though she would not know it.

In the evening Leda asks me at once, 'What did you see?'

I hesitate. I wonder how best to explain in a way that she will understand. This immortal with her egg-children. I say at last, 'I saw a child. Unhatched.'

'Did you unpeel him from his mother?'

'Yes.'

Leda is quiet. The room is still.

'In the normal way of things, the child mourns for the mother. But these two shall be together always,' I say.

I look at Leda surrounded by her children, and know that she does not understand. She is a goddess, and her children are suspended in time. They will neither grow up nor leave her.

'Did you learn the great mystery?' whispers Leda. 'Where real women keep their life force hidden?'

'No. We only saw that two lives were stopped. They were perfected and ended, yet together. They will not grow old.'

'Like us.'

'But they will wither and rot.'

Leonardo joins us, and sits examining his sketches. After a time I ask him to colour the child in the womb. He almost never colours his drawings but, this once, it looks wrong to me in grey; it doesn't evoke the life force of the child. He does as I ask, and the boy seems to hover before the page, warm once again. The boy's life was spent when we glimpsed him, but the marvel of its power was not. At once he is transformed; on the page, he lives again. No longer a dead boy plucked rudely from his mother's womb coffin, but a foetus waiting to be born, pushed out into a noisy world, toes wriggling, fists curled, coiled with potential. The dead boy will be buried with his mother. The living boy on the page belongs to me.

At the Chateau of Fontainebleau is a portrait at life size on wood in a carved walnut frame of a half-length figure and it is a portrait of a certain Gioconda. This is the most complete by Leonardo da Vinci to be seen, since it lacks nothing but speech.

Cassiano dal Pozzo, 1625

Fontainebleau, 1594

Autumn

We return again to the Queen's Cabinet at the great palace of Fontainebleau, where I watched the court come and go from my easel. I waited alone, feeling my paintwork threatened with damp and wondering if I should simply rot and slough away. I do not like coming back to this moment. I was miserable and lonely. For nearly seventy years I could only hear Leda and never see her.

My visitors were the kings and his court. Yet they all die in the end. Kings are still flesh. Francis. Henry. Francis. Henry. The gallant. The just. The good. The lascivious and the wicked. After each sovereign's death, the mourners came. The bathers stopped for a month, and then returned naked but for a band of black – unfortunately worn on the arm and not any lower. Another *roi* was crowned, until at last came the end of the Valois kings and the beginning of the House of Bourbon. To me, in the fog-filled salon of the bathing suite, all kings looked alike – pink and flushed and bare-cheeked.

The latest king, another Henry, was repurposing the *appartement des bains* at Fontainebleau, and workmen and builders hurried from room to room. For the first time in half a century the salons were cool, emptied of steam and heat, and without the miasma the leprous plaster on the walls and ceiling was quite apparent. The Carrara marble statuary was wet and grey with dirt; even Flora and Venus looked ashamed at their slovenly appearance. I looked at a Raphael of the Madonna in the garden, and observed with horror that she was bowed and cracked, the frame wormy and rotten. The ceiling and walls drip-dripped, stained green with florid mould like a grotto. I worried about the damage inflicted upon my paintwork. There was no mirror near, and I could not see what had happened to me. Every so often a smut fall would flutter down past me from my frame and I feared that I too was infested with worm or termites. Would I still know myself? My face might splinter and then disintegrate into noth-ingness. I did not know what would happen to me if I faded or broke apart.

'Leda?' I called. 'Are you still here?'

'Yes,' she replied. 'They haven't come for me yet.'

All of us were to be taken from here and hung in a grand gallery, the Pavillon des Peintures. I was relieved; if we remained, we would all decay. This fetid *appartement* was no place for a painted lady. For decades, Leda and I had called to one another, never in the same room, sep-arated at either end of the bathing suite. Yet every night, once the mortals left us, we called out to one another, and walked together in our dream house. Sometimes we swam in the River Adda, but other evenings we sat on the loggia in the gathering dusk while Leonardo and La Cremona watched the fishing boats and talked and drank wine. It was years since I had glimpsed Leda outside our visits to the dream house, and I longed to be with her once again. To look upon her face. My Leda. My adored and beautiful girl.

I was unhooked from the wall and carried through the palace. I cried out with joy. I hadn't left this captivity in decades. The doors were thrown open to outside, and I could see the woods at the edge of the estate beyond the parterre, the flush of autumn leaves. A chill wind rumpled the trees, so that the colours changed as if with an unseen brush, blended from red to yellow and gold and back. Swallows circled high above, skating on the plumes of air. I hadn't seen a swallow for years. The birds made me think of Leonardo and his dreams of flight. Even decades after his death, the thought of him pierced me. I was glad he could not see what I had become.

A workman in dirty gloves conveyed me through shuttered corridors and back stairs until we reached a grand gallery of double height lit with many windows on both sides and dozens of spinning chandeliers. The ceilings and walls, where they were not adorned with paintings, were highly gilded so that the room streamed with light, appearing almost to shine. Paintings were laid out on tables and, when those were full, on grubby sheets upon the floor. I was placed on the ground between a Judith by Rousse and a Virgin and Child from the Italian school. A foreigner in peculiar dress stood at a table before a window, as a footman carried each painting over for his inspection while a bespectacled clerk took notes of his observations. The foreigner danced upon his toes, cheerfully announcing his verdict – reprieve, punishment or death.

'Copy of the Raphael *Madonna in the Garden*, warped beyond repair. Nothing to be done. Pity. She's a decent copy. Once upon a time anyway. Mark for destruction,' the foreigner declared.

With horror, I saw a footman pick up the Madonna and carry her over to a large pile of paintings propped against a trestle table and dump her there unceremoniously.

I was plucked from the floor and transported to the foreigner for my trial, without any chance of speaking in my defence. I could only wait for my sentence. The man wore a grubby wig askew, long robes and loose-fitting hose – not in the French style, although after decades of being subjected to parades of endless nudity I was relieved that he wore any clothes at all. He scrutinised me, then gave a mew of pleasure and, a moment later, coughed with annoyance.

'The Mona Lisa herself. Not one of the many mawkish copies. Her walnut frame is absolutely putrefied. It's sodden.'

He flipped the blade of a knife beneath the edge of my frame and it disintegrated at once, crumbling away into mulch and shards of wood. White commas of maggots and deathwatch beetles wriggled across the table. He flicked them away with his knife, revolted. I lay on the table, naked and exposed.

'What a wretched place to leave a painting such as this!' He picked up a magnifying glass, and peered at me through his giant pupil. 'The steam has caused craquelure damage to her paintwork. I'll restore her myself.'

His voice was filled with a glee and zeal that I did not like. He stared at me like I was a thing to be consumed and eaten. I wished I had legs that could run away. The clerk carefully inscribed notes into a book, while the footman lifted me with care and placed me to one side of the gallery, gently propping me against a table, so that I had a convenient view of the magnificent chamber. All around me were paintings requiring greater or lesser restoration. In the unflinching sunlight, all our flaws and the sufferings inflicted from years of moisture were apparent – twisted wood and flaking oils – a Madonna swaddling empty blankets, her baby quite gone, stolen away by damp.

There was a pitiful cry and I looked to see two footmen carrying a painting into the gallery. The bright rays dazzled me, and it took me a moment to recognise that it was Leda. She was badly hurt; her walnut panel had split into three separate pieces and, where it had come apart, her paint had chipped away. She was shuffled so her right hip and leg now lay on the wrong side of Jupiter's wing, her babies sliced in half, the paint on their shells worn down to the *imprimitura* white-lead base. I was shocked to see her so mutilated, but knew at once I must hide my disquiet, for fear of frightening her.

'Mona!' she cried, her voice brimming with panic and anguish. 'Mona, what is wrong with me? What have they done to me?'

'Leda. All will be well,' I called, willing it and wanting it to be true.

I was frantic to have her close to me, to be able to comfort her. The footmen carried Leda over to the trestle inspection table before the window, and placed her down in front of the foreign doctor. I was filled with rage at the idiocy of kings. They hung us in their *appartement des bains* to parade us before the court and ambassadors, and Leda – the loveliest, the most cherished of us all – was despoiled. All three pieces of Leda lay on the table, and the foreigner surveyed them with disgust.

'This was a Leda? She's beyond repair. The destruction pile.'

'No! Mona, please,' she cried out for me in desperation and despair.

I was overwhelmed with rage and self-loathing at my helplessness. I couldn't even offer her consolation.

'My darling,' I called.

'Mona,' she said, panic rising. 'Am I no longer beautiful?'

'To me,' I said, 'the most beautiful in all the world. Until the end of days.'

This was no comfort to Leda who was used to being the most beautiful picture to all admirers. And it was not enough to save her. She cried out in terror. The vanity and foolishness of mortal kings had turned a Spartan queen into a warped and broken thing, and I hated them for it. What would they do to her?

'No!' I was beside myself.

But this was a century of fools and no one could hear me.

The footman plucked up the separate panels under his arm and tossed them down in a heap with other doomed paintings. In my anguish it took me a minute to notice that an argument was taking place between the foreigner and another man, who I recognised as the Keeper of the King's Pictures.

'It doesn't matter that she is in poor repair. She's a Léonard de Vinci. In France that means something still. Restore her. That's what we brought you from the Low Countries to do.'

The foreigner clucked like a chicken. 'Poor repair! She's in three pieces! When they lifted her from the wall, the panel split apart.'

'So put her back together. That's what we hired you for. If you can't do it, we'll find someone more qualified.'

The Keeper of the Pictures snapped his fingers, and to my joy the footman lifted Leda up, and brought her to rest beside me. He did not, however, pay much attention to how he placed the panels, and Jupiter's wing lay skewered inside Leda's body, her toes in the clouds, monstrous and mismatched. I didn't care. She was with me. She was safe. Her panel was nuzzled up against me. We were together again, side by side, broken or not. Leonardo had painted us to be together. I could not be without her. I would not.

I lay on the block in the restorer's apothecary, awaiting surgery. I stared up at the Dutch restorer. He had donned a pair of weird magnifying lenses so that he resembled a bug or beetle of some sort with giant antennae. The room was bright and lit again with lamps, and reeked of astringent chemicals. Leda and several other paintings waited their turn, propped against the walls. The man peered down at me, baring his grey teeth. There was a piece of spinach lodged between them.

'What have they done to you, Mona Lisa?' he muttered with sympathy.

I agreed. They were buffoons.

He took a swab of cotton and picked up a jar of clear liquid and poured some of the contents onto the swab. I needed to be brave. Leda was watching, waiting in dread for her turn. Whatever the man was about to inflict upon me, what he must do to Leda would be much worse. I must endure it smiling, serene and without a murmur of discomfort. I must not frighten her and increase her suffering. He placed the balled-up fabric upon my eye and began to scrub at the iris. I did not think. I only screamed. He rubbed away at me, panting with the effort. He pulled out each of my eyelashes in a pitiless attack, scratching away at my flesh, with his fingernails and rags steeped in chemicals raking at my painted skin. My cheeks, my lips, my fingertips and finally my eyebrows, until by his assault they too were rubbed away into nothingness. I wept and howled in pain and humiliation. No one heard but Leda.

He stared at me, sweaty with satisfaction, his tongue protruding wetly. 'There,' he said. 'Much cleaner.'

I sobbed. I had quite forgotten to be brave.

He reached for a foul-smelling pot and then with a brush daubed upon me thick layers of viscous lacquer. The world dulled. I stared out through brown mucous.

'What have you done to me?' I asked.

He could not hear, but even to myself, my voice sounded muffled and odd. He was staring at me, not entirely pleased with his work.

'Your colours are not as bright as before. It is a pity, but necessary. The varnish will protect you from further harm, Mona Lisa.'

'You simpleton! The varnish is the harm,' I hissed.

If Leonardo was here, he would have mended me with his own brush. He wouldn't have let them spoil me, make me drab and wretched. But we always knew he couldn't protect me after he was gone.

The foreigner moved away from me, as if half-afraid to look at what he had done, the damage he'd inflicted through idiocy upon a masterpiece. I felt bruised and broken.

An assistant laid out Leda upon another table in her three parts.

'No,' she whispered in terror. 'Leave me be. I'll stay broken. Please.'

'I'm here,' I said. 'Whatever he does. I'm here with you and I love you.'

He flipped her onto her front, and called to the footman. 'Hold her steady.'

I watched aghast while he pulled out a hammer, nails and batons and proceeded to pin the pieces of her back together. She yelled in pain and anguish.

When they turned Leda the right way up, she was mismatched; her face had slid as though she'd suffered a palsy.

'Am I better? Am I lovely again?' she demanded, a note of fear and panic rising.

'Yes, darling,' I soothed. It was only half a lie.

After a few days to allow the lacquer to dry, we were carried out of the restorer's tomb and fixed high upon the golden walls of the gallery. All comers continued to stare at Leda; even misshapen she was a creature of wonder. One day I would hang near the Venus de Milo, who despite her missing limbs was celebrated as the epitome of Roman sculpture, and that is how it was with Leda – men gazed at her, trying to put her back together in their minds, as if through love they could mend her, make the puzzle of her whole again.

I was overjoyed to be reunited with Leda. We hung side by side, but on the wall opposite us was a vast gilded mirror so, to my delight, I could see her. At first I thought that, together once more, we would have no more need of our dream-house game. Yet for the best part of a century, after the mortals had gone to sleep, we had roamed its halls every night or lingered in the dappled shade of the gardens, and to my surprise I found that I longed for it still.

'Mona,' said Leda softly. 'Can we?'

'Yes,' I said.

We stepped out into our villa. It was there waiting for us. In our dreams we were flesh and blood. I felt sunlight on my skin. A breeze lifted the strands of my hair so that it brushed against my cheek. Summer edged into autumn, and wisteria leaves lay like inlaid fishes in the rills that flowed down to the river. It was warm and our long-dead friends sat at the table on the loggia, eating bread and cheese and picking up melons, sniffing at them to see if they were ripe. Leonardo smiled to see us, beckoning us to join them. La Cremona stood and kissed us both, slipping her arm through Leda's. She poured us wine.

'Sit, eat, drink.'

We sat.

'Now,' said La Cremona, raising her glass, midway through her story, 'several people were talking in Florence and each was making a wish for the thing that would make her happy. The first wanted to be a pope. The second a queen. And third was Cecco here, who said, "I wish I were a melon."'

Cecco interrupted with a frown, saying, 'A melon?'

'Yes,' said La Cremona. 'Because then everyone would smell your bottom.'

The table erupted in laughter, tears running down Leonardo's cheeks in appreciation of the bawdy joke.

La Cremona handed me a slice of melon; it was perfectly sweet, and the juice tickled my chin.

Leonardo opened his arms for me and I nestled closer to him, laying my head on his shoulder. He tugged my earlobe and planted a kiss on the top of my head. I inhaled deeply and breathed in his scent of linseed oil and rosewater. He passed me a napkin to wipe away the spilled juice of the melon.

'Where do you go, my Lisa, when you're not here with us?' he asked.

I shook my head. 'Nowhere. Nowhere important.'

His beard was grey but not yet white, and his eyes creased when he smiled. He was full of vigour and ideas, his fingertips stained with paint. This was my and Leda's dream and we invoked them as we wished them to be – vital and happy.

'Soon, shall we walk down to the river?' he asked.

'No,' I said. 'I want to paint you. My portrait of you isn't finished.'

Leonardo pulled a face and pretended to grumble. 'You know how I hate to sit still.'

'Just for a little while, my love. And you'll need to help me with your hands. However hard I try, I can't get them right.'

He sighed which I took as agreement. As I watched, Leda looked out across the garden to where her children lazed in the sunlight. For the first few years of our *fantasia* they'd remained babies, unchanging, infants clinging to her legs. But then Leda decided, in our dream house at least, her children could grow up. They were now beautiful youths, Helen and Clytemnestra arguing over poetry. Irritated, Helen threw the book at her sister. It hit her on the forehead, leaving a small red mark. The boys wrestled, punching and kicking one another, viciously, and then, suddenly tiring of the game, anger fled, they flopped back, still tangled in one another's limbs.

'Come with me, Mona.' Standing, Leda held out her hand and led me into the villa. Every wall was now frescoed with trees and flowers. Chestnut, larch, branches of oak and birch. Star of Bethlehem, blackberry, Job's tears, sprigs of guelder rose and sedge. It was a house of laughter and such charm. It also smelled of paint, the tempera not quite dry. Once, Leonardo conjured us out of his imagination, and now we brought him back to life in ours. In our dream house, we were real women; we breathed and we were made of flesh and bone and always, everybody we loved, lived.

Fontainebleau, 1678

Autumn

*U*nder Louis the Sun King the Palace of Fontainebleau became the nursery of mistresses, or, as I heard the Spanish Ambassador mutter to his envoy, the most expensive brothel in the world. Leda and I revelled in watching them all. Fontainebleau was devoted to pleasure and echoed with the popping of champagne corks and the snuffling and yapping of the royal dogs. Louis adored them, and the polished parquet floor of the gallery below us pattered with the sound of their claws, until it was scratched and scuffed. When he had his favourite pointer and spaniel painted, Leda was appalled lest he have them hang beside her. She would not be rivalled by a floppy-eared, wet-nosed pup.

The King had ordered a new palace to be built near Paris, at Versailles, but many at court still preferred the hunting in the vast forest surrounding the chateau at Fontainebleau. The King adored the hunt. Deer, wolves and women. His adoration and pursuit of women meant that the court was forced to accept two queens: the pious Marie Thérèse, who preferred Mass and prayer to dancing;

and the queen of his affections, his mistress Madame de Montespan, a woman of fierce wit and passion. She swept into the gallery, plump and pretty, but she was now in her late thirties with real threads of grey beneath her wig, aged for a mistress, and the King had to rouse himself and pretend joy on seeing her. She sucked on a sugared almond.

'She's always eating,' I said to Leda. 'Her teeth will rot like the Queen's.'

Queen Marie Thérèse had beautiful white hair and unblemished fair skin but black teeth from her incessant eating of fruit.

From our gilded vantage point on the gallery wall, Leda and I had been observing Madame de Montespan, who had just returned to court after her most recent confinement – she'd borne the King another son – and noticed she seemed ill-tempered and on edge. Her famous wit had given way to a jumpy irritability. I thought of all the children she had given the King tucked up in the distant nursery, cared for by another woman, the young and exquisite Françoise, rumoured to be a new favourite of King Louis. Madame de Montespan was not supposed to visit the babes too often. She did not belong to her children. They, like their mother, belonged to the King alone. All of us women, flesh or painted, were property of the King, one way or another. She stared at me blankly and, beneath the layers of rouge, I could see that she was tired and frightened. There were cracks upon her skin, just like on mine.

'We are the same, Madame,' I called. 'You are not so alone as you think.'

'Why do you bother?' asked Leda. 'They never hear us.'

'I exist in hope,' I said. It was no longer a source of pride that only those gifted with divine *ingegno* could hear us, but of sadness and despair.

Madame de Montespan turned away from me with a sigh, adjusted her pearls and her smile.

A feast had been prepared to celebrate her return to court. Orange trees bearing candied fruits, mountains of jam and marzipan, a castle of sweets in the shape of Fontainebleau itself was set up in the grand gallery. The King sat down beside the Queen and ate with the Dauphin and Dauphine, while the rest of the assembly watched. When they had finished, it was the turn of the court. Courtiers savoured a few treats, but Madame de Montespan tucked away handfuls of marzipan and *macarons* while Louis looked on appalled and revolted.

He stood beside her and placed a hand upon her shoulder.

'Madame? Is that not sufficient? You are very fat.'

She glared at him and hissed, low enough that only Leda and I who were just above could hear.

'My liege, your power is great, but your sceptre is small.'

He stepped back from her, as though stung by a scorpion. I glanced around the array of powdered faces and saw that they were steeped in pleasure, gratified to see the King's favourite rebuked.

'She has borne him six children,' I said to Leda. 'He ought to have a little patience. She is unhappy.'

'So many children breaks a woman's body and animal spirits,' agreed Leda.

Madame de Montespan reached out defiant for another tiny soufflé and stood to eat it, unable to sit in the King's presence. Yet I could see that she glowed with humiliation. I could not blame her for her ill temper and irascibility. I glanced along the ranks of court women in their gleaming diamonds and silks, armoured into their corsets, and knew that they sensed weakness. Madame de Montespan's jewelled grip on power was loosening, and there were many here who had suffered from her wit. The King was tiring of her; she had borne him half a dozen living children, miscarried more, loved him and had overripened from plumpness into corpulence through the exertion of it all. Yet he bore her no gratitude; instead he glanced along the ranks of fluttering painted fans, like a flotilla of butterflies, surveying the assembled countesses and duchesses. The King was ready for another mistress, but it was the task of the new mistress to depose the old.

The night was full of blood. The King had spent much of the day hunting with four packs of hounds, and later there was to be a ceremonial feasting on the spoils by the dogs on the torchlit lawns. But first, Louis wished to take his favourite ladies into the forest on his two-wheeled *soufflet* to listen to the rutting of the stags, weaving through the trees in the murk at speed with the skill of the best coachman, the ladies crying out in terrified pleasure. The ladies held their breath – waiting, to see who he would choose. He selected the most beautiful of all. He looked up to Leda and blew her a kiss.

'Your Majesty, I would that you would do me the honour. A Spartan queen, for a French king.'

Leda laughed, pleased. 'I belong to Jupiter.'

Louis had already turned to his old mistress. He spoke without warmth or pleasure.

'Madame de Montespan.'

She smiled with relief, filled with shame at her earlier rudeness, and eagerly took his hand. The King had not finished. He looked at the slight, pretty woman beside her. The governess of their children.

'Françoise, Madame de Maintenon, you will also accompany us.'

It was not a request but a command. The young woman bowed her head. Montespan flushed with humiliation.

I looked over towards Queen Marie Thérèse, but she had quit the gallery with her ladies-in-waiting.

'She doesn't even notice,' said Leda. 'She doesn't care at his unending faithlessness.'

'Oh but she does,' I said.

I knew she cared. I was too old and had seen too much. I understood that there was only so much degradation and dishonour a woman could bear.

The park was luxuriant with elm, oak, beech and swaying limes. The windows were all cast open to the cool night air. Even in the gallery, Leda and I could hear through the dark, the pistol crack of the stags' antlers as they fought. The lawns outside were lit with hundreds of torches and the carcasses of the slaughtered deer had been dragged into the centre, leaving a bloodied, blackened trail. Hunting horns began to sound and horses careered back from the forest, dozens of them, a stampede of hoofs upon gravel while the moon floated serene and white above it all, unblemished. The King in his *soufflet* screamed into view, hurtling along the path as the music of the horns called again and again. The Grand Veneur whistled for the hounds, and at once, with a frantic howling and baying, two hundred dogs hurled themselves across the lawns so that it was seething with black backs and snapping mouths. In the blazing torchlight I saw Madame de Montespan shriek and clutch at her rival, Françoise, Madame de Maintenon, terrified that the hounds would tear her to pieces instead. The King threw his head back and laughed at them both. The lawns were bathed in fire and blood as dogs ripped apart the carcasses of the stags, devouring and disembowelling them as the music played, and the men toasted and cheered the King.

'This is what they do for fun, Leda. This is civilised revelry.'

'And uncivilised. And also of the gods. They hunt and carouse on Mount Olympus.'

Footmen in reeking wigs held open the doors and the nobility swarmed the gallery, helping themselves to cups of hot chocolate that were set out on silver trays. Madame de Montespan took two, swallowing them like medicine, leaving a slick brown deposit on her chin. I noticed the bottom of her gown was spattered with blood and gore. Her hand shook as she drank. Two dukes stared at her with open distaste. A month ago they would not have dared, but they all sensed the King's regard for her slipping, like clasped hands around an oiled rope.

'Why do you still gawp? Have you not seen a fat woman before?' she yelled, with a stamp of her foot. It was still swollen, jammed in its slipper. It was not long since she gave birth. Her cheeks were puffy, water-logged; her bosom strapped but heavy and hard with milk that was not to be suckled. Her newborn son had been snatched from her. She must not nurse him, but be back on show before the court. I ached for her, as the others curdled with vitriol and spite. We were both creatures of reluctant display.

Spring

The parterre was filled with marigolds and daffodils, geometrically ordered in their beds. Servants opened the door and Queen Marie Thérèse walked inside with King Louis, the breath of spring chasing them.

'I haven't seen them together for months,' I said.

'Years,' replied Leda.

They were an odd pair. The white-haired, pious queen looked more like the King's mother than his wife now. Yet, despite his infidelity, she remained devoted to him and resolutely loyal. She fixed her blue, guileless eyes upon him.

'Monsieur le Roi, when you choose the next one—'

He winced and took her hand, trying to hush her, but she threw him off.

'Let me speak, monsieur! You owe me that. No one is listening but Mona Lisa and Leda,' she glanced up, 'and I've never heard them tell a secret.'

Louis grimaced but let her continue.

'Monsieur, because I tolerate your behaviour, do not believe I am the dupe the court imagines. I see things clearly but I am prudent.'

Louis, a man of feeling as well as impulses, was moved. 'Madame, you are an angel.'

'Monsieur, I am not! I am a woman. And your actions wound me.'

Marie Thérèse swallowed and sought to regain her composure as her husband stiffened, offended. He was a king and therefore could bear no criticism, however just.

'Please, I beg of you a simple favour. Please, when you choose the next one, and we both know you will, I ask only that she is not one of my women. Do not choose one of the women of my household. I ask only that.'

I looked at her, whey-faced and proud. She refused to beg; she merely asked.

Louis took her hand again and brought it to his lips and kissed it. 'Madame, I—'

'Do not swear to it,' I called. 'Do not promise her, unless you can keep it!'

The King stopped, startled by a fit of coughing, his vow caught in his throat like a fish bone. His eyes watered and a servant rushed forward with a glass of wine.

'I swear to you, madame,' he said at last.

The Queen smiled, satisfied.

'He cannot keep his word,' said Leda.

'I know,' I said. 'This will not end well. Some other poor soul will pay for his crime of passion.'

Leda and I spied on them both through the open windows, watching as the King paced the parterre outside the gallery with Françoise, Madame de Maintenon. Françoise was a slight, serious woman of twenty-five. She owed her position entirely to the benevolence and favour of the Queen. They spoke earnestly and low, and we could not hear.

'She is pious and discreet and will resist him,' said Leda.

'No one can refuse the King,' I said. 'It is impolite and impolitic.'

As we observed, he stooped to pick a posy of spring tulips with his own hand.

'You see?' I said.

Yet a moment later, to our astonishment, he stopped the sedan chair of the Queen and thrust the blooms at her. The chair continued on as the Queen partook of her morning constitutional.

'You see?' said Leda, triumphant. 'She's persuading him to pay attention to his wife.'

I was not convinced. The footmen held open the doors to the grand gallery, and Françoise and Louis stepped inside. Françoise was endeavouring to keep her distance from him, skipping lightly away. He pursued her as a fox would a hare. She stared up at him, imploring him.

'My great and Christian King, I would ask that you honour your wife, the Queen. Be kind and good.'

He clasped her hand and ran kisses along the flesh of her arm.

She whisked it away. 'The Queen, Your Majesty. We are both women of God. She longs for you to go to Mass with her.'

The King emitted a most unholy groan.

'And Madame de Montespan,' continued Françoise. 'I look after her children. Your children. Do not forget her, Your Majesty.'

The King regarded her longingly. 'You are good, too good, Françoise. I will be kind to the Queen, and to Madame de Montespan, and then I think you will be kind to me.'

Françoise for the first time looked cornered, her face flushed with anxiety. She gestured up at Leda.

'I am nothing. No one. You deserve a woman such as she. A queen.'

'I do,' agreed Louis, looking up. 'Leda? Will you have me?'

'No,' said Leda.

'She doesn't answer,' said Louis with a playful shrug. 'But in any case I prefer you.'

But Françoise, Madame de Maintenon had already made a hasty curtsey and was running down the gallery, her frantic footsteps echoing upon the parquet floor, the King's pointers baying at her heels.

Summer

*F*or the first time in many years, I saw the Queen smile. Usually, she took great pains to hide her rotten teeth, but she couldn't help it. The King accompanied her to church, Françoise, Madame de Maintenon walking dutifully in the procession behind, with all the King's bastards trailing alongside her. Yet what Leda and I agreed had pleased Queen Marie Thérèse most of all was that Madame de Montespan had been pensioned off. He had a new case of jewels made for her, to thank her for her service, with stones of every colour; but we all understood it for what it was – a parting gift. The King still called upon her after dinner for ten minutes, but he no longer visited her bed. For the first time in more than a decade, there was only one Queen.

Leda and I glimpsed Louis and Marie Thérèse just beyond the window – the King walked alongside the Queen's *châtelet*. He was always full of vigour and energy, unable to bear being cooped up in a carriage on a bright

June morning. The Queen leaned out of the carriage and smiled – first at her husband, the shy, tender smile of a bride; and then, turning, she searched for Françoise, and smiled broadly at her friend and lady-in-waiting, unable in her joy to hide her black teeth. It didn't matter. In happiness, she was radiant.

A dinner was held in the gallery. The King, the Queen, the Dauphin and Dauphine all sat at the long table and sampled processions of lobster, oysters, beef, six poussin, four plump capon, pigeon tart, six turkeys, wood snipe, sliced pineapples and quails' eggs, *au grand couvert* before the court, as the assembled nobility stood to watch. The Premier Maître d'Hôtel du Roi tested each dish for poison. The Queen was served fricassees, minced meat and soups to make it easier for her to chew.

'I never wish I was able to eat more, than when I am here,' grumbled Leda.

I had to agree.

The King wore a coat of gold brocade so covered in diamonds that under the chandeliers he appeared to be made of light. Everyone was forced to stand, except duchesses and princesses and me. I always sat. The King glanced up at me and beamed, a slick of butter running down his chin.

'Mona Lisa, you must be a duchess at the very least. Or else, I must make you one. You are granted the honour of the tabouret, so you may sit in the presence of the King, and watch him eat.'

The court laughed, convulsing with laughter, edged with cruelty. Tonight, Madame de Montespan was being granted that honour – the tabouret. The right to sit on a stool opposite the King's table to watch him feast. Madame de Montespan glowered at me with resentment: pipped by a painting. She had been retired from the royal bedchamber, and was now receiving ceremonial gratitude of the highest order, but the King was mocking her, bestowing it upon me first.

'I did not ask for the honour, Madame,' I said. 'We are not enemies. In fact, I am one of your few friends in this court.'

Madame de Montespan sat on her tabouret stool opposite the King and the royal table amongst the princesses of the blood, watching the royal family eat pastries and salad and mutton, the laughter echoing around her. She bit her lip and she clasped her pudgy hands into fists. I had spoiled this occasion for her. She had lost the King's affection and also his esteem; he felt free to tease her before the court.

The Queen studied the King, amazed.

'She thinks he has returned to her,' I said.

'Even after all these years and all these women, she still loves him,' said Leda. 'A queen and a fool. But perhaps we are all fools for love.'

The King smiled at his wife. He enjoyed all admirers, and he was fond of Marie Thérèse. In all the long years of their marriage, she had caused him no trouble. He reached for a silver tray of green beans.

'Madame, would you like to try this dish?'

She beamed at him as if it was a platter of pearls and oysters rather than a humble plate of garden vegetables.

'Monsieur Roi, *oui*, I would love to.'

She sucked on a bean, gazing at him unblinking. He patted her hand and fed a scrap of pigeon to one of the spaniels with equal affection.

Autumn

*T*orches blazed in the park outside, shining like extra stars. All was still. Leda and I listened to the shuffle of mice. A door banged. Shouts and running bare feet. Françoise careered into the gallery in her night robes, weeping.

'What's happened?' I called. 'Are you all right?'

The Queen followed close behind her. On seeing Marie Thérèse, Françoise threw herself at her feet.

'Madame, forgive me. I had no choice. He is the King.'

Leda laughed. 'She's found Françoise in his bed.'

I didn't find it funny in the least. Even in the dark, Marie Thérèse looked stricken, grey with grief. 'He's been the kindest, the most attentive in years, and it was all because of you.'

'It was. It is. You are good and you deserve respect and kindness.'

The Queen flinched, and withdrew from Françoise's caresses. 'Madame, I thought you were my friend.'

Françoise wept openly. 'I am. I am.'

Marie Thérèse stamped her foot. 'No. You are not. You are his. Everything and everyone is his.'

The King erupted into the gallery, accompanied by a flurry of courtiers and servants, and berated his wife. 'You cannot behave like this! Interrupt my bedchamber! I come to you when I desire your company.'

The Queen turned to him, for once holding her ground. 'I asked you for one small thing. Do not choose a woman from my household. Françoise belonged to me. She was my friend.'

'She's very fond of you. We both are.'

The Queen gave a cry of despair. 'That makes the humiliation worse.'

She shook the kneeling Françoise off her with disgust and stepped away. She began to pace the gallery, pain and degradation giving way to anger. She looked around the gilded room with its beautifully carved furniture, pictures by Raphael, frescoed ceilings and Gobelins-made solid-silver chandeliers.

'What do you love?' she demanded of Louis. 'Your women? Your dogs? Your children. You love them. And your paintings. Yes, you love your paintings.'

She moved a chair towards Leda and me and, standing on it, unhooked Leda.

'No! Mona! No! What is she doing?' cried Leda.

'I can't hurt your women, I wouldn't touch your children, but this will hurt you,' spat Marie Thérèse.

Clutching Leda tight, before the King or anyone realised what she was doing, she ran outside with Leda in her arms to where the torches were blazing on the lawns.

With considerable force and rage, she smashed Leda upon her knee, and Leda snapped easily, where she'd broken before, and split again into three pieces, screaming out in terror.

'Mona! Mona Lisa! Save me!'

I could not. I was only real in our dream house. In the world itself I was helpless. I called her name. Leda. Leda.

Leda. My love. My life. And then, I could only listen and watch as she died.

Marie Thérèse hurled Leda onto the grass and grabbed the nearest torch and set her alight. She ignited instantly. Her walnut panel was old and dry, the lacquer flammable. The flames licked her skin. Her paint bubbled and blistered. Jupiter's white feathers were scarlet flares. Her babies burned in their shells.

'Leda! I love you.'

Leda screamed in agony, agony only I could hear.

'Mona!' Her cries became animal howls. She called my name again and again, and then there was silence and charred skewers of wood and dust.

The King stood beside his wife, aghast. Shocked at her sudden violence. He offered no rebuke. To him it was vandalism. Only I understood it was murder. They watched for a few minutes, and then Louis led the weeping queen back into the palace by another entrance. Françoise padded away into the darkness.

I was alone.

'Leda!'

I called her name and wept.

'They have killed you. Leda! Leda!'

She suffered as she died and I watched uselessly, neither able to save nor comfort her. I was bereft and disconsolate, horrified by the knowledge of her pain. I wished that I had hands so that I could claw my face, score my own paintwork; that I had a voice whose screams they must notice; but there was no one left in the world who could hear me. Instead, I would be forced to mourn alone, mute, watching her murderers day by day, untroubled, unpunished for their crimes.

My last connection to Leonardo was severed. Leda and Leonardo. I chanted their names as an incantation that only I could hear. Soon everyone who had seen Leda and witnessed her remarkable beauty would die, until only I remained. I, who could tell no one. Her beauty was a myth already fading as her ashes cooled in the rain that was starting to fall upon the palace lawn.

That night, I walked into our dream house alone but I found it a smouldering ruin. Only the burnt-out shell was left. I raced through the empty halls, frantic, and saw that all the frescoes were ruined and smudged; the branches of oak and sweetly flowering bramble and guelder rose smoke-stained and blackened. The house was silent. I called out for Leda but she did not answer. Every room was deserted, the furniture twisted and fire damaged. The walls encrusted with soot. The roof was fallen away, the bare beams contorted into ribs.

I ran from room to room, calling and calling, but again no one answered. My voice echoed. Everyone was gone. I stepped out into the garden where it was neither night nor day but some strange, unearthly twilight. No birds sang and the wind did not blow. The river was gobbled into blackness and fires burned. The scorched remains of fishing boats floated on its surface, the fishermen vanished. I was the only living creature in this ghastly, godforsaken place.

I searched for traces of Leda and her children but there was nothing, only smoke and emptiness. I sat down and hugged my knees and wept. Leda had died a second death. And without her, I could not linger in the dream house we had made. For nearly two hundred years we had played here together. Here, we had been real. Or believed we were. Without her, I could not make Cecco, Giovanni, Tommaso, La Cremona or Leonardo live once more. They were all dead and I was nothing but a lonely painting. I would never come here again.

Versailles, 1780

Summer

A hundred years passed. I waited to fade away from grief and unhappiness but I did not. I could not. There was no longer anyone left who could hear me, so I no longer spoke. Yet somehow, I remained, listening, watching, on the walls of the kings.

Marie Antoinette peered at me closely and with considerable disdain, leaning so near that the feathers protruding from the muslin of her hat tickled my nose. She had ventured into her husband's apartments, lured by the promise of a card game. I'd hung in the Petit Appartement du Roi for a century, mostly ignored by courtiers jostling to attend the King in the waking and sleeping ceremonies. The Queen had taken care to dress so that she toned exquisitely with the decor of his state rooms, in a gown of dusty pink silk, with striped ribbons and trimmed with frothy cream Point de France lace. King Louis XVI, concerned at his beloved's tendency to win and lose entire fortunes, had banned her from playing cards in her own apartments. Frustrated, she'd persuaded him to allow her an intimate game for twenty in his rooms. A green baize table was set up beneath me.

'I don't like the way she's looking at me. She's watching my hand,' she complained, adjusting an ostrich plume in her hair as she sat back down. 'I'm not sure she isn't going to give me away.'

'*Non*, my love,' said the King. 'Mona Lisa keeps her secrets.'

'I don't like her at all. Too brown. Too dark. And she stares too much.' Marie Antoinette gave a dismissive wave.

I felt that beside her I was wearing the wrong dress to the party. She was a rococo reverie, in the finest damask silk, while my dark gown had become darker still beneath the layers of lacquer; the exquisite embroidery upon my bosom was evidence of a painter's genius but was nothing to a queen.

'Why is she in a black veil? Is she a widow? Who is she mourning? Did she bore her husband to death?' she demanded.

I was not in mourning when I was painted, and yet I had come to be grateful for my veil. I grieved for so many souls. I'd had a hundred years to weep for Leda, and yet I wept for her still. My veil was a miracle, painted and yet giving the illusion of absolute translucence. The Queen chose not to see.

The King laughed. 'Madame, my great-grandfather, the Sun King, admired Mona Lisa so much that he kept her in his bedchamber, and blew her a kiss each night before he went to sleep.'

The kiss was apocryphal, but the rest was true. After witnessing the wrath of Marie Thérèse and her destruction of Leda, Louis decided he needed to keep me safe. He removed me from Fontainebleau and took me to Versailles. He had me placed where he considered most secure of all – the Roi's bedroom suite. It was a dubious and unwelcome honour. I was forced to witness the gruntings and false protestations of pleasure of the young women of the court, unable to refuse the King's propositions. The Sun King, much like Salaì, enjoyed his carnal performances to be observed. I was a reluctant and weary audience, just as the women were compelled into being players.

The present Louis appeared much diverted by Marie Antoinette's animosity towards me. 'It's said that my great-grandfather confided to her all the important affairs of state.'

'Because he didn't have to listen to her advice.'

This was remarkably astute. I refrained from giving the Sun King the benefit of my wisdom. He wouldn't have listened even if he could have heard me. He was a king and they heed no one.

The royal party returned to their card game. The Queen lost. The King winced. He must pay her debts. The nobility around the table held their breath; they would be paid, but it was uncomfortable, they longed to leave. Footmen poured chilled champagne and brought dishes of sorbet. A line of perspiration tingled upon the King's upper lip. The Queen glared at me, as though it were all my fault.

'She is so superior. And so *brown*.' The Queen gave a fretful sigh and wrinkled her nose. 'She lacks joy. She knows too many things, none of them good.'

This much regrettably was true.

'I want her out of your apartments. Have her put somewhere else where I don't have to see her again. Choose a Fragonard or an Elisabeth Vigée Le Brun to put in her place.'

The King took her hand and kissed it, all embarrassment and irritation at her debts forgiven, charmed by her eccentricity. 'Madame, my love, it is done.'

Versailles, 1791

Winter

The office of the Directeur Général of the Palace of Versailles was gloomy and dank. He kept several cats who were ineffective at keeping away the rodents who had free rein, and were frequently my only company. I endured more than ten years, relegated to obscurity, half-hidden behind a door, only able to glimpse the triangular greens of the parterre through an unwashed window.

I listened to the distant thunder of the Revolution from my dusty corner. The Directeur Général disappeared one day. New people came and went again. The ineffectual cats remained. The mice popped in and out of their holes, unconcerned about the change in regime.

One morning, I observed that the grounds outside were full of carts and wagons, men lugging paintings and sculptures from the palace into the waiting vehicles. The wind blustered, grabbing at the coverings on the pictures, tearing away rags from the sculptures, revealing naked arms in the freezing December air. The mirrored pools of the park were solid with ice, slimy and unreflective. The chateau hummed with activity, teams of soldiers and workmen helping with a colossal removal task. The royal family had been permitted to take with them to their imprisonment in the Tuileries Palace their preferred paintings and furniture and treasures, but this was a consignment on a vastly different scale.

I strained for snatches of conversation. My corridor was out of the way, the vanguard of rodents and long-departed servants. After several hours of waiting, two workmen at last shuffled past. From their footsteps, lugging something heavy.

'*Merde*. Don't think much of this one. Proper ugly.'

'Do you think? Wouldn't stick him in a museum. But the wife would like him, I reckon.'

Then another voice, raised in outrage.

'It doesn't matter what you think! It only matters what Citizen Fragonard decides. He chooses what's coming to the Paris *musée*. If he declares it's no good then it'll be auctioned off next week. Your missus is free to bid on it then.' The voice dissolved into laughter.

Citizen Fragonard. The name was like the ringing of the duomo bell. The Queen's former favourite artist, disgraced and then imprisoned. His style had fallen out of favour in the fervour of the Revolution, but somehow he still had friends to help him into freedom and a position in the new people's museum in Paris. Yet it seemed that he would not find me tucked away here. Like Leda, I was falling out of living memory. Soon I too would be little more than a rumour. The name Leonardo da Vinci no longer mattered as it once had except to me. I tried to accept my fate. I too would be auctioned and end up on the wall of a tavern or perhaps a brothel. I had endured worse.

The voices faded and the footsteps disappeared. No one came near my room for the rest of the day. I watched as painting after painting was lifted onto a caravan of wagons. Afternoon slid into early evening. Horses huffed steam, and pawed the half-frozen mud. Men pulled their coats tightly around them. Dusk fell like a heavy curtain. The red eye of the sun glowered in the sky, and then slid angrily below the horizon, leaving me in darkness. The last of the wagons left. The palace was empty, the silence sepulchral. I listened to the scrape and skitter of the mice.

A little later, I heard the shuffle of footsteps. A tramp, perhaps. They came here occasionally. He entered the office, holding a lamp, a yolk of light in the gloom. His clothes grimy and tattered. His overcoat was patched and the scarf pulled up high around his cheeks was riddled with holes. A tramp indeed. But with a lamp? I was puzzled. He padded slowly to the window and looked out, staring down at the black triangles of the north parterre, and sighed. He remained there for several minutes, apparently lost in reverie, watching the blanched moon suspended over the water. As he turned back, I felt the thrill of recognition. He was not a vagrant, but Jean Fragonard himself. He must be on a last perusal of the chateau. Before the Revolution, he came to Versailles as a guest of Marie Antoinette. He had withered since – his cheeks were sunken and his coat hung from thin shoulders – but it was the same man.

'Jean-Honoré Fragonard!' I called. It had been more than a hundred years since I'd tried to speak, and when I did, my voice was cracked and strange. A croak, a creak of wood. 'I remember you, do you remember me?'

He hesitated, and for a moment I thought he heard me, but then he shrugged and tugged his scarf tighter and moved towards the doorway. I was desperate. He was going to quit the office without seeing me. I remained hidden behind the open door. In the murk he didn't notice I was there. Then a fat rat scuttled across the floor. Bold and fearless, it paused in the middle of the room and sat up on its haunches. Fragonard startled, disgusted. He looked around for something to hurl at the creature. There was nothing.

'Be gone!' he yelled.

The rat watched him, unafraid.

Fragonard reached for the door handle, and slammed it shut to smash the rat out of the way. The creature scarpered. Fragonard shuddered with relief. Wiped his forehead, and then glanced up. He saw me.

'Mona Lisa. It's you! I thought perhaps you were stolen or lost. Nearly forgotten, but not quite by everyone.'

He brought the lamp closer and contemplated me intimately, and then smiled. It had been many years since someone smiled at me with rapture.

He chuckled. 'You know. You're so lifelike. Perhaps it's the light. But it makes one want to chat with you.'

'Good,' I said. My voice was still rasping and odd. 'It's been a long time since anyone spoke to me at all.'

'I'm almost tempted to keep you,' he muttered. 'You're the most precious of all the collection. And no one would ever know I took you. But if I did and they caught me stealing, they'd kill me for it.' He gave a low laugh. 'Now, that would be something worth dying for.'

He thrust his hands into his pockets. 'But I can't do it. More people than me ought to see you, Mona Lisa. Better men than I have loved you. Greater men than I will love you again. I'll make sure they take good care of you. The very best.'

I was moved and I thanked him, even though he only heard the rustling of the wind banging against the window frame.

I had been relegated to the office of the Directeur Général by the Queen because I was not a Fragonard, and yet it was Fragonard himself who saved me and sent me to the new gallery in the Louvre Palace. Despite the beauty of many of the other paintings, they were poor companions. They were not friends but shadows. Some I'd known in Fontainebleau and Versailles, and several were painted by my old friends Raphael and Michelangelo. Yet, for all their beauty, they were silent. None of them could listen or see. No other picture was like me.

For several years, Fragonard would visit me in the Louvre, and come and sit sadly beside me, and I listened as he talked of the old days when he was loved by Marie Antoinette. He liked my company. He was broken and bewildered by the new art and the new France and he was soon dismissed from the *musée*, but he would call in all the same to see me. Then one week he did not come. Nor the next. And I understood that he would come no more and this friend too was dead. No one else spoke to me. In the years and decades that followed I began to forget that I had ever had a voice at all. I felt myself placed in a prison, of walls and also of silence. Yet I watched and listened, searching in the faces of those who came to the gallery for the vestiges of those I'd known. The sun rose and set. I survived.

The painter makes his work permanent for very many years, and of such excellence that it keeps alive ... those parts which nature, for all her power, cannot manage to preserve. How many paintings have preserved the image of a divine beauty which in its natural manifestation has been rapidly overtaken by time or death!

Leonardo da Vinci, *On Painting, Codex Urbina*
1482–1518

Florence, 1515

Winter

*I*t's time for us to return again to Florence with Leonardo. Although I did not want to leave Rome, if I must come to Florence, then I am glad it is to Lisa's garden. I have not seen Lisa del Giocondo for more than ten years and I'm curious to meet her once more. Time has softened my animal spirits, if not my appearance, and I'm almost pleased at the prospect of seeing her. Lisa is the shell from which I emerged, long since discarded and set aside, but once she nurtured the seed of me. I know Leonardo wants to call upon her, and I love him too well to deny him this pleasure.

Leonardo carries me along the walkways in my oak case. He takes me everywhere with him now; we are never parted. It's also ten years since I last visited the Giocondo villa. Even in the thin November light the garden is a place of mystery, a labyrinth of pleasure, of dark green hedges and running rills. We are secluded from the world as the low winter sun glints off the orb of the duomo roof. The honied tiles of the city roofs are far below. Skinny cyprus trees shiver in the wind, and the statues glower at us from icy pools, where drowsy fishes slink amongst fleshy clumps of sodden leaves. The earth is bare and smeared with frost, and the garden whispers of death. The trees are stripped and scalloped. All life is hunkered deep below the soil. In the breaths between the wind, the silence is glottal.

Then Lisa calls out for us to join her on the pavilion. A servant has lit a brazier for warmth, so she and Leonardo can eat outside while admiring the garden. Leonardo sets me upon an easel, tenderly away from the flames. Lisa stands before it, examining me with little pleasure.

'I wanted to see her,' she says at last, wringing her hands, 'and now I wish I hadn't. She looks like I used to, not so long ago.'

Leonardo replies with a rueful smile, 'Oh painting, you keep alive the transient beauty of mortals! But, Madonna Lisa, your beauty hasn't fled yet.'

It's true, it has not. And yet we are no longer mirror images. Our characters were always different but our faces were almost the same. In truth, she was always the greater beauty. Now we are sisters perhaps and she is the elder. We do not yet look like mother and daughter. That is still to come, but there has been a parting of the ways. Time has moved on for her, even though it never shall for me.

Two servants appear and spread the table with a fine linen cloth, and Leonardo and Lisa sit down in readiness. She appears subdued and preoccupied, forgetting her role as hostess, and it falls to Leonardo to make conversation.

'Your husband is well?' he asks, always polite.

Lisa nods, thanking him for his kind solicitations. Francesco del Giocondo is not here or Leonardo would not have brought me, although the silk merchant must have given up hope of gaining possession of the painting of his wife many years ago. I am safe with Lisa. She does not want me. I remind her too much of her mortality. So many covet me and yet the woman who inspired me does not value me or even like me. Perhaps I should be hurt. I am not. It is a relief to be looked at without being coveted.

I glance out over the garden while the servants bring the two of them plates of food and set them down upon the tablecloth. Oranges and roasted eels rubbed with spices, salads of bitter leaves and walnuts. Even if Leonardo painted me a tongue, I still could not taste. In Rome he took me many times to the Ospedale at Santo Spirito. There I have seen a tongue laid out upon the table as on a butcher's block, pulled out by its roots, blue and red and foaming with spittle. I have watched as he sliced it in half and prised apart its layers. With Leonardo I have peeped into the secretive parts of the human body, but afterwards in the *bottega* while he drew a cross section of the human tongue, and I helped him annotate it, it did not help me to eat.

'Mona Lisa, you are very quiet,' he says. 'What are you thinking?'

'It doesn't matter,' I say.

He has forgotten that we are not alone, but it's of no consequence as Lisa del Giocondo believes he is speaking to her. She is touched. Men do not often ask her what she is thinking.

'You are here with Pope Leo?' she asks.

'He does me a great honour. I am charged with the designs of the *entrata*.'

Leonardo moves his chair so that the sun is no longer dazzling him. He has fashioned himself a pair of blue spectacles in order to better examine solar bodies, but on occasions such as this, it also protects him from the sun's glare. Lisa laughs to see him look so peculiar, and holds out her hand for the spectacles. He obliges with a smile and she tries them on.

'You look charming, Madonna. Perhaps I should add them to your portrait.'

'No thank you very much,' I say.

She passes them back to him, but he doesn't put them back on, instead placing a hand upon her arm, sensing that she is troubled. Her fingers are like needles weaving in and out of each other.

'I am looking forward to the *entrata*,' she says, her voice falsely bright. 'It's to be so spectacular, I hear even Michelangelo and Raphael have come to watch.'

He shakes his head. 'No, they're simply here as part of His Holiness's grand retinue to impress the young French king. Michelangelo is always foul-tempered but even Raphael has lost his usual sweetness at being ordered to Florence.'

The Pope adores Leonardo's spectaculars. His designs for costumes are the most inventive and his staging and pulley systems the cleverest. No one else will do, for what must be the greatest pageant of all to mark Pope Leo's summit in Florence with the French king, the absurdly young Francis. He's barely twenty-one, and he's conquered Milan and the Pope is nervous. Authority must be asserted. The pageant must be astonishing enough to humble a young king with a penchant for empire building. No one but Leonardo can be trusted with such a task. The Pope is residing just outside the city, waiting until the last day of November; only then, on the day of the celebration itself, will he ride into Florence in triumph on the back of an elephant, gifted to him by the King of Portugal. Leonardo has promised to place me somewhere I can gain a glimpse of this most magnificent of beasts.

'His Holiness was a gentle boy for a de' Medici. He loved music and candied chestnuts. But his brother—' Her voice trails away.

'Giuliano de' Medici. Il Magnifico?'

'Yes. Giuliano de' Medici came to see me recently with Lorenzo de' Medici.'

'His nephew?'

'Yes. Do you know him? He rules Florence now. Sympathetic. A good man, I thought. But it seems after all that he isn't very good, Leonardo. He should ask someone to pray for his soul.' She is speaking very fast, and she shoves her plate of eel away from her, revolted. 'They came here to see my husband, but when they found he wasn't here— Oh, it doesn't matter. It doesn't matter at all.'

The needles of her fingers have become frantic. Leonardo leans towards her, his face creased with concern.

'Of course it matters, it matters to me.'

She sees his affection and distress for her and relents.

'It was nothing. Please don't trouble yourself. Really, it was nothing at all. A joke. A silly joke, to them at least. Giuliano wanted to see me. In all honesty, I don't think he wanted to see my husband at all.'

She pauses to catch her breath which is coming fast, in gasps, and she is pale, but her cheeks are blotched and her throat mottled. She cannot meet Leonardo's eye.

'He – il Magnifico – talked about your painting. About her,' she points to me, full of accusation. 'He said that he couldn't ... have ... a painting. That *she* wasn't real, but I was, even if I was old. And that he'd have me instead.'

Her voice is steady and soft as though she is describing a dream.

'He and Lorenzo told me to come with them to the pagoda. I didn't want to. I told them Francesco would be back any minute but they kept laughing and pulling me along. What could I do? They're Medici. I'm only a del Giocondo. What might they have done to my husband if I didn't do what they said?'

'Did they dishonour you?' asks Leonardo, stricken.

'No. I pleaded with them and at last they let me go. Only my pride was wounded.'

Her hands flutter at her throat and chest like tiny birds. She is trembling as if from fever.

The servants appear to clear the table and Leonardo dismisses them, impatient and irritable.

'Madonna Lisa, I am glad you were not hurt.'

I stare at her, and I see that Leonardo is wrong. Both of them are wrong; she is wounded, only we cannot see the injuries except in the shaking of her body, and the frantic flickering of her fingers.

She looks across at me, jabs her finger towards me, full of resentment. 'I wanted to see her again. I kept thinking that somehow the error was mine. That I had committed some sin. But I see now that I had not. It's her. She leads men into madness and sin.'

Her voice tremors and cracks, and she balls her thin hands into fists, and her tongue darts along dry lips.

'No,' says Leonardo, firm. 'It's Giuliano and Lorenzo who chose to sin. No one made them. If you blame my picture then you must blame me, for I painted her. Do you wish to accuse me of the assault?'

She hesitates, but only for a moment. She adores Leonardo for he is her friend and a man of great *virtù*.

'No. Of course not.'

'Did you tell your husband?'

'Yes. He confronted them.'

'Good. I'm glad.'

Lisa turns and stares benignly towards the evergreen pagoda where the seduction took place, as though trying to see if the events are printed upon the twisting trees and the dark canopy. There is nothing there. Only the breeze and the eddies of ash rising from the brazier and drifting downwards.

Lisa looks at Leonardo. 'I don't want to see her again.'

To my surprise I experience a flicker of sadness; then, like the feathers of ash, it's gone.

I've never seen Leonardo so angry. He is a firestorm of fury. Thunder-lit and incoherent with curses. He paces, spitting out his worries about Lisa, his contempt for our patron, his fate at being harnessed to the whim of fools. At our lodgings Salaì and Cecco reason with him to temper his rage before he speaks to il Magnifico. I plead too, my affection for him heightening my anxiety; he must not enter the Medici court until he has calmed himself, but Giuliano has ordered Leonardo to bring me to the Palazzo Vecchio, where he has honoured guests who wish to see and admire *La Gioconda*.

Il Magnifico waits at the palace, overseeing the plans for the *entrata trionfale*.

'Where is Leda?' he demands, irritated.

'In Rome, *illustrissimo mio Signore*, I brought only Mona Lisa to Florence.'

I miss Leda too. These weeks are the longest we've ever been apart and time drags. I wanted her to come, but Leonardo refused. Her panel is too large and difficult to transport. He doesn't want to risk damaging her just because I pine for her when I'm not with her.

Giuliano grunts in annoyance. 'I hope you have brought drawings at least. His Holiness wishes you to show them to His Highness, Francis, the Most Christian King of France.'

Leonardo assents, but I'm vexed on his behalf. He, Raphael and Michelangelo are here as a more distinguished version of the Pope's buffoons. They are no different from the captive elephant, here to perform and dazzle.

After Giuliano's companions have duly looked upon me, sloppy with admiration, and been led out to feast upon further Medici treasures, Leonardo confronts him with Lisa's accusation, and Giuliano smiles fondly, as if amused by the recollection. It does not occur to him that Leonardo or his *garzone* would be anything other than warmly diverted by his account.

'Ah, Lisa del Giocondo. Lisa. I called on her with my nephew Lorenzo. She was in the garden all alone and so sad, in that charming villa above the city. It was our duty as gentlemen to offer her company and amusement.'

Leonardo turns very white as Giuliano speaks, until he resembles one of the bloodless corpses in the Ospedale di Santo Spirito.

'We led her to a pretty little hut in the wilderness at the bottom of the garden. We tried to tempt her honour, but she refused.'

He describes her refusal with bemused indignation and wonder.

To my disgust, he makes it sound like an Arcadian ritual, a pair of gods descended from Mount Olympus to seduce a pretty yet ordinary mortal, only to be amazingly rebuffed. Yet I see a woman, frightened and repulsed by the probing fingers and tongues and lechery of two men of power. Lisa Gioconda, mother of six children, the roses in her cheeks withering, but still she is not protected from men like Giuliano. Their influence makes them entitled to pluck fruit where they choose. I marvel that Lisa managed to refuse them. He speaks of her attempted seduction as though it is a joke, some scene in a comedy that the pontiff's buffoons will enact after the more holy cardinals have retired, and the rest have drunk sufficient wine to be leery enough to yearn for bawdy entertainment.

Giuliano grins. 'But the best part of the story is yet to come. Listen.'

Leonardo looks agonised. While Lisa posed for him, he became extremely fond of her. He cannot bear to hear of her distress from the man who inflicted it, and for whom it means nothing. Even Salaì looks uneasy and he adores the lewdest of capers. But no one can interrupt or contradict il Magnifico when he's mid flow. He starts to splutter with laughter, only just managing to spew out his words.

'Lisa must have recounted what happened to her husband, as Francesco del Giocondo came to see us in Florence a week later, demanding an audience. I'm amused, not worried. What's he going to do? Bring his sword ready for a duel?' Giuliano pauses to wipe a tear, so amused by the memory. 'Anyway. It's better than I could have hoped. Francesco wasn't angry with us but thoroughly put out with his wife. He came in, all sweaty and holding his cap, gasping with obsequiousness. He's worried that Lisa's rejection offended us. He was tripping over himself as he grovelled, swearing that he's one of the Medicis' close friends.'

'That does indeed sound like the noble Francesco del Giocondo,' I say, appalled at the account. 'Concerned that his wife's virtue and her well-being might get in the way of his ambition.'

'What did you say to Francesco, Magnifico?' asks Leonardo, frowning.

'Oh, I told him that he was indeed one of our most valued servants.'

Only servant, I note, not friend. Everyone despises Francesco del Giocondo, even the despicable Giuliano de' Medici.

'*Vostra Eccellenza*,' says Leonardo with a bow, 'I beseech you, do not see Madonna del Giocondo again. Do not approach her alone or in company. Do not seek her out. Pretend as if she is a stranger to you from this day, I beg of you, *illustrissimo mio Signore*.'

Giuliano's mild gaze curdles to instant spite.

'You forget yourself,' he says. 'You are not her husband. You're certainly not her lover; from what I've heard, your interests lie elsewhere.' He looks at Salaì with antipathy. 'A repugnant deviation of holy law that up till now, we've been content to ignore.'

The silence hangs in the air, dangerous.

'Apologise, Leonardo from Vinci.'

Leonardo hesitates, bows. 'I beg mercy for any offence I have caused you, *Vostra Eccellenza.*' He looks up, studies Giuliano's face beseechingly. 'And I beg once more that you do not see her again. Please, do not hurt her.'

Giuliano's neck turns red with anger. 'How dare you address me so? You presume too much. You are a painter not a prince. Do you wish to fight? Will you duel me with your brush, old man?'

Suddenly, he stops and his fury dissipates into laughter as though Leonardo is not worthy of his wrath, only ridicule. The servants in the room eye us like frightened cattle.

Giuliano stalks across the room until he is staring at me, his lips almost brushing mine.

'The likeness is uncanny, or was,' he says. 'If I kissed this Lisa, licked her, she could not object.'

'The latest layer of varnish is not dry,' says Leonardo. 'Your spittle will spoil the lifelike effect.'

This is a lie. He has not worked on me for weeks. But unlike Francesco del Giocondo, Leonardo will do anything to protect those he loves.

I stare back at Giuliano. He smells of the tripe he had for supper. His face might be handsome but there is cruelty beneath the charm. He is a Medici like all the rest.

Leonardo has refused food or drink, turning down even a cup of lentil soup. He relaxes a little as he draws, studying his dissection sketches, adding another observation in his left-hand scrawl, his face creased with concentration. I notice, tucked in amongst them, the drawings of my boy, the tightly furled foetus. Leonardo has envisioned him from another angle: face on, his ankles crossed, the bulb of his head nestled upon the nubs of his knees, the seed-pods of his toes, the wavering fingers, the nip of his heel and the tiny brine-stung hole of his anus.

A visitor has come to call. Tonight he is not welcome. We hear the servant open the door, and hope that he has simply come to deliver some message, but the leaden footsteps thrust themselves inside.

I will him to go away. The footsteps descend the stairs. Leonardo glances up, startled, annoyed to be disturbed.

'Da Vinci!'

Michelangelo. Rarely has a visitor been so unwelcome. He stands in the lodgings amongst the cascades of paper, and takes in Leonardo drawing in the firelight beside the high window.

'So, we're all here for this absurd *entrata*. To watch a pope parade upon an elephant,' he says.

'This pope needs an elephant,' I add quietly.

'I hope all is well with you, Michelangelo,' says Leonardo, setting his work aside and pouring him wine from a carafe.

'It is well with me only when I have a chisel in my hand.'

Michelangelo takes the wine, sips, and then, still cross, looks about for something else to be annoyed by.

'You hardly ever call upon me in Rome.'

'Are we friends? Why would I come, Michelangelo?'

'Everyone does. They come when I'm working and ask stupid questions. It's aggravating.'

'Then it's good I don't,' says Leonardo.

Michelangelo has weathered like a statue left out of doors over the last decade. His frown is permanent and he wears his restless disquiet like a rash upon his skin, scratching at his arms and face. Despite his vast renown and corresponding riches, his clothes are ragged.

'Can you not order some new boots?' I ask.

'I like these,' he shrugs, indifferent. He steps closer and peers at me. 'I see he's brought you back to Florence.'

'She comes everywhere with me. We're never apart,' says Leonardo.

'And yet you're still not quite finished, are you?' says Michelangelo.

'I'll never be finished with her,' says Leonardo.

'I mean, you're remarkable, Madonna Lisa,' says Michelangelo, 'but you have to admit that, in the time he's painted you, Leda and a pile of sketches, I've done the Sistine Chapel, and about a dozen sculptures. Now I've started work on the tomb of Pope Julius.'

He gloats without humour.

'Not even the heavens set the limit to your ambition,' says Leonardo, his eyebrows also rising heavenward in exasperation.

'The greater danger for most of us lies not in setting our aim too high and falling short, but in setting our aim too low, and achieving our mark,' replies Michelangelo.

'And yet, despite all your remarkable achievements, you have never succeeded in creating a picture like me, old friend,' I chide.

He hesitates, pride pricked, and then for a moment the old smile of sweetness cracks the stone of his countenance.

'It is true. You've got me,' he says and bows in deference. 'Everything pales next to you, Mona Lisa. I've tried and tried but I can't give a painting life like you. They all want speech. I've begged and pleaded with my statues to talk but they cannot answer. It takes a great miracle to make a painted woman a real one.'

I don't tell him that Leonardo has made another one since we saw him last. He hasn't met Leda. Since it already seems that, for a moment at least, the arrogant man is humbled and forlorn.

'The Sistine Chapel and Hebrew Slaves are miracle enough,' says Leonardo.

Immediately Michelangelo glowers, stiffening. 'I didn't come here to beg for compliments. Keep your scraps.'

Leonardo feels his rebuke and says nothing more. No one gets anywhere quarrelling with Michelangelo. We watch him warily. It's like having one of the lions chained in the Piazza della Signoria visit the studio. His stink is almost as bad. He prowls, inspecting, picking things up, and setting them down with a derisive snort. I observe the watchful faces of Cecco, Giovanni, Tommaso and Salaì eyeing him from the stairs and note that none of them are brave enough to venture down.

He picks up a sketch Leonardo made of Salaì posing as St John. Salaì had been standing nude for hours and, bored, had begun to play with his cock, and so Leonardo had drawn him exactly so. A naked, rigid angel, with the smirk of Bacchus. Michelangelo studies the drawing with contempt. Leonardo tenses.

'This is wicked. It's also ugly,' complains Michelangelo.

'It's a piece of fun. A joke between friends,' I say.

'All of Rome knows they are more than friends.' He turns to face Leonardo. 'You make the word Florentine a filthy pun,' he spits.

Coming from Michelangelo this strikes me as unfair. The *garzoni* in his *bottega* are chosen for their beauty every bit as much as their talent. He and Leonardo share that in common. Although I don't believe he has taken a lover amongst the fellows in his workshop. He seethes with too much anger and self-loathing; it coats his skin like another layer of stone dust. I heard that he found his Sistine Adam while roaming a building site seeking out the handsomest of men. I wonder if I ought to remind him. I decide not.

'Michelangelo, I know you've found God since we last saw you. But did you have to lose your sense of humour?' I complain.

He stares at me confounded, and also pleased. 'Did I have a sense of humour?'

'Yes. You were always conceited and unbearable, but you were also sometimes funny. Even on purpose.'

For a moment it looks like he might smile.

'For her, I'll say nothing to the Pope about this,' he says, waving the sketch of Salaì. 'But when we're back in Rome, come and see my studio sometimes. Have some respect.'

He stands up to leave, and I think we're safe, but then he stops. He glances down and notices the drawings of the unborn child. My adored boy.

'What blasphemy is this?' he whispers.

'Knowledge isn't sacrilegious,' says Leonardo softly. 'We saw to it that they were buried together. Two beings, one soul.'

Michelangelo turns ashen. 'Are you saying that the child has no soul? If it has no soul it cannot enter the Kingdom of Heaven. That is heresy.'

'They share a soul,' I say, trying to placate him. 'They enter together.'

He stares at me, his face contorted with agony. 'He has fouled you. Filled you with sin. I'm sorry. I cannot save you. Not from this.'

He runs his fingers through his hair, leaving a slick of dust in them. He looks tormented. 'I said you were a miracle. I always thought you a gift from the divine. Touched by God or Our Lady. I'm not certain that you're not something darker. Sorcery or witchcraft, sent from the devil himself.'

'Don't be absurd!' I object, incensed. 'We're old friends, you and I.'

'No longer.'

'Please, calm yourself,' I say, provoked and frightened. 'We'll buy a papal indulgence for the sin you say we have committed.'

'No.'

He strides towards the fire and it looks as if he will toss the drawings into the blaze. The red of the flames shines on the foetus and the child seems to glow warmer still, pulsing with life. The paper shakes in his hand. Michelangelo can't do it. The drawing might be blasphemy but it is also beautiful and, while he is a man of God, he is also an artist. He slams down the drawings on the table beside Leonardo.

He leaves without another word.

Leonardo reaches for a glass of wine. His hand trembles and he spills drops in his beard; against the white, they look like beads of blood.

'What will happen now?' I ask.

Leonardo steadies himself with another drink. He gives me a rueful smile.

'Michelangelo will denounce us to the Pope for heresy and blasphemy.'

It is the last few days of November, and Leonardo is busy overseeing the preparations in the city for the greatest *festa* it has ever seen. The French king declined to travel as far as Rome and, in truth, the pontiff was not sure he wanted to hazard inviting the young conqueror into the heart of his empire. So, instead, Leonardo has metamorphosed Florence into Rome, erecting reproductions of the Eternal City's landmarks in the piazzas of Florence. Hercules now stands beside Michelangelo's David in the square outside the western door of the Palazzo Vecchio, demanding all onlookers recall the glories of Rome's past beside the brilliance of her present. Eight vast triumphal arches have been constructed across the city along the route of the procession.

The day before the *festa*, the papal summons arrives. I insist Leonardo takes me with him; perhaps by reminding His Holiness of the sheer brilliance of his skill, his sentence might be commuted. We ride out of the city, the master, Salaì, Cecco and I, in a melancholy, doom-laden procession. The Pope is staying in a villa at Marignolle, a small village just beyond the city gates. A groom takes our horses. The papal court is squeezed into the villa, which although commodious appears cramped with the vast entourage. Tents have been set up across the gardens for the overspill and I see miserable-looking Swiss Guards standing to attention in the mist. Leonardo is ushered into the papal presence where half a dozen musicians crowd onto a loggia, the music wafting across an open landing. A fire smokes with damp wood and seven cardinals cower before it, warming their hands as the logs sputter and spit crimson sparks. I notice Giuliano de' Medici picking his teeth at the back of the hall. He ignores Leonardo.

The Pope himself is jammed into a wooden throne, and heaped with blankets. He is sweating like a buttered onion, but does not ask for the covers to be removed. He smiles to see Leonardo.

'Everything is ready for tomorrow?' he enquires. 'We are most looking forward to it.'

'Yes, Your Holiness. Rehearsals have been going well. We nearly ran out of gold paint, but more has arrived from Venice.'

The Pope nods with little interest. Shortages of gold paint do not concern him. He waves vaguely towards a table brimming with bacchanalian morsels, set too close to the fire and starting to wilt. 'Are you hungry?'

Leonardo shakes his head. He is not here to eat. He wants to know his fate.

Pope Leo grunts. 'You have entertained me. But there are accusations of your unseemly conduct and even witchcraft.'

Leonardo opens his mouth to voice his objections, but the pontiff holds up his hand for silence and Leonardo dare not interrupt.

'The rumours of witchcraft are, I believe, without foundation. I have never heard a painting speak. Has anyone else?' He glances about the court.

No one says a word. There are a few sniggers, and ripples of laughter.

The Pope continues. 'You have rivals amongst artists. Your work as a painter is indeed marvellous if slow. And that which provokes envy and whispers amongst your peers gains you friends amongst your betters.'

The Pope pauses, waiting for Leonardo to acknowledge his gratitude, which he duly does with a deep bow.

'Your skill at creating scenery and clever designs for our carnivals is unsurpassed. And so, on account of your skill as a painter, as a conjuror of theatre and spectacle, I shall not heed these rumours and grant you some measure of clemency.'

With trepidation, I watch Leonardo who has turned ashen.

The Pope's voice is loud and clear, spittle flying. 'But I forbid you from going to the Ospedale. No more anatomy or dissections. No more alchemy and experiments. No more investigations of the human body. Some knowledge belongs only to God. You fly close to heresy. Fly closer and you will be burned.'

Whether His Holiness means that literally or figuratively isn't immediately clear.

He smiles coolly. 'We are fond of you and your festivals. Stay here and produce them for us. But nothing else. Nothing else is wanted, not by us, and not by God.'

To return to Rome and make papier mâché suns and moons and not investigate the secrets of the universe, to paint in fear that the subject is not holy but heretical, is a bleak and unhappy prospect. Leonardo glances in desperation towards il Magnifico, his patron and the man who once called him brother, waiting for him to plead for leniency. Giuliano meets his eye, and gives a tiny smile and says not a word. Leonardo has no friends here.

We leave in silence. They have humiliated Leonardo. We stumble out into the cold air. He looks up at the leaden sky. 'The Medici made me and destroyed me.' His eyes are filmy with tears. I do not know how to comfort him.

The weather is fine. A thin, steely light and no rain but a wind as sharp as broken glass. The actors in their costumes shiver, lips tinged with blue. Carmine rouge is doled out, to bloom their cheeks and mouths. Leonardo has brought me in my case so I can witness the *feste* by his side in the Piazza della Signoria. Thousands of men have laboured for a month to ready the city, making things that will last for only a day. There is a massive paper castle at the edge of the piazza held aloft on twenty-two columns; it buckles in the wind and rages like a living thing against its rope tethers. Along the streets are screens decorated with gods and goddesses, and the unfinished eastern façade of the duomo is masked by a colossal tapestry.

Here in the piazza each triumphal arch is ready with the shivering actors assembled, the musicians poised while the crowds are gathered twenty deep. Flags flutter from every window – Medici red and blue, and gold for the House of Valois – and faces crowd beside them for a view of the piazza. Cannons have been wheeled into the centre of the city poised to herald the arrival of the great men with fire and thunder. Veiled noblewomen in dresses of velvet trimmed with bobbin lace and laden with furs and jewels pace the empty platform set out for the Pope. Many of them, overcome at the prospect of a blessing from His Holiness, sob with joy and clasp their children close.

Yet the beacon signalling that the Pope and Francis, the Most Christian King of France, are beginning the

procession has not been lit. The crowd jostles and murmurs. They are cold and restless. A trickster of a gust
hurries through the square, lifting the women's skirts and
tossing hats. A boy pokes one of the thin, ragged lions
sleeping in its cage and it roars, angry and disconsolate.
The sound is raw and feral, and for a moment hushes the
crowd which panics at the animal and savage brought
into the city. Then the rumpus builds again, impatient and
restive.

'What's happening?' hisses Salaì.

Leonardo shakes his head and gathers his cloak around
his shoulders. He does not know. The duomo bell tolls
the half hour. The impatience of the crowd is turning to
anger. There isn't even a hanging or a flogging to amuse
them and the wind bares its teeth. A sweating and breathless papal courier arrives with a note for Leonardo and
presses it into his hands. Leonardo tears it open and reads,
scowling.

'King Francis declines to take part in the *entrata*.
Absolutely refuses. He won't take the role planned for
him. He declines to mount the white charger and ride
behind the Pope. He says, apparently, "I care not a whit
for processions."'

'Perhaps someone ought to have checked?' I say.

'Of course they did! Everything was agreed with courtiers over weeks of interminable discussions. This is a
monarch's display of power.'

'Yet it's very similar to a child's tantrum.'

'Well, I shan't tell him that,' replies Leonardo.

We glance at the crowd with unease. Then, as we
wait, a train of horses ride out into the piazza with a
thunderclap of hoofs upon stone, not along the

processional route but through a narrow corridor of a lane at the rear of the square. At once, the piazza swirls with soldiers and cavalry bearing the colours of the Valois kings. There are cries of confusion and terror, irritation and discomfort, instantly given over to fear – it's an invasion, a surprise attack; the brilliant and scheming young French king has sprung a siege upon the city. Yet I can see there are only a dozen cavalry gathered around Francis, swords still sheathed. The soldiers appear bored, intent more on breakfast than on war. This doesn't look like an attack to me, but something else. Amongst the Valois-liveried warriors are several of the Pope's Swiss Guards in Medici gold and scarlet. Then I see Giuliano de' Medici riding amongst them on the white stallion intended for the King.

Il Magnifico himself leads the French king into the Palazzo Vecchio. Neither man, Medici prince nor the great king, dismounts. The King rides his black charger up the steps flanked by cavalry on either side. He is tall and slender, broad-shouldered with thick black hair, his plumed cap making him appear yet taller still. He wears a suit of black, embroidered with silver thread, and his golden spurs wink in the morning light. He seems half-man and half-god. Michelangelo's *Il Gigante* and the copy of Hercules appear to salute him as he rides into the palazzo, but the young king doesn't even glance at them.

A papal usher has sidled up unnoticed beside Leonardo. 'His Holiness desires your presence in the palazzo. His Grace, Francis, the Most Christian King of France, has expressed an interest in your company, Master Leonardo.'

The usher leads the master and Salaì through the crowd, shoving people aside. Glancing upward, we see the beacon is lit and hear the distant sound of music. Despite the King's sudden reluctance, the *festa* has begun and the pontiff has mounted Hanno the elephant and commenced the procession. I wonder whether the pontiff's determination to press ahead is a political calculation, designed to match Francis's demonstration of power with an equal showing, or whether it is instead a childish inability to face disappointment.

The French court has swarmed the Palazzo Vecchio. Inside it hums and seethes with people. All is chaos and uproar. I wonder whether we shall glimpse the *entrata* at all and I had so wanted to see Hanno the elephant. I'm nearly knocked out of Leonardo's hands by the tide of courtiers and the stench of sweat, and we find ourselves borne up the grand stairs of the palace. The King and his court have taken over the Hall of the Great Council. I glance around with interest, able to survey the vast chamber from the privacy of my specially converted box. The crowd conceals most of the view, but through the gaps I glimpse ruins of Leonardo's fresco of the Battle of Anghiari. It has not been painted over. Beside it is Michelangelo's cartoon, which remains pinned to the plaster, the paper ragged at the edges. It appears he also never finished his commission and did not transform the cartoon into a mural. Leonardo fidgets unhappily. He does not want to be here, face to face with his greatest failure, forced to look upon the limits of his ambition and genius.

The room is so overstuffed with people that the walls are running with condensation and I am half-afraid that the floor will collapse. I spy il Magnifico glowering in a corner, playing surly and reluctant host. Then, upon a wooden seat, sulks the French king. Even seated and hunched over, he's tall. He's almost handsome, with a pallid face, black hair and a long, bulbous nose, too prominent for any painter to flatter away.

We wait. For hours. Leonardo has been summoned here by King Francis, but the Most Christian King neither speaks nor looks upon him, and does not invite him into the royal presence.

It appears that the Pope won't let the King's refusal spoil the lengthy festivities. We are all trapped in an interminable game between a king who won't watch and a pope who won't rush. His Grace, the Most Christian King of France declines to permit anyone from the French court to watch the festival either. There are rows and rows of windows in the palace all facing out upon the piazza and the sound of the festivities rises upward like smoke, filling the air with singing and lutes and joy. Leonardo and his assistants spent months in Rome on the plans for the arches, designing pulley systems for the moving parts as well as the costumes, and here we are, unable to even peep at the carnival. We are blind men, hearing from others' distant shouts the scale of the triumph. No one dares so much as glance towards the windows; they are sealed not with paper but fear. Giuliano de' Medici simmers in the corner, festering with rage. He has been ordered here to act as ambassador until his brother the Pope arrives, but he's bored and slighted, yet even il Magnifico himself lacks the courage to stroll ten paces to the flapping window and watch the elephant lumber into the piazza. No one speaks or sits as there are very few benches. The room clacks with dread.

The King idly surveys the chamber. He settles upon Leonardo, who has been standing for some time.

'Leonardo from Vinci?'

Leonardo steps forward and kneels; then, to his embarrassment, finds that tired from standing he has difficulty in rising.

The King is furious, but not with Leonardo.

'Who let the great Leonardo stand for hours? Do you not know who he is? Find him a seat! He's not a young man. Treat him with honour. Give him wine and food.'

Two courtiers help him onto a chair and give wine, plying him with a plate of duck, truffles and sweetmeats. Colour returns to his cheeks.

'You were charged with this pageant? In my honour?'

'Yes, Your Majesty,' says Leonardo.

It was planned to honour the King and Pope in unequal measure – in the pontiff's favour – but this is not the moment to quibble.

'Assist Leonardo from Vinci to the window so he can witness his triumph,' orders Francis. There is a note of mockery in his tone, but again none of it appears directed at Leonardo whom he regards apparently transfixed.

The courtiers, the two burliest, simply lift Leonardo up in his chair and carry him with me in my box still clasped on his lap and set us both down on the raised platform beside the row of windows. Leonardo watches the window bleakly. Threads of duck flesh are caught in his beard.

'Can you see?' asks the monarch.

'Yes, Your Majesty,' lies Leonardo.

The windows are far too high.

The King laughs fulsomely, throwing back his head. He rises.

'Come. We will see the end of this absurdity. We will watch the Pope ride to us on his elephant. We do it for Leonardo who has planned and sweated in our honour.'

The point of refusal has been made. Leonardo is merely an excuse. No one is fooled. King Francis sweeps down the staircase, il Magnifico just behind, the court thronging at their heels. Leonardo and Salaì join the crowd; the pair of French courtiers are waiting to attend us.

'Do you need the suitcase?' asks one, looking at my box, baffled.

'Yes,' replies Leonardo frankly.

The courtiers thrust the herds of onlookers out of the way and, as we emerge from the Palazzo Vecchio into the chaos and fury of the piazza, they find Leonardo a place to watch on the edge of the regal platform behind the King of France who sits on a throne, head in his hands, feigning disinterest. The noise is reminiscent of a battle, thick with shouts and screams and cries, not of agony but ecstasy. The Pope approaches. A crimson tide of cardinals like a blood river sashays through the crowd, tossing silver coins to the wailing masses. There is the Pope himself, borne upon the back of the hulking grey elephant, wearing white robes and a white and gold crown – more god than king. The crowd leaps back, terrified of the massive beast, and then edges closer again, eager to brush the papal robes. At the head of the procession, on a gold-painted wagon pulled by two horses, is a towering pedestal where a young winged boy stands naked and gilded entirely from head to toe; the curls on his head are coils of molten gold as if he had been touched by King Midas. This is the Golden Age of Florence and the Medici. Even King Francis stirs and murmurs his approval, apparently moved. A tear falls from the eye of the Pope but, as we watch, the boy squirms and wriggles, scratching at his arms and tearing at his wings as he flails and chokes. A moment later, he falls, a golden angel or Icarus diving down to earth, and crashes onto the cart below. Men rush forward and seize the child, attempt to revive him. Salaì runs to discover what has happened.

He returns, downcast.

'The boy is dead. Suffocated from the gold paint.'

I shudder. The pigments that brought me to life have killed the child.

His Holiness and the King send silver florins to the child's mother. The Pope is trying not to be annoyed that the boy's audacity at dying has spoiled his *festa*. It is not a good omen for the Medici. In the Hall of the Great Council, surrounded by courtiers from both courts – the papal and the Valois – the two men make endless professions of insincere friendship. Both are angry and displeased. This meeting is intended to set out more cordial relations between two men of formidable power and lay the foundations of a treaty of concord, but they each simmer with resentments. Francis wants Naples and a dukedom. And he presses Pope Leo to surrender Parma and Modena. I listen with interest, but Leonardo sits on his chair, leaning against his cushions, listless, hearing nothing. His face is painted with guilt at the death of the gilded boy. To have a golden angel was part of his design, another death marked upon his conscience.

The young king stands, towering over the corpulent and glistening pope, who perspires freely in his robes, and kneels with a smirk, kissing his hand. His Holiness blesses him through his teeth. Francis springs to his feet.

A cardinal shuffles forward and presents Francis with a gleaming golden box set with diamonds, emeralds, rubies and topaz. Painted saints with lapis eyes gape mournfully from the lid. Francis stares at it, his lip curling with his lack of enthusiasm.

'This is a symbol of our friendship and our esteem for you, most high and excellent Prince, By the Grace of God, Most Christian King of France, Duke of Brittany; Duke of Milan, Count of Asti, Lord of Genoa; Count of Provence, Forcalquier and the lands adjacent,' says Pope Leo, eyeing the box with unchristian covetousness.

The King makes no remark.

The Pope's neck-rolls turn red with fury like strings of blood sausage in a butcher's shop. 'It's a reliquary with a fragment of the true cross,' he explains, outraged that such a treasure should require parsing.

King Francis gives a nod of cool and indifferent thanks. 'If you truly wish to demonstrate your regard, but do not wish to present me with Naples, then I desire to possess Leonardo from Vinci's Mona Lisa. And her sister Leda.'

I'm relieved that Leda is safely tucked up in Rome and this fierce boy-king cannot seize her. To glimpse her is to need her and he hankers after her already.

'I've heard of their beauty even in France,' continues Francis. 'These are works of art beyond all compare. They have been touched by God, so it's said.'

The Pope struggles to his feet, after finding himself momentarily wedged into his chair.

'The true cross was actually touched by God!' yells Pope Leo, then remembers himself, swallows and blinks.

'The Mona Lisa and the Leda are indeed remarkable but,' he winces and searches the room for Leonardo, 'they are not mine to give. If they were, then of course I would bestow them upon Your Grace in a moment.'

'In that case,' says the King, with a chuckle, 'it appears I must persuade all three – painter and his paintings – to accompany me back to France.'

The entire Valois court gathered behind their monarch on the left side of the hall erupts with obedient laughter. The papal court does not. Pope Leo stares at Leonardo with fury; any satisfaction at the *feste* has dissipated, only anger remains. Leonardo has humiliated him before the French king.

We sit in the receiving room in our lodgings. Leonardo huddles on the high-backed settle before the fire. No one speaks very much. The shutters keep out the streaming rain but not the ghosts; the night thrums with them. Leonardo frets over the dead boy. The landlady carries in food that no one eats. Cecco tries to tempt the master with morsels of salted fish and eggs, but he pushes it all away. Salaì is flushed with wine and pours another glass, slopping it on the table. He glares at me, stiff with resentment. He does not want to share Leonardo with any rival – not with another man, a woman; not with whatever I am.

'You are celebrated, Mona Lisa, even beyond Italy,' he grunts. 'And you are making the master famous.' His voice glitters with danger like a whetted blade.

He is jealous that I am bringing Leonardo renown across Europe. Leonardo rouses himself to look at his protégé. 'It should be you, my *garzone,* who garlands my reputation. I do not need to collect my own laurels.'

Salaì shrinks like a kicked dog at the rebuke. He lacks much skill as a painter. Yet even little Cecco fades like a candle placed next to the sun, when compared to Leonardo.

There is a rap at the door, and the landlady hurries to answer it. A courier appears, not in papal livery but Valois blue, and presents a letter to Leonardo. It's marked with Francis's own seal. The master studies it for a second before opening it and reading. Once he has done so, he looks up at us – Salaì, Cecco and me – his expression bewildered.

'Francis, the Most Christian King of France, desires us to go with him to Amboise. He wants me to be his court painter. He offers me a "most commodious manor, servants, and to accord me the esteem, respect and adulation that he fears I am not accorded in my native Italy".'

'It's true. You are not accorded,' I say.

'How much?' demands Salaì.

'A thousand florins each year.'

'I bet he offered Michelangelo more. And Raphael.'

We all stare at Salaì who preens in the attention. 'Oh yes, the Most Christian Arsehole asked them both first and they turned him down. Too busy. Too adored in Italy.'

Leonardo is third choice. Salaì watches the master and his face contorts on seeing Leonardo's hurt expression. The master pricked Salaì's pride, and Salaì struck out in revenge like a viper, and yet he loves Leonardo, and he is both satisfied that he has wounded the master and agonised that his barb has caused him pain.

'It doesn't make a difference,' I say. 'There is no future for you here. You have not only made an enemy of your patron, il Magnifico, but also Pope Leo. You cannot stay with all the Medici against you.'

I, Mona Lisa

He stares at me, expression full of sorrow. 'I fear you are right.' He sighs. 'We must make friends with France.'

For the second time, I find myself persuading Leonardo to leave Florence, but this banishment will not only be from Florence but Italy and this time he shall not return.

Alpine Pass, 1516

Autumn

We leave in early September when the sun is still warm on our faces. The mules are loaded with crates and boxes. Leda and I are carefully wrapped, placed in our cases and strapped onto mules. I'm relieved to have her with me again; we've never been apart so long, and we call to one another. I do not know then that the time will come when I must endure existence without her. But I'm young and only filled with excitement at this new adventure. The mountain rocks look blue and the thin air makes them appear bluer still – particularly in the shadows, according to Leonardo, who insists upon frequent stops so that he can draw. He is diverted by the livid moss and violet and ochre tones striping the strata in twisting patterns. Leda is entranced by the shining wild strawberries amongst the alpine rocks, like those sprouting beneath her toes, and Leonardo has Cecco grind up beetles so he can brighten those around her, casting painted sunlight upon them. She's enthralled and can't stop admiring the new berries.

We walk through days, then weeks. The light shifts. The sun cools and the air thins further as we climb. I hear the men huff and see them sweat. The path narrows and then disappears until we need a guide to seek out the way. Whether it is all the pauses so that Leonardo can sketch, or the slow pace of the overloaded mules, picking their way through the ragged paths, but the first flakes of snow fall as we reach the Aosta Valley. Our progress slackens and Leonardo catches a ragged cough that he can't shake.

Our guide leads us on through tracks beside streams and pine trees. We are leaving Italy and approaching France. Snow flurries cover the stone quarries and hide the meadows. The wind picks up and hides our tracks. If it wasn't for our guide, we wouldn't find our way. Cecco sings to keep up our spirits and Leda joins in, her voice sweet and clear. Leonardo coughs and coughs, and stoops hunkered over his mule in silence, his cloak pulled up around him, trembling with cold. His fingers are blue every evening when he tugs off his gloves. We spend each night in wooden chalets along the road, bare but hospitable, where the master sleeps in a pallet beside the fire and is given soup and bread and warm milk. We can hear the snort and huff of the cattle just through the wooden partition, and the stink is ripe. Leonardo eats less and less each time, and he looks wan and feverish. Leda and I beg him to take a day and rest. I hear Cecco and Salaì arguing with the guide.

'We need to slow down. He's an old man. He needs a few days to recover,' pleads Cecco.

'*Non*,' replies the guide. 'We must cross the pass before real winter. These are only the first flurries. We're already too slow.'

'You'll kill him with this pace,' says Salaì.

'He'll die on the pass if we wait,' says the guide. 'Or you must hold up till spring.' I look at Leonardo, but he's already asleep in his clothes, his food uneaten, a blanket tossed over him. His skin is stretched taut and I can trace the shape of his skull, the outline of death already marked upon his face.

We trudge on. The snow continues to fall. I see it catching upon the men's eyelashes. The mountains disappear. We only know they are there. The road has gone but the guide finds the way from the trickling of the stream, not yet frozen. All is white. We stumble onwards. We make our way through the shelter of the high forest, but just above us lies the bare back of the Alps, rocky and desolate, wearing nothing but snow, devoid of life. When the clouds clear, we see the bruised gleam of the glacier, tall and deep and otherworldly. Leonardo does not speak. His lips crack and bleed. We have to coax him to sip from the mountain streams like a baby sparrow. The sky is grey and threatens more snow.

'We need to reach the church of Notre-Dame de la Gorge for shelter,' says the guide, looking anxiously at the sky.

We cross the gorge itself, an old Roman bridge spanning the river, the waters smashing against the rocks below. Leonardo rouses and shudders, staring at the torrent, transfixed. The air is solid with snow, white and blinding. It patters against the luggage. The mules flick their tails and ears and slog on, uncomplaining. Leonardo slips from the back of his mule, unable to sit. Cecco clambers down and walks beside him, pinning him in place. We lumber onwards. At last, through the pines, there is a light.

Huddled among snow-covered trees is a painted church, a lamp lit in the high windows.

'Help me with him,' yells Cecco. 'He's having some kind of fit.'

'What's happening?' I call, only half-able to see him through the slits in my box.

Salaì and Cecco half-carry, half-lug Leonardo into the church, shouting for assistance.

The guide unhooks the cases containing Leda and me – he has been schooled by the others we are all that matters to the master – and conveys us into the building. I peer out through the eyeholes in my box, getting used to the gloom of the church. A lamp shines in the nave, but otherwise until we erupted through the doors, all was calm and still. A crude Madonna gawps from behind the altar. We've fractured its tranquillity. Hearing Cecco's shouts, two nuns bustle out and rush to aid Leonardo. He tries to walk, but when he does so, he drags his right foot and his right hand hangs. Leonardo attempts to speak but his mouth sags and slackens, then he stumbles. He collapses onto the floor of the church, pale as the plaster saints around the walls, and for a moment I think he's dead. His lids are half-closed. The nuns, sheathed in their dark robes and woollen shawls, take charge.

'He must be put to bed and kept warm. He's having a palsy.'

Salaì and Cecco pick him up and carry him through the back of the church to some simple rooms. The guide, who has been taught never to leave me unattended, brings me too. One of the nuns points to a cot near an empty grate and lays a fire.

'Tuck him in. I'll make a poultice.'

'What else can we do?' demands Salaì.

'Pray,' says the nun.

Salaì mutters something crude under his breath. He has little patience with God.

Leonardo cries out and mumbles and tries to sit up and point. He's gesturing towards my box. He wants me. He needs me.

'I'm here, maestro!' I call. 'I'm with you.'

Leonardo continues to fuss and whimper, until Cecco unfastens the straps around my case and releases me. The instant Leonardo glimpses my face, he relaxes and at once falls asleep. The guide carries in the second box and takes out Leda.

'Mona, is he dying?' she whispers.

'I don't think so,' I reply, willing it to be true. 'Not today.'

One day, but not yet.

The nuns nurse his body. They force him to sip poultices steeped with herbs, and blessed with prayers to the Virgin and St Sebastian. Salaì mutters and paces. He has no patience with either potions or prayers. The snow melts during the day and freezes at night. Winter stalks closer. Soon, if he doesn't recover, we shan't be able to cross the mountain pass. We won't reach France this year. Mostly, Leonardo sleeps. He wakes only to try a little soup, and it dribbles from his slackened lips, and the nuns feed it to him like an infant. Then, before he has finished half a dozen mouthfuls, he is asleep again.

He wakes in the middle of the night through drifts of sleep with a sob. The dying logs in the grate glow orange.

'Il Magnifico!' he gasps.

'He isn't here,' I soothe. 'He's in Florence. You're quite safe.'

Leonardo is bathed in sweat and he stares, frantic and unseeing. 'He drowns in the Great Sea.'

'You are safe and warm and dry and a thousand miles from the Medici,' I soothe, wishing I had arms that could embrace him, hands that could stroke his fevered brow.

'Dream only of me,' I murmur.

In the morning when he wakes, I see with relief he is stronger. He's returned to the world and to me. Every ordinary thing he does is precious. He sits up and eats oatmeal. The spoon tumbles when he experiments with his right hand, so he returns to using his left. Leda cries out, overjoyed.

'You look so much better, my friend! But you have grown old. Like a prophet. Cecco must trim your beard.'

It is good that Leda frets about his appearance; it shows that he is better.

The nuns come in and start to clear away the breakfast tray, pleased. Leonardo frowns, grappling with a question.

'Giuliano de' Medici. I dreamed of him last night. That he had crossed the Great Sea.'

The nuns fall silent and start to fuss with a basket of logs. They look at Leonardo with anxiety.

'Il Magnifico is dead. For some weeks at least, for us to hear of it here. You must not dream of death, or it will steal you away while you sleep. I do not think il Magnifico can have been a friend of yours, for him to try and take you in your sickbed, asleep, before you can even call for a priest!'

'He was no friend of Leonardo's,' I agree, troubled.

I shall not pray for Giuliano's soul. Yet I can see it is not so easy for Leonardo. He despises him for his cruelty towards Lisa, but he is a man of mercy and compassion. He is haunted by his dream. Giuliano was not so old and only recently married. Perhaps he is stranded in the netherworld. If so, it is no more than he deserves.

The guide comes in and perches uneasily by the fire. We must decide whether to wait for spring, or else we must leave within the week. Winter is snapping at our heels. The Bonhomme Pass will be too dangerous soon, piled high with snow. Impassable until April.

'We wait,' declares Cecco.

'I agree,' says Salaì.

'We cannot go,' I say to Leonardo. 'It's too dangerous. I won't risk you.'

'No, we must wait. What is a single spring?' asks Leda, pleading.

'Ah, Leda. Nothing to you. Time moves differently for you, *topolina*.' He leans back, exhausted. He looks old and thin. 'Three days and we leave. I shall not wait here. I am going to France. The life I have left, I spend there.'

We emerge into the ghostly white light. The snow lies in patches; it has receded like teeth from sickened gums and much of the earth is laid bare. Leonardo is swaddled in furs and strapped to his mule so he cannot fall. Above us looms the spear of Mont Blanc massif, swirling with cloud, sharp and sinister. Behind us crouches the small church of Notre-Dame de la Gorge, its cheerful yellow-painted façade sunny against the clumps of snow, marking the end of the road and the start of the mountain pass. Leda and I are fastened back onto the mules. Our little party moves on, silent except for the steady snorting of the animals. The end of Italy and the beginning of our journey into France. Far across the Alps lies the green Loire Valley, Amboise and a new life.

She is no longer so young ... life's finger has left its imprint on the peach of her cheek. Her costume, through the carbonising of the pigments, has become almost that of a widow ... but the expression, wise, deep, velvety, full of promise, attracts you irresistibly and intoxicates you, while the sinuous, serpentine mouth, turned up at the corners, under violet-tinged shadows, mocks you with such sweetness and grace and superiority that you feel wholly timid like a schoolboy before a duchess.

Théophile Gautier, *Guide de l'Amateur au Musée du Louvre*, 1882

Paris, 1911

Spring

The square hall of the Salon Carré of the Louvre was full of copyists, poised before their easels and painting canvases destined to sit beside carriage clocks and photographs of Grandmama above bourgeois mantelpieces. I took pleasure in observing the painters. Titian's *Three Graces* had the largest crowd in winter as the copyists could contrive to place their stools close to one of the gallery stoves. As the days lengthened, they swarmed the Raphaels, and to my dismay lifted the paintings off their hooks and placed them on easels in order to trace them more readily with chalk. I scoured the length of the gallery for the guards in their gold and black uniforms, but sometimes I wouldn't see one for hours, and even when they appeared, they tended to be more interested in the charms of the lady copyists than any chance one of them might have taken off with one of the paintings. In age, I'd grown irritable. I had a few admirers of my own who came to copy me: not as many as some of the other Italian pictures, yet the suitors I had were passionate in their devotion.

'Here I am. Did you miss me?' demanded Picasso.

'No,' I said.

This was only half a lie. I was always wary of Pablo. His charm was edged with cruelty and disdain. He stood before me smirking, paint-specked, worker's hands splayed on his hips. His hair gleamed, lacquer black. He was squat, thick-necked and waited with feet apart, more like a bullfighter than a painter. Yet I had been friendless a long time. Solitude chips away at your soul. I had almost forgotten that I had a voice at all when he first spoke to me. I had not tried to talk to anyone since Fragonard more than two hundred years before, and I had almost forgotten how. Then Picasso had called out to me like a lover, crooning to me, 'Oh, Mona Lisa. Gioconda! You are no painted lady but a woman of blood. Tell me, what are you thinking? No one has talked to you for a long time. Too long, I think.'

When at last I'd answered him, discovering my voice again, he didn't appear astonished in the least.

'Why weren't you surprised when I first spoke?' I demanded later.

'Ah, I knew you could speak, my Lisa,' he said. 'I was only waiting for you to remember.'

I always shuddered when he called me 'my Lisa'. Only one man was allowed to call me by that name and it was not him.

Now he leaned forward and blew on me softly with hot breath that smelled of Pernod. 'You are thrilling, Mona Lisa. Reality must be torn apart. I am going to remake you.'

Pablo Picasso stirred, amused and exhausted me. Sometimes he frightened me, but even the fear was exhilarating. With his open-necked shirt and sly grin, he appeared out of place in the golden splendour of the Salon Carré, its crimson walls and vast domed skylight held aloft by ornate plaster angels. He sat before me with his sketchbook and drew and talked, but it always seemed that he cut out pieces of me and reassembled them on the page before him. He was an artist and a monster. He demanded to know everything about Leonardo and Raphael and Michelangelo and when I declined to tell him, needing to keep some parts for myself, and pretended I couldn't re-member, he would become angry, then pout and sulk. When he left I felt as if I had been visited by a vampire and I was weary, relieved that the Louvre was closing. And yet, if in the morning he did not come back and see me, I felt bereft and stricken, worried he might not come again. What if I had irrevocably displeased him? What if this time I had pushed him too far? I was filled with self-loathing and acrimony, and when he next appeared, with his swagger and grin, with his greeting of 'Mona, did you miss me?', I experienced a flutter of relief as well as fear.

I did not feel about Pablo the way I had about Leonardo. I did not adore him as I had Leda. I never fooled myself that this was love, but I yearned for his company, the smell of his skin – sweat, aniseed, coffee grounds and the tang of paint thinner and sex. When he was not there the Salon Carré was dull and empty. I was impatient and irritable with the tedious crowds who I'd endured mute for more than a century. Pablo had woken me up to colour and noise again, and now I had someone to talk to, I couldn't bear to be abandoned to silence. He understood his power over me and gloried in it. He was the same with me as with all his women – witty, charming and diabolical. I was smitten.

I watched dawn break through the domed glass roof, the cleaners dawdle by with their brooms and rags in agonised slowness, and then at last the admission of the public in twos and threes. He was never amongst the very first visitors. Sometimes I wondered whether he was deliberately late to prolong my suffering. I listened and watched for him with the eagerness of a schoolgirl for her crush. It was mucky and humiliating, but that is what I had become. I heard his footsteps, the sauntering gait. His voice as he greeted a guard. He strolled up to me, whistling, his large canvas bag slung on one shoulder, hands thrust deep into his pockets.

'You waited for me,' he said, chewing on a toothpick. 'That's kind.'

'Go to hell,' I said, furious that I was ecstatic to see him.

He glanced over his shoulder, then leaned forward and whispered, 'And the others think you're a gentle Renaissance lady. Demure and godly.'

I laughed.

He unpacked his things. Canvas seat. Folding easel. Flask of coffee. Paints. Palette and brushes. Beer. A sausage and baguette rolled in a newspaper.

'I'm going to paint you,' he declared. 'And when I start, I shall not stop. Not ever. I'll paint my other women, all my lovers, but they will all be you, my darling Mona Lisa.'

I smiled. 'I've been copied hundreds of times,' I said. 'Why will yours be any different, Pablo?'

He threw up his hands in outrage. 'Because those are mere copies! I am not copying you! You have not been painted before and certainly never by a god! Leonardo da Vinci painted Lisa del Giocondo in order to create you; now I am painting you and I shall make something new.'

'I'm sorry,' I said. 'I forgot that you are a god.'

'Good. Please remember,' he said, wagging his pencil.

He drew for a while, and then paused to eat his lunch and drink his beer. Eating in the Louvre was supposedly forbidden but no one admonished Picasso. Some of the guards knew him by reputation, but even those who did not were wary of his sudden temper. They daren't throw him out. He brushed the crumbs onto the floor and drained the bottle, and gestured to a pair of women perched on stools before Titian's *Man with a Glove*, carefully copying to order, and groaned loudly, throwing wide his arms.

'The fools don't know what to look at! The Titian is good. Is very fine. But not next to you. You're an old lady but you're full of fire!'

He stashed his beer bottle under the bench; it clinked as it joined a dozen more he'd deposited there over the previous weeks.

'I don't mind,' I said. 'Some peace, for an old lady, isn't too bad,' trying to mean it.

He chuckled, not deceived. 'One day they'll see you again, Mona. It will take some calamity, some great event, but they will.'

As he said it, I realised that I hoped he was right. Now I'd found my voice, I didn't want to lose it. I was tired of being forgotten, of being mostly ignored while viewers hurried past on their way to admire Rembrandt or Caravaggio or Velázquez.

'We're revolutionaries, you and I. We're going to remake the world.' He leaned forward as he spoke, a frenzied glint in his eye. In those moments, I adored him. He was no Leonardo, he lacked his gentleness, but there was no denying the man's *ingegno*.

One afternoon, an hour before closing, a small thin girl appeared in the Grand Gallery. She lurked beside a Rembrandt, half-afraid. Her clothes hung from her, and she seemed like a china doll, with vast brown eyes and spiderish lashes. I almost mistook her for one of the vagrants who sometimes haunted the museum and tried to sneak in before closing and find a quiet, dry corner to pass the night, except her clothes were too fine. She watched Picasso hungrily, but daren't approach.

'You're being stalked,' I said.

Pablo didn't turn around but continued to study me. 'Eva. I told her to come.'

'Then why doesn't she join us?' I said, trying to tamp down a surprising spike of jealousy.

'I didn't say she could. I'm busy with you, my darling. My remarkable Mona. You, who are more alive than most women. You know, there are only two kinds of women. Goddesses and doormats.'

I hoped for Eva's sake that she was the former or I feared for her health. She was now sitting on a bench, hands neatly folded on her lap. She was as pallid and still as porcelain. She smiled at me. I smiled back, shy. My jealousy ebbed away, like pollen upon the tide. Abruptly, Picasso stood and stalked over to her, and sat beside her, pulling her into his arms and smothering her with kisses, whispering to her in Spanish and

French so that she blushed and giggled. He glanced up at me.

'Eva, this is Mona. Say hello. It's only polite.'

Eva stuttered, embarrassed to speak aloud to a painting; but used to Pablo's demands she acquiesced.

'*Bonjour*, Mona Lisa,' she mouthed.

'Hello, Eva. I hope he's kind to you,' I said.

'She says hello,' said Pablo to Eva. Then he turned to me, growing annoyed, 'And of course I'm kind. And wicked and passionate and everything in between. I'm Picasso. It can't be helped.'

Eva stared between us both, bewildered.

Picasso stamped his foot, losing his temper with his beloved. 'Can't you hear her? Of course you can't. You're much too stupid. Sit back over there till we're finished.'

Instantly, Eva stood and fled to the back of the gallery and sat near a Bellini Madonna, biting her lip with humiliation and fury.

'You're a bastard. She'll leave you,' I said.

'She won't. I'll make it up to her later,' he said, unconcerned. 'I met her in a café. She belonged to someone else, but I loved her at once and now she's mine. She's Eva, you see, and I'm Adam.'

He turned and regarded her with benign adoration, and at once Eva seemed to bloom again, a flower unfurling in the eye of the sun.

'You make her suffer. You *are* unkind.'

He shrugged with apparent indifference and turned back to his sketch pad. 'Women are machines for suffering.'

Too angry to answer, I thought back to the women I had known – Lisa, Bianca, La Cremona, Queen Marie

Thérèse, Madame de Montespan. It was true that they had all suffered but if women were machines of suffering it was men turning the handle. My Leda had endured agonies too; to me she was a woman, and the best of them, just not a mortal one.

Picasso was a genius, but, unlike Leonardo, he seemed to take macabre pleasure in women's pain. He needed to inflict torment upon us in order to create his art. I was filled with repugnance. Beside Pablo, Michelangelo seemed a gentle, agreeable fellow. Eva leaned against the wall, so pale she looked ill, almost asleep. She was drained, and by him. Picasso needed blood to sign each of his paintings but not his own. He needed the blood of the women who loved him.

A few days later Picasso and Eva came to see me. They strolled into the Salon Carré, but as always, despite the sumptuous grandeur of the gallery, the symphony of golds and reds and winged angels, it was Pablo in his ordinary jacket and shirt and slicked hair who exuded animal glamour. As he and Eva strutted in, small and dark, every visitor stopped looking at the pictures, and eyed the couple instead, before returning to Titian or Velázquez.

He had brought a painting to show me. It was large and he unwrapped it and propped it up on the floor. At first I couldn't understand. All I could see were shapes in grey and green and brown, but then I realised it was also a naked young woman, but in the identical *contrapposto* pose as me, her hands clasped in her lap.

'It's you and Eva at once,' he grinned.

'And Picasso,' I added.

'Yes. Always Picasso,' he agreed with his usual frankness.

I hated and loved the painting at the same time. It was like nothing else I had ever seen. As he had promised, he had broken me apart and remade the world. Leonardo too had changed how people saw when he first painted me, long ago. I glanced at Eva, silent beside Pablo. It was as if he had taken her living essence and put it on the canvas, and now there was less of her in the world. With growing horror, I understood that I was the only one who could survive him; I was not like the other women. I am older and stronger. Whatever I felt for him was not love. It was closer to obsession but I would always love another and it meant that Pablo could not shatter me.

That day, after Eva and Picasso had held a little picnic at my feet, toasting the new painting and me with champagne, I watched him wrap up the painting of me and Eva, two women in one, and they both left the Salon Carré. As they passed through the Grand Gallery, I observed Picasso pause beside a pair of ancient Iberian sculptures of some heads. He glanced around for a moment; then, seeing that there were as usual no guards, set down his own painting, picked up the prehistoric heads and slipped them into Eva's picnic bag. She said nothing. She either did not notice or was too frightened of him to object.

I called out to the guards. There were none to be seen, and even if there were they would not hear me. Picasso turned around and gave me an insouciant wave and walked away with Eva out into the Paris afternoon.

Summer

*A*s it was Monday, we were closed. Picasso hadn't come to visit me for some weeks. He was working on another painting, a subject that did not involve either me or Eva. I wondered if it had anything to do with the Iberian heads he had stolen. As far as I was aware, no one had even noticed they were missing. The shelf from which they were taken was dusted. No one inspected it or commented that it was empty. Everyone assumed that the ancient heads had been taken to another part of the gallery for cataloguing or restoration. I speculated how many other treasures had been quietly pilfered over the years.

That Monday, the gallery was peaceful except for workmen in white overalls who strolled through the rooms, taking down paintings that were due to be cleaned and varnished. I hoped and prayed to the Virgin that I was not amongst them. I noticed that a short man, so small in stature that at first I mistook him for a child, kept staring at me. He had greasy hair and an uneven moustache puckering his top lip. He was busy fetching other pictures, but every hour or so, I would find him watching me, open-mouthed, wet-lipped. I didn't like the intensity of his stare. At the end of the day, the workmen filed out. I was relieved the little man too had gone.

Then, to my dismay, he reappeared. He was standing right before me, perspiring and bright-eyed with eagerness. He reached out and unhooked me, fingers trembling so fiercely with apprehension that he nearly dropped me. I cried out, but there was no one to hear. He laid me face up on one of the plush benches, took out a knife, and for a moment I thought he was going to stab me with the blade, but instead he flipped me over and used it to prise me out of my frame and, once he had done so, picked me up, naked. He held me aloft and scrutinised me with frank admiration. I longed to hide.

'You are even more beautiful like this, Mona Lisa,' he said, in Italian.

'You are an idiot,' I replied, but of course he could not hear.

Quickly, he removed his white smock, and smothered me in it. It stank of sweat and cheap wine. Clutching me in his arms, still wrapped in his overalls, he hurried through the Grand Gallery and past one of the custodians, and scurried down a back staircase. He tried the door at the bottom, but to his dismay and my relief it was locked. He set me down, and started to unscrew the door handle, rattling it in desperation.

A janitor appeared. I was saved!

'Are you all right, mate?' he asked.

'The door's locked,' said my assailant, thrusting his hands in his pockets and trying to appear casual but perspiring freely. I waited for the janitor to sound the alarm and summon the gendarmerie.

'Ah, no problem,' replied the janitor, rattling a large key fob and unlocking the door, without so much as a glance at me, badly concealed in the bundled overalls on the floor.

The vagabond picked me up and fled out of the museum and into the street. No one stopped us. I had not been outside for many years and was torn between terror and a thrill of exhilaration. Who had ordered my abduction? Was I destined for some great collector? My admirers, though few, were devoted and sometimes fanatical. Dread and trepidation lodged deep within me.

My kidnapper hurried along the pavements, clutching his parcel, but no one stopped or questioned him. He gripped me tightly, his fingers sweating through the fabric. I tried to picture in my mind the route we must be taking. The Tuileries Garden, the statues staring at us inquisitively, and the Jardin du Palais Royal, the lawns parched and brown, lovers lazing on benches in the late-afternoon sun. We rushed on. Eastward, I guessed. I envisioned us brushing passers-by on pleasant strolls, all of whom must have given a wide berth to the per-spiring man clutching his overalls. I could feel the heat of the pavement and smell the summer city – the river, rotting garbage. He walked fast, never pausing to catch his breath which came in ragged gasps. At last, in a little more than half an hour, he stopped and, unlocking a door, darted inside. In a fetid, unlit hall, he climbed a staircase to the first floor, and slid the key into another door.

Removing the overalls from me, he placed me lovingly against a grubby pillow atop a bed. I looked around a cramped, grimy and poorly lit bedsit. My skin crawled. The bed was filthy and unmade, the sheets unwashed and stained. The ceiling sagged ominously with damp.

'It is not much, my beloved Gioconda,' he said, lying next to me, still speaking in rapid Italian. 'Will you be all right here?'

'No. Take me back this instant. The Louvre is tedious but this is repellent. What were you thinking?' I spoke out of frustration and fury, knowing he could not hear.

He sighed. The sigh of a demented lover. For the first time since my kidnap, I was properly afraid. He reached out and stroked my cheek. I shuddered.

'You are so real. You shouldn't be in Paris. You should be in Italy where you belong. I will take you back home. Just not yet. I want you here with me, for a little while.'

He propped himself up on his elbow and searched my face, stroking my hair with affection.

I didn't want to go back to Italy. Everyone I loved there was dead. I certainly didn't want to be here in this filthy room with this peculiar, mawkish man.

He began to unfasten his trousers and reached inside with short, damp fingers.

'I adore you, Gioconda. And one day you will love me too.'

I stared at the sagging ceiling, disgusted, trying not to listen to the quick gasps of his breath, and not notice that, when he had finished, he wiped his hands on the sheet beside me. He smiled at me, his face creasing with tenderness.

'I wish we could lie together all evening, but I have to go to work again, and so I must keep you safe.'

To my dismay, he pulled out from under his bed a leather trunk. He had made it himself and, when he opened it, he revealed with pride that it had a false bottom, carefully fashioned to fit me, and imprison me inside.

'You'll be safe here, until I come back. I'm sorry, I have to leave you. Only I have a key to my room, but just in case.'

He picked me up and slid me into the trunk, encasing me in darkness, and closed the lid. I screamed and shouted and wept, but it did no good. I was trapped.

*

I lay in the gloom, dreading and hoping for the sound of his footsteps. I despised the man I came to know as Vincenzo Peruggia but I longed to be out of the trunk. To be released from the dark confines into the watery light of the small room. Hours dragged by. The key turned in the lock. Immediately, he unfastened the trunk and lifted me out and laid me on the soiled bed. His hands were shaking with excitement.

'They know you are missing! It took them a day to notice. Can you believe it? But now all of Paris is in shock. See?'

With trembling fingers he held before me a copy of *L'illustration*, open on a double-page spread of a photograph of me. I'd never seen myself in the paper before. He held aloft another in *Le Petit Parisien*. It took me a moment to realise that it was a photograph of the empty space where I had hung in the Salon Carré.

'The Louvre is closed. And they are to stay shut for an entire week. The French borders are closed. We are famous!'

He had forgotten that, for now at least, no one knew who had kidnapped me. The fame was mine alone. I did not want it.

Each day he returned, more and more eager, with armfuls of papers discussing my kidnap. He lay on the bed beside me and, after pleasuring himself amongst them, read the pages aloud to me like poetry. When the Louvre reopened he was the first in line, queueing around the Tuileries Palace in order to admire the faded space on the wall and my empty frame. He even bought a postcard of me from the Louvre shop, which he placed on the dust-ridden mantelpiece. No one, it seemed, even suspected for a moment that a diminutive, nationalistic workman in the Louvre might have taken me. I was glimpsed in Switzerland. Germany. In an antique shop in London. No one considered that I might still be in Paris, hidden in a trunk less than three kilometres from where I had been snatched.

He lay on his side, propped up on one elbow, beaming down at me.

'Soon, you'll be happy in Italy, where you belong. Just not yet. We need a little more time together, just you and me.'

He described my return to the motherland as though I was to be picking grapes on a Tuscan hillside or luxuriating in the gardens at the Giocondo villa, but I didn't believe he had considered a plan. He was enjoying his secret infamy too much. The squalid room was littered with newspapers, from which, after reading to me, he carefully cut out every reference to my abduction and stored them lovingly.

He studied me unblinking, frowning and fiddling with the ends of his moustache. He had tried to grow a beard, which remained stubbornly sparse, although his moustache was thicker and now carefully waxed upwards into a circus master's swirl. I wondered if it was part of a deliberate attempt to alter his appearance, or rather a display of flamboyance as a consequence of pleasure at his secret infamy.

Much of my kidnap was dull. Endless hours left alone in the dark, imagining how I might die. I worried that I would be lost for all time. When before I'd considered how I might end, it was not like this, discarded at the bottom of a trunk. Forgotten and in all likelihood accidentally destroyed. Tossed out with the rubbish when Vincenzo died or was arrested for larceny or drunkenness. The secret bottom of Vincenzo's grisly trunk was more likely to result in my annihilation than my safety.

I wondered if Picasso missed me. Despising myself, I hoped so. I doubted if he was amongst the crowds gazing at the empty space on the wall in the Salon Carré. He would view the entire spectacle as gauche – most of the visitors to the Louvre had not noticed or cared for me before, so why the exaggerated display of sentiment now? But he had cared for me, and I had mattered to him, so my absence must trouble him at the very least. I wondered if he was looking for me. I couldn't imagine Pablo putting up posters. It was beneath him.

When Vincenzo lay beside me, and fumbled with the buttons on his trousers, I tried to lose myself even as he sought to meet my gaze. He could not possess me because I was not there. His hot breath was but the wind across the Adda, his stink the river tang of mud and netted fish on the boats. I remembered Leda and Leonardo on the loggia of Villa Melzi watching swans come in to land on the surface of the river, the lightning crack of their wings, the flash and glare. 'Here they come again,' cried Leda in delight. 'Another! So white. A summer blizzard.' Leonardo added a feather to Jupiter's powerful serpentine neck with his brush. Leda laughed at the swans above. The beauty of them and of love.

'Stay with me,' said Vincenzo. 'Look at me.'
I did not. I would not.

*

'You look unhappy, *tesoro mio*. You need to go out,' announced Vincenzo with a sigh one evening. 'And I know just where to take you. You're starring at the cabaret.'

He unfurled a crumpled poster and held it out. There was a drawing of several dancers wearing low-cut, short dark dresses and veils, flashing their frilly crimson knickers as they swarmed a photograph of me, which had been altered to make it look as if I held my hand to my mouth in shock. I'd never seen a picture of myself satirised before. The line on the poster exclaimed: I SMILED AT THE LOUVRE. NOW I AM MERRY AT THE MOULIN DE LA CHANSON.

'You want to see yourself, *amore*?'

Before I could wonder what he meant, Vincenzo was stuffing me into a canvas bag, padded with shirts and other items.

'I'm sorry, *amore*, it isn't dignified, but necessary in case someone peeks.'

I thought it was only marginally less dignified than spending my days locked in a chest. Humming to himself, he combed his hair and shined his shoes, and as soon as the sun slid below the rooftops opposite, he slung the duffel bag over his shoulder and hurried down the stairs.

It was a relief to be out of the seedy apartment. He walked at a rapid pace with the bag heaved across one shoulder. I listened to the rattle and whine of the taxi cabs and omnibuses, the jangle of the dray carts and the knock of horses' hoofs against the cobbles. In those days there were still more carriages than motor cars. He jumped onto a tram to take us up to the Moulin de la Chanson, and I glimpsed a rush of yellow light through a gap in the bag's zip, a carousel whirl of Paris; then he fastened it again and all was black. I cursed him.

It was early enough at the cabaret that there was no queue, and Vincenzo ambled straight inside. The cloakroom attendant hailed him.

'Hey, monsieur! Wanna put your bag away?'

'*Non, merci.*'

'It'll be quite safe. We're used to travelling salesmen.'

'Really, *non.*' He clutched me tighter.

The cloakroom attendant coughed in irritation, inured to eccentrics and skinflints unwilling to pay her tip. Vincenzo marched on before she could accost him further. Ribald music from a large band played out into the room. I heard applause and laughter. The *maître de maison* glided over.

'*Bonsoir*, monsieur. Would you prefer to sit at the bar, or may I show you to a table?'

Vincenzo hesitated for a moment and then declared, 'A table. Why not?'

'Of course. Follow me, monsieur.'

The scrape of a chair. Vincenzo sat, and slid the bag under the table; and, as he did so, to my relief unfastened a corner of the bag, whether by accident or design, allowing me at least a partial peep at the club and the stage. I had a snail's-eye view, which mostly gave me an excellent view of the dancers' high-heeled shoes and elaborate knickers as they kicked up their legs. I could see enough of the club to make out that the floor was unspeakably filthy, covered with a confetti of cigarettes, and I had a partial glimpse of a sleek and gleaming mirrored bar where I could hear how a barman shook cocktails in time to the beat. Marie Antoinette would have adored his panache.

The music was Ravel, with two pianos and frantic peeling chords, and it was at least another hour before a line of girls in high heels and short, frilled skirts appeared, this time to the sound of Saint-Saëns performed on strings as well as piano.

'Here you come,' said Vincenzo, and unzipped the bag a little more.

I saw a poster of me wheeled into the centre of the stage. The crowd, which had swelled, whooped and went wild. Hundreds of feet stamped in approval. A singer wearing a longer skirt but split up to her thigh appeared on the stage and, as she sashayed out, the crowd whistled. The girls danced, kicking their legs.

The singer crooned into the microphone, 'I'm Mona Lisa, a fun-loving girl, a little bored at the stuffy Louvre. Hi, *mon poteau*, give us a kiss, I ain't coy, I was dead bored in that dreary ol' palace. One evening, when the guard yelled "closing time", I said "up yours" and made myself scarce.'

The club erupted with hooting laughter and applause. Vincenzo was on his feet, yelling and thrusting money at the dancer who came round in her high heels and no skirt and proffering a hat for tips. Perhaps I ought to have been flattered by the outpouring, but it left me only bemused and wondering what any of it had to do with me.

Could Picasso be here? I knew that he frequented this place. From my few glimpses, it seemed that many of the women were dressed in black and were wearing veils, in imitation of me. In order to become an icon, I only had to disappear. And yet, I knew with ghastly certainty, I would end the evening stuffed into the bottom of a trunk.

Autumn

*V*incenzo took me out in such a frenzy of excitement that he clattered me against the side of the trunk, chipping at my paintwork. He barely registered what he had done, such was his agitation. He laid me on the bed and sat down next to me.

'They have arrested Pablo Picasso! For stealing you. He is a thief, it seems. He stole a pair of Iberian sculptures from the Louvre. So why not the Mona Lisa herself?'

He was almost shouting, so thrilled was he at this latest twist. I stared at Vincenzo in disgust and confusion. He ran his hands through his hair and then proceeded to read aloud from the *Paris-Journal* how Picasso had been brought before magistrates, and confessed to having the Iberian heads, although he claimed that it was his friend Apollinaire who had stolen them and given them to him. A story that Apollinaire did not deny – I thought it was typical that Pablo evoked such devotion amongst his circle that they would go to extraordinary lengths to protect him.

'And Picasso kept the statues in his sock drawer,' declared Vincenzo with glee. 'He and Apollinaire panicked after you were stolen and took them in a bag and tried to dump them in the Seine. But they couldn't do it.'

Of course they couldn't. Pablo was a man of feeling. He could also be a monster but, like Michelangelo, he could not destroy a work of art.

Yet, I was also hurt. After my disappearance, it appeared that Pablo was preoccupied by his own guilt and his misfortune rather than concerned about mine. I knew I ought not to have been surprised at evidence of his selfishness and egotism. Perhaps, I told myself, I needed to be forcibly removed from his company in order to break the dubious hold that he had over me. I always knew he was a powerful and entertaining presence but a cruel one. Nonetheless, I still did not want to see him punished for a crime he had not committed. I couldn't bear the way Vincenzo slathered over the news of Picasso's arrest with such gruesome triumph.

Each evening for a week, Vincenzo read me further snippets, sitting curled up beside me, picking at his toenails.

'Picasso is in a panic and a flap! He denies ever having had the statues, even though they were found in his apartment. What an idiot!'

For the first time, I pitied Pablo. The god and the genius, diminished, and made to lie. When I thought of him, it was now with anxiety and commiseration. On the sixth day, Vincenzo arrived back at the house in a fury, dropping his keys in a temper. He wrenched me out of the trunk and dropped me on the bed, yelling, 'They have released Picasso! Not enough evidence. So they say. His high-up friends in the art world have made a fuss at his detention, that's what it is.'

He raged and stormed and drank a good deal of cheap wine as he bellowed about the inequity of the class system. If he could have heard me, I would have told him that Pablo was working class too. He'd earned his place upon the Left Bank and I'd have reminded Vincenzo of the absurdity of his position – he, of all people, knew of Pablo's innocence, but Vincenzo wasn't interested in truth or reality. And, while Picasso had been released, I worried that I'd never be free.

Over the next year, the mourning for me became hysterical and then began to fade. Obituaries were written. It seemed that I was lost forever. The Louvre bought another painting, *La Femme à la perle* by Camille Corot, to hang in my stead. I had been replaced. I was removed from the Louvre catalogue. Soon, it seemed, I would be forgotten.

Florence, 1913

Winter

I could tell that Vincenzo had run out of money, as his nationalistic fervour suddenly increased. He began to pace his dingy room and declare in zealous and rambling speeches how he wished to return me to the bosom of Italy – and collect a handsome bounty. Of course, the greatest reward would be to see me where I belonged but he'd also accept the hard cash of a grateful nation. I was relieved, as each time my captor took me out of the trunk to feast upon me with hungry eyes, I had begun to fear that I was doomed to remain his hostage. For the first time in more than two years I had hope.

We travelled to Italy by train, me concealed in the trunk as baggage. Guards opened it at the border and searched it carefully but found nothing except some linen, clothes and items of Vincenzo's trade as a restorer – brushes, a ruler, a small palette and some iron tools. I called out for help with little optimism. Sure enough, after a minute or two, my trunk was slammed shut without any of the border guards discovering my secret compartment.

On arrival in Florence, we hired a cart from the station and Vincenzo took lodgings in the Hotel Tripoli. He allowed me out of the trunk in the hotel room only for a few minutes while he changed his shirt and combed his hair. He prattled on in tremendous excitement about how I ought to be grateful to him for returning me to my place of birth. I ignored him.

It was over four hundred years since I had last been in Florence and it sounded different. The train station was new, yet already grey with smut and coal dust. The city held the rattle and clang of modernity. Yet, beneath it all, I felt something familiar stir. The Hotel Tripoli was located close to the Baptistery of St John where the newborn Lisa del Giocondo had been brought in swaddling clothes to be blessed at the door by the priest, before dangers or devils could steal her eternal soul. The cobbled streets were the same; here the feet of my friends had walked. Along here Leonardo had carried me to the Piazza della Signoria to glimpse Pope Leo's *festa*. In the raised voices outside the windows, not angry but ardent, I heard echoes of Salaì and men I had known. The Florentines themselves were unchanged. Then I heard the tolling of the duomo bell. It pealed low and deep, ringing through time, pealing through the years, splitting them open like the layers of an onion. We were close to Leonardo's *bottega*. I could almost persuade myself that I could smell the linseed oil and hear little Cecco grinding red beetles with a pestle to make cochineal.

And then foul Vincenzo seized me and kissed me on the lips with his rank breath. I wished I could wipe my hands across my lips and scrub away the feeling of his mouth on mine.

'My Mona, *mio amore*, the time is coming for us to be parted. I am sorry for us that I must share you with the world again. I do this for Italy,' he said.

'And for the cash reward,' I said.

He placed me back in the wretched trunk with muttered apologies. Then stashed it under the bed and hurried out, leaving me alone in the room.

Later that afternoon, Vincenzo returned, accompanied with, from the sound of their voices, two other men.

'Where is she?' asked one.

'Here. Like I said,' replied Vincenzo.

The trunk was yanked out from under the bed. He unlocked it and, revealing the secret compartment, carefully lifted me out and handed me to one of the men.

'There she is, Dr Poggi,' said Vincenzo, a note of pride in his voice. 'La Gioconda.'

I stared up at Dr Poggi as he held me in his arms, and as the small, polite man stared down at me, he pinked in wonder and delight, and then quickly drew a mask over his features. The other man, curly-haired, well fed and wearing an extraordinarily well-cut suit, came and peered at me over Dr Poggi's shoulder, his mouth forming a round 'o' of surprise, which he turned into a nonchalant whistle. Neither man, it appeared, wanted Vincenzo to know they were agitated.

'Well, Alfredo,' said Dr Poggi, 'what do you think?'

'She's certainly very like the real *La Gioconda*. But I'm only a humble art dealer. You're the expert, Giovanni.'

'We need better light to examine her. Can we take her to the window, Leonard?' asked Dr Poggi.

I looked around for the fourth man, Leonard, and then realised to my amusement that they were talking to

Vincenzo who'd picked an absurd false name for subter-fuge. Vincenzo/ Leonard shrugged and leaned against the door, studying his nails. He knew I was the genuine *Mona Lisa* and was not interested in their scrutiny. Alfredo Geri and Dr Poggi retreated to the window, cradling me with loving reverence. I smiled up at them. They smiled back and then quickly concealed their expressions again. Dr Poggi took out a magnifying glass and started to look at me closely. I noticed that his neck flushed carmine beneath the starch of his collar.

'She really is uncannily like the genuine *Mona Lisa*. But I must take her to the Uffizi to be sure,' said Dr Poggi.

'Of course it's her! Any idiot can see!' exclaimed Vincenzo.

'Yes, but lots of idiots have claimed to find her. I had ten last week. I need to compare the craquelure on her face with the photograph of the missing picture,' said Dr Poggi, patient.

I wondered what the Uffizi was. I'd never heard of it. I guessed it to be a museum like the Louvre. It didn't exist when I'd last been in Florence.

'Bring her to the Uffizi, okay?' he said to Vincenzo. 'We want to see her properly. Let's do it now, Leonard.'

'Then you can collect your reward,' added Alfredo.

There was a long pause. Vincenzo stared at me in the two men's arms. For a moment it seemed that he might cross the room and snatch me back. Everyone waited. The air felt hot. I felt Dr Poggi's grip around me tighten.

'All right. We'll go now,' said Vincenzo.

Dr Giovanni Poggi and Alfredo Geri watched in dismay as Vincenzo wrapped me up, cringing as I was smothered in a sheet.

'Do you not have anything more suitable?' asked Dr Poggi, unable to bear it any longer.

'No. Unless you want to pack her away again in my travelling trunk.'

Dr Poggi peered at me. 'Not the trunk. See, it's chipped her varnish.'

'Well, did you not bring something, if you care so much?' demanded Vincenzo, annoyed.

They had not. They were not truly expecting to find me here in this railway hotel. They would not return to the museum and leave me alone with Vincenzo in case he vanished with me again. The sheet must suffice. Our peculiar caravan, me still clasped in Dr Poggi's arms, left the hotel room and climbed down the twisting stone steps to reception. As Alfredo opened the door into the street, the hotel manager scurried out, shouting with alarm, gesticulating wildly at me, wrapped up badly in the sheet.

'What are you doing, signori? You can't take our pictures! They're hotel property. I'll summon the *carabinieri*!'

'Signora, I assure you, the painting is not the hotel's,' replied Poggi, perfectly calm. He handed me to Alfredo, and he then must have handed his card to the manager, as she read his name aloud. 'Dr Giovanni Poggi, Director of the Uffizi. Ah, of course. Apologies, signore.'

'None necessary,' he said, lifting his hat.

I merely observed ruefully that the security of the Hotel Tripoli was considerably tighter than that of the Louvre.

We took a horse-drawn carriage to the gallery. I at least was glad that the covering was inadequate as it meant I could see. Even the names on the shopfronts had not changed so much. In a few minutes, I was back in the

Piazza della Signoria after so many years. Here was *Il Gigante*, haughtily ignoring all admirers. Yet the giant seemed different, wrong, blanched and battered. He'd aged worse than me. As I looked again, I realised he was a copy. Leonardo had got his wish in the end. The real *Il Gigante* no longer loomed over the piazza.

In the cloisters of what they now called the Uffizi, I observed a statue of Leonardo himself, while Michelangelo glowered back at him. With rueful pleasure, I saw that I was surrounded by old friends. Alfredo paid the driver and handed us down. The square was quiet and a chill wind blew, grasping at my covering. I glanced around for the lions, but I knew they weren't there – their stench had gone. I smelt only the Arno, coiling through the city, which clung to its back on either side. Opposite us was the ominous red brick of the Palazzo Vecchio. I was tracing my own past. Glancing up, I saw a kite circling in the sky high above and I felt for a moment as if Leonardo himself was watching my return. I longed to linger, but immediately I was torn away and taken inside.

The building was cool and dark and hushed. Half at a run, as if afraid Vincenzo would change his mind at any second, Dr Poggi led us deep into the museum, twisting and turning through corridors until we reached his office. Everyone who saw us stopped to greet him, but he barely registered them, such was his hurry. As we entered, he and Alfredo removed the last vestiges of the sheet. The room was meticulously neat and well ordered, with books stacked in symmetrical rows.

'Help me set her on the easel,' commanded Dr Poggi to Alfredo.

They produced a torch and a magnifying glass, and a photograph sent by the Louvre, and began to mutter with excitement as they examined my craquelure. I winced inwardly. No woman likes her wrinkles scrutinised.

'Now, help me turn her.'

The two men reversed me with the utmost care and studied the back of my panel. I heard Alfredo rustle paper and murmur, 'It's the Louvre catalogue number. It's her.'

Vincenzo muttered, 'I told you it was her already. I stole her from the Louvre for the glory of Italy.'

Alfredo turned me around again and beamed at me. 'My apologies, Mona Lisa, you shouldn't stare at the back of an easel. You've suffered enough indignities.' He glanced at his friend. 'Any more damage?'

Dr Poggi peered at me. 'She seems to be in remarkably good condition, despite her ordeal. She's a survivor, this one.'

Alfredo was busy behind the desk with the telephone.

'Can we talk about the reward? Two million lire?' whined Vincenzo.

The afternoon was broken by the wail of *carabinieri* sirens.

To my disgust, though not surprise, Vincenzo was prosecuted for theft not kidnap. Some even considered him a patriot and his punishment was a pitiful twelve-month prison sentence. I resolved never to think of him again. I had endured and survived. I listened to the curators discuss my venerable age and the fragility of my woodwork and the historic damage inflicted by worms and beetles and grotesque varnish by ignorant restorers, and I thought how little they knew. I have endured centuries of assaults by men and miasmas and insects. I am chipped, scuffed, eaten and I have suffered, yet I am unbroken.

I was put on display in the Uffizi before being returned to Paris. Now I was back in Italy, I was glad to remain for a little while. I wanted the scent of spring, to breathe in orange blossom and magnolia and to hear the first larks call. Thousands wanted to see and admire me. Now that I'd returned like Persephone from the underworld, they wanted to pay tribute, certain I'd been lost for good. A curator in white cotton gloves carried me with the utmost care and solemnity into a cordoned-off section of the gallery, partitioned to make way for the crush of the expected crowd. My new fame now required a pilot ship to clear the way for me. As the curator conveyed me into the room, I glanced around the chamber displaying lapis Madonnas with flat noses and lumpen babes, and the Magi on their wooden horses come to adore the squirming, wormlike holy infants. I was nothing like any of those Renaissance pictures, even though they were supposedly my contemporaries. Leonardo had painted me and together we changed how everyone saw the world. Art wasn't the same after me. I would have been embarrassed for these Byzantine atrocities, but they were asleep.

Then one painting caught me by surprise and, amazed, I cried out.

There, on the wall opposite me, was a Leda. My heart faltered. She was almost as old as me. Was it possible? By some magic had I willed her back to life? Here she was – naked and flawless while Jupiter the white swan slid his wing around her waist. Could it really be her? With a sigh of anguish, I realised it wasn't her at all. I was staring at a lifeless echo of my beloved. This was merely a sixteenth-century copy of my Leda.

So many artists had visited us in Milan while Leonardo was painting Leda, and like everyone else they had been transfixed by her beauty and had sought the master's permission to copy her. I tried to consider who might have painted this Leda. Cesare da Sesto? Bernardino Luini? It did not matter. The copy was very good. Almost excellent. He had made careful variations. Dandelions and violets and buttery primroses bloomed around her toes. The blue-tinged mountains were replaced by a cavern or grotto. None of these details mattered. She was silent and un-seeing, her expression blank and voided. Exquisitely pretty but devoid of the sharpness that gave the true Leda such sweetness and vivacity, as if she were but a moment away from glancing up. It seemed as if I was staring at a wax death mask of my Leda. This version was but a lifeless doll. I couldn't bear to look at her, and yet I found myself transfixed. She was like her, and nothing like. It was torture and the sweetest relief. If I looked too long, would the flawed, dead features of this Leda replace the perfect Leda in my memory? Still, she reopened the wound of my loss. In the evenings when the gallery was empty I heard my Leda laugh, and I watched her burn, cry out for me, call my name and die again. I was haunted by my own mem-ories, summoning my own unhappy ghosts.

The months in the Uffizi were almost unbearable, filled with bitter charm and regret for my lost friend and love, and I was relieved to leave. Then, when the moment came, I was suddenly sad to go – eager for one last glance. I called out farewell. She did not answer.

*

When I returned to Paris, they put me behind a thick and suffocating layer of glass. I was enraged. Isn't the victim supposed to be freed? The queues of people lining up to see me were even longer than those in the Uffizi. To my surprise, Picasso came on the first day. He arrived a little before closing and, ignoring the guards, came right up to the glass.

'Oi, monsieur, *s'il vous plaît*, stand back! Not so close.'

He took no notice. He was still Picasso.

'I'm glad you're home. I missed you,' he said.

He held his hand up against the glass, and then pressed his lips against it, placing a smacking kiss. Standing back, he unwrapped a large parcel he'd brought, and lifted up a picture to show me. It was me and not me, rendered in black and white. I sported a dashing hat, and my round nipples were displayed like the puckered buttons of a tightly upholstered armchair.

'See, I painted you again. Do you like it?'

'Yes and no. Do you care for my opinion?' I said.

'Yes and no,' he answered, smiling.

I laughed, glad to see my diabolical friend. In the time we'd been apart, and during my ordeal, I had changed. I was glad to see him, but no longer frantic that he return tomorrow. Whether I saw him in a week, or month or even a year, I would be satisfied. It was a relief because, as with all my friends, there'd come a time when I would no longer see him again.

Our master went with the rest of us to one of the precincts to see Messr Leonardo da Vinci, an old man of more than seventy, the most outstanding painter of our age. He showed to His Excellency three pictures, one of a certain Florentine woman portrayed from life ... most perfect, though as he suffers from paralysis in the right hand nothing good can further be expected. He has successfully trained a Milanese pupil who works well enough. And although Messr Leonardo cannot colour with his former softness, yet he can still make drawings and teach.

The Travel Journal of Antonio de Beatis, Canon of
Molfetta, 1517

Amboise 1517

Autumn

I want to return to Leonardo for almost the last time.
Even now, I can tell there aren't many days left
together. Time's beat is starting to hurry, however much
I will it slow. We're nearly at the end. Not quite yet. But
already I can feel death's cold breath upon our necks. I
want to stay here as long as I can, for while I'm here, he
lives.

Late-summer sun ignites the tips of the chestnut leaves,
burnishing them in the evening light. The cattle have
nibbled away the lower branches evenly on all the trees
leading down to the river, so that they sway and float like
the twirling dresses of ladies dancing at a court extrava-
ganza. The air is grey with puffs of gnats and the cattle
huff and flick their tails. We sit on the long loggia surrounding Clos Lucé manor – a handsome building of red
brick and light stone – looking out towards the green-
mantled pool and the swirling insects. It stands on rising
ground above the Loire, and only a short distance from
the royal chateau at Amboise. We are all here, Leonardo's
family: Leda and I reclining on our easels; Cecco perched

beside the master, in case he should be needed; and Salaì sipping wine, his feet propped up on a stool.

'Here he comes,' announces Leda.

Leonardo rises to look. 'Ah yes, so he does,' he says, pleased.

A black mare ridden by Francis in shining silver spurs, the Most Christian King, is galloping across the water meadow separating the royal chateau from our manor. Leonardo stands and watches his progress, leaning against the stone barricade of the loggia. He adores horses, and loves to watch them run. Picking up a piece of black chalk and some paper, he starts to outline the movement and flow of its forelegs, capturing the animal's speed and rhythm. He's lost in his task, and doesn't notice when His Majesty draws up, dismounts and, handing off his horse, climbs the stairs to the loggia. A servant, frightened by the master's lack of courtesy, reddens and, stuttering, prepares to announce the King but Francis waves away his concern, hushing him. Leonardo is his established favourite. He doesn't wish him disturbed. During these evening visits, he leaves the court behind and comes with only the barest of retinues. They linger scowling at the bottom of the stairs, forbidden from intruding. He moves in closer and watches Leonardo draw.

'While running, a man puts less weight on his legs than when standing still. And in the same way, a horse which is running feels less of the weight of the man it bears,' murmurs Leonardo, his chalk hurrying across the page.

The great king smiles in happiness. This is why he has come. He watches for a few more minutes and then slumps on a low chair and stretches out his legs, squinting against the sharp glare of the sun. He notices the paper slip from the fingers of Leonardo's right hand. It flutters along the terrace, catching wing, and Cecco snatches it and returns it. Salaì doesn't move. He continues to sip his wine, staring ahead, insolent. The animosity between the two assistants is turning into a canker. The King tolerates Salaì for Leonardo's sake, but I also wonder if they have some private agreement. Salaì disappeared on a trip back to Milan in the summer and reappeared with several paintings by Italian artists which he presented to the King. Francis adores all things Italian. Leonardo, Leda and me. I notice that he is staring at me now with frank, male admiration.

'Reconsider selling her, Leonardo,' he says. 'Five hundred scudi for Mona Lisa and another three hundred for Leda.'

Leonardo glances at me with disquiet, and forces a smile. 'No, my great and noble king. They are not for sale. They are my family.'

He pretends to drop his chalk and fumbles for it with his wrong hand, unable to grasp it between his fingers. Francis is not fooled but winces nonetheless. The King is still not even twenty-three. Leonardo has aged. His beard is as white as the dandelion-seed clocks billowing on the breeze, and although he is still tall, he's stooped, windbattered. He has an old-man's thinness to him, in his face and in his hands – his artist's instruments.

'You do not need to work,' declares Francis. 'Just to talk with you is joy enough. I do not believe a man has ever been born who knows as much as you, Leonardo. Not only of painting but of sculpture—'

'Don't tell Michelangelo,' I mutter.

'—of architecture, and you are a very great philosopher,' continues the King, for a moment the awed adolescent and not the monarch rampaging across Europe.

Leonardo smiles and bows his thanks for the compliment. 'I can still draw with my left hand. And I must continue; iron rusts when it is not in use. Stagnant water loses its purity. Inactivity saps the vigour of the mind.'

We all glance about the loggia which is littered with evidence of the day's work. He and Cecco have been trying to order his papers, Cecco taking notes and acting as his amanuensis, with me reminding Leonardo wherever I fear he has forgotten something important. It is a considerable task, one that ought to take years, but we know that he fears he doesn't have that long – Leonardo is preparing his legacy.

Francis smiles. 'Of course. You are free to do as you please.'

Salaì is conspicuously silent. He drains his wine, signalling for another bottle. His only concession to the presence of the King is to remove his feet from the stool. The King, whose temper is irascible and who can bear no slight, offers no rebuke. I wonder again as to the nature of their arrangement.

Later in the evening, Leda and I are removed to inside the manor to protect us from the damp and dew. We are placed in one of the halls, with a large inglenook fireplace and huge oak-beamed ceiling, and tiled floor. A tapestry of a forest scene covers one wall. Dried lavender set in vases fills the air with the sweet herbal scent of late summer. A pageant is being prepared for the entertainment of the King, and Leonardo has the plans. He's designed mechanical falconets to fire carnival missiles of tissue paper and balloons from the battlements. A crowd gather on the lawns outside to watch the display. Music begins and bonfires burn.

'Here he enjoys the parties,' says Leda. 'He hated them in Florence and in Rome.'

'He always liked parties, just not when they were the only thing he was allowed to do,' I say. 'Here Francis adores him. Leonardo draws. He writes. He's allowed to pursue whatever interest or fancy takes his desire. And he likes inventing things – even mechanical oddities for carnivals. Here his great genius is recognised and saluted.'

At that moment, from outside there is a raucous cheer and the sound of clapping as, with a series of bangs, the mechanical cannons start to fire.

'Sad to be missing it?' I ask.

'No,' says Leda. 'Once you've seen one falconet cannon fire paper and balloons, you've seen them all. Oh Mona, if we could dance, and join the revelry and feast, then I would go!'

I'm silent, considering her with concern. Now and again there are moments when Leda yearns to be real, when she is not satisfied with watching, listening. I wish there was a way of pleasing her. I want her to be happy. She exists because of me.

A few seconds later a footman runs in, red-faced and flustered, quickly followed by another. Hurriedly they start to change out of their livery and into festival costumes.

'I told you we was supposed to do it before,' complains the first.

'I thought Piero was the lion.'

'No. I told you it was us.'

Soon, suitably attired, the two men race out across the lawns, leaving their uniforms on the floor. Leda and I watch the crowd through the window, only half-interested. We have seen so many of Leonardo's festivals and inventions that they have lost their awe. He pretends not to be hurt by our disinterest and places us close to the window in case we change our minds. The light is fading and the lines of bonfires glow red and amber. Someone else creeps into the chamber. Not another footman, but Salaì.

'Why isn't he watching the carnival?' asks Leda.

'He's probably seen enough too,' I say.

Then, to our disgust, after checking carefully that the room is empty, he starts to go through the discarded clothes of the footmen. There is nothing to be found in the belongings of the first and he grunts with disappointment. He glances over his shoulder, making sure no one has come in, and then continues his hunt.

'What's he looking for?' wonders Leda.

Delighted, he pulls out a purse from the hose of the second footman.

'Money. Always money,' I say. 'Salaì: vagabond and thief.'

I inform Leonardo the moment he comes inside from the pageant, pink-cheeked with triumph. He listens as I tell him of Salaì's duplicity, joy ebbing from his face, and summons his favourite at once and presents him with the accusations. Salaì stares at him, furious and bewildered.

'No one was there. I checked and then I checked again! Who was spying on me? I'll fight him. God damn it, I will.'

Leonardo says nothing, his face sagging with disappointment, noting Salaì's lack of denial. Salaì is red-faced with choler, whirling round as he scours the hall for hidden spies, as though they may yet be concealed amongst the heavy furniture and draperies. Leonardo is very still. He loves this man and has forgiven him many times for countless transgressions. But Salaì is no longer a boy. We are in the employ of a king, and Leonardo is the painter du Roi. He has no other friends left. He is content in France, revered and cosseted, and yet Salaì would risk it all for petty greed. Even now, as Salaì stands in the half-light full of rage and fury, he is a discarded angel; long, disordered golden curls tumble around his shoulders, his skin bronzed from the sun. He is muscled, and has lost the leanness of youth, but is not running to fat. His eyes are keen, watchful. He never relaxes for an instant. Even when he sleeps or sits, it is with the restlessness of a fox with one ear cocked.

'I tell you, I searched the place. There was no one here but Leda and Mona Lisa!' He hesitates and then scowls, spitting, 'Ah, did the footman tell you? Loathsome whining wretch.'

Leonardo shakes his head. 'No,' he says, his voice weary and betraying an uncharacteristic sharpness. 'No, don't be absurd; a servant would never dare to complain. Accuse you, the chief assistant of the King's favourite, of petty theft?'

Salaì falls silent, and we can see him thinking, ready to protest again that the room was empty, and then he slowly turns to stare at me. Leonardo has told him a thousand times that I speak. He has listened to the master talk and argue with me, but he considered it as another facet of his genius, and my voice not real but a *fantasia*. Now, finally, he understands or thinks he does. He looks at me, full of loathing.

'See the man is repaid,' says Leonardo. 'And, when His Gracious Majesty asks you to return to Milan on business, do not hurry back.'

Salaì does not answer. He only continues to stare at me, dry-mouthed with bile and hate, wordlessly considering his revenge.

October is mild. Leonardo has us carried out into the gardens surrounding Clos Lucé. He has us placed in the physic garden, a secluded part of the kitchen gardens to the west of the house, sheltered by low box hedge and lined with gravel walkways. He says the quality of the light is good for drawing, but he knows that Leda and I like to be outside among the last of the spidery asters and the salvia, purple as a bishop's robe. A few late star of Bethlehem shine luminous amongst the soil like shooting stars fallen to earth. Leonardo spends the morning outlining them in fine brown chalk. They are a flower usually reserved for the Madonna, but he has given them to his Leda.

'Do you like them?' she asks me, her voice bright with pleasure.

'Beyond anything,' I say, pleased that she is satisfied again, distracted with her looks, and not hankering for the impossible. I am filled with love for Leda and Leonardo, and yet love isn't always a universal balm. I am aware of the dissatisfaction and anguish of each. Leonardo's frustration at his ageing body grows day by day, while Leda wonders at the fleshy miracle of mortality.

There are even a few roses still blooming in the garden, their petals not yet browned by frost, and each time the wind blows, the air's breath is sweetly fragranced. Yet we feel the chill of the days to come whenever a cloud passes over the sun. Cecco is inside the studio ordering papers. He scurries outside only when he has a question for the master, or to remind him to eat. The soup is ready. The soup is now getting cold. Then to inform him that Cardinal Luigi and his retinue are here.

'I am ready for them,' declares Leonardo, magnanimous. 'They may come out and meet me in the garden.'

Leda groans. 'Why can't we be left in peace? Why must they always come? You are a stop on the travellers' trail as popular as Nantes or Marseilles.'

Leonardo chuckles. 'I am indeed. That's why I grow my beard so long. I must play the part.'

He rises from his seat and, gathering his cloak about him, peers out across the lawns, to where an armada of between thirty-five and forty clergymen in purple and crimson gowns are sailing towards him at full tilt, their robes swelling in the breeze. He smiles. 'The canons tone with the salvia beautifully. The Cardinal in red clashes. But still, he looks very striking against the grass.'

The fleet of clergy reach us, and Cardinal Luigi of Aragon, son and illegitimate prince of Naples, bestows a chilly smile upon Leonardo. He is of middling height with chin-length black hair and pale skin. His dark eyes flick from side to side like the gecko watching us from the low wall.

'We are most pleased to see you, Leonardo of Vinci. We are told that a journey to France is not complete without a journey to you.'

Leonardo bows and demurs. 'Have you enjoyed your tour of the chateau and the manor, Your Eminence?'

The Cardinal nods. 'We saw a chapel. Pretty enough, but everyone expects that I should want to see it,' he adds, gesturing to his robes.

Leonardo laughs. 'In the same way everyone shows me his child's scribblings, certain I must be interested.'

The Cardinal raises thick black eyebrows. 'We should swap. You can have the chapels.'

'No, no, I think I shall keep the scribbles.'

The Cardinal snorts, amused. He is a man usually feared – it is rumoured that he had his sister murdered, the beautiful Duchess of Amalfi, along with her lover – but, as always, even the most querulous men are charmed by Leonardo. At least until their commissioned painting is late. Fortunately for us, the Cardinal is unlikely to commission a portrait.

Servants have silently appeared and set out dozens of chairs for the party. The Cardinal edges closer to Leonardo's easel, staring at the drawings of plants, and at Leda.

'She is perfect. Living in the sylvan shades of the garden. I'm not entirely sure I can tell where the garden stops and the picture begins.'

Leonardo murmurs his gratitude and adds, 'It is the light. Landscapes exhibit the most beautiful blue during fine weather because the air is purged of vapours.'

He gestures towards the distant chestnut trees, swaying in the water meadow, and the thickets behind Leda in the painting. The Cardinal is enamoured of both. He simply wants to listen to Leonardo, who knows what is expected of him as the painter du Roi. He is painter and philosopher.

'We should linger here a while, for the sun makes such a spectacle when it is in the west. It illuminates all the high buildings of the chateau and the loftiest trees and tinges them with pinkish colour. All the other things below remain in slight relief, because there is little difference between their shadows and their lights.'

The Cardinal grins, delighted; the severity of his expression softens. This is indeed better than either Nantes or Marseilles. The old man was worthy of the detour. The Cardinal sits, fanning out his robes behind him. The canons do the same. Cecco hovers, leather-bound portfolio case of Leonardo's drawings in his hand, proffering them to the Cardinal.

'Most of them from better days, although I can still sketch,' says Leonardo. 'I am fortunate that my weakness doesn't affect my left hand. Still, painting is more difficult now, and slower.'

The Cardinal peers at Leda again, transfixed. The others step closer too, almost touching her with their noses. Here, in the sunlight, she looks exposed and vulnerable. I wish I could protect her from them all.

The Cardinal comes over to peer at me. 'And this one? Who is she?'

'This is Mona Lisa. A Florentine woman painted from life.'

'Who commissioned her?'

'Tell him I was painted for Giuliano de' Medici,' I say to Leonardo. 'He's dead and buried in the Medici tomb. He can't contradict you.'

Leonardo hesitates for a moment. What I'm suggesting is a lie, but he knows the Cardinal will be more interested in me if he believes that I've been commissioned by one of the legendary Medici.

'Giuliano owes us a debt. He owes another to Lisa,' I insist. 'Think of it as a little posthumous revenge.'

'Who commissioned her?' Cardinal Luigi asks again, louder, thinking Leonardo hard of hearing.

'Giuliano de' Medici,' answers Leonardo. 'Il Magnifico.'

The Cardinal looks at me with swelling admiration.

I laugh. Leonardo gazes at me in wonder. Together we're inventing the legend of my creation. We're making my myth. Our fame.

Amboise, 1518

Spring

There are scuffles and twitters emanating from the house martins nesting in the ivy against the eaves. We are observing the sun dip behind the royal chateau, as Cecco attempts to draw the outline of the turrets, the soft Touraine light seeping in at the windows. All is peaceful. Leonardo has decided to apply another translucent layer of vermilion glaze upon my cheek. He holds his finest brush, mixing it with an oil binder to make the pigment extraordinarily fine. It tickles my skin. Still he is not satisfied, and sets his brush aside, and uses his fingertips instead to soften the shadow. We are content. Leda hums. There is the rustle of Cecco's chalk against the page, and the murmur as Leonardo offers him a word or two of correction, and then the door is thrown back and Salaì explodes into the room. Oh, how I wish he'd stayed in Milan! I did not miss him. Yet, to my dismay, Leonardo seems overjoyed to see him. His expression brightens like a lamp that has just been lit.

'Did you miss me?' Salaì doesn't wait for answer. 'Here, I brought presents.'

He conjures squashed Italian sweets from his bag as though they are gold, along with several bottles of Vin Santo, and sets them upon the table. Leonardo is gazing at him as if he is the Prodigal Son returned. All, it seems, is forgiven. Salaì comes and sits beside the master, who runs his hands through the silk of his hair and kisses him soundly. He grips his hand as though, if he lets him go, he might vanish again like a mirage.

'Gifts are not all I brought,' says Salaì, enjoying the attention. 'A man going to Milan had to pay a toll of five scudi to enter the city. He made such a fuss that he attracted various bystanders who asked why he was so astonished. And the man replied, "Of course I'm astonished to find that a whole man can get in here for a mere five scudi when in Florence I have to pay ten ducats just to get my cock in! God save and protect this fine city and all who govern her!"'

Leda chuckles with glee and Leonardo roars with laughter. 'Cecco, get the pen. Write it down. It's delightful.'

Cecco stares at Leonardo to see if he's serious and, to his dismay, realises that he is. Peevish, he retrieves the pen and starts to write.

'Make sure you get it all,' says Salaì. 'I can repeat it if you like.'

'No need,' grumbles Cecco.

Salaì has kicked off his shoes and stretched out before the fire like one of the studio cats, and Leonardo strokes his hair, while Salaì continues to amuse him with gossip from home and more wicked jokes. Cecco is put out. He stomps and clatters, relegated to second best. Salaì cheats and misbehaves and is adored. Cecco is loyal and toils and is appreciated, well regarded, but he is not loved like Salaì. Salaì's return is bad for all of us. I catch him watching me, weighing me up like a prize carp, when Leonardo is not looking.

I can see that Leonardo has become old. There is a fragility to him. He is like a painting that has been restored again and again but I can see the cracks in the panel and at some point the picture must warp and snap, broken beyond repair. I tell myself that I must enjoy him while I can, but in truth I cannot bear the prospect of his dying. I savour the spring with him and worry how many more he will see. On some days his chalk shakes in his hand, and on others it is perfectly steady. The fires are lit in the studio but just beyond the windows the beds foam with forget-me-nots and erupt with tulips and the scented bells of lily of the valley. Yet Leonardo sits close to the blaze, never quite able to feel the warmth; the chill of death already stalks him. In the afternoons we persuade him out into the sunshine but Cecco hovers, ready to catch his arm if he falters. He sits in the sun with a rug on his knees under the elm tree, where he draws for an hour and a half, but then he falls asleep, the chalk slipping from his grasp.

Cecco carries me out and I sit with Leonardo, and he tells me stories as he works, often of his childhood. I treasure them as jewels. Some of the stories are familiar, but he's never recounted them in such detail or with such fondness. He closes his eyes, and breathes in deeply the fragrance of the magnolia and willowherb. I try to remember every word, each phrase, in case this is the last time he tells it to me.

'On days like these we would paddle in the Vincio River. The women would soak the reeds so they were soft enough to weave into baskets. I liked to watch them. Their fingers moved so surely as they made the knots. To me it was mesmerising; they sang as they worked and told stories. The other boys wandered off and wrestled and played – they did not find it fascinating. But to me, the sound and tang of the river, and their fingers, making sweet knots, loving knots, *dolci Vinci*. I'm bound to that place. Always Leonardo from Vinci.'

As far as I know, his mother was an osier weaver, and I want to ask him about her. He never speaks of Caterina, I'm not even sure he remembers her, but as I look over at him, he's already asleep. His skin is grey, colourless beneath the white of his beard. His thin fingers rest on the blanket. His eyelids flutter and his mouth isn't quite closed. Everything tires him.

The King visits in the evening. There are tunnels that link the royal chateau with our smaller manor, and on damp days, or when he wishes to escape the regalia of the court, he comes with only a single bodyguard to sit for an hour or two and talk with Leonardo in his study. The young king is gawkish, and ambitious, busy with strategy, while Leonardo likes to listen. Francis reminds me of the breed of prince Machiavelli envisioned, clever and greedy for power. He would do well to read his book. I suggest that Leonardo recommend it to the King but he refuses. It's probably for the best. Francis doesn't need any help with warfare or winning. Leonardo gently talks about art instead, and one of the studio cats leaps into his lap. He strokes the fur on its belly absently as it purrs loudly, unabashed, staring brazenly at the Most Christian King of France.

'Cecco, bring me the folio of animal drawings,' instructs Leonardo.

Cecco does as he is bidden, turning to find the correct notebook amongst the vast array lining the stacks on the bookcases and shelves. He rummages only for a moment, and then presents the volume to Leonardo who opens it and turns the pages quickly, nudging the cat on his lap, until he finds a page of cat drawings, most of them of the very same beloved and audacious ginger tom. He passes the book to Francis who admires the drawings, while Leonardo picks up the cat by the scruff of its neck, as it mews indignantly, and he tickles beneath its chin.

'If, at night, you place your eye between the light and the eye of a cat, you will see that its eye seems to be on fire,' says Leonardo.

Francis peers into the piqued cat's green iris, searching it like a lover, and then laughs, in that moment not Machiavelli's prince, but a child delighted.

The following afternoon, Cecco is preparing to take me out to sit with Leonardo beneath the elm. It's the warmest day we've had all spring. The first of the dragonflies have hatched and they whir above the green pool like the master's clockwork toys, iridescent wings catching in the sunlight outside the window. Even Leonardo does not ask for the fire to be lit. Salaì comes into the studio, and frowns, folds his arms and tuts.

'Maestro, is the sunlight good for Mona Lisa's paint? On a day like this when it's so fierce and so bright? I worry that it will damage her.'

'Nonsense,' I say, indignant.

But Leonardo is already listening; the worm is crawling into his ear. 'The mineral pigments should be all right, but that's not to say that the binders they're mixed with won't be damaged. I fear you're right, Salaì. I have been selfish in my desire for her company.'

'No! I sit in the shade. Look at me,' I object, 'I've come to no harm.'

'I'll sit and keep you company, maestro,' says Salaì, slippery as olive oil. 'We can discuss the celebration of the Dauphin's baptism.'

'Salaì doesn't care about any festival plans! That's Cecco's task. Salaì never puts himself out. Don't be absurd. He wants something.'

Leonardo sighs and considers me sadly. 'Is it not possible that he might simply want my company? Don't be unkind, Mona Lisa. And he cares for you more than you think. We've been foolish, you and I. It is luck that there is no damage to you, yet.'

'Please. I always sit with you.'

'You don't need to worry. Salaì will look after me today.'

He remains firm. Salaì gloats. I'm outraged and helpless. There's nothing I can do. Leonardo is adamant he's doing what's best for me. Salaì picks me up and places me back on my easel in the cool of the studio, triumphant.

'Stay with me, Mona, *stellina mia*,' says Leda. 'Tell me again the story of how you wished for me, and how I was born.'

Usually I love nothing more than to recite this tale again and again, but now I'm too filled with fear and dread at whatever poison Salaì is dripping into Leonardo's ear. He's set me beside the window in full view of the elm tree. I can see him and Leonardo. They sit close together, deep in conversation. Today, the master does not draw. He does not even lift his chalk. He laughs a little at first, but then he looks drawn and worried; he fiddles with the knots on the rug. They both glance up at the studio window to where Leda and I are waiting.

'They're talking about us,' I insist.

'You are too suspicious,' replies Leda. 'You're missing nothing but dirty jokes, which I do agree is a pity.'

Salaì leans in close and continues to talk, emphatic, and Leonardo listens, unhappy. After a while Salaì leaves him alone, after kissing him tenderly on each cheek and tucking in the blanket around Leonardo's knees, but today the master does not sleep. He only stares up at our window.

Later, in the chill of dusk, I plead with Leonardo to tell me what he and Salaì discussed but he only murmurs ruefully, 'All will be well, my Lisa. All will be well,' and he does not smile.

Summer

𝓘t is the evening celebration of the Dauphin's baptism. The vast royal chateau at Amboise is a marvel of blanched white stone, towering against the widest sweep of the Loire River. The chateau is a medieval city, with a thousand pointed turrets needling the sky, and chimneys puffing out smoke as spits are turned with hogs and game, and cauldrons simmer with white soup for the celebration of the infant prince. As the sun lowers, the bleached stone of the castle is dipped in pink, and the entire frontage glows. The wind blows in from the river, murmuring among the lime trees and causing the flags of the King and Dauphin to snap like whips. Leonardo has ordered a triumphal arch of woven flowers set up on the great expanse of lawns outside the chateau – lilies for France and scented jasmine and laurel for a future king and poet. Beside the arch leaps an effigy of a dolphin, the emblem of the Dauphin, plunging through a hoop of lilies into a limpid pool. The entire courtyard before the palace is canopied in sheets of sky-blue cloth stitched with gold stars in heavenly arrays, along with the principal planets – Mars, Jupiter and Saturn – creating a vast spangled tent spacious enough for hundreds. As it grows dark, servants scurry forth setting five hundred torches burning.

The King and Queen open the dancing, and soon the entire court is filled with wonder and exultation at the joy of the occasion. France has a new heir and this is a celebration worthy to mark such felicity. I watch Salaì. He is drunk and grinning with satisfaction – more pleased than the occasion warrants. What does he care for the future of France? It is he who insisted that Leda and I are brought to the *festa*. More often now, she and I remain in the manor at Clos during parties, but tonight Salaì persuaded Leonardo that we must come. The gold stars on the awning glint in the darkness. The music plays. It's too hot in the tent with all the carousers, and the inside of the canvas runs with moisture. We watch the royal party now seated on the raised dais. Amongst the revelry, I am uneasy. Leonardo sits at a table brimming with delicacies – trout with capers, hunks of boar bathed in Calvados, Muscat grapes and runny cheeses – none of which he tastes, but Salaì guzzles with relish, washing down with brandy and wine. Leonardo is almost entirely vegetarian now, and dresses mostly in linen – he doesn't want another creature to suffer so that he can eat or be warm. A servant brings him a plate of pickled walnuts and vegetables, and he thanks her but toys with the food rather than swallowing it. No one speaks much – it is hard to talk above the noise of the music – but even so Leonardo is subdued and out of spirits. A footman approaches our little group from the King's table.

'Her Majesty requests that Mona Lisa and Leda, Queen of Sparta join Her Majesty Queen of France in viewing the fireworks and spectacular,' he says.

We glance over to the royal party and see that they are drinking wine and laughing. Something about the situation disconcerts me. The King and Queen appear to be expecting Leda and me. There are a pair of easels set up on the royal platform. Salaì is sweating and fidgeting, eager to be rid of us.

'I'm staying here,' I say, and to my relief Leonardo does not press me.

'I should be on the royal dais,' declares Leda. 'Please come with me.'

'I don't think we should go,' I say.

'I'd like a little fun for once,' Leda sighs. 'And the view's better from there.'

Leonardo frowns. 'Cecco will go with her. Make sure no harm comes to her.'

Cecco and the footman carry Leda across to the royal platform, where she is received with mock ceremony and pomp and set upon the waiting easel. Salaì is in high animal spirits, and has imbibed a good deal of wine from the King's cellar. Even in the torchlight I can see the whites of his eyes are bloodied. He licks his teeth, and in the gloom it seems to me like the darting tongue of a serpent.

'Come, maestro. It's time. We have discussed it many times. This is the moment to demonstrate your gratitude to the King of France,' he says.

Leonardo does not reply.

'Are you not grateful for his extreme generosity?'

Leonardo nods, miserable.

'And this, the celebration of the baptism of his son, is the perfect occasion. Agree to the sale. Sign the paperwork. Be done with it.'

He slaps a sheaf of paper on the table before Leonardo with a pen and a container of ink, and stalks off exasperated, in search of another flagon of wine.

Leonardo watches me, his face stricken. He's as white as the painted moon pinned to the inside of the tent.

I stare at Leonardo in horror and betrayal. 'You are selling us to the King?'

He can't look at me, but murmurs, 'You and Leda will stay with me until I die. That is what we agreed with His Majesty.'

'You can't know that! He's a king!' I can hardly speak for shock; my voice is reedy and thin. 'We'll all be at the mercy of his whim. He could seize us at any time. Remove us to any of his other palaces.'

Leonardo still can't look at me. He blinks, swallows hard as though choking on a lump in his throat.

'I trust that he won't. And above all, I need to know that you'll be safe after I'm gone,' he says.

'Don't. Please. I beg you. Leave us to Cecco! He's a good man. He'll take care of us.'

'Indeed, he's a good man, the very best, but he isn't a king. What about after Cecco has left this world? After this king has gone, there will be another and another.'

'So? You believe we'll be safe in a royal collection?'

He doesn't answer, for he cannot know we'll be safe. He only hopes and wants for it to be true. He has been persuaded by Salaì into treachery and foolishness. I seethe with rage and hurt. What has he done? He sits before me, shrunken and grey, fiddling with the linen of his tunic, lost and tormented.

'Leonardo, I don't want you to sell me. I'm not an object, a mere thing. We've been together for my whole existence. Whatever happens to me afterwards, you cannot sell me as if you don't know what I am. What I am to you.'

Leonardo stiffens, angry. 'I have never willingly been parted from you, from the moment I created you. This thing I do, I do for you.' He pauses, considering, and when he at last looks up, he nods. 'Very well. It is your choice, Mona Lisa.'

'I will not be sold by you. Whatever happens to me after, I will take that chance.'

Salaì stumbles back with a jug of wine, slopping some. He looks down at the unsigned papers on the table.

'Salaì, I will not sell her. She does not wish it.'

Salaì pales with fury and frustration. 'I shall inform His Majesty that you have changed your mind.'

The King is disappointed but he claims to understand. He loves Leonardo. But the affair has taken its toll on the maestro. He's exhausted and develops a bad cold, full of phlegm that rattles in his chest as he breathes. The King dispatches his own physician to bleed him, but Cecco sends him away. Leonardo refuses to be bled. We give the doctor five gold ducats not to tell the King. He pockets them and informs the King in any case.

We all try to soothe the master, coax him into getting well, to balance his vital humours. All of us except Salaì. He barely sits with him. He stalks the manor grounds, and will not speak with Cecco, except when his stipend is due. He simmers with resentment, grieving for his lost commission. I'm vexed with the maestro. Instead of showing disappointment towards his favourite, Leonardo appears to be full of self-reproach. He could not please us both. He chose me and humiliated Salaì before the King, revealed the limit of his influence. Leonardo rises from his sickbed to sign deeds gifting him a farm and vineyard in Milan, which Salaì receives coolly as his due. Leonardo showers him with money. Salaì thanks him thinly and leaves for Milan.

To my relief, we do not see Salaì again this year. I believe this is the end of his trying to sell me and Leda to the King, and that afterwards he will let us go with Cecco. But I am young and foolish.

Autumn

As the leaves fall, Leonardo recovers some of his strength. He seems more like himself. The further Salaì is from him, his influence weakens, like a magnet upon a body of metal. By October, Leonardo is strong enough to leave his bedroom and is helped into his studio, and sits before the fire. The windows are open during the day, to allow for fresh air, although we close them securely at night against vapours. Cecco has been tirelessly attempting to order Leonardo's writings and drawings, but the master keeps changing his mind on how he wishes them categorised – according to year or theme or subject.

Should all inventions be grouped together? All animal drawings? Should all horses be in one collection, or rather the cavalry that were part of the *Anghiari* cartoons be kept with those preparations? Cecco works without complaint, shuffling, ordering and reordering. It is a journey through the master's mind, labyrinthine, chaotic and brilliant.

He wants all the dissection drawings and writings to be published together. Surgeons need to study his work, to examine his discoveries and learn from them in order to understand the human machine. From death, we can learn about life. He needed the drawings of muscles and blood flow and death to create Leda, to make her wondrous. She is positioned behind him with her children in all her devastating glory. I look at them both side by side and I understand that we are a family. Every day with one another is more precious than the layers of gold leaf in the studio.

As we study the sketches and writings, we revisit our life together and Leonardo is wracked again with remorse at considering selling us. He pleads for our forgiveness.

'I do forgive you,' I say. 'What you did, you did out of love. You did what you thought was best. Even though you were wrong,' I add.

Leonardo laughs. 'Even in forgiveness, you are unyielding, Mona Lisa.'

Leda forgives him grudgingly at last. But I always loved Leonardo more. Even as I adore her, I know that I have learned to be more human than her. I accept human flaws and frailties. I love a man. I didn't fuck a swan.

Leonardo asks for me to be brought into his room at night. I talk to him as he falls asleep, trying to comfort him. He sleeps fitfully and wakes often from bad dreams.

I ask him what he dreams about, but he either can't remember or won't tell me. He keeps chalk by the bed, and sometimes in the dawn he sits up in bed and sketches. The very act of drawing consoles him. Then, one morning, he wakes early, startled and distressed.

'Peace! You're here, all is well,' I call.

'No, Mona,' he says, 'all is not well. I am caged in this prison.' He gestures to his body. The slack and weakened right side. He fumbles for a drink. 'In my dreams I am young. I am with my father and I walk in the hills and I do not tire. And then I wake into this.'

'Stop,' I say. 'It's not so bad. You can draw and talk. You are loved.'

He does not answer and we listen instead to the ribald chatter of the dawn birds. The shutters have been left open at his request and the sky is streaked with broad strokes of carmine, yellow lake and vivid cinabrese. A kite soars across, its wings tipped with gold in the light. Leonardo smiles to see it.

'A kite. Hunting for breakfast. The poor mouse doesn't know what's coming.'

'See?' I tell him. 'We are here, we listen to the birds, we watch the kite flying.'

He is quiet for a moment and then he says, 'Have I told you the story of the goldfinch?'

'The goldfinch?'

'Yes.'

'I don't think so. You told me about a kite and how it visited you in your cradle.'

'Ah, yes. My earliest memory. This is different. This is a fable. The goldfinch was out hunting for worms, early one morning, like our friend the kite today. When she came back to her nest with the breakfast, she found her children had gone. She hunted for them everywhere. The forest. Amongst the olive groves and the vines. The whole countryside resounded with her call but no one answered.

'Finally, one morning a sparrow piped up, "I think I spotted your babies at the miller's house."

'The goldfinch flew off, her heart pitter-pattering with hope, and quickly came to the watermill. The wheel was turning in the water, but she couldn't see the miller. She fluttered down into the yard where it was still and silent. Then, as she turned her head, she saw a cage hanging outside the window of the mill. It creaked and swung like a gibbet. Her children were prisoners inside.

'As soon as they saw their mother, the babies began to cheep, hopping up and down and pleading for her to let them out. She rattled the bars of their jail with her beak, and shook it with her talons, but it did no good. Then, with a cry of agony, away she flew.

'The following day, the goldfinch flew back to the cage where her children were trapped. She sang to them, and watched them for a long time, before feeding them breakfast through the bars of the cage, her heart breaking with sorrow.

'She had given them a poisonous berry, and each of the little birds died, one by one.

'"Better death," she whispered, "than the loss of liberty."'

'That's a horrible story,' I say. 'I'm glad you haven't told it to me before. Please don't tell it to me again.'

I loathe the fable because I know why he's telling it to me now. He needs me to understand that if his body becomes a cage, he wants to be free.

'Not yet, Mona Lisa,' he says softly. 'We have a little time.'

He reaches for his chalk and starts to draw in the rosy light. I watch the chalk move surely across the page. He's not drawing the bird I expect. It's neither a kite nor a goldfinch, but a girl. She is reminiscent of a young Lisa del Giocondo, and slowly, stroke by stroke, takes shape on the page. The spirals of her hair blow in unseen winds, and she clutches at her gown. Her feet are bare and she dances on a dark riverbank amongst the bulrushes. A furtive smile plays on her lips. She's pointing the way. I do not ask to where. I know. She points to death. Not yet, but soon.

She is older than the rocks among which she sits;
Like the vampire,
She has been dead many times,
And learned the secrets of the grave;
And has been a diver in the deep seas,
And keeps their fallen day about her ...

Walter Pater, 1894 ed. W. B. Yeats 1936

Paris, 1938

Summer

*T*hrough the glass roof I glimpsed the cobalt-blue sky, and the tilt of lead-white clouds. Only Michelangelo or Leonardo himself could render them as weightless. I watched as a spider climbed on an invisible thread upwards to the heavens, passing the curved buttock of an angel in the plasterwork of the ceiling and persevering upwards until it abseiled down again, pausing precariously high above the ground. None of the other visitors noticed the tiny sightseer, swinging like a pendant over their heads.

Many of them had come to peer at me. I stared back. I was now a fixture in the travel guides and on the organised Cook's tour of Europe. A trip to Paris was not complete without a visit to see me. I was like the obligatory maiden aunt with whom one must take tea when in town. Whether I accepted my fate or raged against it, there was nothing I could do. Like Marianne or Joan of Arc, I was ranked amongst the first women of France. I was no longer an individual painting with her own history but a cipher. I did not belong to Leonardo but to the hordes. They could not hear me and they no longer saw me for myself.

My respite was Picasso. Pablo was now a man of fifty-seven. The liquorice-black hair had thinned, turned white and receded, but his eyes retained their fury. He was as powerful as ever, rolling on the balls of his feet, twitching with energy and resolve. He came to call on me most weeks, elbowing the tourists out of his way with irritation and disdain. I glanced about for him since he'd said he would come – apparently he'd a painting to show me – but he usually came just before the museum closed and I could not see him.

Only the usual crowd stood before me, chattering. I tried not to listen. I'd heard it all a thousand times. *She's a disappointment. Too small. Too dark. No, you're quite wrong. She's tremendous. A melancholy sphinx. No. Definitely a let-down.* I speculated whether the tourists ever considered that they were a disappointment to me, when after looking for less than half a minute they scurried off for a postcard of me as proof of their visit. They were, in the most part, poor company. I watched an elderly man lingering at the back of the throng, leaning on his stick. He stared at me for some time, standing perfectly still, looking and looking, unhurried. I smiled back at him. He had grey hair and a trimmed beard and an elegant hat and small round spectacles. The young teemed around him, but he remained motionless, watching.

At last, as the next guided tour was ushered on, he shuffled forward. We were alone together. He studied my face closely for several more minutes and then eventually he spoke, not in French but German with an Austrian accent. After all my years in the gallery listening to conversation, my ear was excellent.

'So, Mona Lisa. They call you "the First Lady of France" but really you are in exile.' He gave a hopeless shrug. 'I am in exile now too. I left Vienna this morning with my wife. We go to England tomorrow, and so, from this day on, I'm a foreigner.'

He looked so forlorn and lost, I longed to offer him some words of consolation. Something about his voice was familiar, but I did not recognise him. He gave a rueful smile. 'I wanted to come here. Look upon you one last time. You know, I have solved the Leonardo problem?'

Immediately, my sympathy shifted to impatience. I was unaware that there was a Leonardo problem.

Another group of tourists had started to gather around me. One of the women amongst them apparently recognised my admirer, and nudged her companion, and the elderly gentleman raised his hat in acknowledgement.

'Herr Freud,' she said, in a tone of awe. 'Would you do us the honour of telling us something about psychoanalysis?'

Sigmund Freud. I examined him again and searched his face for one I'd known long ago. I'd thought the cadence of his voice was familiar. He had spent a summer visiting me many years before but in those days he had been young. He leaned on his silver-tipped cane and smiled benevolently at the enquirer.

'Madame, would you like to know a little something about Leonardo da Vinci? Perhaps we ought to take him as our patient?' he asked.

She flushed with pleasure. 'It would be a privilege.'

I choked with annoyance.

Other visitors began to drift over to join the small gathering and listen. Freud cleared his throat.

'In his earliest memory, or possibly a dream, Leonardo recalls a vulture visiting him in his cradle and tapping him on his lips with his tail feathers,' he said.

'It wasn't a vulture,' I objected. 'It was a kite. What godawful translation of Leonardo's works are you using?'

Freud gestured to the far end of the Grand Gallery, saying, 'He even painted the vulture in his *Virgin and St Anne*. You can see the bird itself in the robes of the Virgin if you look closely. Quite unconsciously done, I believe.'

I laughed. 'There is no bird. The draperies on the robe are bleached. We are old ladies, I'm afraid. Not quite as we were when the master first put his brush to us.'

Freud and his audience considered me for a moment in silence, and several of the more gullible drifted away to search poor St Anne for the imaginary vulture.

Freud continued, 'It's not surprising that he rendered the vulture from his unconscious. After his dream of the bird, he was terrified of being eaten. It's a common phobia.'

'He wasn't terrified of being eaten! He wanted to fly. Leonardo dreamed of flying. Of being free.'

Freud talked on. For an analyst, he was quite unable to listen.

'But the vulture in Egyptian culture is also the mother goddess. Leonardo was tapped on the lips by the bird's tail feathers. Which also represents the breast. The phallic mother. It repels and attracts. It's desirable and also very threatening. And very possibly marks the beginning of his homosexuality.'

There were murmurs of appreciation and awe from the gathering crowd. It was beyond exasperating.

I stared about the Salon Carré in desperation. Apart from the throng around me, the visitors were thinning out, and I searched for Pablo to rescue me. He was nowhere and Freud was unstoppable.

'He loved his mother perhaps too much. Then he was taken away from her when still very young. And we can see in his work that he paints himself an ideal mother again and again. Those glorious Madonnas. The Virgin with St Anne – two mothers at once. Then this perfect Mona Lisa. The best of them all. Since his life was tied to the problem of his mother's lips, he was forced to paint all womenkind with the same mysterious smile.'

He leaned back with triumph upon his silver-tipped cane. I stared across at him in horror.

'I am not his mother,' I said, appalled.

To my profound relief, Picasso arrived. He surveyed Freud, his coterie and then me. 'Why are you in such a snit, Mona Lisa?'

'I'm being forced to listen to how Herr Freud has solved "the Leonardo problem".'

'Is there a Leonardo problem?'

'No. But there is a Sigmund Freud problem.'

Pablo laughed, a low grumble. The press of tourists glanced between the analyst and the painter with delight; they'd come to the Louvre on the obligatory visit, and instead were witnessing a far more amusing encounter. A young fellow was already rehearsing it in his mind for his dinner companions later that night.

Pablo set down his parcel and looked at Freud. 'Are you finished with them?' He gesticulated dismissively at the visitors.

'Unless they have questions?' said Freud politely.

'They have no questions,' said Pablo. 'They are leaving. Out.'

Grumbling, the tourists moved away, as Pablo shooed them, commandeering the assistance of a Louvre guard in his endeavours. Once they'd left he turned to Freud.

'What's this idea about Leonardo, then?' demanded Pablo.

Patiently, Freud recounted his theory. I tried to object, but Pablo kept shushing me.

'You speak to her as though she's real,' said Freud. 'Interesting.'

'You do not. That's stupid,' snapped Pablo.

'Don't be rude. There's no need,' I admonished.

'She spoke to you again? What did she say?' asked Freud.

Pablo hesitated. 'She told me not to be rude.'

'How fascinating. She's like your better self. A good mother who admonishes.'

Pablo swore.

'Tell him that I don't like his theory about Leonardo,' I said.

'She thinks your ideas about Leonardo are shit. *Merde.* She should know. She knew him.'

Freud appeared unconcerned by the dismissal. He studied Pablo evenly.

'And what do you think, Monsieur Picasso? Since you do not feel the same way as Mona Lisa who is real.'

Pablo shrugged. 'I don't give a fuck one way or the other. Anyway, I'm a degenerate artist. What does it matter what I think?'

There was real anger and resentment in the way he pronounced degenerate; both Freud and I heard it. An exhibition had been held in Munich the year before, denouncing his work alongside that of several of his friends and paintings by Jewish artists. He'd raged to me about it many times. There was little consolation I could offer.

'All the best artists are degenerates, or so I hear,' said Freud. 'It's the greatest honour.'

I decided that Freud was a terrible art critic but a good man, and I chose to forgive him. He sat down on one of the benches, and looked tired again and lost.

'I am sorry you must leave. Exile is not as bad as you fear. Some of us choose it,' said Pablo.

Freud sighed and tried to smile. 'Ah, yes. But you were a young man when you left Spain. It was an adventure. I am old. If I ever go back to Vienna, they will murder me. I shall not see home again.'

Pablo took two beers out of his pocket, popped one open and handed it to Freud, who looked at it with surprise and then sipped. Pablo drank from his own and then toyed with the string on the large parcel wrapped up in brown paper propped against the bench beside him.

'Is that for me?' I asked.

Pablo nodded. He stood and began to peel back the layers. Freud observed for a moment and then started to help. The gallery was almost empty now, except for the Louvre guards, but they were used to Picasso and always allowed him to stay for a short while after closing. When the picture was unwrapped, he propped it up so I could see, standing to one side.

'It's my darling Dora Maar and, as always, you, my darling.'

I stared at the painting of a woman seated in a chair wearing a plaid skirt; she had long black hair, and was half-turned towards the viewer in the *contrapposto* pose. Her eyes were huge, and of a sensitive expression; her mouth in a mournful half-smile. She leaned on the arm of the chair with one elbow, her hands painted with vibrant scarlet nail polish.

'It's Mona Lisa with red nails,' declared Freud, excitedly.

'I do very much like those,' I agreed.

Picasso grunted and started to wrap up the painting again. I had seen so many of me and his women over the years, but I did particularly like this one of Dora as me with long red nails.

'You have a few days in Paris and you came here?' asked Pablo, looking back at Freud.

'A single afternoon and I only came to see Mona Lisa.' He took another sip of beer. 'How is it in exile, Mona Lisa? You left Italy a long time ago.'

'You see!' said Pablo with a laugh. 'You talk to her too. It can't be helped.'

'Did she answer my question?' asked Freud.

'No,' said Pablo, noting the guards signalling it was time to leave. 'She did not answer. The gallery is closing – I'll walk you out.'

They did not hear my answer, as I did not speak it aloud. I had lived in exile for centuries; but not from Italy – from another age. I was a fossil from another era, like a shard of pliosaur bone, encased in a limestone tomb cracked open and washed up on the shore after a storm. Visitors contemplated me in wonder and awe. I was as foreign to them as the Roman relics along the corridor. I was a remnant, a slippage from history, fallen through the centuries as if through a gap in time, but I was no time traveller, as I could never return. The trip was one way. I had outlived my age. I did not tell Herr Freud how lonely exile is nor how hard it is to bear.

Paris, 1939

Summer

*A*t five p.m. the Louvre closed as if it were simply an ordinary August night, but the moment the last visitor departed, a small army of museum staff – curators, cleaners, guards, the coiffured ladies in the gift shop and café – students, artists and assembled volunteers poured into every hall and corridor of the gallery. Louvre director Jacques Jaujard assembled a meeting with them all in the Salon Carré. They gathered around and listened. Jaujard was immaculately dressed as always, but gaunt and drained.

'Germany and the USSR have signed a non-aggression pact. This evening we begin.'

I looked down at more than a hundred empty packing crates waiting to receive paintings and sculptures from the Louvre's collections, the instant the director decreed it was time to evacuate the treasures from Paris and hide them across France. Yet, ungainly and untidy as they were, the crates themselves were not the most incongruous items in the Salon Carré that evening. Propped up against them were at least two dozen copies of me.

Some were aged and delicate renditions from the Renaissance. There were clumsy sixteenth-century imitations, and clever nineteenth-century ones pretending to be sixteenth-century ones, except that they were painted on canvas and not on wood. Some bore a subtle resemblance to me – a distant cousin perhaps; others were hideous and ungainly. A few were much too big. In several, I was too young. I felt as if I was gazing into a strange and distorting mirror and seeing warped versions of myself. Some Monas simpered, others smirked. Yet more were prettified into blandness. They were all vacant and dumb. The Salon Carré had metamorphosed into a Mona Lisa factory. The director of the Louvre stalked amongst the copies, inspecting them, accepting some and dismissing others. Dozens of Mona Lisa eyes seemed to follow him.

'Passable. Wrap these and label. *Non*. Send back to storage,' said Jaujard, glowering, cigarette in hand. 'We want it possible that people could be fooled. For whispers to start.'

Some of the copies I even recognised. One or two had been accomplished during the maestro's lifetime. Others had been executed while I sweltered in King Francis's *appartement des bains*, or in the Grand Gallery in Fontainebleau, and the paint on these copies had darkened horribly from too long in basements and attics. There, hidden at the back, was Salaì's grotesque Mona Vana with the wooden tits, leering at me. She too was placed beside a crate and labelled as 'Mona Lisa, da Vinci'. An insult to us both.

'Write on every decoy box "Mona Lisa" in red ink,' said Jaujard.

'And on the box with the real one?' enquired his assistant.

'Mark it MN in black without letters or numbers. Don't even put the Louvre catalogue number on the crate.'

The assistant stepped forward and made to lift me from the wall, but he placed his hand on her shoulder and stopped her.

'Not yet. Call the post office. Ask them to disconnect telephone and telegraph wires to allow our trucks to pass underneath.'

She hurried off to make the call, leaving me with Jaujard and the myriad versions of myself. They stared back at me, smiling and uncanny.

Under strict orders from Jaujard, the legions of helpers began to pluck paintings from the walls, prise them free from their frames to wrap and crate them. Typists were ready to record in lists the catalogue numbers of every painting and item of sculpture and the corridors rang with the staccato rattle of the keys, in an eerie prelude to the coming war. The paintings were all carried into the Salon Carré to be packed and assembled, and checked by Jaujard who placed a yellow dot on the boxes of most of the collection, green on a few significant items, and red on the most astounding paintings. I observed as he anointed the box containing Raphael's painting of the Madonna in the Garden and Leonardo's *Virgin and St Anne* with two red dots. The task of packing up the collection was Herculean. There were thousands of paintings to be moved, and only hours until the first of us needed to be gone from the city. Picasso and several of his friends arrived to help. He waved at me, but in a few minutes was busy with a team heaving the vast *Raft of the Medusa* from the wall. The moment it was safely down, he was back up a ladder and retrieving another painting, fearless and inexhaustible. Jaujard moved amongst them all, pristine, unruffled and determined. He eyed Pablo warily – perhaps concerned he might take the opportunity to steal another priceless relic.

The undertaking was such that men from the Parisian department stores had been summoned to assist. I watched with interest as they packed the paintings beautifully with delicacy and panache, folding the paper quickly and lightly. To my amusement, I noticed that not only were the shop assistants wearing the same long smocks as other workers but also splendid striped caps and mauve tights that were identical to those sported by the jesters in the medieval painting that they were currently wrapping, and it appeared as if the characters in the scene were packing up themselves.

After the paintings were removed from the walls, the frames were traced around and the number and name of the item scrawled on the vacant space in chalk. In a few hours the walls were bereft of art, and daubed with chalk scribblings – it was a gallery filled with ghosts. The army of volunteers had been working for some time, and the light was starting to fade. One of the guards moved to flick on a switch but Jaujard called out to him, 'Non! They might see us! We must take every care in case there is a raid. Portable gas lights only.'

The gallery flickered with the yellow glow of the lamps. Everyone worked with anxious determination. Masterpieces lay propped against crates or simply flat on the floor. I cringed with fear lest some well-meaning soul stepped back into the middle of a Velázquez or Titian. A young woman stood near Jaujard, watching him and then me. She had luminous skin and a heart-shaped face, framed by pencilled eyebrows that might have been drawn by Sandro Botticelli, and a Cupid's bow of a mouth. She stepped up close and scrutinised me.

'We will do everything to keep you out of harm's way, Mona Lisa,' she said. 'Whatever happens, France needs to know that you are safe.'

Something about her tone made me certain that she believed it, whether or not it was true.

My moment had come. Jaujard himself lifted me from the wall. Picasso, dripping with perspiration, came to stand beside me.

'You see, you travel in style?' he said, pointing to a custom-made case that had been designed to fit me, fashioned from poplar wood and lined with crimson velvet.

'A box is still a box,' I said.

I tried not to think of the trunk where I had been entombed for years. This was intended not as a kidnap but an attempt to keep me free. Jaujard placed me with reverent tenderness in my handmade coffin.

'Mark her crate with three red dots,' he ordered.

I watched as they anointed it. Picasso crouched down beside me.

'Good luck, my friend. When all this is over, we'll meet again, you and I.'

He blew me a kiss.

Jaujard slid the box shut and it went dark.

I could see nothing. My velvet box was sealed into absolute blackness. I listened. I was lifted and carried, placed into a vehicle. Urgent voices. *Mona Lisa goes in the first vehicle.*

She leads the convoy. An engine. Loud. The rattle and shake of the van. I had no sense of hours passing. My box muffled light and time.

I was unloaded. Checked for damage and hidden away again. But not for long. A few days at the royal chateau at Chambord. I was never safe. The wireless hummed with bad news. *War declared, but they'll never take Paris.* They slid me back into my velvet case and drove me away in the night. I was lifted out of my box in another golden salon and inspected for termites. A week at the chateau at Louvigny. The wireless played as curators re-dressed the silk lining of my box. *Paris has fallen. None of her citizens will meet the eye of the invaders. Paris is now 'the city that never looks at you'.*

I was glad I was not there. Not only did I not wish to be seized, I could never look away, no matter the horror.

Jaujard came to check on me and my painted companions, and sat in a corner of the salon, smoking cigarette after cigarette, his fingers drumming with anxiety.

'It's our duty to keep her safe. The Germans must not find her.' He frowned, troubled. 'But I've been told by one of our agents that there are already Nazis officers hunting her.'

So I was wanted in the Reich, a trophy of conquest to be mounted on a wall in a castle like a shot stag. We had to play a game of hide and seek all across France.

Jaujard stubbed out his cigarette. 'I've been ordered to return to Paris. I've to ready the Louvre for its reopening.'

I imagined the Louvre emptied of its treasures, and strolling through its long galleries alongside Jaujard with nothing but chalk outlines marking where its riches used to be, mocking the intruders. No *Venus de Milo*, only a vacancy where *The Raft of the Medusa* and Titian's *Man with a Glove* once enraptured all admirers. The soul of France, of liberty, hiding. I pitied Jaujard. He was compelled to pay court to monsters, obliged to stand beside a plaster mould of the *Venus de Milo* and agree with Goebbels how art displays the best of man and that without it we are nothing, all the while knowing that these were the men who destroyed paintings that displeased them. The true collection of the Louvre had to stay hidden in rural France like bulbs beneath the soil, ready to bloom when it was safe to return, and men were ready to see once more.

Every day the jackboots stomped closer. We heard the crack and boom of war. I must be rushed away again. Northern France was not safe for me. We joined the ragged caravans of escapees. I was just another refugee on the road trying to flee the black tide gobbling up Europe. We travelled south, to the hidden Chateau de la Treyne, perched precipitously on the banks of the Dordogne River thundering in the ravine below. We arrived on a cool, sunlit afternoon and Jaujard explained to the chatelaine that the pictures must be aired; too long sealed away and our paint begins to darken. The chateau was well concealed, at a distance from the village, and Jaujard and the curators, with the help of the chatelaine, unpacked us from our crates and set us all on the terrace overlooking the river. It was a magnificent spot to sunbathe, a moment of calm amidst the chaos of war. I lay cradled in the gentle heat, between a Poussin and a Millet, gazing at a pair of plump Rubens stretched out on the grass opposite, basking nude.

Jaujard paused, sweating from the effort. 'When I return to Paris they want the *Mona Lisa* to come too. If they get her, that's the last we'll see of her.'

'What will you do?' asked one of the curators.

'I must dally and delay. Be inefficient. Until they are preoccupied with something else. Soon you must move again. She can't stay long in one place. They mustn't catch her.'

'No,' I agreed. 'They mustn't.'

'And,' added Jaujard, 'we'll send them one of the decoys. Or perhaps even better, we'll let them discover one.'

Late one morning Jaujard returned from Paris to check on us all. He paced the terrace as we were laid out in the easeful sunshine. A young woman arrived; I recognised her from the last evening at the Louvre – the one who looked as if she had stepped out of a Botticelli painting. Jaujard's grey and exhausted face was suddenly illuminated with happiness, and he greeted her with a lover's kiss. I watched them with interest.

'Jeanne. Is it true?' he asked.

Jeanne looked at me and smiled. 'Yes, our Mona Lisa is safe for a little while. They caught her further north. She's heading to a salt mine in Altaussee. Or they believe she is.'

She grinned and Jaujard kissed her again.

I hoped that it was Mona Vana that the Germans had found. She deserved to be buried in a salt mine. I should have liked to have been saved by Salaì in the end. It was too much to wish for. I knew it was almost certainly a pretty sixteenth- or seventeenth-century copy of me that had duped the Nazis, but still I dreamed. If it weren't for the other stolen paintings hidden there too, I should have longed for the mine to collapse, burying Mona Vana and the last piece of Salaì.

Aveyron, 1944

Spring

I still wasn't safe. Jaujard insisted that I be moved again and again. Jeanne, as Agent Mozart, had heard whispers the Germans weren't convinced they had the real *Mona Lisa*. I could stay nowhere for long. My next hiding place was the ancient abbey at Loc-Dieu, nestled at the bottom of a marshy valley in the middle of a deep forest. While many of the paintings which travelled with me were stored in the Gothic chapel at the mercy of the humidity and swampish air, the chatelaine and her husband took me into their bedroom. It was considered too dangerous for me to be left alone, day or night. It was a comfortable chamber with a four-poster bed, a vast inglenook fireplace and windows looking out towards the unbroken green forest. Yet the woods were not as empty as they appeared. Resistance fighters haunted their shades.

The chatelaine cared for me as if I were her own sick child. Half a dozen curators from the Louvre lived in the chateau and Jaujard himself visited each month. He brought news from Paris and fretted over the damp atmosphere. As soon as he arrived, he came to my room and searched my face like an estranged lover, checking me for harm, and then when he had finished, he sat at the table and sipped a cup of coffee, made from bitter chicory leaves. The curators – a young woman, and an older, balding man, with a nose like an eagle – sat and listened. Jaujard sighed and ran his fingers through his hair.

'The Gestapo massacred paintings this week. They made a vast bonfire of pictures in the garden of the Louvre, doused it with petrol and set it alight. Four or five hundred works of art. Miró. Klee. Ernst. Picasso.'

'Picasso?' I wondered to myself, seizing upon the name of my friend.

'All considered degenerate artists,' continued Jaujard in disgust. 'Most of them stolen from their Jewish owners. A few confiscated from our museums.'

He gestured towards me. 'There was a Picasso of a woman sitting in an armchair, which reminded me very much of Mona Lisa here. She burned too. The smoke from the Tuileries Garden filled the sky in Paris for hours.'

I thought of Picasso's picture in flames, on a vast pyre with all the others. I considered the other version of myself ablaze, ashes floating through the blackout above the city. It only took a few hours to burn a nation's soul.

Jaujard turned to the chatelaine who had entered the bedchamber.

'And, s'il vous plaît, never light a fire here, madame,' he said. 'The soot alone, never mind the risk of a spark.'

The chatelaine flushed with anger. 'I am afraid to even breathe, for fear of stirring the air! To think I would light a fire.'

Jaujard bowed his apologies.

*

352

Yet the danger to all of us at the abbey was not fire but rain. A huge summer thunderstorm blew across the Midi-Pyrénées. Spears of lightning split the sky. Tiles hailed from the abbey roof and splintered upon the ground. Rain spittooned through the new holes. Curators and the few elderly servants raced through the attics with buckets and rags and mops but it was hopeless. We were under siege from the sky itself. Ceilings began to collapse beneath the deluge. Paintings stored in the upper rooms were moved to lower floors, but that was only good for a few days; pictures and sculptures were all jostled in together and the stone walls reeked of moisture. It was clear that, once again, we must seek another refuge.

I listened as Jaujard, summoned urgently, sat in the driest salon and discussed where I should go.

'Where is the best place to hide her?' he asked. 'Apart from the dankness of the marsh, the abbey was perfect. Nicely concealed in the woods.'

I was set upon an easel in the corner. The other pictures remained stashed in their crates.

I listened as several destinations were suggested. The abbey at Saint-Guilhem-le-Désert. Montal. Jaujard said nothing. Jeanne sat amongst the most senior curators. She wore a thin summer dress and her mouth was a gash of red lipstick.

'You don't like any of these places?' she demanded.

Jaujard shook his head and asked, 'Jeanne, did you make contact with the British?'

She grinned. 'Oui. They said to tell you "Van Dyck thanks Fragonard".'

Jaujard winced. 'I'm Fragonard? I would have preferred Delacroix or Degas.'

Jeanne clicked her tongue. 'We let them know when we're moving paintings to a new location and they won't bomb it.'

'How will we know they've got the message?' asked Jaujard.

'Apparently we listen to the BBC.'

Jaujard sat back in his chair, troubled. Jeanne toyed with something in her pocket. Jaujard held out his hand for it and she passed him a brooch. It was an emerald-green bird, escaped from the bars of a golden cage, its wings spread wide and free.

'Cartier?'

'*Oui, bien sûr.*'

'You shouldn't have this, Jeanne. It's dangerous. If the Germans capture you, they'll know you're Resistance.'

Jeanne shrugged. 'Sometimes a thing of great beauty is worth a great risk.'

I looked back at the emerald bird in Jaujard's palm, its wings spread. The bird free from its prison. It made me think of Leonardo and his goldfinch. *Death rather than loss of liberty.*

'So where do we take Mona Lisa?' asked Jaujard.

'Somewhere they won't think to look.'

She leaned forward and whispered something. Jaujard gave a slow grin.

'Signal the British the location,' he said.

We listened to the BBC for three days, alarmed that they wouldn't receive Jeanne's message; then, on the last day, as we listened to the news bulletin we heard: *We hope that, despite what is happening in France, and wherever she is, the Mona Lisa is still smiling.*

It was time for me to move once again.

*

I was packed away into darkness in my poplar box. Hot and airless. Time faltered and drifted. I was cocooned into a void. The constant clamour of the diesel engine. Then silence and stillness which I took as night. Voices and the racket of the road. Hours or days. I could not tell. Then we stopped. My crate unstrapped. My box opened. I was lifted free.

It was so bright. I could not see at first. The light. The blue-grey light of the Loire. I knew this place. Of course I would be safe here. Our last home together. Clos Lucé. The very name was like a spell to bring him back to me. Here we had been together. Here we had been happy in those last ragged autumn days. There was the elm whose shade we had sought, stouter now and grown venerable. Upon that loggia we had waited on summer evenings for the King to ride out across the water meadows amongst the huffing cattle. If I listened, I could almost hear the percussion of the horses' hoofs upon the ground. I searched about for Leonardo. His presence was imprinted upon every brick and stone, on each blade of grass. This was his rose garden. Up there was the studio window where Leda and I looked out to the copse beyond. The bees buzzed amongst the chestnut candles and the blossom fell from the trees like snow. Time whirled forward and back; and its knots, its bonds, came undone.

He is here. He is here. I am filled with joy and gladness, which I never thought would come again. I am remade. Without him, existence was simply waiting. 'I love you,'

I call out to him. I thought I must wait forever, without hope. I was wrong. I call out again.

My love, my Leonardo.

Amboise, 1519

Summer

The hour has come at last. I can't delay telling you any longer. Perhaps you don't even remember the promise that I made? But I'll keep it all the same. And now that we're here, there's some relief amongst the pain as I relive it for you.

'Leonardo!'

He's too busy to answer. Apple and plum blossom is set all around the bedroom in vases but he isn't drawing it, only visions of the deluge. Pages are scattered all upon the bed, cataclysmic storms overwhelming the earth. A city lies in the distance, helpless before the wreath of darkness that is about to engulf it. All is whirling chaos. Time spins.

'Come back to me,' I say. 'Where are you?'

He looks up for an instant, startled, then drops his chalk. He will not pick it up again, but we do not know this, he and I.

'You are here,' he says, comforted. 'I thought you'd gone.'

'I'm with you. Always.'

He lies back against the cushions. He is gaunt and his skin is lead tin yellow. His beard is soft and white like puffs of cloud.

'All is well,' I soothe. 'I am here, my love.'

His speech is slurred as if he has supped too much wine. 'When I sleep, I dream of a deluge. Sucking men to their deaths. They drown in muddying foam and blood. But now it is me who drowns. I'm drowning in time. Too much or too little.' He scratches at his throat.

'You will not drown. I'll jump in after you and haul you out.'

He laughs at my absurdity. 'But this is not the worst of it; you are alone in my dreams. I don't want you lonely, Mona Lisa. Who will hear you speak?'

'I won't be alone. I have Leda, maestro. You have given her to me. We will have each other always.'

He closes his eyes. 'Yes. You have your Leda. Two women of grace.'

I think he's asleep again and then he mutters, 'Don't leave me, Mona Lisa. Not for a moment, not until the end.'

He reaches out for me, forgetting that I am not real.

I curse my lack of hands. Of lips.

He mostly sleeps. Cecco and the King's physician take it in turns to watch him but I never leave him. Leda and I are placed on either side of his bed. Leda sings him lullabies. Her voice is like the wind. He is never alone; he has us. The windows are thrown open to the sound of the birds. In the evening, I hear a nightjar and from dawn the bustle of the larks.

*

I, Mona Lisa

We are waiting for him to die. He neither eats nor drinks. I measure time only in the rise and fall of the frail rigging of his chest. His fingers are tightly curled upon the sheet. His eyelids flutter. He is neither in this world or the next. He waits on the banks of the River Styx. The ferry boat will not take him yet. The pauses between each breath are the gaps between worlds. I wait and wait; he is gone, and then a gasp. He is still here. The will to live is strong, even at the end.

And then, in a spasm, he reaches out with his arm, brushes my cheek with his fingertips, and in that moment, for just a second, I feel the warmth of him. The miracle of his fingers. A pulse. Our heartbeat, and in that second I live with him. My cheek is warm and flushed with life. The roughness of his skin against mine. I flutter. I gulp a breath. I am. I am real for a single moment. I am full with life and love and I can't bear for him to leave me and I can't bear for him to suffer. And then he's gone. His life is spent. And I am cold once more.

Paris, Today

One day I too will be dust. I too shall join the ether. I might be the Universal Woman, but I am still just a woman painted on poplar wood from cinnabar and white lead and gesso. I must perish by fire or flood or worm in the end. I don't know which vision of death or the beyond is true for me; whether my soul shall ascend to join Leonardo with St Peter, or my atoms rejoin the carbon of the stars. He's painted me a place to wait so I can exist in his presence. He has rendered the universe all around me. The entire firmament, his vision of the world is here with me. The rocky earth. The blue rivers and winding path, the tufa and open sky.

In the translucent glazes upon my cheek, there is the mark of his fingerprints. Like Eve from Adam's rib, I am rendered from parts of him. I look out at the world through the eyes he painted me, and all around me are his ideas. I am suffused in his existence.

Art is the eternal part of us. Leonardo da Vinci is dead, but as I look at his landscape rendered in exquisite beauty all around me, I catch a glimpse of a piece of his soul, his very essence. Leonardo will always be here on this earth, so long as I am. It has taken me many centuries to understand this. Leda is not lost so long as I remember her. She lives on in love. Look for her in me. Search for her in Leonardo's drawings of the whorls of her hair, in his studies of her slow, sad smile. Like the echoes from a dying star, you can find traces of her still.

Long ago, Leonardo gave me a voice but now I speak for him across the ages. Because of me, his name shall live forever; we made each other immortal. Yet I am not alone in my immortality. I feel him with me. Until it's my time, I'll wait. Come and see me. Look at me. But remember, I'll be watching.

ACKNOWLEDGEMENTS

Nearly all of this story is true. While dates have been tugged here and there and events consolidated for fiction, the story is based in fact. The beautiful Salaì was Leonardo's 'little devil' and Francesco Melzi was Salaì's bitter rival. Salaì died in 1524 in a brawl, killed by a shot from an arquebus fired by a mercenary under murky circumstances, and soon after the paintings known as the Mona Lisa, Leda and St John were sold off to the King of France, Francis I. The painting of Leda and Zeus in the guise of a swan was reputed to be the most magnificent da Vinci ever painted. It vanished from the French royal collection at Fontainebleau in the seventeenth century during the reign of King Louis XIV, the Sun King, and his Queen, Marie Thérèse. The closest surviving copy is at Wilton House near Salisbury. Picasso was indeed arrested for the theft of the *Mona Lisa* in 1911 and admitted possessing two ancient Iberian heads stolen from the Louvre previously. Freud wrote an infamous essay on da Vinci where he mistranslated 'kite' (aqualone) as 'vulture'. While, if it wasn't for the bravery and ingenuity of Jacques Jaujard

Acknowledgements

keeping her safe and on the run during the Second World War, the *Mona Lisa* might have been lost in a salt mine in Germany alongside many other priceless treasures stolen by the Nazis.

This novel would not have been possible without the remarkable work of historians, most notably the Leonardo scholar Professor Martin Kemp of Oxford University, whose books and research have been invaluable. He patiently gave sensible answers to absurd questions, helped me reimagine the lost Leda, and corrected the Leonardo mistakes in the manuscript. Any errors that remain are firmly my own. Thanks are also due to Donald Sassoon, Charles Nicholl, Martin Clayton, Maurizio Zecchini, Dianne R. Hales, Giuseppe Pallanti, Catherine Fletcher and of course Giorgio Vasari. Sabine Schultz and the team at Neri Pozza kindly helped with the Italian translations. Thanks also to Stan.

It takes a village to raise a book, particularly in these times, and Mona has been fortunate enough to have a village of editors championing her and listening to her voice. Huge thanks to Charlotte and Laurie, her first fans, Rose, and to Ailah who has picked up the baton. Thanks also to the wider team at Hutchinson Heinemann: Amelia, Najma, Linda and Lydia. I'm lucky to work with you all.

Huge thanks to Sue Armstrong and Meredith Ford, who first read Mona and became amongst her loudest cheerleaders. I couldn't be more grateful to you. You're the best.

I wrote this novel as, like Mona, I felt I'd lost my voice for a while. So thanks to all my friends and family – you kept listening, even when it was hard to do so. Thanks in particular to Laura, Lea, Ros, Emilie, Sophie, Rach,

Acknowledgements

Ali, Catty and Mat, and to my sister Jo and my parents. Special thanks to my husband, David, and my children, Luke and Lara, who are thoroughly sick of Leonardo da Vinci and the *Mona Lisa* but win any trivial pursuit question on the topic when it comes up. I couldn't do anything without you.